CONTRARY WARRIORS:

Opposite Sides of the Coin

CONTRARY WARRIORS:

Opposite Sides of the Coin

by
Sheryl Wright

New Voices Series v. 33

FAP BOOKS
FLORIDA ACADEMIC PRESS, INC.
Gainesville, FL

For Dawn . . .

> *you called me back from Spirit World . . .*
> *you always knew I had more to do!*

> *. . . nea:we — kowa*
> *kohyonhowane: kahènta (Kahnyàn'kehaka)*

Published in the United States of America by
Florida Academic Press, Inc. Gainesville, FL 32635
April 2015

Front cover picture designed by Christina Cozart by permission
Text and cover by David Greenberg Communications, Inc.

Library of Congress Cataloging-in-Publication Data

Wright, Sheryl, 1961-
Contrary warriors : opposite sides of the coin / by Sheryl Wright.
    pages cm. -- (New voices series ; v. 33)
  ISBN 978-1-890357-52-8
1. Women intelligence officers--Fiction. I. Title.
PR9199.4.W7535C66 2015
813'.6--dc23

                        2015008464

My Gratitude . . .

To Michelle Barrett, Sharon Hogarth, Kyra Dorward, Vicky Furman, Dr. Barbara Montgomery, Dr. Cathy Kivi, Sheila Collins and Olivia, and Elizabeth Payea-Butler for your insights and unlimited support. I can't thank you enough.

To the Darlington Palace troop; Tracy and Simon, Heather and Keith, Kerry-Anne, Lynn and Eric. Thanks for making it fun!

And to the Gypsy Squadron; the best flyers I have ever had the honor of knowing, Leslie Preney-McChesney, Eileen Hobbs, and Lori Pearce.

To Dr. Sam Decalo, Florida Academic Press for taking a risk on a genre crossover from a first-time fiction writer. Plus Linda and all the Staff at FAP for their support. I would especially like to thank David from Greenberg Communications for the design work and cover, but more than that, for his patience and vision.

For the spirits who headed west before I could finish, thank you for this day . . . Nanny Connie, Nanna Doreen, Auntie Dee, Dad, Loretta, Rae, and Kim . . . slow down guys, I can only type so fast.

And finally, to the readers who took a chance on *Contrary Warriors*. I look forward to your comments and views. Please drop me a line at info@ sherylwright.com, or visit me at www.sherylwright.com

Principal Characters

The Americans

Mike Perkins, London Station Chief for the Central Intelligence Agency (CIA).
Hank Darian, retired Deputy Director of Operations for the CIA.
Kenneth Butterworth, Major, United States Marine Corps, Marine Aviator and
    aviation specialist. Military Attaché to the U.S. Embassy in London.

The Brits

Victoria (Tori) Braithwaite, The Honorable Viscountess Dufferin, Royal
    Navy Captain and MI6 officer, currently commanding the Special
    Operations Executive, a CIA/MI6 joint taskforce.
Sir Richard Braithwaite, Admiral of the Royal Navy and head of the Security
    and Intelligence Service, also known as MI6.
Rodney (Rod) Nelligan, retired Command Chief Petty Officer, Royal
    Navy, MI6 officer and deputy commander of the Special Operations
    Executive (SOE).
Darcy Gerrard, Doctor of Psychiatry working for the Security Services and
    assigned to the SOE.
Allan Bashir, MI6 officer and Middle-East analyst assigned to the SOE.
Siobhan O'Reagan, MI6 staffer, assigned to the SOE.
William (Will) Green, retired Royal Navy Chief Petty Officer, proprietor of
    the Loyal Archer Public House.
Nigel Wren, Regimental Sergeant Major, Royal Marines, Lead Accident
    Investigator for British military and Civil Aviation incidents. On-call
    member of the SOE.
Parminder Dutt, Clothing designer and proprietor of the London dress
    shop: All About the Dress.

The Canadians

Étienne Ste. Hubert, Colonel, Canadian Armed Forces, currently serving as
    the London Station Chief for the Canadian Security and Intelligence
    Service (CSIS), previously served as a United Nations Peacekeeping
    officer.

Robert Robilard, Major General, Canadian Armed Forces, currently serving as Her Majesty's Canadian High Commissioner to Great Britain.

Hans Semple, Captain, Canadian Armed Forces, currently serving as Communications officer at the Canadian High Commission in London.

The Israelis

Genevieve Schilling, Israeli Ambassador to the United Kingdom.

Ari Ben David, London Station Chief, Mossad, and leader of the Ambassador's protection detail.

Jacob Huffman, Major, Israeli Defense Force, and Mossad officer.

Aryeh Perec, Officer Candidate, Israeli Defense Force, and demolitions expert.

Hanna Bergeson, Medical Officer, Israeli Defense Force, currently assigned to Shachar 7 detention center—a joint CIA/Mossad black site.

The Iranians

Yusuf Suyfias, Major, Iranian Republican Guards, Islamic Republic of Iran's Intelligence Ministry, or VAGA, currently serving as a counter-intelligence officer.

Hasid Mosaddegh, previously served as a Sergeant of the Iraqi Guards, currently an asset of the VAGA.

The Mohawks

Cleopatra (Cleo) Deseronto, retired Captain, Royal Canadian Air Force. She is completing a promotional tour for her book on Persian Vernacular Architecture.

Boudicca (Bo) Commanda, retired American Marine, FBI Agent assigned to the US Embassy in London.

Albert Mackenzie, Staff Sergeant, US Army, Black Hawk crew chief and private pilot.

Cyril Johnson, apprentice aviation maintenance engineer and son of the Grand Chief of the Mohawk Nation.

A Word on the Quick Reference to Acronyms, Short Forms, and Localized Slang, Plus the Mohawk Nation

A glossary of military and aviation acronyms and slang is included at the end of this book. I have taken some liberties to help simplify this very complicated world. Readers unfamiliar with this setting will notice that some conventions are particular to the nations and services involved. For example, most readers know that a Captain of Marines is not equal to a Navy Captain in any nation, although both fall under the auspices of the Naval Service. The equivalent of a Navy Captain in the Army, and most but not all Air Forces, would be Colonel. Whenever this type of differentiation has gotten too cumbersome, I've taken the liberty of applying the simplest forms available. For example, in 1974 the Canadian government combined their military services into the Canadian Armed Forces, and only recently reversed this decision. Even though the title Royal Canadian Air Force or RCAF was not yet restored to regular use during the period of this story, I found it made more sense than constantly citing "Her Majesty's Canadian Armed Forces—Air Element—Air Transport Command."

The HM prefix for Her Majesty may be a revelation to many Americans and more than a few Canadians. Canada is a member nation of the British Commonwealth, an association of countries that were once a part of the British Empire. Most of these member states recognize HM, Queen Elizabeth II, as their sovereign, Canada included. Many aboriginal nations within Canada, still recognize their connection to the British monarchy as well. The Mohawk Nation has enjoyed a particularly long allegiance with the crown, with treaties created between the British government and the Mohawk Nation still in effect. A legacy of military service to the crown is well documented and surfaces in many areas including literature. James Fenimore Cooper's *The Last of the Mohicans* touches on the Mohawk service to Great Britain and stands as testament to the large numbers of Mohawk Warriors in service to the crown. Of course, this relationship has evolved over time. The last and least known interaction between these two allies occurred during World War II. Sir William Stevenson, under the direction of Winston Churchill, and Lord Hankey, Chancellor of the Duchy of Lancaster, created the Special Operations Executive.

On paper the SOE was a service office located in Rockefeller Plaza, New York, and concerned with processing applications from American businesses interested in supplying the growing war materials market. In actual fact, and completely unbeknownst to the Canadian Prime Minister, the SOE was tasked with recruiting, training, and deploying counter-intelligence operatives behind enemy lines. Bletchley Park, home of the Government Code and Cypher

School, today known as the Government Communications Headquarters, was named Station X, while Camp X was established on the shores of Lake Ontario, on a farm nestled on the border of Oshawa and Whitby. Interestingly, the first American to receive training at Camp X was a US Army Colonel named William Donovan. Colonel "Wild Bill" Donovan was a regular visitor to the camp from its inception until well into 1943. Not a man to waste time and money reinventing the wheel, Donovan modeled the Office of Strategic Services after his experience with the SOE, even going as far as to name the OSS training facility "Camp B." Some historians have speculated that this base was co-located on the Roosevelt retreat, now known as Camp David, while others cite "the farm," the CIA's training base in Virginia, as the actual location.

Prologue

In the spring of 2004 the United States of America, with the United Kingdom and the Coalition of the Willing, were at war in Iraq, while also deeply involved in the NATO commitment to Afghanistan. When accusations surfaced that Iran, with nuclear ambition of its own, had begun a secret weapons program, Americans, and the world at large were unwilling to act on speculation alone. With the public believing they had been duped into supporting the Iraqi war, with faulty Intelligence over the existence of Weapons of Mass Destruction, politicians knew they would need undeniable proof before linking the words Iran and Nuclear Weapons together . . .

Chapter One

Heathrow International Airport
London, United Kingdom

Stepping from the vehicle at Heathrow's Terminal One, Tori Braithwaite was pleased to see Darcy waiting for her, without an entourage of Airport and Customs officials. The last thing she wanted was another barrage of useless questions, much less the risk of being recognized. Usually that wasn't an issue. For some reason, the public rarely made the connection between the suit-wearing bureaucrat she portrayed while working, with the hat and dress popularity of her peerage persona. Airport officials, and especially customs Warders, were often the exception. In the public eye she was The Right Honorable Viscountess Dufferin, granddaughter of the now-departed Earl and Countess Dufferin, with all the civility and frivolity that entailed. Her cover story, created for days just like this, named her Commissioner, for something called the Special Officer of the Environment, an unpaid consulting appointment to the Security Services. Why the Security Services needed a "green" advisor was simple, or at least it was assumed, she had received the nomination as a make-work project from dear old Dad. The gossip rags speculated that Sir Richard Braithwaite, Head of the Security and Intelligence Service for the UK, had created the position to keep his daughter out of trouble, whenever she was not attending to her peerage responsibilities. The fact that Tori was a serving Naval officer completely escaped the public eye. After 9/11, a few feel-good pieces showed up in magazines like *Hello* and *Royal*, depicting the Right Honorable Viscountess Dufferin in uniform, glad-handing the troops. There was no mention that Tori was actually an officer of the line, commanding a cruiser in the Persian Gulf. When Tori's name was offered as a suitable replacement to head the newly re-commissioned Special Operations Executive, or SOE, her father was dead set against it, while the Joint Intelligence Committee was equally divided. When the nomination was confirmed, she suspected certain members of the Joint Intelligence Committee were more interested in discrediting Sir Richard than improving counter-intel capabilities. Under Tori's command, the new SOE had been quickly positioned as a counter-intelligence think tank, and as its World War II namesake had been, was hosted by MI6 and financed by the CIA. Sir Richard had warned his daughter before she accepted the posting, that political scheming was just as much a motivator behind the appointment, as her command experience.

Like her father and her grandfather, Tori's Navy service was just part and parcel of the whole Dufferin gig, and a convenient cover for the family's other business, the Security and Intelligence Service. At thirty-seven, she had successfully divided her time between the Royal Navy and MI5, the Domestic side of the Service, since graduating from Uni. That wasn't actually accurate. Tori, like many teenagers in the UK and Commonwealth, had paraded weekly with the Sea Cadets and the Navy League before that. To this day, Sir Richard still kept a photo on his desk of a keen nine-year-old Tori, in her seaman's Flat Top and blues, standing next to her dad and his crew aboard the flight deck of the "Rusty B." It hadn't surprised Richard that his only daughter would love the Navy as much as he did. They had hashed out the differences on many occasions. One evening, half in their cups, she had enthused to her father, "It's completely different. When I'm at *Five*, it's like I've something to really sink my teeth into, it's very focused. But when I stand on the bridge of that ship, the world comes alive, and I feel is if I can finally breathe!" He understood it better than most, and admitted as much to her. Heading the SIS, he explained, was difficult. Running the SOE, with oversight by the UK, the Americans, and the half dozen Commonwealth countries, would be a real test. Never one to back down from a challenge, Tori accepted the job with all the inherent strings attached, and gave up the Navy command that had meant so much to her.

Never one to second guess her decisions, she did however think unkindly of the JIC, and the CIA, as she made her way through the terminal to the Customs and Immigration holding corridor. This latest operational proposal was one more example of the Americans dumping unrealistic requests on the SOE, and the JIC's constant desire to tie her hands. Even worse, this proposal required she involve CSIS. The Canadian Intelligence Service was young, naïve, and hog-tied with conflicting directives. With Canada involved in the Afghan conflict but opting out of Iraq, any involvement on Intel gathering required every operation be run up the flag pole, and often more than once.

Tori shook off her frustration before following Dr. Gerrard, the SOE's Human Psychology Specialist into the observation room. Once the door to the corridor closed, and her eyes adjusted to the darkness, she surveyed the analysts gathered. Ordering, without preamble, "Report."

When Tori took up the reigns with the SOE, the first change she invoked was participation from all hands. To encourage everyone, she always began with the most junior member of the team, then worked her way up the hierarchy. "Siobhan?"

"What surprises me most is how calm and compliant she's been. I'm not sure what I expected but this woman's been, as they say, on-ice for three hours . . . longer actually, without a peep. I've not seen her move a muscle, except when the Matron took her to the loo. Even then, she didn't say a word. By now, I would be banging on the walls demanding answers!"

Tori moved on to the next team analyst without comment, "Allan?"

"I concur with Vonnie. She almost seems too calm and relaxed."

"What, like she's hiding something, or just putting us on?" Tori prodded.

"No actually." Allan, struggling for an explanation offered, "It's as if she's acting calm, or perhaps as if she's unshakable in that calm. I'm thinking she might be assuming 'a calmness,' as if she knows she's nothing to worry about."

"I might categorize it as a trust in the system," Darcy offered. With a nod from Tori to explain, he added, "She knows she's done nothing wrong and has clearly decided the best course of action is to cooperate fully. To that end, she has chosen to remain calm and wait until the situation has been presented to her before reacting. As for Allan's observation of calmness, I am much more impressed. I do believe this young woman is not as calm as she appears, I would judge that she very much dislikes confined spaces. I'll attribute her calmness as the mechanism she uses to control her discomfort. If anything, I would suggest she is practiced at controlling her outward emotions. It's practically Buddhist and quite remarkable."

Tori wasn't sure what she thought about the "quite remarkable" comment. Although the woman she was watching through the one-way glass, did seem unnervingly still. "Let's see if we can shake this up a bit. Siobhan? If you would be so kind and read us the dossier summary."

"Yes mum." Siobhan said, opening the SOE file folder to the top page. "Deseronto, Cleopatra Isabella. Captain—retired, Royal Canadian Air Force. Her last posting was as a pilot and Flight Commander, with Air Transport Command, and mostly flying the Lockheed Hercules in which she has some 14,000 hours. Before joining the Air Force, she attended the Royal Military College, graduating with honors. This she completed, after serving with distinction in the Canadian Militia, and as a United Nations peacekeeper. Before that she joined the Air Cadets and received six-months-time in rank for completing the entirety of the youth program. Awards include the Canadian Decoration, the Meritorious Service Medal, the George Medal, the Canadian Peacekeepers Service Medal, and the UNDOF ribbon. The George Medal was awarded instead of the Conspicuous Gallantry Medal. I checked on that, the CGM was discontinued the year she was nominated, so they must have given her the GM instead. By the bye," she added with a cheeky grin, "the nomination for the CGM was signed by a Royal Navy Commander named Braithwaite! Just thought you'd find that interesting." Flipping back to the summary page, from her detailed notes, she continued in her soft Irish lilt, "She is thirty-nine years old. She joined the RCAF from Montreal?" Confused by that last fact, she turned to Tori for guidance.

Without explaining, Tori turned to Darcy. "What have you got?"

"Still nothing from Canada House, other than that one pager, Vonnie just read. The FBI did send over their security summary, along with the Warrant you requested. It's not much but it is interesting."

Tori caught the inflection in the "interesting" and knew it was his way of suggesting the info may be best disseminated in private. She accepted his judgment without comment. Picking up a folder bearing the emblem of the Foreign and Commonwealth Office, and her fake credentials, she grabbed the two passports Customs had seized from Deseronto, before adding the US Federal Warrant for Arrest to the pile. "Anything else? Before I head in?"

"Actually," Darcy interrupted. "There is something I would like you to try?"

When she finally entered the holding room, it was with an air of bureaucratic indifference and displeasure. She dumped the folder, Deseronto's passports, and the Arrest Warrant on the table unceremoniously, before setting down a large takeout cup of black coffee. Rather than acknowledging Deseronto, she removed the lid of the steaming brew, allowing the smell of burnt coffee beans to fill the small space. When she finally turned her attention to one Cleopatra Deseronto, RCAF retired, it was with an air of impatience, displeasure, and a wee bit of judgment to boot. Ready to play her roll, she wasn't prepared for the complete openness of the woman sitting across from her. Easily schooling her reaction, she launched in as planned. "Miss Deseronto, I'm from the Foreign and Commonwealth Office." Her tone, while posh was stern sounding. "A Warrant for your arrest has been issued by your government. Do you understand how much trouble you're in?"

Deseronto's face read like an open book. *Well, she clearly can't school her emotions, or is she allowing me to see her trust in the system, as Darcy suggested?* Tori caught something else in the woman's expression and smiled inwardly. Deciding she knew what Darcy's interesting information was all about, she relaxed her expression slightly, taking the time to push her long blond hair back behind her ear. Trailing that same elegant hand along her collar and neck, she watched Deseronto's reaction, before placing her hand back on the stack of papers, and laughing to herself. *One ping and one ping only!* Deseronto's eyes had followed the movement of her hand, lingering on Tori's long neck, and the barest hint of cleavage her power suit allowed. *Darcy will be so disappointed to know I picked up on this before he could tell me.* Launching back in, as if scolding a small child, she explained, "The United States Embassy has requested that we hold you until transportation to Washington may be arranged." She was about to say something else when Deseronto cut her off.

"Did you say the US Embassy?"

Tori nodded, handing over the Warrant and suggesting, not unpleasantly, that Deseronto read it herself.

Deseronto scanned through the folded document quickly. "They issued a Federal Warrant under the Indian Arts and Crafts Act? Are you kidding me?" she asked, before something else on the page caught her eye. "This is only valid in the United States," pointing to the information on jurisdiction.

Tori gave her a sympathetic look but answered, as a matter of fact, "Since 9/11, it has been our policy to hold American citizens for whom warrants have been issued." Watching Deseronto assimilate the situation was interesting. She was obviously trying to choose her response carefully, but in contrast to her earlier openness, she gave nothing away. Tori knew her best offense was to interrupt whatever process Deseronto was working through. Quickly standing, and scooping up the paperwork, she turned for the door.

Deseronto stood, extending her hand, "Please call me Cleo. I don't like Miss. Besides," she asked, "isn't addressing officers by rank the customary practice in this country?" Deseronto's cheeky grin gave away her strategy.

Tori didn't respond. She knew the question had nothing to do with etiquette and everything to do with what the Foreign and Commonwealth Office actually knew. The question was a gauge, designed to establish just how much homework they had done. *Well, I wasn't expecting that. Good for you Captain. I'll give you that point!*

Cleo Deseronto lowered her outstretched hand but stood quietly. Tori decided the best defense was ignorance. Her response was non-verbal, and clearly indicating she had no idea what Deseronto was asking.

"Okay," the woman offered, "Let's start again. My name is Cleo Deseronto, and I'm a member of the Six Nations of the Iroquois Confederacy. I also live and work in Canada. Therefore, I formally request the assistance of the Canadian High Commission, and I expect the United Kingdom to honor their Commonwealth status."

"You are also an American Indian!" Tori challenged, holding up the yellow-colored Six Nations passport as proof. "I'm afraid the Americans believe this puts you squarely in their hands."

With a sigh of surrender, Cleo admitted, "I'm also Canadian."

Tori watched as Deseronto drew herself up, practically standing at Attention.

"Ma'am, I have served honorably in Her Majesty's Canadian Armed Forces as both an officer and a non-commissioned member. I will not take responsibility for, or accept punishment from, a foreign government who has chosen to squat on the lands titled to the Six Nations by our Grandmother, and Sovereign!"

"You truly believe that?" Tori asked, letting her surprise show. *This is interesting! Fiduciary responsibility is not an everyday defense. Very clever, Captain. Bonus points for obfuscation!*

"Have you any idea how many Mohawks have died over the last four hundred years in defense of British North America?" Deseronto had raised her aboriginal identity like a shield of honor. "The Indian Act may now be upheld by Canada, but it was created and enacted here, in the House of Lords. Those good Lords and Baronesses, peers of the realm, took fiduciary responsibility for all Indians. Are you really ready to negate your duty to us, your aboriginal children?"

Bleeding hell! I couldn't have scripted this any better. Tori turned and left without answering. It was all she could do to maintain a straight face, as she slipped back into the observation room. While eager to hear Darcy's insights on Deseronto's course of action, she nevertheless stuck to protocol, "What's everyone make of this little development?"

Siobhan, the Intern and PA who had been manning the video camera, stepped into the team scrum. "Is it true? What she said about us being responsible for the Red Indians?"

"There is a long and amicable relationship between the Crown and the Mohawk Nation. That is true. As is her reference to the Indian Act. Of course, times change and so has our relationship with America, whether she wants to accept that fact or not."

"If she's no law acts to support her challenge?" Allan asked, "then why the history lesson?"

"Good question. What say you Darcy? Are we witnessing simple obfuscation or does she actually believe that bullocks she's spouting?"

"She is completely believable in her assertion. Her logic is flawless. If we answer her challenge, it forces us to call the Home Office for direction. They would probably send over some octogenarian with experience dealing with aboriginals.

Either that or we would have to call Canada House for direction. Either way, it brings new players into the situation, thereby diluting the American threat."

Both Allan and Siobhan were confused by the comment. Tori, ever the history major, filled in the blanks for her junior charges. "The Home Office managed the Indian Act, well actually the entirety of the British North America Act until 1984. That's when Canada became a full-fledged nation."

"What, I don't understand that," Siobhan asked, clearly confused. "I thought they were a nation for . . . more, what, since before the Potato Famine?"

Tori nodded, "Yes and no. Canada was granted Dominion by Queen Victoria. Back in the day, they were slow to actually pick up the reins. They didn't establish a citizenship Act until just before the Second World War. In my opinion, the BNA was only repealed to smooth the troubled waters between the French and English citizenry. With little effect, I might add."

"Well that explains the Indian Act," Allan noted, adding "and the role of government as father, but it doesn't eliminate the American connection. She is still an American Indian. Isn't she?" he asked, clearly unsure of his assessment.

"Yes and no."

"If I may," Darcy interjected. At Tori's nod to continue, he smiled. "I'm starting to form an impression of how our Canadian Officer thinks, but first, to explain the citizenship issue . . . the Home Office briefing package on these people was twenty years out of date. That however, did not diminish the revelations it provided."

Tori gave him her private signal to skip to the pertinent info.

"Well, the important point is that we have three nations in dispute over sovereignty. Canada, the USA, and the Iroquois Confederacy, which *is* recognized by the United Nations. Those Red Indians living within the overlapping territory can often ignore this dispute, but once you leave, the parent states assume fiduciary responsibility for the individual. The Americans and the Canadians have long since espoused a policy of dual citizenship for aboriginals. That of course serves our purposes, but remains an issue for those involved, and affects how other nations look at these people. For example, beyond North America, and exempting ourselves and the entirety of the Commonwealth, most nations, and especially those throughout the Americas, will adhere to the UN policy and recognize the Iroquois' sovereignty, with all the rights and responsibilities therein. To that point, our officer here, has said and done everything that would support that position."

"But she was asking for Canada House for help," Siobhan noted. "Doesn't that mess things up a wee bit?"

Knowing the answer, Tori turned to the next senior for his observation. "Allan?"

"Right. I think she knows she needs to ask for assistance from one or the other of the parent nations, at least here, since we've no Red Indian Embassy!"

"Darcy?"

"Quite right. And, asking for assistance from Canada and not the US Embassy, whether that is her prerogative or not, was smart. The Commonwealth connection, and the historic legacy, deliver layer upon layer of bureaucratic mishmash. Again, a smart strategy."

"You think this is an intentional tactic?" Tori asked.

"Intentional or accidental, she has achieved the same result. She has stated her rights, and our responsibilities reasonably, and is now waiting patiently for the wheels of justice to turn."

"And if they don't?" Tori prodded.

"And if they don't? Well, that will be interesting to watch."

"All right then," Tori glanced at her watch. Her team had been at this since early morning. They had been on hand to witness Deseronto's seven a.m. arrival, subsequent apprehension, and had been observing her ever since. "How about we get some lunch in. If I remember correctly, the staff canteen serves up a good sandwich. Allan, why don't you and Siobhan head down first?"

Allan stood, and turned for the door before Siobhan stopped him, "Maybe we could bring something back for you lot, save you the time and the walk?"

Tori nodded, knowing the young Intern would know exactly what she wanted. After Darcy had given the pair his lunch order, he suggested they pick up something for Deseronto too. After explaining what he had in mind, Tori nodded her approval, waiting for them to leave before asking him, "What precisely have you learned?"

Before explaining, he pulled an inch-thick folder from his satchel. "She has a rather extensive FBI file, which Major Butterworth was willing to share with me."

"It didn't come from Mike Perkins directly?"

"No," he admitted. "Evidently, Mike told his number two, to provide me with anything I deemed relevant. The major was quite proud when he explained that Mike had 'let him off the leash,' as they say."

"American Marines and their Bulldog euphemisms—always entertaining, and in this instance very helpful. What have you learned?"

"You mean, other than that little fact you discerned earlier?"

Tori smiled, "Noticed that, did you?"

He smiled in response and set the FBI file before her. "So did the FBI. Although it's not an issue in the Canadian military, it did prevent her from joining the American Marines when her cousin did."

"I didn't know she applied to join the American Forces. As a matter of fact, I'm quite sure Agent Commanda is unaware of the rejection as well. She has been quite vocal in her criticism of Deseronto for just that reason." Staring openly at the woman sitting quietly in the holding room, she asked reflectively, "How did they find out? The Marines, I mean. How did they learn she was a lesbian?"

"Evidently, when asked she said, and I quote, 'I'm only seventeen. I don't know what I am yet, but a homosexual could be a part of me.' "

Tori snuffed at that. "Interesting self-insight for a child."

"No disrespect mum, but weren't you a serving Midshipman by seventeen?"

Amused by his insight and the fact that he had called her out, she smiled, nodding the point to him. "All right, explain the coffee and the fact that you have Siobhan scouring the terminal for a vending machine sandwich, when she and Allan are already visiting the canteen?"

"Ah, the food issues, yes it's all right here." Darcy flipped the pages of the file to the relevant section. "She and Agent Commanda have a number of food allergies and sensitivities to the standard American diet. It's evidently quite common amongst their race. Reactions can be quite severe and are atypical in most cases."

"Explain?"

"To begin with, the introduction of sugar has caused an epidemic of Diabetes, with levels of affected persons reaching as high as fifty percent in one generation . . ."

Tori held up her hand to gently cut him off. "I look forward to reading your full report, Doctor. For now, may we fast forward to Deseronto's particulars?"

"Very good, mum! Deseronto, obviously aware of her dietary risks, refuses to eat several of what we would consider staples. What is interesting, is that many foods are quite noxious to her, usually resulting in severe nausea and sometimes vomiting. The Flight Surgeon has prescribed a cancer medication for the nausea. Evidently, while very expensive, it is the only effective pharmaceutical solution."

"You disagree?"

"No, well yes and no," he admitted. "I believe there is a psychological element in the food issues. The coffee for example, is an instant catalyst for the nausea. Evidently, just the smell is enough to affect her."

"It says that?" Tori asked, surprised by the level of detail he had garnered from what was supposed to be a security file, not personal medical information.

"Again no," Darcy admitted. "There are comments regarding her service commanding a C-130 Hercules in Canada. One that caught my eye, was a complete prohibition of coffee on board her aircraft, while allowing tea to be served. Evidently, she stocked an ice chest for the crew on every flight. While the other Flight Commanders were spending their meager discretionary funds on pizza parties and pub nights, she outfitted her crew with new aviation headsets and custom flight jackets. There is a mention of complaints from the Quartermasters. She reportedly hounded them relentlessly, to insure her crew had the latest safety equipment, and flight paraphernalia."

"So, she's a conscientious officer. That doesn't explain the coffee."

"I assumed it might be one of the catalysts mentioned, although there is no list of what they might be. As you noted, she did not react to the coffee when you were in the room. However, once you departed, she quickly recapped the takeout cup and carefully placed it in the wastepaper bin, then moved that as far from her as the room allows."

Tori harrumphed her acknowledgement. Before she could ask more, Allan and Siobhan knocked, then re-entered the observation room. Siobhan, always conscious of her job as Personal Assistant to Tori, set out the plates of sandwiches and crisps before handing over a takeout cup of coffee. "Double milk not cream?"

Taking a cautious sip, Tori nodded her thanks before turning her attention back to the team's psychiatrist. "All right Darcy, we've not much time. Not if we're to review the surveillance footage and hope to meet our briefing as scheduled."

Without further prompting, Darcy grabbed the cellophane packet from the table and headed out the door. Minutes later a Customs Warder entered the holding room and unceremoniously tossed the vending machine sandwich on the table and left. Interestingly enough, while Deseronto had acknowledged the Warder, she had not asked him anything or objected when he left without comment. The team munched quietly on their lunch while watching Deseronto in the adjacent room. She sat quietly for a lengthy moment, before inspecting the packet label and unwrapping the sandwich. Carefully disassembling her lunch, she set the bread and cheese on one half of the open wrapper, and the ham and buttery lettuce on the other side, and carefully inspected each. Taking her time, she munched quietly on the lettuce and ham slices. It was interesting to watch Deseronto eat. The cheese and bread went completely ignored, as if they didn't exist. What remained, had become her entire focus. Appearing completely satisfied, it would be difficult to imagine her enjoying a five-star meal, more. As they watched, Deseronto, finished the ham then the lettuce and began licking the butter from her fingertips before suddenly stopping, perhaps conscious of the surveillance. Any discomfort she may have experienced appeared to be quickly dismissed, as she quietly resumed her patient vigil.

"She's tossed the makings, the bread and cheese?" Siobhan questioned.

"So, what's she doing now?" Allan asked, "Just waiting?"

They all wondered the same thing. They speculated on her strategy, or if she even had one, for the next half hour. Then Deseronto surprised them all.

Standing up, she walked around the interview table and wrapped her knuckles on the one-way glass. She looked to the camera, in the upper corner of the room, before announcing, "I know what's going on. Send her back in."

Tori waited ten minutes before returning to the interview room. While she waited, she listened as Darcy challenged each of the juniors to speculate on Deseronto's next move.

Back in the holding room, Tori silently reclaimed the chair across from the woman.

"You're not from the Foreign and Commonwealth Office!" Deseronto challenged, adding, "A low-level officer wouldn't know much about Canada, or Indians for that matter, or even the BNA Act, but you're not a low-level officer. Are you?"

"Why do you say that?"

"A low-level officer would never say *our policy*," Cleo explained, hammered the point, "Our Policy! Not British policy. Not UK policy. Not even the more correct, policy of Her Majesty's government."

Tori's continued silence forced Cleo to push on. "My guess is that your clearance level is way out of my league and as for who or whom you actually represent . . . my guess is that you work for the Security Services. MI5, MI6, I really have no clue which one but it's there, something's there. Now . . . tell me what Her Majesty's government wants with a washed-up transport pilot, who now makes a living hawking books, and trying to survive on a broke-down farm in Canada?" A long silence followed, but Deseronto seemed determined not to break it.

Wanting to shake things up, Tori, with a very straight face said, "You forgot to add the part about being a poor suffering Red Indian!"

The shock on Deseronto's face was evident for all to see, then something changed. It was as if she was suddenly aware of the game at hand. "So, you have a sense of humor! How about you tell me your name?"

Again, ignoring the question, Tori appeared either out of patience, or simply disinterested.

"So . . . if you're not willing to tell me your name . . ." Deseronto said, with a crooked grin, "I'm guessing there's little chance of you joining me for dinner?"

Too experienced to let even that little irony show, Tori announced "Miss Deseronto," before correcting herself. "Captain Deseronto, your cooperation has been appreciated. A driver is waiting to take you to your hotel. He will have all of your belongings." Standing, and clearly indicating the interview over, Tori signaled for Deseronto to head through the door first.

"Wait," protesting with a growing smile, Deseronto challenged amiably, "That's it. Here's your hat, what's your hurry? Can't you tell me anything?"

Tori guided her by the elbow, escorting her into the hall. Once clear of the room, she turned a disarming smile on her interview subject. "There was some question regarding your loyalty," she explained gently. "Nothing to concern yourself with. I'm quite confident Sir Richard will explain everything tonight and at some length." With that said, she indicated to Allan, who was standing a discreet distance away. "This young man will escort you to a waiting vehicle, which will take you to your hotel." Allan picked up Deseronto's single suitcase, and without exchanging a word, signaled for her to follow him to the promised car.

Tori watched as Deseronto, without further question, followed Allan from the security corridor to the main terminal. *Not what I expected would be a vast understatement.*

Security and Intelligence Service (MI6)
Vauxhall Cross, London

Part of being a good analyst is the ability to see the big picture with only a few pieces of the puzzle in place. Allan Bashir was particularly adept at seeing the big picture. His weakness, which he was always the first to admit, was behavioral analysis. "Who could understand why anyone did what he or she did," he would say, often putting it down to fate. Of course, Dr. Darcy Gerrard, the touchy-feely member of the team, would always have a retort. Allan hated that. He figured psychiatrists should be treated much like other people's children: seen but not heard. Focusing more on the subject of the video, than anything Darcy was saying, Allan interrupted the good doctor. "All I am asking is, can she do it?" The smallest hint of a Persian accent made his voice distinctly aristocratic.

"Can she do it?" Darcy repeated. "Bleeding hell Allan! Have you not heard a word I've said?"

"Of course I heard you," Allan answered, resenting the constant chiding. "I was just wondering when you would get around to making your point."

"Well, let me put this plainly," Gerrard said without condescension, simply needing to have the last word. "Your officer here, looks to be quite capable of managing most situations. However, much of her confidence comes from a belief that help is on the way." Darcy paused to insure he had everyone's attention. "As long as she can retain that hope, she will do quite well. But . . ."

"But?" Sir Richard asked. He and Tori had been listening intently to the psychiatrist's evaluation of Cleo Deseronto's behavior at Heathrow. Sir Richard had approved the field evaluation they were reviewing. He believed it an unfair trial but a necessary one.

Darcy halted the playback and selected another clip from the surveillance video. He waited for Sir Richard's signal before continuing. "Here we see something interesting," he said, maximizing Cleo's face and eyes. "I believe this is an extremely discrete survey of the holding room. Miss Deseronto begins by examining only one small section of the wall. Here, watch the eyes," Darcy said with emphasis. "She follows a line then stops, waits a discrete amount of time, before moving on to a new area." His tone had an air of admiration. "And here," he said again, pointing to the magnified eyes on the large screen.

Sir Richard looked to Tori, "Did you notice this?"

"No," she admitted, shaking her head with surprise and growing respect.

"Darcy," Sir Richard asked, "your final evaluation is that she will survive if captured?"

"No! What I'm suggesting is that she will survive for as long as she has hope. When all hope is gone, she will take matters into her own hands. And regardless of what the Americans say, in time they will wear her down enough, and she will lose hope."

Tori had to ask, "You're saying that once they break her, she'll what? Kill herself?" As uncomfortable as the question was, they were all thinking the same thing. "Darcy?"

Dr. Gerrard raised his hands to stop the questions. "No, no, no," he said patiently. "What I meant is that she will attempt to escape without our assistance and at all cost. There is a spiritual element at play, which is difficult to gauge, and a calm that borders on disassociation. Even here in the vids, Captain Deseronto is clearly claustrophobic yet continuously assesses the situation, makes a plan, and stays calm for over five hours!"

Tori, still finding his evaluation incredulous, interrupted, "I don't understand. If she's claustrophobic, why wait to take a runner? Besides, it's a fool errand, that room is escape-proof."

Even Sir Richard smiled at her assumption.

"We all know it's completely secure, but she does not." He pushed ahead knowing Tori was somewhat doubtful of his evaluation. "At this point nothing has happened that would impinge on her confidence. Having said that, you should know she is still hard at work assessing her options." He looked back down at the list he had made of pertinent clips and clicked the mouse to open another file. As the new video clip was buffering, he took the opportunity to magnify the area around Cleo's eyes. "Tell me what you see?"

"She's looking at something directly in front of her," Tori answered.

Darcy gestured for her to continue with her scrutiny. Tori Braithwaite, the SOE Commander, wasn't considered an expert in Behavioral Analysis although she was determined to learn and recognize micro-expressions and improve her body language skills. The psychiatrist offered her a clue. "Tell us what is in front of Miss Deseronto?"

"Just a wall," Tori answered, her confusion obvious, before clarifying, "The observation room one-way glass."

"The observation glass," Darcy repeated. "Was the observation glass upgraded?" He asked without waiting for an answer. "Look carefully. Now watch how she surveys the room . . . and look at how she has begun to make comparisons to the other walls. Is there a discernible difference?"

Before anyone could say more, a loud cackling roar burst forward from the back of the room. "I told you she's a bright wee lass!" Rod Nelligan, the resident Scottish Bard and old man of the pack had entered the briefing late. He wasn't interested in what Dr. Darcy Gerrard had to say. As far as he was concerned, the only thing that mattered was how one Cleopatra Deseronto behaved under fire. "My guess," Rod said, "is that our girl here has noticed that those cheap bastards at Heathrow, only upgraded the observation wall, and the one-way glass. She'd be out of that room faster than those arses in observation could trip over their feet to chase her."

Tori, a little insulted by the arses-in-observation comment, wasn't so convinced. "Chief," she said, addressing him in the tradition of his Royal Navy rank of Chief Petty Officer, "you're a loyal man but a bit generous in your estimation, don't you think?"

Before anyone could comment, Allan interrupted them with a question. "Perhaps we should discuss the real issue. Knowing she will survive until rescued is not the point. The real concern is *if* she will be rescued?"

"Allan's right," Sir Richard answered, effectively putting an end to the debate. "If we ask her to do this, she needs to know the SAS isn't waiting in the wings." That was enough information to turn a few heads. Only twelve people outside the room knew anything about the plan they were considering. While the American plan was far from being presentable to the Joint Intelligence Committee, Sir Richard knew in his gut they needed to make it work and Cleo Deseronto was the foundation they needed to build on.

"Isn't this the reason the Americans are suggesting we make use of her Indian Status?" Tori asked. "They believe it will provide a shield of sorts for her and Agent Commanda?"

It was Dr. Gerrard, ever the sci-fi enthusiast, who voiced the common concern in his own special way. "If Iranian Intelligence decides they want to keep her, it won't matter if she and Agent Commanda are Mohawks. As far as Iran may be concerned, our two Indian Princesses could be invading Klingons. The issuer of their passport will be inconsequential if anyone suspects them of espionage. And, there is the issue of history," he added. "While most nations throughout the Americas recognize the sovereign rights of their aboriginals, the rest of the world has taken to accepting the notion that these people, and their tribes, are long extinct." Darcy had hit the mark with his assessment, although a few eyes rolled at his Star Trek parallel. Would the Iranians see Cleo and Bo Commanda as Americans or aboriginals still living under the subjugation of the west? Everything hinged on that perception. It was a question that had to be answered quickly. A detailed workup of the plan would require all parties involved.

Sir Richard surveyed the somber faces in the room. "Do we bring her in?"

Before Allan could formulate his thoughts, Rod Nelligan was on his feet. "You've just stewed over five hours of tape. You haven't learned any more than I've been telling you from the start! She's a wee little thing in person, and a giant under fire. It's all yah' need to know!"

"What exactly happened between you two?" Darcy asked Rod pointedly. Everyone else would have considered the question impertinent, knowing that Sir Richard had also been involved in the same operation. They all knew that close to twenty years ago, a squad of Canadian peacekeepers, which included Cleo, had been called in to rescue the two men. They had been flying a Sea King avionics test-bed helicopter, and had crashed on the northern border of Israel. The team had never been apprised of the details and no one had asked until now.

Before Rod could respond, Sir Richard stood. "Do we proceed?" he asked the room, cutting off the debate and halting any probe into a past that included Cleo Deseronto.

Allan answered first. "Yes. But we must bring her in now."

"Agreed," Darcy chimed in without further comment.

They knew the Chief's opinion on the matter. That left the final say with Tori. Not that her view would halt the planning now, but her opinion did matter. The organizational chart listed her as the Commanding Officer of the Special Operations Executive. Her work as an analyst as well as her extensive field experience made her one of the most knowledgeable officers in the building. That combination was invaluable, even if she was Sir Richard's daughter. "I'm not convinced," Tori said. Respectfully she added, "but we should still brief her on the plan. Perhaps we should consider asking Agent Commanda to take the lead?"

"What?" Rod Nelligan said with disgust. "You want us to entrust a second rate *G-Man* with a mission like this? Tori-girl," Rod said, appealing to his goddaughter, "why would yah' ask us tah' do that?"

Rod and Tori went back and forth for a few minutes, arguing with vigor and respect. While everyone looked and listened, it was Darcy's job to scrutinize the behavior of both speakers. While Tori seemed confident of her opinion, he began to think that she was just going through the motions with the chief. Uncharacteristically, Tori didn't appear to care if she won the debate. Was that because she knew the rest of the team was positive about Captain Deseronto or because she wasn't actually sure about the American FBI agent? If she didn't think Commanda was the person to lead the operation, then why fight for her at all? He sat back in his chair, making a mental note to question her later. He had a sneaky suspicion about her motivation. *If I'm right, do I confront Tori, or inform C?*

C was the code letter for the head of the UK's Security and Intelligence Service, or MI6, as most people still preferred to call the ultra-secret agency. Sir Richard wasn't particularly fond of the tradition that saw him constantly referred to as C. The moniker had begun with Captain Sir Mansfield Cumming

RN, the first head of MI6, who signed documents with just the capital of his last name. When Ian Fleming, once a member of MI6, began writing his spy adventures he included the code letter theme but changed the boss's initial from *C* to *M*. The current C turned for the door, announcing as he left, "Rod and I will brief her tonight. Then we'll see if she wants in."

All about the Dress
Camden, London

The car stopped three doors down from the shop. Cleo grabbed her book bag and her suitcase and thanked the driver before heading for the door. The rain had started up again and a young English woman practically collided with her before she could drag herself and her luggage inside.

"Allo! Can I help you?"

Smiling at the shop clerk, Cleo explained apologetically, "I'm a few hours late. Will you let Parminder know I'm here?"

"Whaut?" the girl asked, looking at her with confusion. "Ew yew on about?"

"I'm looking for the boss?" Cleo pointed to the design studio door, at the rear of the shop. "Parminder?" she repeated, when she realized the woman really had no idea who she was asking for.

"Oy," was all the young woman said before turning to the same door Cleo had indicated. Hauling it wide open she called out, "Mindy! There's some nutter out here askin' for cheese!"

Parminder Dutt popped around the layout table, calling out in her pleasant East End accent, "Is that the voice of a noble savage?"

"I have come from the land of rivers and lakes and claim this place for my own," Cleo announced in her best Hollywood Injun voice.

"Well you can claim all you like," Parminder offered cheerfully, entering the shop with a smile. "The real trick will be having you explain it to the Council."

The shop clerk watched the exchange with absolute dismay. "Two nutters! I'll put the kettle on then," leaving Parminder and Cleo to laugh at each other.

"You are late!" Parminder said unassumingly and with a big affectionate hug. "How do you expect me to run a professional shop with customers like you?"

"You won't believe it! Customs grabbed me over some bogus complaint."

"You're joking?"

The sound of the whistle from the kettle grabbed their attention. Parminder signaled for Cleo to follow. She grabbed the handle of Cleo's suitcase, heading for the studio. Once there, Cleo plopped herself in a chair while Parminder joined her shop clerk in the adjoining kitchenette. She listened contently as her friend instructed the other woman in Cleo's preferences.

"Whaut! No milk! Who drinks tea with no milk?" The shocked young woman carried a full cup of black tea and set it on the layout table in front of Cleo. "Nutter," she repeated to herself, while shaking her head, as she carried her own milky version back to the showroom.

Once the door that separated the studio from the store was closed, both women howled with laughter. "That poor girl will never be the same," Cleo said, barely able to spit it out. The ridiculousness of the moment fit perfectly with the theme of the day.

It took them both a few minutes to settle down. That's when Parminder raised her concern again. "So, what happened at Heathrow?"

"I'm not really sure! At first I was accused of trafficking in Indian artifacts."

"Indian?" Parminder asked. "Oh, you mean North American Indian, I assume?" She nodded, letting Parminder continue. "Please tell me you're not talking about that kit you brought the boys last year?"

"Hey! I made that stuff for them. And just because you are not fond of your brother-in-law does not mean your nephews should go without."

"I wasn't suggesting they go without," Parminder corrected her friend. "Besides, the boys chat up everyone they can about the real Red Indian, who came to their house and could take bad dreams away."

"Take bad dreams away? Oh yeah, the story of the Dream Catcher. How is Leo, anyway?"

"The pediatrician can't believe the difference in him. He sleeps every night and his confidence is growing in leaps." Parminder was extremely proud of her nephew. He had been a difficult baby who had grown into a frightened little boy. When Cleo heard Leo's story she wanted to meet the boys. She had even frightened Parminder with tales of malevolent spirits who sometimes attached themselves to the souls of small innocent children. On her first visit, the boys were dazzled by the stories and gifts, and couldn't wait to tell everything to their neighbors and friends. Of all the stories, the shortest and probably most important was the teaching of the Dream Catcher.

Cleo waited until bedtime, giving Parminder and her brother-in-law time to hang the Dream Catcher in the boys' bedroom window. She had made two of them, not knowing the kids shared a room. The spare one now became a useful visual aid for the storytelling. With the kids tucked in, the adults, eager for some grown-up time withdrew, leaving Cleo to deliver the bedtime story. When Parminder came up to check on her friend, she found that Harry had joined Leo in the lower bunk and Cleo was sitting cross-legged, discussing magnetism with them. She had given each of them a magnet, that had come from who knows where, and instructed them to connect the ends. When they did, the two magnets snapped together firmly, requiring Cleo to help pull them apart. Once separated, she had Harry, the older boy, turn his around, changing the polar orientation and instructed him to connect it with Leo's magnet again. This time they couldn't make the two magnets bond and the effort stirred up a little giggle fest. Cleo let them laugh it off before asking what had happened.

"They don't work when the letters are the same!" Harry said, taking the lead as expected. When Cleo looked to Leo for confirmation, the little guy explained by pointing to the North marking on his magnet.

"Wow, you guys are smart." Cleo said, sincerely impressed with the quick comprehension. "So they can only stick together when they are opposite?" Both boys nodded. "Well, that's exactly how the Dream Catcher traps bad dreams and lets the good ones go through. The string in the web has good medicine. When a bad dream tries to come in it gets stuck just like the magnets were stuck and can't escape. Now when a good dream flies in, and meets the good string, the dream gets sent right through!"

"Do they stay in there? The bad dreams?" Leo asked, almost in a whisper, while pointing to the spider web-like net.

"Actually, bad dreams get sucked inside the magic string. They can't get out, even if you touch it." Cleo did just that with the spare one, tracing her finger in different directions on the webbed circle. "They're stuck inside until the sun comes out. Every time the sun comes up, it pulls the bad dreams into the heat of its rays where they melt away. Once a bad dream is stuck in your Dream Catcher, it can never bother you again." She chided herself for that one. If any part of her story failed, just one nightmare would do it, and Leo would lose confidence in everything she had said and done.

"Wow, I can't believe that was almost a year ago."

Putting her cup down on the layout table, Parminder challenged her. "I do believe you're stalling? Now if you're not going to tell me what happened at Heathrow, just say so."

Cleo put her cup down too, shaking her head. "It's not that. I just don't want to bore you with my family crap."

"So that's it? The next installment of Boudicca's Revenge. Or perhaps you might prefer Boudicca Strikes Back!"

"Oh, I like that!" No matter what was going on, she always enjoyed Parminder's perspective on things. "Actually, I did have a thing . . . sort of."

"You met a girl!" Parminder said with astonishment. The way it came out of Parminder's mouth, made it sound more like curl than girl.

"Are you still a girl if you're over thirty?"

"I think so. At lease I think I will always be a girl!"

"Really?" Cleo said, mocking her friend. "You don't think you'll always be a girl. You're just hoping you'll always be girl enough to chase one."

Parminder took the last sip of tea from her cup and smiled over the rim. "I can't help it if I pull all the women. Besides, we were discussing you meeting someone. Anyone, actually!"

"Well, don't get too excited. It's typical. You meet someone who interests you and they don't even notice you exist. And, don't give me a hard time about being shy. I even asked her out."

"You?" Parminder was stunned. "How very scandalous," she said, adding, "she must have been something?"

"Putting aside the fact that I don't know her name, and she wasn't interested, I will only admit to being slightly smitten. Actually," she confessed, "she really got to me."

"Now that is something. My mate Cleo may just be human after all. I was beginning to think you might grieve forever," she said gently, smiling at her friend. "There may be hope for you yet."

"Well . . . I figured it would just be a matter of time."

"A year or two would be a suitable amount of time after losing a beloved partner. Four years?" Parminder added with raised brows, "is a very long time to be without love."

"You mean without sex," Cleo shot back at her closest friend, regretful the minute she said it.

Parminder took it in stride, shaking off the crack with a laugh, "I do believe we were discussing your love life!"

Golestan Café
Tehran, Islamic Republic of Iran

Yusuf Suyfias was a cautious man by nature, but it was his training in counter-intelligence, that made him dangerous. Standing in a shaded doorway, steps from the market he had just sauntered through, he watched carefully for signs that he had been followed. He had made this type of spot-check several times during his morning sojourn. Now confident that he was not shadowed, he cut back through the market, heading to a small café. Once inside he took a seat near the front window, and sat with his back to the wall and both exits in clear view. There would be no surprise amongst his colleagues if he ran into anyone he knew, after all, this was his morning ritual, and everyone in the VAGA, the Islamic Republic of Iran's Ministry of Intelligence, knew he daily traversed the backstreets and markets of Tehran for dead-drops and markers. In the ten or so years he had served within the Counter-Intelligence section of *Vezarat-e Ettela'at Jomhuri-ye Eslami-ye Iran*, he had also inserted himself as the "go-to" man for all things desired by his higher-ups. It was this unofficial duty that had brought him to the café and the unsavoury business at hand.

From where he was sitting, it was easy to watch the man making his way across the street. While Suyfias had never met him, he had compiled a complete dossier on one Hasid Mosaddegh. Suyfias stood when Mosaddegh entered the restaurant, quietly beckoning him over. The two men eyed each other carefully, "As-salamu alaykum."

Mosaddegh nodded solemnly, "Wa 'alaykum al-salaam," he replied before offering his hand. When Suyfias hesitated to accept his outstretched hand, he offered his own opinion of the situation. "Like you Major, I only serve those with such needs. I find this business repugnant as well!"

That seemed to comfort Suyfias somewhat. He offered his hand in a friendly sort of shake. "Please sit," he said, indicating the empty seat across from him. "How do you know this request, or 'needs' as you called them, are not my own?"

Hasid smiled, "Major Suyfias, like you, I do my homework. From all that I have garnered, you are a good man, loyal to Allah above all. In many ways, you and I share many of the same duties. We are both responsible for finding that which will please our superiors."

Suyfias's smile was tolerant, even if he didn't like what the man said. "My duty is to VAGA and the safety of Iran."

"Of course!" Hasid agreed. "But sometimes to serve the greater good, we must placate the powers that be. There is no shame in that, Major. No shame at all."

The intense scrutiny Suyfias focused on Hasid was usually all it took to put his lessers on shaky ground. Hasid Mosaddegh was either too stupid to realize he was dealing with someone far his superior in intellect and power, or he was a far more connected criminal than Suyfias had imagined. Scrutinizing the man seated across from him, he noted professionally that his suit jacket and trousers were mismatched, the collar of his shirt, while clean and pressed was frayed and worn, as were the winter gloves that sat on top of an old winter jacket Hasid had strewn across an empty chair. *What are you*, Suyfias asked himself. *You dress like a sheep herder, but you talk like a soldier. Yet nothing in my research indicated military service.* "Where did you serve?"

There was no masking the astonishment on Hasid's face. "Ah! I was told you are a very receptive man. I was a tank sergeant with the Republican Guard, Iraqi Republican Guard. Are you surprised?"

Ignoring the question, the counter-intelligence officer in Suyfias, struck at the heart of his concern. "Did you abandon your post like so many cowards did?"

"What? No, of course not! My unit fought until ordered to surrender. My commander ordered us to the border where we set fire to our tanks. We buried our ammunition in several caches, then crossed the border."

While his explanation was reasonable, there was little chance the major could verify much more than if, and when, he had crossed into Iran.

"Major! I work now as I did then, for my commanding officer. This unsavoury business we have taken on, has one purpose, and one purpose only: The complete removal of the infidels from Iraq and the restoration of Islam."

After long consideration, Suyfias nodded his approval. "You are a good man, Hasid. Tell your commander that I will need detailed maps of the weapons caches, and you will have a friend in VAGA."

Chapter Two

The Bombay Bicycle Club Restaurant
West London, United Kingdom

The Bombay Bicycle Club or the *other BBC*, as regulars referred to it, was one of the best-kept secrets in London. The small walk-down was barely noticeable against the myriad of signage for the fashionable shops above and beside. The regular clientele, an exclusive bunch, were more than enough to keep the place hopping.

Cleo hadn't wanted to be late but she didn't want to end up being so early she would have to wait at the bar. She always felt like she had entered enemy territory whenever she entered a straight bar. Even though she had spent her entire career almost exclusively working with men, she still felt uncomfortable in social situations. She was especially uncomfortable around civilian men, who often lacked the code of honor instilled in military personnel. A bar, she believed, was the worst-case scenario. Cleo was sure that the rules of social conduct were compromised with every drink served. It was always easy to find some guy who had drunk more than was acceptable, and had the mouth to prove it. Somehow, for a certain type of guy, the principle of equality was an invitation for rude and aggressive behavior.

Groaning at her own trepidation, she pushed the restaurant door open. The Interior, was something else, with polished oak panels, leaded glass pane dividers, and a volume of artwork that invoking a theme of Flemish Masters. She smiled recognizing a reproduction of a Rubens she was particularly fond of. Succulent odors wafted from the kitchen while a uniformed Maître d' smiled at her, from behind an oak lectern. Without realizing it, the tension in her shoulders began to dissipate.

"Mademoiselle Deseronto." The Maître d' surprised Cleo by addressing her personally. "The gentlemen are waiting in the Green Room."

The *Green Room* seemed a strange name for the ornate dining room. From her perspective, the only thing green was a pantsuit worn by a ruddy-faced woman, and a very healthy ficus tree. Perhaps the room had once been green or the name had come from some long forgotten tradition. The Maître d' signaled for her to follow. As they made their way through the room, Cleo scanned the tables but didn't recognize anyone. After reaching the far side, she was sure he had made a mistake, but before she could ask, he opened a door that had been completely hidden by the elaborate wood moldings.

Inside the restaurant's private dining room, Rod Nelligan was the first on his feet to welcome Cleo. Dressed in a Scotsman's Tuxedo, a kilt and short black dinner jacket, he swept her into his strong arms with great enthusiasm. There was always an air of joviality about the chief that she so admired.

"Chief," she hollered, trying to control a squeal of delight. Chief Petty Officer 1st Class, Rodney Nelligan, Royal Navy (ret.), was one of Cleo's all-time favorite people, and had been ever since their first meeting almost twenty years earlier.

"Aye lass," Rod crooned in her ear, "how is it yah look better and better every year? And wearing a dress too! Bless ye'r heart."

"Charmer!" When the chief finally released her from his bear hug, Cleo turned to meet the other guest in the room. A tall slender man, in a charcoal suit, reached out to shake her hand. "Étienne?" she said with shock and joy, "You're here?"

Étienne for his part, seemed delighted that she recognized him, after so many years of mail-only correspondence. He was surprisingly overwhelmed when Cleo bypassed the outstretched hand to deliver the second bear hug of the night.

"You are not upset with me?" Étienne asked, with sincere concern.

She was staggered by the question. "What am I supposed to be upset about?" Étienne gave her a weak smile but said nothing.

When the chief realized he wasn't going to explain, he motioned for Cleo to take a seat. The small dining room included one round table, elegantly set for five. When she turned to look where he was signaling, she found the room also housed a grouping of leather wingback chairs and a well-worn nail head chesterfield. Cleo sat down with Chief Nelligan. Over the course of their friendship, he had asked her to call him by his first name on umpteen occasions, only to receive the same reply: "Okay, Chief!"

"Cleopatra, my girl, what our dear Frenchman is not saying, is that he is very sorry for the way those lairy yods at your Defense HQ treated you."

Before the chief could explain more, Étienne set drinks in front of them. Cleo was about to turn down what looked like a gin and tonic when he explained, "it is Soda only," adding, "and some lime. *C'est comme vous l'aimez, non?*"

"*Oui*, perfect. Wait! How did you . . ." Cleo looked back and forth between the two men, "What's going on?" When they didn't immediately answer, she questioned them again, this time with what she did understand. "How is it that my old CO, whom I have not seen in twenty years, knows what I like to drink? And don't think you're off the hook, Chief. How is it you know so much about my floundering career? The career I am now retired from?"

The two men looked at each other. Étienne hunched his shoulders and signaled for the chief to explain.

"We pulled your PersFile," Rod said, with some embarrassment. Explaining, "Sir Richard has an idea that yah just might want'a consider."

"You'll have to do better than that. The last time I checked, you, Chief, had retired and Colonel Ste. Hubert here, had been appointed to head the

SIU for the Canadian Forces. *Non?*" she turned her attention back to Étienne, her one-time troop commander.

"Cleopatra . . ." he pleaded, in his heavy New Brunswick, Côte du Nord accent.

"Don't call me that!" she snapped, quickly losing patience.

"Cleo," Étienne said, correcting himself, "you 'ave a right to be bitter. Your instinct made my career and damaged you. I was very sorry for that, but I 'ave a way that maybe will put you back in!"

She looked at him for a long moment. When they had first met, she was a Trooper. A cavalry rank equal to a Private First Class. As a qualified member of the Canadian Forces Reserve, Cleo had volunteered for duty with the United Nations. She was accepted and assigned for six months to a platoon of peacekeepers in Syria, along with a newly minted Lieutenant, Second Class, Étienne Ste. Hubert. On paper, Cleo was posted as a Military Driver in a time when most female peacekeepers were Radio Operators or Administration Clerks. While she took her driving duties seriously, keeping "her G-Wagon" safe and clean, she had actually been selected for the posting because of her secondary trade qualification.

As a thirteen-year-old Royal Canadian Air Cadet, a sort of Boy Scout of the Air Force, Cleo Deseronto had taken an interest in photography. The Commanding Officer of her cadet squadron, wanting to encourage her, placed a request with Air Force Training Command for one photographic training kit. He was sure nothing would come of the request, knowing full well that training kits were rarely issued to reservists, much less young cadets. To his surprise, a large crate arrived several weeks later. The sturdy plywood box was larger than a steamer trunk. Stenciled on the crate lid was a description of the contents: MOC 541: Photo Tech: Training Set: Complete. With no other kids interested in the subject, the entire kit was issued to Cleo as a self-study project. By the time she was old enough to attend the cadet summer photography camp, she was already more experienced and better qualified, than most of the professional instructors provided by the Armed Forces.

When Cleo volunteered to serve with the local Militia Regiment, she learned that Photo Tech was solely a trade of the Air Force, forcing her to choose from primary occupations specific to armored regiments. When the Warrant Officer in charge of recruiting offered her a spot as a clerk, she handed over her cadet trade certificates and her civilian driver's license, which clearly showed that she was qualified to operate any truck up to five tons, with or without air brakes.

"I would like to volunteer as a Vehicle Tech," she said. "There are other MOCs for which I qualify, but I believe I can serve best as a driver." Twenty minutes later, her application was approved, making her the first female driver in the Regiment.

Way back when she had first arrived in Syria, Étienne explained that she would work double-duty as both Driver and Photographer. She would never forget the hours they put in, updating the UN operations plan, including updating all the large binders of photographic documentation. They had worked well together.

"Stop right there," Cleo said. "The first thing you guys need to know is that I'm okay with how my career turned out. Yes, I miss flying, but I was ready to move up from the Hercules. We all know they were never going to give me an Airbus, not even if they had allowed me a promotion board. Now Étienne, I do not regret, not for a minute, blowing the whistle on the officer cadets who were being recruited by the nationalists. I knew I'd get burnt eventually. So stop thinking you're somehow responsible." By this point, she was back on her feet, and seriously considering making a break for it.

"Cleo, my girl . . ." Rod said, standing to join her.

She cut him off before he could say more. "Please, Chief! I'm not sure I want to hear what it is you two have cooked up. Honest to Gods, I don't have a problem with either of you. Chief, I love you and I think of you like a dad. A really good one! How could I be disappointed with you? Even if I thought you or even Admiral Braithwaite could somehow influence my career, you can't think I would have asked?"

"Of course not," Rod Nelligan said, now beaming with stouthearted pride. "This morning certainly proved that ta' all parties interested!"

"This morning?" she said, repeating it more than asking. "This morning!" This time it was an accusation. She'd been hauled in at Heathrow, and her military personnel file had been pulled, but by whom and why? Special Investigations Unit, Canadian Security and Intelligence Service, the British Security Service, Military Intelligence . . . MI6? *What the frack?* "Gentlemen," Cleo said flatly. "I think I've had enough excitement for one evening. Please excuse me." Without another word, she turned to leave, but was stopped dead in her tracks. Admiral Sir Richard Braithwaite was standing in the door with a guest. She had expected Sir Richard, and recalled seeing the table set for five. Now the fifth guest appeared amused and very aware that she was blocking Cleo's escape route.

Cleopatra Deseronto stood in the center of the ornately decorated private dining room, completely lost to her surroundings. She was standing less than an arm's length away from the nameless woman from Heathrow. Her hair was pinned up elegantly, showing off a delicate, milky white neck. Her dress and heels were the color of moss and beautifully offset the amber sparks in her hair and eyes. Cleo sensed the woman was talking but couldn't decipher a single word said. As her shock dissipated, she tried kicking her brain back in gear.

"Captain Deseronto!" Sir Richard announced formally, finally breaking through her mental fog. "Lady Dufferin, may I present Captain Cleopatra Deseronto, of Her Majesty's Canadians."

Recognizing the smirk on Sir Richard's face, Cleo knew there was more to come.

"Cleopatra, I wish to introduce you to, Royal Navy Captain, the Right Honorable Viscountess Dufferin." His introduction of Cleo, to her Ladyship, was an obvious reminder of Cleo's lower social ranking, The inclusion of her rank in the introduction acknowledged the mystery woman's higher military standing too. A Royal Navy Captain was equal to a full Colonel of the Canadian Armed Forces, or any military force for that matter, and that's when Sir Richard delivered his third salvo, "Of course, you know Lady Dufferin is my daughter!"

If the shock of actually meeting the woman who had interrogated her at Heathrow threatened to unraveled Cleo, this last bit of information landed like a ton of bricks.

Navy Captain Victoria Braithwaite—the Right Honorable Viscountess Dufferin—extended her hand. "I'm Tori," she said informally, with a tender and inviting smile. "I can't tell you how long I've wanted to meet you—properly that is. Father, and the chief, have said so much over the years that I feel we've already met."

Cleo was lost somewhere in Tori Braithwaite's eyes, and could barely breathe. Instinctively aware that everyone was watching her, she tried forcing a reply. "Hi." It was all she could muster. She did manage to take Tori's outstretched hand and shake it. At the feel of her soft warm skin, she was practically overwhelmed with sensation. Suddenly aware she had been staring wordlessly, she relinquished her hold on Tori, and stepped back to allow her and Sir Richard to join the group. Predictably, it was the old man of the party, Chief Nelligan, who began to put things right.

"How 'bout I play bar keep," Rod said, "while our Tori here, briefs everyone on the situation."

With everyone in agreement, they waited for Tori, then Sir Richard, to choose a chair before joining them in the cozy sitting area. Cleo, still very much off balance, sat down at the far end of the leather sofa. What happened next confused her even more. Tori got up and joined the chief at the sideboard. They chatted for a few seconds before she returned to the group, with her drink in hand, and another soda for Cleo. This time though, Tori chose the wingback chair next to her.

Once Étienne and Rod took their seats, it was Sir Richard who actually kicked things off.

"Cleo," he said, beginning with her, "you are familiar with some of the information about to be discussed. Other information, depending on how sensitive, will be made available to you as is necessary."

"Sir Richard," Cleo interrupted, "before you continue, I'm sure my security clearance is out of date. Is that why Étienne is here?"

Sir Richard looked at Étienne and then Rod Nelligan. "You haven't told her?"

Étienne confessed before Rod could say anything. "We had just begun."

Before he could explain further, Rod Nelligan started laughing, "You see lass, our baby boy here has gone over to the dark side. He is now the Intelligence Attaché at Canada House! Aye," the chief beamed, "A prouder papa there never was."

"CSIS Station Chief," Étienne said, explaining the chief's convoluted congratulations.

"Wow," was about all Cleo could say. Then something else dawned on her, forcing her attention back to Tori. "And I suppose you're in the family business too?"

Tori nodded. "You were quite correct in the assumptions you made at Heathrow." Now beginning her briefing in earnest, "You may remember that Cleo provided Étienne with some very interesting pics from her travels in the Middle East last year?"

"More than a year now. Is that what this is all about?"

Tori reached over and touched Cleo's arm in a gesture of patience. "Those photographs contained layer upon layer of data that took months to analyze. Frankly, we have been unable to convince anyone of our findings."

She stopped for a moment to take a sip of her drink, before turning her full attention to Cleo, "Without support amongst the intelligence community, we have been unable to act. That is, until now. With the increasing instability in Iran, we have decided, with our Intel Partners, that a more detailed reconnoiter of the area around Q'on is necessary."

Everyone sat quietly, waiting for Cleo's reaction.

"What's the plan?" Whenever it came down to crunch time, all Cleo really wanted to know was how to successfully complete the job at hand.

"We send you back in," Tori said. "Your pretense will be a new book. This time, you will have a larger budget from the publisher, which will be your excuse to loiter in the region for a longer period of time and hopefully provide you the opportunity to document the building in question."

"I know you guys are all up to speed," Cleo said. "But why can't you get what you need from one of your fancy satellites?"

"We can't get the angle low enough to provide confirmation of our analysis," Tori explained.

Cleo thought about that for a second, the fog that had consumed her only minutes before was now gone. "Are you telling me you can't get the necessary declination?" Then something else hit her. "Can you tell me what the analysts say I found?"

Tori looked to Sir Richard for approval first.

"A bunker built to house a centrifuge capable of generating enriched plutonium."

Cleo almost whistled as her head raced through all the variables that situation might present.

"Okay . . . Here's everything I know about nuclear stuff. There are three or four types of reactor, each suited to producing energy or isotopes according to the size of centrifuge. The grade of isotope generated is controllable but not variable and that again is related to the size of centrifuge."

"Which means . . ." Tori prompted.

"Which means, you can turn a reactor designed to produce medical isotopes into one capable of producing weapons-grade plutonium, but not without a huge increase in scale."

Before Tori could provide feedback, Sir Richard chimed in. "We need a closer look at that bunker before we can press Inspectors on Tehran."

"So," Cleo continued, thinking out loud. "You want me to what, backpack around Q'on, taking pictures of mud and brick huts, while trying to secretly uncover a hidden bunker?"

"Hidden bunker?" Étienne asked somewhat confused.

Once again it was Sir Richard who chose to explain. "When you sent us Captain Deseronto's photographs, your analysts had suggested Cleo had photographed an old fuel bunker. Our Intel says it started out that way but it has now become something much more dangerous."

"Cleo," Tori asked gently, "do you have any questions?"

"Questions?" She had flown too many missions both in peacetime and otherwise to not have an excellent grasp of the complexities of operational planning. "I have hundreds of questions." Then it occurred to ask the most important. "Will I have access to the satellite reconnaissance Intel and the photo analysis?"

"Yes," Sir Richard said. "You may access any materials you wish."

That turned a few heads. Up until that moment, Sir Richard had declared Cleo only needed access to the basic briefing pack. It included the type of high-level information a politician might see in a security briefing but none of the details on how the information had been collected or by whom. Sir Richard was a man who never ignored his gut, and on this occasion everything in him said to give the final planning to Cleo. After all, she would be the one who would need to make it work.

"Tori," he said, "get Cleo set up in the Tutor Room as soon as she is available." He then turned his attention to Étienne Ste. Hubert and Rod Nelligan. "I assume you two can arrange code word clearance for our Cleopatra. And Rod, I'll expect you to smooth things over with the Americans."

That caught Cleo's attention. She had shrunk slightly from Sir Richard's use of her given name but the fact that she might have to deal with US intelligence hit her harder.

"The Americans are involved? You're kidding me, right?"

"You need not be concerned," Sir Richard said, leaning forward to stress his point. "If you can devise a workable plan, count on having the choice to lead the team above any other party. You also have their assurance, and my own, that there will be no repeat of that Israeli nonsense."

For a moment, Cleo tried to think about what that would mean, completely losing her concentration when Tori touched her hand again.

"Perhaps I could join you tomorrow and bring you into Vauxhall?"

"I have a book signing tomorrow," she said, explaining her reluctance to set a time.

"At Waterstones, I understand. Would you mind if I popped by? I could queue up and get my copy signed. If you're not against it?"

At that moment, Sir Richard stood and the door to the dining room immediately opened. Two waiters, and what Cleo supposed was one of the chefs, marched in and began setting covered serving trays on the sideboard. Sir Richard invited everyone to take his or her seat at the table, and thus began one of the best prime rib dinners Cleo had ever enjoyed.

* * *

Hours later, alone in her hotel room, Cleo sat cross-legged on the bed, supporting her head in her hands, elbows resting on her knees. The evening had been more than enjoyable. She couldn`t remember the last time she had spent time with friends, and she couldn't recall ever meeting anyone like Tori. *I can't imagine a more beautiful and charming dinner companion. Tori is beautiful,* Cleo thought, *beautiful, and smart, and way out of my league.*

Cleo groaned to think of her behavior. She had been so shocked to meet the woman from Heathrow again, she was instantly overwhelmed and felt witless and shell-shocked at the same time. Learning that she'd been hauled in at Heathrow as some sort of test, should have been a wake-up call, but coming face to face with her enthralling interrogator had muted the warning horns blaring in her head. *Tori Braithwaite is Sir Richard's daughter! Go figure.*

Sir Richard was one of her oldest professional acquaintances. Someone she had come to think of as a friend. They had met under harrowing conditions, just minutes after Richard's Royal Navy helicopter crashed on the northern Israeli border. Finding the downed chopper had been the first test. Getting the three-man crew out of the wreck, seemed like a cakewalk in comparison, until one of her fellow Troopers stepped on a landmine. In that instant, everything changed. Cleo had charged from her cover position, to her friend's side without a second thought. Patrick had been supporting a wounded Richard Braithwaite in a fireman's carry when he took his last step. Richard had been shielded by Patrick's body from the spray of shrapnel, but the percussive wave had ripped open his already tended wounds. With Étienne's help, she had dragged Richard back to the van to join Rod Nelligan, the chopper's wounded crew chief. Once the bodies of the dead co-pilot and her best friend were on board, they made a successful hot retreat. In his After Action report, Richard had been emphatic in praising her role in the rescue, stating unequivocally that Cleo's individual actions had made the difference in their survival. They had become friends and had stayed in contact ever since. *If you were such a good friend, Richard, why did you wait twenty years to introduce me to your daughter?*

Over drinks, she had listened to the high-level briefing on the American plan, with polite interest. It had been more than a year since completing her one and only trip to Iran. The research tour had been approved solely for the study of traditional Persian architecture, and created the backbone for her second volume. The resulting manuscript was now in her publisher's hands and due for release within months. With the book now complete, she couldn't imagine going back. She had done her part, passing her photographs on, as a courtesy, and out of respect for her old friend Étienne. She wasn't an analyst and couldn't see how she could add any value to the information they had already collected.

Pulling herself from the bed, she walked to the window of her hotel room, moving the heavy curtain aside. With a single bedside lamp lit and the street in darkness, she was greeted with her own reflection. *Perfect*, she grumbled, taking in the eerie and indistinct likeness of herself. The street lights, adding a layer of shadowy overlap, only underscored her mood. Like staring at the ghost of Christmas past, Cleo stood patiently, waiting for some spark of insight. Was there some key that once turned, would move everything silently into perspective?

Instead of some epiphany, a wave of guilt washed through her, leaving her feeling stripped of the façade she had maintained all evening. This wasn't the first time a woman had turned her head, but never had it felt like this. She remembered everything in painstaking detail. The intelligence in her eyes when she spoke, the feel of her hand when she would reach out and touch

Cleo when making a point, or the smell of her perfume whenever she would lean closer to playfully conspire. Then there was the electricity. The constant surge of something she couldn't name, something she'd never known. To say "hand-in-glove" would be a massive understatement. Her grandmother had, years ago, told her of a medicine woman of great respect. "The river of life flows through her," she remembered hearing, and the idea fit the sensation. In Tori Braithwaite's company, she felt buoyant and alive. She was airborne again and without a hunk of tin to make it happen. Cleo had never loved anything more than flying and the realization produced even more guilt.

Closing her eyes to remember how many times Samantha had come to her when she was in this dark place. She remembered the way Sam would slide up behind her, slowly snaking her arms around Cleo's waist, saying, "I've got your six covered, fly girl," before retelling some story that would underline her confidence in Cleo. *Oh Sam, what the hell am I doing?* She groaned at the memory. *Samantha would probably just smile and give me one of her "God works in mysterious ways," maxims. Frack me!*

Waterstones Books
Trafalgar Square, London

As uncomfortable as she was in social situations that involved meeting strangers, Cleo had grown to enjoy these book signings. Her publisher had warned her that she would miss the interaction with both the proponents and the opponents of her philosophy. Writers were the last to agree to a media tour, and often the first to admit that, even though they were exhausted, they were disappointed it was over.

Tomorrow, Cleo would deliver her last lecture, a slideshow she called 100 Mile House. The concept went beyond the sustainable owner-builder housing. The idea was to limit the materials used to build a home to only those items available in the local region. What was the point in building a Straw-bale Home if you had to truck the straw in from the other side of the country, or if the Portland cement for the natural plaster had to be shipped from another state?

"Vernacular has to mean more than *by the people*," Cleo would often explain, using the Latin root. "Vernacular has to be *of* the people, of our Communities, and of the very sacred ground that sustains us, each and every day."

Parminder Dutt, who had volunteered to help out, was fluttering around the signing table, leaning in close, she whispered mischievously, "You have a special guest, a lovely woman is asking to meet you!" While teasing, Parminder was also curious. "She says you're old friends from Heathrow? Perhaps when you're done?" she suggested, signaling with her eyes to the last few readers waiting in line.

Cleo smiled. "No problem." She couldn't help but like the fact that Tori had shown up. She finished up her signing duties before turning to find Parminder and Tori chatting amiably. Tori was flipping through a copy of Cleo's book and clearly discussing some aspect with interest. Mindful of the cover story provided by MI6, just that morning, she joined the pair taking time to properly introduce them. "Parminder, this is Tori Waite, she's investigating the Trafficking of . . ."

"Squirrel!" a dark woman wearing a bureaucratic blue suit called to the group. Instantly, the color in Cleo's face drained away. Suddenly a study in stone, the temperature around them began to plummet.

The flash of ice Parminder was witnessing was uncharacteristic of her friend. "Cleo, what . . ."

"No *gor-am* way," Cleo hissed at Tori, turning to face her straight-on, and with teeth still clenched, she repeated, "No *gor-am frackin'* way!"

Suddenly worried, Parminder immediately demanded to know what was going on.

Tori, with the pinch of Cleo's outburst still on her face, finished the introductions. "This is Bo Commanda." Absent was any enthusiasm for what should have been a happy reunion.

Both Cleo and Tori could hear Parminder curse under her breath. "You must be Cleo's cousin," she said, now visibly embarrassed for having missed the obvious familial features. Ever conscious of her friend's issues, she was anxious to either terminate the meeting or move somewhere else to privately sort this bullocks. "I think we could all benefit from a quiet cup? I know a place close by . . . where we all might profit from a little less distraction?"

Tori agreed. This was the last place she wanted the cousins squaring off. Aside from the embarrassment of a public confrontation, the security risks under the circumstances were incalculable.

Security and Intelligence Service (MI6)
Vauxhall Cross, London

Sir Richard waited patiently for his daughter to report on the reunion at Waterstones. He had been notified of Her Ladyship's return to Vauxhall. It was now just a matter of time before she reported to him. Their SOP was for her to check in with her team, the Special Operations Executive, then walk up the two flights of stairs to his office. Whenever she skipped her team and reported directly to him, he knew someone had thrown a spanner in the works. The objective of today's meeting had been to get Cleo and Bo Commanda to sit down in a casual atmosphere and observe their interaction on a social level. Tori had been warned that tensions existed between the two, but had been assured those difficulties could be overcome. To be fair, Bo herself had said that their old animosities were long forgotten.

Sliding into the chair across from Sir Richard, Tori sighed, signaling her deep frustration. "We may have a problem," she said without elaborating.

For his part, Sir Richard was enjoying one of the quietest days he had experienced in years. He had more than an hour until his eight o'clock dinner engagement, and had just sat down to enjoy a drink of twenty-year-old scotch.

"Join me for a drink?" he asked. Tori nodded. Scotch neat was not her preference, but Sir Richard was sure she would appreciate something stiff.

"I take it, the reunion between our cousins did not go well?"

"Go well?" Tori said flatly, lamenting the whole farce, "these two have more issues than the Parliamentary Gazette."

Sir Richard sipped at his scotch. "Perhaps we should put them together with the good doctor. See what he can do to smooth things out."

Tori thought about his suggestion for a moment. "I'm not sure," she confessed. It was not as if they wouldn't benefit from time with the resident psychiatrist. "There is more to this than we've been told. I'm not at all sure we can solve the issues between them. If we hope to bring Captain Deseronto on board, we must create an atmosphere of trust." Tori had a method of verbally working her way through complex problems. She and her father had practiced the problem solving technique ever since she was a tot. The practice provided immediate feedback when trying to solve a problem. "Perhaps we should take another look at the SAS?" Tori suggested, lamenting the turn of events.

"The Special Air Service wouldn't get within twenty kilometers before being detected and we just haven't the data to support our actions. I may be willing to risk war with Iran but the Prime Minister will not. At the moment, the only plan we have requires Captain Deseronto. And I need you to make that work, whatever it takes."

Over the years, one just assumed that male officers in the field might be required to serve their country through intimate personal contact. For women officers the same commitment was sometimes necessary, although this uncomfortable reality would normally involve serious consideration long beforehand. Sir Richard had sent his only daughter into harm's way more than once, but had never considered asking her to get personally involved with anyone. How the world had changed. He needed Cleo Deseronto and there wasn't a single man around who could do what he needed of his own daughter.

"Take her out. Get her to trust you. You have to find a way to get them talking. I would think that much easier on a social footing," he added, taking a slow sip of his scotch. "Do remember, we need to keep the Americans in on this too, if for no other reason than to pick up the tab when all is said and done."

Tori nodded, her voice noncommittal. "Whatever it takes? Is that it?"

"As your father," he started, then stopped. What could he say? Go shag a woman I respect? Go shag the girl from Canada who saved my life? Gain her trust—break her heart? Richard Braithwaite sighed, as boss and head of the service, he expected her to do everything necessary for the success of the mission. On the other hand, as her father . . .

"What about a briefing?" Tori asked.

"Let's bring her in tomorrow afternoon," Sir Richard answered, looking over a copy of Cleo's agenda on his computer. "We need to push ahead. Set a full briefing, with all hands on board. She's giving a lecture tomorrow morning. It may prove interesting." Which was Sir Richard's way of telling her to be there. "In the meanwhile, I'm meeting Mike Perkins this evening. Let me take care of that end of this business," he said, watching quietly as his daughter finished her scotch. "Perhaps, when this is all sorted you might join your old dad for a meal?"

Tori just laughed and shook her head, "I am always available for you. Besides, we live in the same house," she reminded him then considered his mood. "You're a tad sentimental this evening?"

"I was just thinking, that other than you, and your dear departed mother, I have never cared for anyone as much as I do this particular young woman."

"It's not surprising. She saved your life."

"Victoria," reverting to the full Christian name her mother had wanted. "She kneeled in that van, with one hand in my chest and the other holding the hand of a dead boy. We were under constant fire and every lurch and jar of the truck felt like it would be my last." He swirled the dregs of his scotch absently. "Do you know she made me tell her nursery rhymes? I imagine the effort was to keep me conscious. The irony was that she'd never heard a bloody one of them! Can you imagine?"

"Where was Uncle Roddy?" While she stuck to *Chief* everywhere else, when they were alone, Tori still addressed Rod Nelligan as she had since childhood.

"He was strapped to a litter, out cold," his grin sentimental. "Their Med Aide died. We were flying Nap-of-the-Earth. We lost the tail rotor, and hadn't enough altitude to autorotate. My stomach still roils at the memory. As we teakettled, end over end, the main rotor blade slashed through the windscreen, killing my co-pilot instantly and knocking me out. My next memory is of a clean-faced boy cutting me free of the wreck. He taped me up, all smiles and jokes, then hauled me over his shoulder with hardly any effort. Three paces later, he was dead and Cleo was dragging me, one frightening step at a time. She took over the medical duties. You see, the boy who died was their medic, not to mention Cleopatra's best mate. She decided to knock your Uncle Roddy out and keep me talking. It was pure instinct. She had little training," he said, remembering every detail vividly. "The doctor said it saved my life and Rod's."

"Land mine?" Tori silently considered his positive response. "How does one stay so focused after witnessing such loss?"

"I asked her once. I wanted desperately to let her know how sorry I was about the boy's death. I remember there was such forgiveness in her eyes. She said simply, 'Tend to the living first. The dead will always wait.'"

"Incredible, really, and with such character I can't understand how her career has progressed so poorly ever since. I've read her entire personnel file and the security files and I can't find any real problems, just unconfirmed innuendo. If she had served here, I imagine the RAF would have made her a Wing Commander by now and given her a NATO or UN command. Bullocks," Tori reflected in a disapproving tone. "If she had chosen to serve in the US, as did Bo Commanda, surely she would be a full Colonel by now or more likely a Brigadier Air Marshal?"

Sir Richard listened to his daughter, knowing her evaluation was spot on. "After she returned home from the Golan Heights, she filed three applications; direct enlistment, Regular Officer Training Plan, and one to the Royal Military College, and was rejected by all three."

"Rejected?"

"She then did a preparatory year at the University of Toronto, which she paid for out of her UN service wages. She finished at the top of her class, but could not convince the Tribe to assist her with tuition for a second year. So, she applied to RMC again."

"Not rejected again?" Tori asked. "Surly not, I've seen the marks from her application testing. She ranked Superior, the highest level!"

Sir Richard grunted at that. "Étienne tells me that they used to grade the secondary schools of all the candidates. At the time, the school she attended had the lowest academic ranking in the nation. As I understand it, one did not graduate as much as survive, Sackville Secondary School."

"But she did attend the Royal Military College?" Tori was now confused.

"Yes, but not RMC proper. The Canadians also run a French language Military College at Saint-Jean-sur-Richelieu. Back then, Saint-Jean had a much a lower academic standard, and our girl worked the system. From what I understand, she used her maternal grandmother's address in Montreal. That action instantly transformed her from an Anglo applicant who also spoke French to the status of a fully qualified bilingual candidate."

Tori had to stop him from continuing. "Did you say the Tribe would not pay for her education? I thought that was a guarantee of sorts?"

"Mm hmmm, but there is always a limit. Back then, I kept a discrete watch on her career. She flourished at RMC Saint-Jean. She was liked by the instructors and respected by her peers. Then she started hearing rumors that the separatists were quietly surveying French-speaking Officer Cadets to see which side they would choose if Quebec were to separate from their Confederation."

"Good God," Tori said, practically hissing. "That's treason!"

"That's exactly how our girl viewed the situation. By the way—the separatists refer to themselves as Nationalists. When challenged in Parliament, the French Nationalists called it good manpower planning. According to Étienne, the military establishment never forgave her for blowing the whistle, and made it their mandate to hold her back."

"And how exactly did Étienne survive this apparent loyalty crisis? Did he side with his French compatriots?"

"He's not French," Sir Richard said, realizing only then that his explanation made no sense. "What I mean is, Étienne is not from Quebec. He is French Canadian but from New Brunswick, and for some reason that makes him unappealing to the separatist enthusiasts of *La Belle Provence*."

"Bloody hell!" Was all she could say. Taking the last sip of her scotch, she put her empty glass on her father's desk. "And I thought the Irish troubles complicated!"

Chapter Three

Field Office
Mirdamad Construction
Tehran, Islamic Republic of Iran

Hasid sat on one of several foldout chairs stacked in the office trailer. He had an old topographical map of the Iran/Iraq border laid out on a folding table and was making painstaking comparisons to the new, and ironically US-issued, version. After carefully adding the few updates from the US map to the Iraqi Army issue version, he drew in the places where weapons had been hidden. Carefully indicating if they had been stored underground or in adjacent building. Once done, he retrieved a sheet of tracing paper from the cabinet and laid it over the US map. Once secure, he made the same annotations on the tracing paper, before removing it and taking the page to the fax machine. Before pressing the Send button, he disconnected the machine from the landline, and retrieving a company satellite phone from another cabinet, connected the two. He entered a number from heart, listened for the telltale response from the fax unit at the other end, before pressing Send. Once the tracing paper spit out the exit tray, Hasid disconnected the Sat phone and returned it to the cabinet, where a half dozen of the portable units were stored. With that done, he reconnected the landline, before retrieving the tracing paper and setting it on fire. Once he had witnessed its permanent demise he emptied the ash into the chemical toilet, returned the trashcan to its regular place and pocketed the Army map for hand-off to Major Suyfias.

The Islington Urban Gallery
East London, United Kingdom

The International Society for Vernacular Architecture had invited Cleo to submit a paper on her *100 Mile House* concept. Unfortunately, she had to advise them that she couldn't hope to make their submissions cut-off while still on her book tour. She did however have two open days, while in London, where she would be happy to come by and answer questions. The College of Chapters jumped at the chance to include an aboriginal speaker in their summer lecture series. Cleo's lecture, or slideshow as she preferred to call it, was scheduled as a kick-off event for the annual fifteen-day conference for professionals from the international architectural community.

Tori's quickly assembled media credentials, identified her as a journalist for Forbes Publishing. She had always found a press-pass provided better access than her security credentials. The trick was to choose a respected media outlet, but not one that would generate much interest. Today's participants would take little notice of a writer from a business magazine. Taking a seat unobtrusively near the back of the room, she was surprised to see just how many people were interested in Cleo's work. If this was any indication of her success, she began to think that Cleo might not need their offer to set her career back on track. If anything, it looked like Cleo Deseronto had done that all on her own, albeit, on a very different track. She was certainly a survivor and on that, everyone agreed.

In the lecture hall, the lights were dimmed and the introductory slide popped up on the double presentation screens. Tori had attended umpteen lectures over the years from Oxford to Vauxhall, and they all started out the same. The presenters would dim the lights and start the first slide, which introduced the topic and the presenter. Many also unscrupulously promoted their latest work or business affiliation using their first and last slide. Like everything else she was learning about Cleo, this was a woman who consciously chose to do things differently.

The first slide, a photograph of a green highway sign, read:

100 Mile House—100 kms

"The first person to figure that out gets to buy a copy of my book." Cleo joked as she made her way to the front of the room. "*Sago*, and good morning to everyone." Continuing from the raised platform that served as a stage, she began by introducing herself. "My name is Cleo Deseronto and I'm here to talk about a renaissance of locality, or the idea of living, working, buying, and building, within the bounds of our communities. In other words, within one hundred miles of our homes. So, before we get started, I just want you to know I'm not some tight-ass. If you want to ask questions while I'm talking go ahead, though there is a chance I'll throw something at you if you start to make me crazy," she offered to polite laughter. "Okay, before we can build the hundred-mile house, I would like to start with some sacred teachings from the Seven Grandfathers of the Ojibwe First Nation."

The next slide depicted the progression of personal growth through circular layers akin to Shrek's *layers of an onion theory* but from the inside out. Cleo went through the stages applying the teachings to community development. Tori sat quietly, letting Cleo take the room from the teachings of the Elders to the building materials used in traditional aboriginal lodges.

The teepee portion delighted the artists in the group with her astounding photographs of painted canvas or smoked-blacked Buffalo lodges. The vistas included starry nights, rolling grasslands, and parched golden mesas. The true reveal came when she displayed a technical drawing, something akin to what the architects in the room used every day. The blueprints depicted everything from heating and ventilation to the working aspects of the envelope design. Cleo, clearly detailing the principles behind the design, pointed out many aspects that had never made it into historic records of the efficient shelter.

Tori watched the audience go from politely interested to willing supporters in only minutes. One architect stood up complaining that to buy the canvas needed to build a teepee, he would have to break the hundred-mile rule. Cleo wasted no time shutting him down.

"The point here is that by restoring the artisan base to the community, the local talent needed to produce the materials would flourish." When she saw he didn't get it, she explained patiently. "Let's look at it this way: if we had local weavers we would choose canvas because it was available. Now, historically the plains teepee was made of bison hides, a ready and durable commodity of the day. Canvas became a modern and inexpensive substitute when the Buffalo disappeared. Canvas was never the best materiel for the job, but successfully replaced animal hides after the attempted extermination of the plains bison." To drive home the point, she pulled up a slide of a teepee-style lodge *skinned* in birchbark.

"Here's a great example. This is a Mi'kmaq lodge." Cleo paused to let the group take in the photograph. "The traditional territory of the Mi'kmaq is the Northeastern United States and Canada. This is a region with an abundance of paper birch trees and very few large prey animals." She looked over her audience carefully, not wanting to proceed until she had eliminated any confusion. Satisfied, she said warmly, "I think it's an eloquent adaptation of the hundred-mile rule."

At the end of her presentation, Cleo invited anyone interested to join her in a traditional cleansing ceremony called a Smudge. Tori stood patiently with those remaining, while a handful of people asked questions or got her to sign their copy of her book. Her publisher had made sure to have a PA on hand with a stash of books just in case anyone was interested in purchasing a copy. Once Cleo had finished with the impromptu book signing, she led the remaining group outside to a small parking area behind the building, explaining that the medicine she was about to burn might set off the smoke detectors. Organized into a small circle, Cleo lit a fist-sized clump of prairie sage and began to move from person to person. Reciting the teachings that went with the Smudge, she led each participant as they washed themselves in the sacred smoke of Woman's Medicine.

When everything was finished and only a few people remained, Tori decided to approach Cleo. While she participated in the Smudge, she had hung back once they had finished. "Is it too late to ask you to sign my book?"

Cleo smiled at the familiar face. "That might be difficult. What, without a book and all."

Embarrassed that she had actually forgotten to bring her copy, Tori winced at the gentle rebuff. "I do have one," she said, protesting. "Actually, I've read it. All of it."

"Really!" Cleo said with some delight. "Okay, then. Here's the deal, if you buy me lunch, and answer a skill-testing question, I will sign your unread book as soon as you remember to buy one."

"Miss Deseronto!" Tori said in pleasant protest.

"Oh no you don't! Calling me Miss? Now that's gonna' cost you. I might even make you buy me lunch."

"I thought I was buying lunch?" Tori asked with a wry smile.

"Of course, but only because I wasn't serious about the skill-testing question."

Tori was starting to appreciate Cleo's sardonic sense of humor. "I'm beginning to understand that no matter what deal we strike, I'll be buying lunch, is that it?"

"Oh my, you are good!" Cleo smiled at the woman walking beside her. "Tell you what, if you can find us a place to eat soon, I'll cancel the essay portion of the skill-testing question."

Tori shook her head, pointed to a place across the street. "And I thought skill-testing question meant one question. Singular? Not an entire bloody exam!"

"For you, Lady Dufferin," Cleo said with appreciation, "I will cancel the whole damned thing."

"Except for buying lunch?"

"Except for buying lunch!"

Seri Thai
Islington, East London

Cleo and Tori were enjoying lunch in a Thai restaurant just a block from the gallery. Over crispy beef and sticky rice, Cleo answered questions about her interest in architecture and her lifelong commitment to the medicine path. Tori had always been curious about the use of the word medicine in aboriginal culture. She had first become aware of its prevalence as a young teen during the Duke and Duchess of York's honeymoon tour of Canada. She had been watching BBC World News when they reported on the couple's visit to Medicine Hat, Alberta. She had thought that quite funny, Medicine Hat! Sir Richard agreed, but true to form, took the time to explain what he knew.

The word medicine had many meanings among the Indians. The two interpretations he knew and partially understood were "sacred" and "magic." In her mind, Tori had always pictured Medicine Hat as the place where Frosty the Snowman must have melted one spring and come back to life the next year.

Cleo laughed when Tori told her that, explaining that she had often thought the same thing. As for her use of the word medicine, Cleo meant it as a lifelong commitment to honor, duty, and respect, for herself and everything around her. She called it walking the *good red path*. She also admitted that many people considered her a hypocrite, first for spending her entire career in aviation, a carbon-contributing industry, and more painfully for having spent those years plus several more in the military. Military service, for a Six Nations member, was considered an honor, although the Canadian or American citizenship that went with it was a hot issue within the Mohawk community. Worse, her mother and her mother's French Canadian family were unfathomably ashamed. Cleo had learned to shrug them off. As she explained it, "when you land in some shit-hole with food and medicine, and see a couple-a-hundred kids running after the plane, any concerns you may have over someone else's feelings dissipate pretty quickly."

In time, Tori turned the conversation to her days in the militia, when Cleo and Sir Richard had first become acquainted, and the choices she had made when she returned home. "How was that?" Tori asked. "You know, going home after all that happened."

Cleo didn't seem to want to answer, then without prodding changed her mind. "To be honest, I don't know what I expected. So, I guess I wasn't that disappointed when no one showed up at the disembarkation point. I remember taking the Inter-Base Bus from Trenton to CFB Downsview."

"That's in Toronto?" Tori asked. "Or was," she said, correcting herself.

Cleo nodded, continuing. "Eight of us got off the bus. We thought we were sooooo tough. We had been in the rough and we wanted everyone to know it. We even formed up and waited until our families showed before falling out."

"How long did you wait?" Tori asked, knowing full well how things had turned out.

"Four hours! I have no idea what I thought I was waiting for," she admitted honestly. "I ended up with a room at the old Orchard Park Tavern down by Greenwood racetrack. I think I spent most of the night crying over my pretty-blue UN beret and the Medal your father gave me. The next day I pulled together all the photos and drawings I had done in Syria and Israel and marched down to the University of Toronto. From that point on, I never looked back or at least tried not to."

Tori was shocked to learn that Cleo had actually been pursuing Architectural Studies at university. Cleo's only explanation for not continuing after her prep year was a lament that she hadn't saved enough money from her part-time militia salary. Tori didn't need a calculator to know Cleo wouldn't have earned enough money to cover her tuition much less living expenses from what part-time soldiers were paid, not even from the wages a part-time soldier would earn serving full-time. It probably took everything she had just to get through the first year.

"I was wondering, doesn't Indian Affairs pay for health and education? I think you mentioned 'Fiduciary Responsibility' the other day?" Tori was smiling quite mischievously until she noticed a momentary flash of ice. She watched, as Cleo appeared to search deep inside, only answering after appearing to consider her options.

"They try, but there's only so much money to go around. And, to be fair," Cleo said, "they try to cover the kids still living on the reserve first. They need it most."

"Did that happen to you?" she asked, watching Cleo intently, noting how quickly the internal debate flashed in her eyes then disappeared.

"It was a tough time for educational funding. Some of the kids on the list were facing very heavy tuition fees. At first there was some talk of splitting the funds evenly between the applicants, but in the end they realized that an even split wouldn't begin to cover the basics for the kids heading off to the States, so . . ."

"So," Tori continued, "some kids got everything they needed and others went without."

"It wasn't too bad for me," Cleo explained. "I got into the military college at Saint-Jean and let the Canadian Forces pick up the tab. Not a bad deal, the way I see it. It certainly made more sense to me than taking on forty thousand in student loans."

Interesting, was how Tori saw it. She was well aware that Bo Commanda had attended Cornell University in New York State, all expenses paid. In her research of the two women, it had occurred to her that they might both hail from the same Indian Nation, but they had chosen separate sides of the border to live their lives. That not only entailed different rights and customs, it meant vastly differing financial systems. She had looked up the exchange rate for Canada and the United States and found the two currencies almost at par, but when she made a historic search of the exchange rate, for the time when the two women had attended university, she was shocked to find the Canadian dollar worth only half of its American counterpart. No wonder the Mohawk band office experienced so much difficulty with the education budget. As the Canadian government did not account for fluctuations in applicant numbers and made no consideration for where the students would study.

"I'm curious about one thing," Tori asked even though the thought of pushing Cleo for any more information made her feel sick. "What criteria did they use in making their final choice of who did and did not receive funding for school?"

Cleo smiled at her. "Criteria? Viscountess Dufferin, that is a big word. If you must know, when it came down to the final names," she sighed, answering with simple honestly, "I think they just went alphabetically."

Tori shook her head, automatically thinking, *C—Commanda, D—Deseronto.*

Bo Commanda, Cleo's paternal first cousin, skipped grade thirteen and joined the United States Marine Corps. She spent the three years of her enrolment sorting files at Fort Leonard Wood in Missouri, and went home a hero. In contrast, Cleo had stayed in Toronto and finished high school. Instead joining the Canadian Militia while still a student, and was later posted to the Middle East. As a peacekeeper, she ended up in several nightmarish after-action clean-ups, saved Sir Richard's life, watched her best friend step on a land mine, and finished up in a foreign prison. When she finally made it home, no one even remembered she had been away, or cared that she had served with valor. The parallels didn't stop there. Bo must have received more than fifty thousand dollars for each of the four years she attended Cornell. Cleo, on the other hand, had been accepted to a fine Canadian University, and for her effort, received no assistance at all. The irony came from the fact that Bo imagined Cleo had been the one to receive all the breaks.

Bo had complained bitterly of how both she and Cleo had worked with their grandfather, a spiritual healer, to learn as many teachings as possible in his last days. He had already invested years preparing three of his own children to take his place. Two of them were now dead, one from cancer and the other from alcohol. The third, his youngest son, was presently serving a life sentence in a Federal Penitentiary. Days before his death, and in the presence of their grandmother, Joe Commanda asked his granddaughter Cleo to take his place and named her a Faith Keeper. Judging by how much Bo whined about the entire incident, she must have complained endlessly to their grandmother. She had been, and was still, completely unwilling to allow Cleo even the smallest success.

From where Tori was standing, she could not think of a single reason why Cleo would consider including Bo in this operation. *Damn the Americans for insisting! And damn the Canadians for giving them cause to insist!*

Security and Intelligence Service
Vauxhall Cross, London

Tori led Cleo Deseronto into the Lancaster Room for the situation briefing. She hadn't told Cleo exactly what or whom to expect. It had been a request from Darcy, who wanted to study how she adapted to changing situations. Whatever Darcy might glean from her behavior, Tori was certain it was no longer necessary. She was starting to find a real connection with Captain Deseronto. One she was surprised to realize did not exist between her and Bo Commanda. She had assumed her lack of connection with Bo stemmed from the casual nature of their association. *Is that what we are, an association?* They had dated; if that was the right term for it. *We drank, we shagged, and it was . . . fun . . . the first time. And, the next was . . . well, it was just sex and not much more, but that's what I expected. Now this . . . What the bloody hell was I thinking?* Tori chose a seat for Cleo, introducing each of the key attendees as they entered the room. She was planning to just skip over Bo and introduce Mike Perkins, the CIA Station Chief, but true to form, Bo was incapable of remaining quiet.

"Squirrel!" Bo exclaimed.

Tori froze in place, preparing for a repeat of the run-in at Waterstones. She need not have worried. Cleo, while slightly terse, was the model of decorum.

"Marine," Cleo ordered, with true military command, "Stow it!"

To Tori's amazement, Bo settled down immediately. Planting herself in the seat next to Mike, she sat quietly and began reviewing her notes. Tori opened the session by introducing MI6's man on Iran, Allan Bashir. The first ten minutes of Allan's briefing was pretty much a repeat of everything Cleo had heard at dinner. Then things got interesting. Allan Bashir had just returned after three years undercover as a Metallurgy Inspector for a pipeline company. The job called for him to travel anywhere oil and metal came together. Allan, or Ali as he was known in Iran, would spend days at remote sites testing for the wear and tear of fittings and assemblies, while taking advantage of his obscurity to spy on a troubled nation.

As bad as things were, they were also changing. While men dominated the national scene, women had quietly become the majority presence in the universities and medical schools. He believed a real power shift in Iranian politics was less than a generation away. What he had to explain now was why he had been extracted.

"Your photos, Captain Deseronto, were so interesting," he said. "I just knew I had to get a look at that facility."

"Any luck?"

"Show her what you found," Tori ordered.

Allan triggered the remote for the large screen and called up several technical and architectural drawings.

"At first I agreed with your assessment and started combing through some of the original production mapping for the oil pipeline. Some of the wells have been pumping since the 1920s with an infrastructure that is almost as old. I found an abandoned switching station near Q'on that may have been used to divert oil to or from that bunker, but I could not find any direct connection, neither physically nor on paper that would explain more. Then I found this!"

The technical drawing was labeled in English and French. "I found it, and more, in the archive at the building standards office in Tehran."

"Holy frack!" Cleo inadvertently swore out loud. "Is that Chalk River?"

Canada's Chalk River Nuclear Reactor was one of the oldest and busiest producers of Nuclear Medical Isotopes in the world. The design was simple and robust, explaining the length of time it had already been in service. It was also scalable. With enough money and space, anyone could increase the size of the centrifuge and effect a change to the quality of the plutonium produced. It was still a long road from creating a 5% pure isotope suitable for medical imaging to the 95% purity needed to reach weapons grade, but now it was possible.

"Étienne," Cleo said to the CSIS Officer, demanding an explanation. "How?"

After a tense pause the CIA Station Chief cleared his throat and answered the question for him.

"Actually," Mike said, "it may have been us. We were working closely with the Shaw at the time, and we may have offered the technology in a trade deal. I'm sure those involved back then had no idea the country would destabilize so quickly."

"It occurs to me, that you guys could have learned a lot from Lester Pearson. I know he strongly suggested you adopt a policy of non-interference." As Canada's 14th Prime Minister, Lester Pearson had sold the United Nations on the idea of creating a multi-national peacekeeping force. His idea came just in time to squash French and English incursions into Egypt during the Suez Canal crisis.

"Look," Mike said in protest, "The United States has done good work all around the world . . ."

"Good work?" Cleo cut him off, truly astonished. "What? Like Iraq? How about Venezuela, Columbia, El Salvador, Saudi Arabia, the Congo, the Philippines . . . The list is endless."

"You want to talk about Somalia?" he demanded, with a raised voice.

"Oh good Gods, we ALL fracked-up in Somalia! At least WE tried to do something in Rwanda, while your people were giving press conferences and trying to make genocide sound like a minor misunderstanding!"

Darcy had just gotten Cleo's inference to non-interference and chimed in, "The Prime Directive."

"See!" A frustrated Cleo practically spat. "Even Trekkies know better than to hand over dangerous technologies to developing worlds. Don't you guys even watch your own TV?"

Sir Richard stood up, putting an instant end to the debate. "Let's take a short break and let Allan go over his findings in Q'on with Captain Deseronto." With that said, he turned to leave the room, calling for Tori and Darcy to follow.

Once they were securely sequestered in the *Tank*, the common work area for the SOE team, Sir Richard let out his frustration. "What in hell's name was that!"

"She's had less than forty-eight hours to process the situation," Tori answered defensively. "And frankly, I believe she's doing quite well."

"Quite well? We haven't time for quite well. What I need is a plan to take up the ladder."

"If I may . . ." Darcy said, interrupting the stare down building between father and daughter. Taking the growl that came from Sir Richard as an invitation to continue, he said. "I think she is asking the right questions. At least what should be considered the right questions for her." Darcy waved an open hand to the chairs they were standing behind. "She is proud. Not good or bad proud, but proud, and the Canadian half of her identity is very much a part of that pride. If we want her to do this, no . . ." he corrected himself, "if we expect her to succeed at this, we will need her to call on every ounce of that pride. Letting her know that the country she chose to serve was not completely responsible for what has happened will go a long distance towards preserving that confidence."

"Queen and Country?" Tori asked. She wasn't completely surprised. After all, Cleo had volunteered to serve at thirteen years of age, when she had chosen the Royal Canadian Air Cadets over all the other distractions available to teens. When considered from that point of view, Cleo had already spent twenty-five years doing her duty for Queen and Country. Tori knew her father would think it contrite but would understand.

"Queen and Country," Darcy repeated.

Sir Richard Braithwaite was a passionate man who believed in what he was doing. Both Tori and Darcy had seen him like this before. If C had his way, Cleo would have been met at the airport, given a short briefing and put on the next plane to Tehran. But Cleo Deseronto was not in the SAS. Hell, she wasn't even an active military officer anymore.

Sir Richard let out a long sigh. "Is there any other way?"

Tori answered with measured patience. "There are always other ways, father, but not always other opportunities."

His expression softened at the advice from his only child. "Remind me to forbid you from quoting the chief." Then he thought of something else. "The PM wants a working plan. I am expected to present that plan at Number Ten on Friday. Have we a chance?"

The question was directed to both Darcy and Tori, and as was custom, Darcy answered first. "Captain Deseronto may be unaware of it, but she has already made a commitment to this operation. Her outburst with the Americans was proof of that. What she needs now is the license to focus on mission planning and deployment. We need only give her some room and support to get things underway."

Tori nodded. "She wants to do it. You can see that, it's just that US involvement is a sore point for her and frankly we were aware of that coming in. We can't undo what happened in Israel, but we can keep the Americans from making more mistakes."

"Anything else?" Sir Richard asked.

"C," Darcy said, "Cleo hails from a warrior society and while she has proven herself ad nauseum, she is being underestimated. The Mohawks underestimated her, her family underestimated her, her superiors at UNDOF Command underestimated her, the Israelis underestimated her, and you and Étienne continue underestimating her. Perhaps letting the world underestimate her is exactly the thing that will give this operation a real leg-up?"

Lancaster Room
Vauxhall Cross, London

Once the briefing had been completed, Cleo asked for time to review the intelligence package in more detail. She also wanted Allan. She knew he would be the best person to get her up to speed. After several hours of tech drawings, blueprints, and satellite recon photos, Cleo had to ask him to stop.

"I need some time to process everything," she told him, and then thought to ask something else about his time in Iran. "Did you call for your extraction?"

"Actually, I had no suspicions at all. I was in the oil company office in Q'on when the phone rang. A woman was on the phone, crying and speaking perfect Farsi. She said my father was dying and I was to rush home to his bedside. I went directly to the airport and managed to board a flight to AR Riyadh. I was lucky to be in possession of the Chalk River material. Evidently, someone in the oil company was aware that I had been in the archives and reported it. Tori was alerted and pulled me out immediately. As I said, I was very lucky."

Tori walked in the room just in time to hear her name. "I was telling Captain Deseronto how you extracted me from Iran."

"Wonderful, because I am now going to extract her for a break, and perhaps something to eat."

"Actually I can't," Cleo explained. "I have dinner plans, sorry."

This surprised both Allan, who expected to be at this most of the night, and Tori who uncharacteristically let her disappointment show.

"If you two are finished for the evening then," she said quite formally, "I'll walk our fearless flyer out."

Cleo accepted Tori's direction, stopping at the door of the room to address Allan. "Should we continue tomorrow?"

Allan thanked her for committing to return for the rest of the review. They set a time, and Tori assured them both that the appropriate credentials would be available. With that solved, Tori left Allan to secure the documents while she saw Cleo out through the maze of departments and security checks.

"I have a car waiting to take you back to your hotel," Tori let her know. "I had planned to take you for another meal but as you already have an engagement . . ." Startled by her own disappointment, Tori tried to wrench her attitude down a notch, instead asking, "are you meeting Parminder Dutt?"

The question brought Cleo to a complete halt. "Why am I surprised?" she asked, her tone defiant. "Tell me, what don't you know about me?"

"Is she your lover?"

"Holy *frack*, Tori!" Cleo looked more annoyed than angry. "She's my friend. A good friend, who was there for me after Samantha died. Have you vetted her too?"

"We had too!" She was well aware that it had only been four years since Cleo had lost her lover. It was the last thing she ever intended to mention. "Please Cleo, I meant no disrespect. It's just that I was hoping we could sit down over a meal and discuss a framework for your bringing Bo Commanda aboard. Consider it a sort of *Rules* setting supper, if you will. I'm hoping we might find a way in which working together would be more congenial."

"Rules?"

"Rules that would make it clear how Agent Commanda is expected to conduct herself while working with you. Think of it as our own *rules of engagement* of a sort."

Cleo sighed. "Rules of engagement, eh? I like that," she replied with a sheepish grin. "Do you like Indian food? And when I say Indian, I do not mean pemmican and bannock! It's just that I'm having dinner with Parminder at her dad's restaurant. If you're interested?"

"In Camden? She won't mind?"

Cleo shook her head. "I refuse to be surprised anymore. And no, Parminder will not mind. She's expecting me at 7:30. Would you like to join me there or is it easier to meet someplace first?"

"How about I fetch you from your hotel? A little before seven should do it. Is that all right?"

"Perfect," Cleo said, with a kind smile. "And Tori, if you want to bring Bo, I can handle it. Maybe this would be a good time to work on those *Rules* you mentioned."

They had walked and talked their way out of the building. Tori, signaling the driver to keep his seat, instead opening the car door herself.

As the sedan pulled away from the curb, Cleo had to fight the urge to turn around. She couldn't help but wonder if Tori had lingered to watch the car drive away.

Taste of Punjab
Camden, East London

Cleo had called Parminder from her hotel room to warn her about the evening to come. As far as she was concerned, it was Parminder's own fault for always wanting to meet Cleo's notorious cousin Boudicca. Neither of them had any idea that Bo had been working out of London for the last six months. Her job as an FBI agent assigned to the US Bureau of Indian Affairs, focused on stopping the traffic of aboriginal artifacts into Eastern Europe. Now someone had the bright idea to match the cousins up. Whoever it was, must have known they had never worked together. Cleo certainly didn't think her time flying a Hercules qualified her for anything the intel boys were considering. Certainly the closest Bo had ever gotten to real field experience was the Crucible exercise during the US Marine Corps boot camp at Paris Island. This operation was a disaster in the making. If they had any chance at success, she knew they would need a better working relationship. *Better*, Cleo thought to herself. Anything would be an improvement over their long-running feud.

Parminder, waiting in the dining room of her family's restaurant, joined Cleo, Tori, and Bo the minute they arrived. While Bo and Tori settled in and read the menu, Cleo headed for the kitchen to pay her respects to Mr. and Mrs. Dutt.

Ever since Cleo and Parminder had been friends, Mr. Dutt had taken every opportunity to question Cleo about her vegetable garden in Canada. He had been quite excited to learn that she had a little farm and planted a three-sisters crop every year. He was fascinated by how Native People made a practice of growing plants that would support one another.

"I have something for you," Cleo told Mr. Dutt, handing him a rectangular paper box. "Be careful opening that," she said. Inside was a sturdy serrated knife with a half-moon-shaped blade. "That's the root knife I was telling you about."

Mr. Dutt smiled broadly, wielding the short blade like a pro. "With this, even the most fractious ginger root will succumb to my desires."

"That too!" Cleo laughed, enjoying his gusto while giving both him and his wife a big bear hug of a greeting.

Returning to the dining room, she was not surprised to see that Bo had already launched into some story about their childhood. When Bo saw Cleo, she did what she always did, "Squirrel!"

Before Cleo could protest, Tori questioned her motives. "Why do you insist on doing that? You can see she doesn't enjoy it."

Never one to accept any sort of criticism, Bo fluffed it off. "Oh she doesn't mind. Do you Squirrel?"

"If you call me that again," Cleo warned, her voice deadpan flat, "I will rip out your tonsils and shove them up your six." That made her feeling on the subject pretty clear. It also made both Tori's and Parminder's eyes pop.

"Don't be like that," Bo drawled, in a sticky sweet voice. "Besides, we both had our tonsils out, at the same time! So, it's way too late to shove them up anybody's ass." Proud of her rebuff, Bo turned her attention to the other women, continuing, "When we were kids, we lived in the city during the school year and only spent the summers on the Rez. It was great being at our grandmother's, but the other kids were always accusing us of being apples and Cleo hated that."

Parminder, enjoying the impromptu roasting of her friend, couldn't help but encourage Bo. "What's the Rez? And what's an apple?" but it was Cleo who made the translation for her.

"The Rez is slang for Indian Reserve or more accurately, lands *Reserved* for Indians. And as for apple," she huffed disapprovingly, "it's a racial slur native people sometimes use to accuse each other of not being Indian enough." When Cleo realized they didn't understand, she sighed again, before spelling it out. "Apple: red on the outside, white on the inside."

Tori winced at that, remembering just how much emphasis Darcy had placed on Cleo's pride.

"What did you do?" Tori asked. Though it was Bo, with zero regard for Cleo's spirit, who plunged ahead with the story.

"You should have seen our girl here. The other kids said she couldn't be a real Indian until she could go out in the bush and kill her own supper." Bo looked at Parminder for a reaction. Part of her joy in telling the story was shock value. "So off she went. Well, you should have seen everyone's face when she came home with a big red squirrel!"

Parminder, for her part, wasn't going to give Bo the satisfaction of thinking she had shocked anyone. Turning to Cleo, she offered, "I would have thought you more a rabbit and wild berries sort?"

Cleo apologized, explaining, "I was only seven."

Tori had to ask, sincerely wanting to understand what had taken place. "How did you kill it?"

"I found some old fishing line on the beach and set up a bunch of clumsy traps, and just by fluke I caught that poor little guy." Cleo didn't like telling this story but she wasn't going to let Bo tell her horror movie version either. "At first I was so proud. That is until I picked him up. He was so soft, but his eyes were open and his little body was still warm. It was like he could see right through me. I cried all the way back to my grandmother's."

"Oh please," Bo interrupted. "It was just a squirrel. Besides, it sealed our reputation as real Indians with the other kids. It was cool!" Bo went on to tell other stories, not bothering to take notice of how Cleo felt about this exposé of their early years.

Throughout dinner and all the way through tea and sweets, Bo told story after story of their childhood and the charmed lives they led. The stories she told seemed a far cry from the personal profiles Tori had read on both woman. The entire evening seemed at odds with everything she knew.

When Tori had taken care of the bill, which was quite difficult to do with Mr. Dutt involved, she left Cleo and Parminder to say their good-byes and joined Bo outside the restaurant.

While they waited, Bo stomped out a cigarette on the sidewalk, and launched into a parody of Mr. Dutt. Tori had pretty much reached her limit with Bo's behavior when she caught something out of the corner of her eye, and turning just in time, grabbing Cleo's arm mid-swing.

"Stop!" Tori ordered.

Parminder, who was behind Cleo, grappled with her other arm, helping Tori wrestle her back.

"That man is my friend!" Cleo shouted at her cousin. "Don't you ever make fun of him, or anyone else for that matter! Understand?" Cleo, now physically under control, shook the other women off, and walked a few yards away to compose herself.

Tori let her storm off, turning her full attention to Bo. "Bleeding hell, Boudicca! Is there no end to your impropriety?"

"What? You don't see me taking a sucker punch at anyone. What the fuck, Tor?"

Before turning her full wrath on one Special Agent Commanda, Tori asked Parminder quietly. "Will you check on Cleopatra?"

"All right, but don't let her catch you calling her that. She's very much liable to take a swing at you too." Parminder joked, before quickly making her way to where Cleo was waiting. Once out of earshot, Tori turned to Bo. "Are you a mad woman?" she challenged. "I specifically told you that tonight was about repairing your relationship, not an opportunity to further alienate your cousin!"

"Relax, I know what I'm doing."

"What you're doing is jeopardizing an already risky objective by alienating the key operative!"

"Okay, okay." Bo acknowledged. "Maybe I came on a little heavy. I'm just trying to loosen Cleo up. Geezus Christ Tor, maybe you can't see it, but Cleo's turned into some sort of tight-ass! How the fuck am I supposed to work with her?"

Tori sighed inwardly. She had explained the facts as she saw then to Bo, repeatedly, and to no effect. The fact was, Cleo had found the secret bunker, maybe by accident and maybe she couldn't do it again, but without her, there was little chance of anyone finding the place where she had photographed the deep narrow valley. *What I should do now is call Mike Perkins and call off this bleeding farce.*

When he had first raised the idea of creating a team of cultural ambassadors, Tori had immediately decided the plan was too complicated and would place the operatives in too high a profile. Wanting to keep things simple, she had suggested they simply return Deseronto to Iran with a photographer or personal assistant in tow, with the objective of continuing her book research. The Americans had not liked her idea but were willing to give it a try, as long as "their" agent was selected as the photographer/ assistant. Their agent had turned out to be Bo Commanda, Deseronto's first cousin. The two had been estranged since Bo Commanda's entry into the US Marine Corps. Commanda carried deep resentment over the division their early career choices had caused. *So, I've an angry washed-up pilot and a resentful FBI agent to mollify. No! Pacification will not be enough, not by a long shot. Conciliation will be necessary to make this work. And how the hell do I do it?"*

Braithwaite Residence
West London

Cleo Deseronto stood in the center of what she could only describe as a perfect English cottage garden. While the complete kaleidoscope of color couldn't be seen in the evening light, the stillness washed away her earlier anger. She stood in silence, inhaling the fragrance of the garden, allowing it to relax her. The place acted like magic on Cleo's spirits. There was no denying, it was time to forgive Bo and herself. She wasn't even startled when she sensed Tori standing behind her.

"There's good medicine here," she said, turning to face her host.

"I am glad you like it." Tori replied, looking around with pride. "I don't always have the time, certainly not the time it deserves, but I try."

"From where I'm standing," Cleo said, gently teasing her, "it looks like you succeed."

"Thank you!"

Cleo tilted her head slightly, watching as Tori moved around the small garden, checking the odd early bloom.

"I like that you can take a compliment."

"I like that you say what you mean. It's a rare quality in my experience."

Cleo smiled at her but didn't comment. She was feeling a little confused by this back and forth thing they seemed to be doing. She couldn't tell if

Tori was interested or just trying to do her job. She wanted to reach out to her, to touch her, but couldn't bring herself to do it. After Sam's death, she had been certain she would never know these kinds of emotions again. How could she, after spending ten years with a woman she knew to be her soul mate. How could she start over? She certainly hadn't been able to date, and with her shy nature, Cleo found it difficult to socialize with other women in the lesbian community. Parminder had been the only one to break through that wall of grief.

Tori interrupted her reverie. "I think we're ready, if you would like to come back in?"

Cleo took a deep breath, "lead the way, oh fearless one."

The first thing she noticed when they walked back into the sumptuous reception room was Bo drinking a beer. Actually, both Parminder and Bo were drinking, and Bo was about to light a smoke.

"You are not going to light that in here!" Cleo growled. She was about to crank on both of them for drinking when she noticed something else. Bo was comfortable here, too comfortable. Cleo knew immediately that Bo had been here before and probably more than once. The thought of Bo spending time in Tori's flat, or more accurately, an apartment in a very large Georgian townhouse, was unfathomable. The whole idea of Bo socializing with Tori somehow made her feel sick.

Relax, Cleo scolded herself. *They work together . . . it only makes sense.*

Tori touched Cleo's arm to offer her a seat, setting a drink for her on the side table.

"Soda and lime," Tori explained, in answer to her unasked question. "You know, I have been trying all night to understand what's happened between you two. If you're both comfortable discussing personal matters, perhaps we might try to sort this?" With no objections, Tori pushed on. "While it is important to the Foreign Office that you both find a way to work on this Artifact Trafficking business, I am not about to force either one of you to do it."

While Parminder was with them, it would be necessary for Cleo, Tori, and Bo to stick to this cover. Tori was playing the part of their team leader, which she truly was, and had ID from the Foreign and Commonwealth Office to prove it. Judging by how easily Tori slipped into her bureaucratic persona, Cleo was sure she had used this cover many times before.

"Well," Bo piped in, turning directly to Cleo, "if we're going to work together, you're going to have to stop being such a tight-ass, and learn to follow my lead."

"Follow your lead?" Cleo asked, stunned by the statement.

"Yes," she announced with authority. "I'm a senior FBI agent with field experience. What have you ever done but fly a plane? I don't know why we need you at all."

Cleo could not tell who was more shocked by this announcement. "Why you need me, AT ALL?" she parroted.

"Bo, we talked about this," Tori said evenly, but it was clear she was upset. "You know the Foreign Office wants Cleo to take the lead. After all, she has flown into some of the airports in Eastern Europe used for such types of trafficking."

Cleo could hear the edge in Tori's voice. She knew how upsetting Bo's attitude could be. There was also the risk of Bo blowing their cover, but it was no surprise when Parminder took things in hand. "What you playing at?"

Bo looked at her. "I'm just stating a fact. Truth is, I don't think Cleo even cares about this job."

"I see," Parminder commented. "A little reverse psychology. You tell Cleo she's not up for it, and she's supposed to what, compete with you? Is that it? Or perhaps you're just being belligerent?"

Tori looked at Bo with disappointment, "Bo, please tell me that's not what you're up to? Competing?"

"I don't know why everyone's so mad at me?" Bo complained. "We didn't know if Squirrel here wanted the job and we still don't. I'm just forcing her to stand up for herself. What's the big deal anyway . . . she's not made of sugar!"

"It occurs to me," Parminder said, "that you two are opposite sides of the same coin."

Bo snapped at her, "what the fuck is that supposed to mean?"

"Watch your gob!" Parminder snapped back. "I know plenty of women like you. They start all the infighting and chaos that make things so inbred in our community. They keep other women down when they could be part of helping each other succeed."

"That's a boat load of crap! In this world, it's every man for himself."

"Is that what the American Marines taught you?" Tori asked.

Cleo watched as Bo got up from her place, pulling a cold beer from a hidden ice chest, in the ornate sidebar. She was clearly enjoying the attention. Walking back to the chesterfield she plopped herself back down, tipping her bottle to the room in a mocking salute.

"The Corps was different. Marines are family, real family," she said, adding, "Sempre fucking Fi," before taking a long loud guzzle of the ice-cold beer.

There was something in that action that bothered Cleo, something beyond the rudeness. "When did you start drinking again?"

"I'm not drinking," Bo said. "I'm having a few beers with friends. There's a difference. And there is absolutely nothing wrong with it."

Tori caught this new information, but said nothing. She knew the FBI had *washed* Bo's personnel file before sending it over to MI6.

"There's nothing wrong with it unless you have a drinking problem. Bo!" Cleo practically pleaded with her. "Have you forgotten your sophomore year? Auntie May spent all summer drying you out. And what about that Rehab the FBI sent you to in New Hampshire?"

Bo slammed her beer bottle down.

"You've got a lot of nerve. Yes, I screwed up a few times, but I was younger then. Now I've got it under control." Bo pointed to Parminder and Tori, continuing her rebuttal. "You have no right to make them think I'm some sort of drunk. I am sick of you doing this to me. You've been nothing but second best since I don't know when, since school, and I'm tired of you taking it out on me."

She picked up her beer again and took a chug before continuing her tirade. "You could have joined the Corps with me and gotten some real military experience but noooo! Your frog bitch mommy wouldn't sign the papers and Uncle George wouldn't either! He knew you couldn't cut it. So what does our girl do? She joins the Governor General's Horse Guards." Bo practically hissed the name of the regiment. "A friggin' militia unit, can you imagine! How fucking embarrassing is that! And then there was university!" Bo waved her arm in dismissive gesture. "I apply to Harvard, Yale, and Cornell. Where does our poor squirrel apply? Ryerson and two other Canadian shit-holes at opposite ends of the country."

Cleo, now strangely entertained by Bo's monologue, helped her along with the names of the other two schools: "Dalhousie, Canada's oldest university and Sir Simon Fraser, in British Columbia, which at the time had the most impressive architectural program around."

"See," Bo said to Tori, "this how she does it. She accuses me of shit then plays the stoic Indian. What about the accident you had out West . . . how long did they ground you for that? And I know about the stress leave you had to take. Did you tell the *Foreign Office* about that?"

Both Tori and Parminder were biting at the bit to say something but it was Cleo who answered Bo's accusations in an even and practiced tone.

"Regarding that accident you keep referring to, I was on the ground helping the crew try and get the hangar doors closed, when a freak storm hit. I was not flying. One of the door panels on the hangar collapsed under the weight of the ice and my foot was crushed. And yes I was grounded for five months while I went through surgery and physical therapy." Cleo held up her hand to stop Parminder and Tori from jumping in. "And yes, the Foreign Office knows all about my stress leave. They know, because the death of my life partner was not a secret. After all, in Canada it's legal to Ask and Tell! Shall I go on?"

When things did not improve, Cleo suggested they leave. Tori called for a cab and chatted amiably with Parminder until the car arrived. When they got up, Bo made it clear she wasn't going anywhere. Cleo was about to drag her out physically when Tori, slightly panicked, suggested that she might be able to sort Bo out if they left her behind. Cleo wasn't happy about that but respected Tori's decision.

In the cab, Cleo and Parminder sat in amiable silence for most of the ride.

"You're not responsible for her behavior," Parminder finally said, "and you are nothing like her, at least not in deeds."

"You think we have a family resemblance?"

"More than enough to pass for sisters."

"You know, there was a time when I thought we were sisters," Cleo admitted plainly. "Auntie May once told me that when our grandfather first saw us as babies, he held us together in his arms and would never do it again. He said he felt like Sky Woman's grandchildren were staring into his soul. In some ways it feels like we are Sky Woman's twins, destined to fight each other to the death. He was always afraid of what would happen if we turned against one another."

"I take it you were destined to be the victorious one?"

"He never would say," Cleo confessed with a grin. "At least not to anyone who would have repeated it to us. He was good that way. He always gave us the choice, never interfering, but always there when we needed him."

"You must miss him," Parminder commented gently.

"On days like this, it's hard not to."

"I have to ask, what's the issue with drinking and your people?"

"Well, there are a lot of issues around it but basically aboriginal people don't metabolize alcohol quite as well as other people, which may simply come from the fact that we have only been exposed to it for a few hundred years."

"Somewhat like your intolerance of cow's milk?"

"Just like that," Cleo said. "The other side is spiritual. Almost all the First Nations have a similar teaching that involves specific medicines being created exclusively for each of the sacred races. Alcohol is one of those medicines. One intended for white people only."

"That's interesting," Parminder said. "There are some parallels to Hindi beliefs. What are the other medicines?"

"Let see, for you my Asian friend, the medicine from the Gods was opium. For white people, or the descendants of Europeans, it's the afore-mentioned alcohol, and tobacco exclusively for aboriginal people. As for Africans, I can't say."

"So, we have tobacco, alcohol, and opium?" Parminder summed up the list. "Three of the world's most devastating drugs, and you say they were a *gift* from God?"

"A gift of sacred medicine not to be abused, not be commercialized, and definitely not meant for anyone other than the people it was created to aid."

Parminder was silent for so long that Cleo imagined she considered the conversation over. When she finally asked, "both you and Bo have white mothers and Red Indian fathers. How do you balance that?"

"I think it's a question every mixed race kid has to solve. For me it was a choice of respecting both. Don't drink and don't smoke. Not smoking in today's health conscious world is not a problem, but not drinking, not even a social glass of wine or a celebratory glass of Champagne, is a hard one, you know that."

"So, you think Bo should have made the same commitment?" Parminder asked sincerely.

"No actually." She was surprised to hear her friend's assumption. "My problem is that she has struggled with it since we were teens. She drank her way through first and second year at university and only stopped when the Band Office threatened to pull her funding."

"I see," Parminder said. "I meant to ask you why your names are different. Your fathers are brothers are they not?"

"You are correct. Rubert and George, twin sons of Joe and Mary Com-manda. I changed my name when I turned eighteen, out of respect for the Mohawk tradition of maternal lineage. It pissed my dad off but he respected my choice when I took his mother's surname."

"So Deseronto is not your mother's family name?"

"I'm afraid not. LeRoux de Cavaliers was just a bit too much for a handle, even for me. Besides, back then I was trying everything I knew to be more Indian and a lot less *that French kid!*"

"Here's my street," Parminder said, letting the cab driver know where to stop. "One day you must tell me how each of you ended up being named after ancient queens."

The cab pulled up to the curb and Parminder opened the car door. Cleo wasn't actually ready to say goodnight to her friend. Their conversation had been a pleasant distraction but it had not addressed the one thing that kept popping into her head.

"They're sleeping together, aren't they?"

Parminder stepped out of the cab before turning back to answer, "I'm sorry, but yes."

* * *

Alone in her hotel room, Cleo sank into an upholstered chair near the bed. A gray numbness began to spread through her.

What was I thinking? I do not care what's going on between her and Bo. All I need to care about is whether this job can be done. Then I will care about how to work with Bo to complete the job. Then I will go home and then . . . And then it doesn't matter. I can worry about the "and then" when I get there.

Home for Cleo didn't really mean much anymore. She loved the farm but it was a lot of work without Samantha, and it wasn't really a home. After Sam's death, Cleo had built a loft in the barn to use as a little apartment. They had purchased the farm for a song, mostly because it didn't have a house on it. They had been deep into the planning for their eco-home when they found out Samantha had cancer. All progress stopped on the new house, while they concentrated on keeping the old house in the city comfortable, while she recovered. When Sam didn't recover, Cleo sold the place in town, and pitched a tent at the farm. She had been flying out of Trenton, and kept a room in the BOQ anyway. Before Sam's death, it had simply been a place to rest after the three-hour drive to the air base from the Princess Margaret Hospital. With Samantha gone, she cancelled the build of the new house and sold the old one. And with no flying duties to take her to Trenton, Cleo threw herself into adding a loft to the barn and making it more comfortable than the tent. When her bereavement leave was finally over, and she was locking up the barn, it occurred to her that the farm was just as much theirs as the house had been. She wasn't ready to sell it yet, but she had been getting closer and closer to the realization that it didn't matter where she lived. The only home she had ever really known was the life she had shared with Samantha Stewart.

Getting up from the hotel chair, and crossing the room in quick-time, she picked up the telephone by the bed. Fumbling though her pockets, she found the business card from the Foreign and Commonwealth Office. It read, Tori Waite, Regulatory Adjudicator. Cleo checked the back to see if she had written a number other than the official listing on the front but found nothing. Undeterred, she dialed the number on the front.

When the line picked-up, a female voice answered "Miss Waite's Office."

"Yes, I need to speak with Tori. It's important."

"Your name please," the woman asked officiously, instructing Cleo to wait on the line. She could hear the sound of the operator clicking keys on a computer, then, "Captain Deseronto, please hold."

Moments later Tori was on the line, asking if Cleo was all right.

"I need to work," Cleo said. "I want to go in. Now. Is that possible?"

"Are you sure?"

"Yes!"

"Very well."

Cleo imagined she heard something else in those words but wasn't willing to ask. *I will not be played!*

"I will pick you up in about thirty minutes."

"No!" Cleo said with force, immediately realizing how that must have sounded. "I mean, no . . . it's not necessary. Or, do you have to?"

There was a long silence from the other end of the line. "I can have Allan meet you, if that's your preference?"

"Actually, is it possible for someone to just find me a room to work in and give me any documents I'm cleared to see?"

"Absolutely, if that is what you want, but you must promise to call me if you need anything or want my assistance, regardless of the time."

Cleo answered more harshly than she would have liked, "if I need something that no one else can help me with, then yes, I'll call."

"All right then," Tori said, still sounding hesitant. "A car will be downstairs in fifteen minutes."

"Thanks." was all she could choke out before hanging up. She didn't want to talk to Tori and she didn't want Tori to know how upset she was. *What the hell is wrong with me? I'm acting like a frackin' teenager.* She had fifteen minutes, *plenty of time to take a fast shower, change and get my gosa together.* If she was going to work on this, she was going to lock herself in until she had an Ops Plan or just downright failed. *And failing is not part of the plan.*

* * *

Tori hit speed dial on her phone, needing less than two minutes to dole out her orders before returning to her company. "Boudicca, if you are actually interested in working for me, there are some things that must be understood."

"Come on, babe," Bo groaned, before Tori cut her off.

"Enough," she ordered. "Have you lost your mind? Why must you antagonize her? I need her and you almost tossed this entire plan in the rubbish heap before we could even begin!"

Bo, stretching on the couch, made a dismissive wave, "relax babe. It's not like we really need her."

"Even you don't believe that, and stop bloody well calling me that."

"Oh, someone's cranky."

"For the last time, enough," Tori demanded. "Plainly, you have misunderstood the situation, Agent Commanda. This evening was about building a new section for the SOE, a section in need of a commanding officer."

"Hey babe," Bo said, standing to pull Tori to her, "I'm here for you."

Tori shook off her embrace, "Do not address me in that fashion again. I command Special Operations at Six. If you're under the impression that you have a place on this team without Captain Deseronto, you are mistaken."

Sporting her most charming smile, Bo snaked her arms around Tori's waist, "Calm down," she purred, pulling Tori in tight. "I know this bullshit with Cleo is just for show. Mike told me everything! You're just covering your ass for the brass. I get it!"

Unlacing Bo's fingers from the small of her back, Tori pushed her away. "You have no bloody idea, do you? Agent Commanda, I am the brass. Your section chief, along with his counterparts from other participating nations, form the core of Section One within the SOE, my SOE. When nations have an overlapping interest, Section One comes together to consider joint operations. The only reason I am considering this preposterous plan from your CIA is because the Canadians have taken a great interest as well. Having said that, no plan goes forward without my approval, I'm in command of the SOE, not Mike Perkins, or whomever is pulling his strings."

Clearly surprised by the information but undaunted, Bo jumped smartly to attention and snapped off a parade perfect salute, "Lance Corporal Commanda reporting for *booty call*, Ma'am."

Tori's face colored but from anger, not embarrassment, "Listen carefully, Agent," she said with flat formality, and a hint of malice, "What happened between us is over. I do not tolerate overt familiarity within the SOE and I will not allow you to undermine my authority. That goes doubly so for Captain Deseronto. She does not need to know about our earlier association. Do you hear me? Nothing is to interfere with her recruitment."

"What the fuck do we need her for?"

Glowering, Tori spoke through gritted teeth. "There is no *we*, Agent Commanda, your presence on this team is neither guaranteed nor fitting. Other than a badge in marksmanship, you possess none of the skills required for this assignment. Frankly the only reason Perkins suggested you was proximity, with you being the only aboriginal within 4,000 kilometers. Cleopatra, however, is a military officer with some experience in the field. While she is not completely qualified, she is a far more suitable candidate that you. If you truly want a position on this team, I suggest you change your attitude. If all the players from across the pond are as intent on making this work as does appear, then I will do whatever it takes to bring her on board, including excluding you from the team, and my life."

"Are you going to fuck her too?" Bo hissed, now angry from the personal rejection.

Tori shook her head, "I did not want this to get ugly. Bo, please, we had fun, but I cannot and will not, continue this with you. Now you may demonstrate your willingness to work for Captain Deseronto, and apply yourself to the needs of the team, or I will order Mr. Perkins to post you to a more appropriate location outside the EU."

"You can't do that," Bo asserted, her professional confidence still intact.

"Yes Bo, I can, that is if Mike wants to stay in the UK."

Bo hesitated, quickly debating the idea that Tori might actually possess that kind of power. Even though she understood she was outmaneuvered, she couldn't stop herself, "what's she got that I don't have?"

Tori's look softened slightly, but there was no mistaking the edge in her voice, "When you can answer that question, you will have earned a spot on this team."

Chapter Four

Newly minted Captain Mateo Perec was ensconced in the belly of a US military Chinook. The heavy lift helicopter group, consisting of two Chinooks and two gunship Apaches on their flank, were flying Nap-of-the-Earth along the Iraqi/Iranian border. Perec, an engineer by trade, had been in the last weeks of his training at the Israeli Defense Force Officer Candidate School when he had been marched in front of the Commanding Officer and asked to volunteer for temporary duty with the US Armed Forces. The posting, it was explained, required a demolitions expert and would last less than thirty days. In return for volunteering his service, Academic officer, or Ka'ab Perec would be immediately promoted to Seren or Captain, and at the successful completion of the operation, be given his own company to command. To Perec, the deal sounded too good to be true but what was his alternative? Besides, he had chosen a military career over simply completing conscripted service and joining his father's company as his older sister had. Confident that the family legacy was well managed, Mateo volunteered as an Engineering officer, completing military training each summer while finishing his degree. Mateo's father had not been happy with his son's choice, but once the two had sat and discussed the future with the family Rabbi, Perec the Elder had agreed with his son's decision. Golem Demolition, the family company was well tended with Perec Senior at the helm and daughter number one as Chief Engineer. Daughter number two, also older than Mateo, was busy fulfilling her family obligations too, and was happily popping out babes with her hubby, who just happened to work for Golem Demolition too.

"Hey Cap?" One of the American soldiers called to him over the loud din of the rotor blades. "What's that thing you write? You know, when you're finished setting the booby traps?"

"Knock it off!" A muscular Latin-looking American ordered the even larger and even more muscular inquisitive soldier. "I told you guys to leave the Cap alone!"

Undeterred, the very large, very black American stood up from the helicopter's netting seat, and crossed the cabin to the opposite bench, before inserting himself between Captain Perec and the Latino. "Come-on Chief! Cut me some slack. I'm just trying to learn a little about the culture. You know—when in Rome!"

The man they called Chief just rolled his eyes. "Whatever, Hotshot! Just don't drive the man crazy." It was an order, Perec noticed, but delivered with a smirk. None of the soldiers on the Chinook with him wore rank or service insignia, while their language and demeanor was all American. Perec had met and studied with Americans at university, but this was his first experience actually being embedded with US troops. Or were they troops? He had been introduced to the team members by surname only, and just the night before. He knew who was in command and who was there to "protect" him, but other than that, he hadn't a clue. Now squished into the bench beside him, the big African/American soldier gave him a friendly elbow, "Cap? That stuff you keep writing on the ground, what is it, a blessing or something?"

Perec laughed, he liked these American soldiers or were they sailors, he didn't know and wouldn't ask. After all, we was sitting in an American helicopter, dressed in the camo uniform of an American Army Engineer. Before leaving for Iraq, he had been advised to only ask questions related to "how" to complete his assignment successfully, and nothing more. At first he had assumed the orders stemmed from a need for secrecy. Now he had to consider that he knew next to nothing about the United States or Americans for that matter. Deciding that being rude to the big American would draw more attention to him than just answering his questions, he offered, "No, it is not a blessing. It is a joke I make at home, when I learned to set charges with my sister. She is demolition engineer too."

"No shit! Oops, sorry there Cap!" The American apologized with a grim and a friendly fist to the shoulder. "So, you got a sister who likes to blow shit up too? Sweet! When can I meet her?"

"Marine!" The one called Chief, growled.

"Aw, come on Chief! A guy can dream!"

"I don't think the captain wants some horny Marine, dreaming about his sister, while he's shaking the sugar-tree!"

Perec laughed along with the good-natured Marine. "I make a little joke, drawing a symbol for the Golem my father has painted on his equipment." At the look of confusion on the big Marine's face, he added, "A Golem is like a funny monster. Like you tell small children, to give them a little scare!"

"What, like the boogieman?"

"Yes! Yes!" Perec was delighted when the Marine made the connection.

"Captain!" the chief interrupted, "The pilot says the last load is on the ground. We're about to land. Any last-minute instructions?"

"No Chief. We will deploy as previously. Once the last hole is dug and the armaments are laid-in, Mr. Hotshot and I will set the charges." He patted the breast pocket of his BDUs for the last of his homemade detonators. Once complete, even the most experienced explosives expert would never guess the charges had been built by an Israeli demolitions expert and not some tank officer from the Republican guards. Except for the Golem squiggle, which Perec and the men all new, would be blown away long before their helicopter was airborne again.

Security and Intelligence Service
Vauxhall Cross
London, United Kingdom

Planning Marathon, Start time: 23:00 Hours, Day 1

The offices of the Security and Intelligence Service functioned at full force day and night. The building itself was quite spectacular, but you had to wait until nightfall to see it lit against the Thames River to really appreciate its aesthetic. In the lobby, Cleo found the volume of personnel was just as high now as it had been five hours earlier. Even with Darcy Gerrard waiting to escort her, she still had to jump through all the hoops required by security, including the surrender of her passport, and a search of her belongings.

Once clear of security, Darcy escorted her to a meeting room. "I've got us in here," he said, pointing at a security door marked Tutor Room. Darcy swiped his pass, opening the door for the two of them.

Cleo was taken aback. "I wasn't expecting a supervisor?"

"Oh I'm not here to supervise," he said, not reacting to her dig. "Tori called me. She suggested I place myself at your service."

"Why?"

"I thought I might help you settle in, maybe answer any questions you might have, or just listen if you wanted to talk."

Cleo studied him for some time before asking, "I'm guessing you're either an incredible tech wizard who is going to help me find everything I need, or you're the resident psychologist, and here for my mental well-being. Which is it?"

"Actually," Darcy answered, un-ruffled by the direct assault, "I'm a psychiatrist, not a psychologist."

"You don't say," her sarcasm was an automatic response to his playful tone. "I feel sooooo much better!" She regretted the words the moment they were out of her mouth. "I'm sorry," she said with a sigh. "Maybe I do need to talk."

"You certainly have an excuse, considering how poorly things went this evening."

"No," she shook her head, ignoring the obvious invitation to discuss everything that had happened. "No! No excuses, I was out of line and I'm sorry."

"I'm the one who should apologize, for not being up front with you, considering Tori's concerns after this evenings lack of progress."

"Did she say that?"

"She was very upset about the way Agent Commanda conducted herself," he reported, without going into detail. "I think you should know she's gone to Sir Richard. She believes this FBI agent will be a liability to the operation."

"This FBI agent . . ." Cleo repeated, noticing how carefully he skirted the fact that they were family. "I shouldn't have embarrassed her." She took a seat halfway down the table. "May I ask you something?"

"Yes, yes, of course," he encouraged, while pulling out the chair across from her.

"As a psychiatrist working for the service, where does patient confidentiality fit in? Is there even such a thing, in this line of work?"

He seemed to spend a lot of time contemplating her question. "It is a bit sticky, but the 'needs of the service' do come first, as I'm sure you understand. I do want to assure you that nothing, other than those aspects that may affect operational readiness, is discussed with senior officers."

"I see. So basically everything goes up the chain of command."

"That is not what I said, but," he grudgingly admitted, "you are mostly correct with one exception, I am a wonderful listener and I understand the pain that follows when private emotions become public fodder. I also know that even the very best officers sometimes need help sorting things." Darcy took her silence as an invitation to continue. "What if I talk and you listen? Then I will have nothing to report, at least nothing that you said to me."

"Does that usually work for you?" she asked him skeptically.

"Actually, it's the first time I've applied this type of logic."

"All right Mr. Spock," with a wry smile and a hint of challenge in her tone, Cleo ordered, "start talking."

It didn't take long for Darcy Gerrard to hit on most of what had upset her. He talked about the airport and how she would have wanted to be properly debriefed on her performance. He commented on her irritation with the chief, about why he had not just called her instead of all the cloak and dagger? Then he talked about Tori and the emotions that often accompany attraction.

"Maybe," Cleo's voice was flat, but the rising color in her cheeks gave her away. "Maybe, but what does it mean when your attraction is involved with someone else?"

Darcy asked quietly, "Do you know who this someone else might be?"

"Not if it has to come from my mouth," she said flatly, reminding him, "that's not the deal."

"No, no! I wouldn't think of it. I do however, need to know just how much you want to hear. After all, some things, once said, can never be taken back."

"You believe that?"

"I do!"

Cleo took a minute to think, trying to pinpoint what was truly bothering her. "Since we were kids, Bo always seemed to catch all the breaks and I didn't mind. I was proud of her. I wanted to see her succeed as much as I wanted success for myself." She paused, as if deciding whether she should continue. "Then she started *frackin'* things up, and I couldn't help but resent the hell out of her. Not because she had problems or needed help but because she didn't care. Not about anything or anyone. She didn't back then and she made it clear tonight that she doesn't care now. Which makes those, what did you call them, confusing emotions, even more difficult to comprehend. It's rough when you fall for someone who's uninterested, but that's life. What I can't understand is anyone getting involved with someone like Bo, someone who doesn't care about anyone or anything?

"Perhaps it was simply a mistake," Darcy suggested, adding, "a mistake she is now trying to clean up as best she can."

"A mistake?" Cleo asked skeptically, slowly letting the idea sink in. "I guess we all make mistakes. It's how we learn, isn't it?"

"It's one way in which we learn, although I find example a more sagacious master."

"Setting a good example is one of the most basic teachings the Elders give us. Although, I think I have learned just as much from the bad examples as the good. So sagacious is not exactly the way I would describe the spirit of example." Cleo watched as Darcy leaned back in his chair, clearly enjoying the conversation.

"Captain Deseronto, you are a born Judician."

"Thank you, Dr. Gerrard. There is nothing more encouraging than a compliment from a Vulcan." Now, ready to get down to work, Cleo wanted to see everything she was cleared for.

Darcy, surprising her, explained that almost all the information she wanted was stored electronically and that she was cleared for everything. In other words, she had received Code Word security clearance, a level above Top Secret. He signed her into the computer taking her to the password screen first.

"You will need to change that every twenty-four hours," he explained.

Once she had entered a new password, he navigated to the file menu, giving her a basic rundown on all of the files, how they were organized, and which commands moved windows to the large screen. Cleo immediately brought up the most detailed topographical map she could find and the analysis of her photos. "Is there a way I can compare the chart and the photos?" she asked. "I also want to bring up the satellite recon with the declination data."

"Right to work then," Darcy said with satisfaction.

Before she could continue, the electronic lock on the door tripped. When the door opened, the computer screens in the room simultaneously shut down, and a freckled face, carrot top of a girl, pushed a cart into the room. Once the door closed behind her, the computer screens lit back up, and Darcy introduced the team's most junior member.

"Siobhan," he said. "This is Cleo Deseronto."

"It's a pleasure to meet you Captain Deseronto," the young redhead beamed.

Siobhan's deep Irish accent delighted Cleo. She stood and offered her hand to the young woman. "My pleasure, Siobhan. Call me Cleo. What have you brought us?" She was expecting Michelin maps and hydration charts, and shook her head when the young woman offered tea and cookies.

"I bought some pop if you'd prefer?" she asked. Once the beverages were handed out, she stowed the wet portion of her cart and hauled several charts and books from the dry side.

Oh the priorities of a civilized world! "You must be the 'everything person' around here?"

Siobhan blushed at the attention. "I try Miss, Captain, sorry!"

"It's okay! Please call me Cleo. That's always my preference," she insisted, ever mindful of the extra discipline often endured by crew mates at the bottom of the pecking order.

Siobhan spent a few minutes going over security protocols for Hard documents, then recited a whole list of services she would provide, from standing guard over everything when Cleo needed to take a bathroom break, to fetching her entire meals from the canteen. Her first priority was to find any other documents Cleo and Darcy might need. Cleo took her at her word, providing a short list of materials that would not normally be part of the intelligence files.

Once she was gone, Cleo turned her attention back to Darcy. "You don't have to stay."

"I wouldn't miss this for the world. I can't wait to see how the hydration data fits in! Perhaps you could just think of me as your research assistant?"

"Be careful," she warned him. "I will take you at your word."

Darcy smiled and tapped a few keys on the computer keyboard. "I have the declination data you wanted to see. Should I put it up?"

"First we have to sort the data by reference point," Cleo said, "then we can look at everything with a declination of less than twenty degrees from the horizon."

After four hours, and two pots of tea, Cleo slouched down in her chair in frustration. "I can't do it like this."

"What's the problem?" Darcy asked.

"Maybe it's the shifting sands in this area," she said, pointing to a place on the chart, "I think my discovery was a compete fluke. Look at the elevation data from the satellite. The elevation has increased by about one hundred and thirty feet from the sightline your guys calculated," she sighed heavily. "No wonder the satellite recon was useless."

Cleo got up from the table. Another cup of tea was the last thing she wanted, instead she chose a bottle of lemon Lucozade from the ice bucket Siobhan had brought them.

"I'm afraid this is the same predicament the planning team hit."

"I'll bet," she answered absently. Then something hit her and she turned directly to Darcy. "You're a Trekkie, right?" she asked, not waiting for an answer, "tell me, why do all Starfleet cadets fail the Kobiyashi Maru?"

Darcy struggled to answer. "It's the *No Win* scenario. They're *supposed* to fail."

"I don't think so. I think it's because they fail to change the conditions of the test. Life is a lot like one big test. And like tests, we often pre-assume the limits or conditions." When she realized he wasn't following, she added, "it's like opening your textbook in the middle of an exam. You wouldn't do it unless you had been told too."

Darcy nodded, following her train of thought. "Because we have been conditioned to take exams without our books for reference. I see where you're going, but I can't imagine how you would change the conditions here."

"I can't," she admitted. "At least, not the way we have been going about this. What we need is a model of the region." With the mouse, Cleo dragged a box around a four kilometers sector north of Q'on. "I don't know how to do that," she admitted, still looking at the enhanced area on the chart.

"Would a computer model work?"

"I was actually thinking of something like a sand table, but a computer model would be amazing," Asking with excitement, "is that even possible?"

Dr. Darcy Gerrard, the resident shrink, smiled at his un-schooled charge. "Please excuse me. I've a call to make."

Ten minutes later, he was back in the room with news. "Guy and Nicola are on their way in." The couple, he explained, worked as the team's tech specialists, or the "tech twins" as everyone referred to them. It wasn't as if they had lost their individual identities when they married, it was just that as a couple they were so completely intertwined in knowledge and experience, they worked as one perfect interwoven entity.

"How long?" Cleo asked. Normally she would have been horrified to drag people in at this time of night, but she was pumped and didn't want to stop.

"They will have a working model for you within two or three hours," Darcy assured her, "but they want a list of all the data sources you need to access."

Cleo nodded, starting to think about what that would include, when it occurred to her, "not everything is stored electronically. What do we do about that?"

"We will need to start a database," Darcy said. "Nic did say to just put that sort of thing in a spreadsheet."

A groan escaped from Cleo. She was not a skills typist and often spent hours upon hours trying to correct the overwhelming number of typos and transposed numbers she entered.

"You need not grouse," Darcy said, knowing exactly where the hesitation came from. "Siobhan has clearance and can type one hundred and ten words per minute."

Cleo relaxed, sitting back in her chair. "I knew there was a reason I liked you."

Reverting to the Vulcan persona she had applied, Dr. Darcy Gerrard answered simply, "a most logical consequence."

Tutor Room

Planning Marathon, 19:00 Hours, Day 2

The Tutor Room had become Cleo's de facto office since her arrival almost twenty hours earlier. The meeting table was strewn with road maps, aerial charts, and geological surveys. Siobhan, busy at the keyboard entering new data, had given up on keeping the room tidy. When Cleo got like this, it was difficult for anyone to keep up.

Guy and Nicola, or Nici, had been working through their third computer model and were finally making progress.

"There it is," Cleo said, looking at a new set of satellite recon photos. "It," was a line on the sand, or more accurately, a shadow of a straight edge. It was the only hint they could find of the bunker, and put its location almost four kilometers east of where they and the experts had been looking. Finding that out had only exposed other errors in the analysis of her photos, explaining why the analysts couldn't find a hint of topography that would indicate an underground facility.

Siobhan, excited by the discovery after hours and hours of repeatedly re-building the database for the computer model, jumped to her feet. "I've got to tell Tori!" Remembering her manners, she stopped and waited for permission from whomever was senior.

Cleo nodded with a smile. "I'm sure she'll enjoy hearing it from you," and with that said, Siobhan was gone. Turning her attention to the tech twins, Cleo asked for an update.

It was Nic who answered first, although they usually finished each other's sentences so you were never really speaking with just one of them. "All the wire frame mapping is done."

"With the exception of the new data Von's working up," Guy added, refer-ring to the new spreadsheet Siobhan was creating.

"We'll have complete 3D functionality by suppertime," Nic added.

"And have the skins laid on by the time you make your presentation in the morning."

"What about sleep?" Cleo asked. "Are you two planning to sleep, ever?"

They both smiled at her as if that was a silly suggestion. The sound of the security lock whirring open, halted any debate.

Siobhan pushed through the door with Tori close behind. "I understand progress has been made?" Tori asked, looking to Cleo for confirmation.

"Well, we don't have a plan yet, but we have a location!"

That confused Tori and she said as much. Since her arrival that morning, she had gone out of her way to give Cleo room to work. It wasn't like there was time or even the privacy to sit down and talk. The Tutor Room had become more than a meeting room—or even Cleo's office, it had the look and feel of a war room, albeit a very small one.

It was Nic who stood up, explaining as she did, "they got it wrong."

"Those wankers down in photo," Guy added, explaining his wife's state-ment. He stood and stretched, then followed his wife from the room. "Cof-fee," he announced from the door.

"You too, Siobhan," Nic ordered, leaving the room to Tori and Cleo.

Tori walked to the end of the table and sat on its edge, taking time to look at the new data her team had collated. "The photo boys were wrong?" She began tentatively, clearly treading with caution, "is there any chance you were mistaken about your location when you took those pics?"

"That was my first thought too," Cleo answered honestly, "but no. I was on the money, but the analysts may have assumed I was wrong, and with good reason." She punched a few keys on the keyboard and brought up a soft copy of the Michelin Road Map with a topographical overlay. "See here," Cleo said, getting up from the chair to join Tori by the large computer screen. "In my re-port I said I was here, on this little knoll, just north of the village. This portion of the north face was visible deep within this valley. Do you remember how I thought there may have been a river down there at one time?"

Tori nodded and pointed to the location on the map that the analysts had identified. "That would put the facility over here, in this valley."

"Except, the night before I took those pictures, there was an incredibly fierce storm."

"Yes, you mentioned that in your report."

"The valley must have been stripped of a large volume of sand, exposing a wet river bed. A condition that wouldn't last long under normal conditions." Cleo turned back to the table and rooted through the piles of paper to find the hydration reports. "According to the 1966 water survey, my valley, this one here," she pointed, "was once a river, the Q'on River which was re-routed to allow construction here," pointing to the line in the sand. "The source of the Q'on is reported to be underground. This is the knoll I was on, and here is the mouth of the valley through which I spotted the bunker. I couldn't tell how far it was, and distances can be tricky in the early morning light."

Tori looked skeptical. "That put you at what, seven kilometers away! It's not possible with the lens you were using," referring to the details Cleo had provided on her camera gear.

"Why not? The sun came up from this direction, just off my right shoulder. It was a perfect angle. I could have taken that shot from the International Space Station and gotten the same results, what with the winter sunrise and all."

Tori looked at her with raised eyebrows, "International Space Station?"

"Okay, so that's a bit of a stretch, but I bet if we send this info back to Photo, they'll agree with me."

"Oh, I agree with you," she said, "but, the implications are frightful. If you were seven kilometers away and not three point eight as predicted, that would mean the facility is almost twice the size calculated. Then there was the problem of a water source to cool a reactor," her tone was heavy with the admission.

"What if the redistribution point Allan Bashir found was part of the original water diversion system?"

"Most probably, but the real issue is the existence of the Q'on River. Now they clearly have a coolant source. Until this moment, all of our allies had dismissed our concerns because we could not solve that particular problem. Now that you have found it, we know the threat is real. We have to take this up to Sir Richard immediately." Cleo was quiet for a minute, forcing Tori to turn to her.

"Would it be okay if you met with him? It's just that I'm dirty and tired, not to mention having a touch of cabin fever. I would really like to go grab a shower and something to eat, at least something that doesn't come wrapped in paper, before I tackle writing an Ops plan."

Tori smiled at that. "Most officers would be tripping over themselves for a chance to present such critical material to the head of the Security Services, but I'll take it up," she said gently. "Take whatever amount of time you need."

"Great," Cleo said, then surprised herself by asking, "will you join me for a bite?"

"You want that?" Tori, caught off guard, looked pained.

"Yah, I mean, if you have time."

"All right then, I know just the place, close by, quiet, and the food is simply wonderful. Or simple and wonderful, as I know you prefer."

Plantagenet Room

Planning Presentation, 10:00 Hours, Day 3

Cleo sat in one of the comfortable briefing chairs while the tech twins bustled about making sure everything was ready for the presentation. Siobhan, from out of nowhere, had managed to find Cleo a very large glass of orange juice, Tylenol, and eye drops. The dinner of sausages and chips she had shared with Tori the night before had left her feeling sluggish. When she added the hours of work, skipped meals, and the earlier emotional joust with Bo, Cleo knew she had earned her exhaustion. Siobhan, together with Nicola and Guy, an eager hand from Darcy Gerrard, and Allan Bashir's firsthand knowledge, had pulled together three high-level options for a close-up surveillance mission in the Bala Valley of Iran.

Cleo was so tired, she assumed that the person who sat down beside her was Darcy, and was startled a moment later when Tori asked how she was.

"Once I finish this," she said, lifting the glass of juice, "I'll be fine."

"That's good, as the Americans just cleared security. They will be up any minute now."

Groaning, she tipped back the rest of her orange juice, before standing to stretch. "I'm ready," she announced, just as Rod Nelligan escorted the contingent into the room. Along with Agent Commanda, and the CIA Section Chief, Mike Perkins, they were joined by a US Marine Corps Major. During introductions, Cleo learned that this tall, black officer with a crisp New England accent was the Military Advisor at the US Embassy. Judging by his youth, Cleo knew he had to be an up-and-comer. *Stars in his future,* was the phase she remembered. After the Americans, Sir Richard and Étienne Ste. Hubert entered the room.

The Plantagenet Room was not so much a meeting room as it was a high-tech briefing room. There were no tables here, and no writing pads. The only papers allowed in the room were Cleo's notes, which now sat on the briefing room podium. There were two other men, who had joined them with Sir Richard, but neither was introduced. Cleo recognized them for what they were; military officers in civilian clothing. She sat quietly while Rod Nelligan began the briefing with an introduction to the situation.

By the time Cleo took the podium, she was back to her old self. The first fact that needed to be discussed was the increase in the estimated size of the bunker and the water table data. "This is the site. We have been referring to it as the Bala Valley for the village of Emameh-ye Bala, seven kilometers away."

Guy pushed several images of the site onto the presentation screen. Some included the pictures Cleo had taken, along with a number of satellite images both new and historic. "As you can see, with an elevation one hundred and thirty feet lower than originally estimated, this valley becomes a flood plain during extreme metrological events. The water source is actually the Q'on River, which flows underground from this point . . ." Cleo paused, waiting for Guy to catch up. A second later, the new image opened on the big screen. "When we went through the books, we found the river runs underground, only becoming visible during spring floods. You may recall that Allan Bashir found a disused supply line and diverter here," she said, pointing to a place on the map. "We all thought it had something to do with the local oil field. We now know it to be part of a water divergence system, that was built in the 1960s, to allow construction in the Bala Valley."

Guy had the drawings up that Allan had made of the diversion station. Before she could continue, one of the unnamed soldiers interrupted.

"You're mistaken," he said arrogantly. "Only oil moves through pipes of that capacity."

"That may be, sir," Cleo replied respectfully, "but once upon a time, that pipe diverted the entirety of the Q'on River, which may not be the Niagara, but she flows like it." Cleo knew this kind of soldier. He would refuse to understand anything she suggested unless he happened to agree with her. "It's like this: When a river runs underground, its capacity becomes fixed, like water in a pipe. The only way to push more water through the pipe is to increase the speed of the flow, or the underground river in this case."

"Venturi Effect," the Marine Major suggested. "The smaller the underground caverns, the faster the water is forced to move until capacity is completely exceeded."

"Wherein, the resulting water flow is pushed above ground. Thank you, sir." Cleo said, noticing the major's wings of gold. "We have now identified a perfect, and fast moving, underground water source to cool a nuclear reactor."

Cleo could have spent all day just going over the site advantages, and the proof that they had discovered a major project, started in the valley some forty years earlier. The fact that security agencies around the globe had forgotten about the site was not her concern. "Operationally, we have come up with three possible plans, all based on the premise that; one—the operation is limited to external visual confirmation only; two—the chance of interception must be minimized, and; three—we intend for the human assets involved to return."

Without a challenge to the preamble, Cleo began the next portion of the briefing. "Okay," she said to Nicola, "let's bring up our computer model of the Bala Valley." The computer-generated model popped onto the screen. Now with all the final additions in place, the appearance was close to that of a CGI world from a video game. Nici turned the 3D image around, rotating both the X- and Y-axis. "Let's set it up like photo seventeen," Cleo instructed the tech twins jointly. "Here we have the same point of view as my photo and in each one this valley looks big, but the satellite data tells us that the valley length, from inside the southwest mouth all the way to the northeast wall, is only eight hundred and forty feet in length. The widest area is one hundred and eighty-six feet at the northeast end, and just over one hundred feet wide at this point, where we believe the facility to be located. Like I said, it's a tight little valley."

Nici turned the axis of the model to face the southeast wall of the valley. "This cliff wall is almost a sheer vertical drop. The geologic data and the lack of large debris at the base suggest a mixed aggregate, most probably too soft to rappel down and absolutely impossible to climb up. The valley entrance is patrolled with a minimum of two squads; one is always on this plateau, overlooking the valley entrance. There are only two other ways in. The first is here, on the northwest side, and involves crossing a highway. Or . . ."

Again, one of the soldiers interrupted her. "That's where we will deploy our team," he said without elaborating on who our team was. "If we land there, we can be in and out of the valley in less than twenty minutes." He actually looked like he was going to get up and leave.

"Do you really think you can land a squadron of helicopters or even a C-130 Hercules on the side of an Iranian highway and not have the whole country immediately know you're there?" He was starting to formulate a retort when she added, "just ask the Americans how that worked for them during the Iran hostage crisis." When he started to get up in protest, Cleo raised her hand traffic cop style. "Look, I know you Army boys aren't happy unless your boots are dirty, but this operation requires finesse, and a cavalry charge down that hill will not work. All you will do is risk your men and jeopardize the Intel gathering objective." The man with no name, while clearly hostile, resumed his seat silently.

"Let's have our three options, shall we," Sir Richard directed, steering Cleo back on course.

She nodded, continuing, "Once we had the correct location, the satellite declination showed us that we don't have to actually get in the valley, we just need to get below the southeast ridge by approximately sixty feet. That works out to, two hundred and thirty feet above the valley floor." She signaled Nici, who added the next layer in the model. "If we want useful Intel, we need to get below two hundred and thirty feet AGL. That makes this even more difficult as Bala is a horseshoe valley, and a small one at that. For a recon pilot, it would be like trying to drop down into a baseball field, and pop back out before hitting the bleachers.

"I wouldn't want to try it," the Marine Major said. "Although it could be done, but not quietly, and if they just happen to have a SAM Battery down there, well, the mission and the pilot would be toast."

"That's pretty much what I thought," Cleo nodded her agreement. She was starting to like this Marine. "So that pretty much leaves us with the need to fly low and slow. Which leads us to: Operation One, Unmanned Aeronautical reconnaissance Vehicle." Guy popped up the USAF, UAV spec page from the *Jane's Defense* database.

"Like most recon aircraft, the UAV hasn't quite got the maneuverability needed to navigate the valley. Which means, as the major explained, if they have SAM's we would get one chance at data acquisition before they detected us. And, we would have to be prepared for the loss of the vehicle." The loss of a four-million-dollar asset drew groans from the Americans in the room. "That's what I thought," she said, sympathizing.

"Operation Two: ROV," Cleo's tone picked-up a little. "Would call for a special surveillance package to be airdropped. The package would be cobbled together from materials already in the system. Namely: a Remote Operated Vehicle, GPS Navigation receiver, a satellite communications uplink, and a digital optics package." That caught everyone by surprise. Even the soldier, forgetting his earlier bruising, wanted to know where they would get an ROV.

"Well," Cleo offered, with a grin, "I was thinking Radio Shack, but if you want, I can shop locally."

Tori turned her head away, and even Sir Richard chose to hide his amusement.

Étienne, often oblivious to Cleo's humor, had missed the joke but not the point. "There is a company in Ottawa, who makes a very good all-terrain rover for the police. They 'ave them on the shelf."

That information did nothing to soothe the arrogant soldier. "And how the bloody hell do you plan to deliver it? You have already ruled out a landing!"

That's where our American friends come in," she said, looking to Mike Perkins. "I'm afraid we'll need a few of those Mars Pathfinder delivery systems. The ones actually designed for testing here on earth."

Mike nodded his head. "You're thinking about the gravitational difference," he assumed, following her train of thought, "but why more than one?"

"I'm thinking the air crew will need more than one practice run. Unless your guys can give us the simulation data for weight, plus vertical and horizontal velocity, for One Atmosphere?"

Before Mike could reply, Rod Nelligan interrupted, "let me see if I understand this," he queried in his deep highland brogue. "You and the twins here want to build a robot on wheels, which we will then drop out of an airplane, presumably from some bloody great distance. It will then bounce its way across the valley in one of those balloon thingies, before tossing them off and roaming about taking pretty pictures. Is that it?"

"Pretty much, Chief."

Nelligan's tone conveyed incredulity but his eyes were full of mischief. "And how would we extract it?"

"Okay, I see where you're going. First, the satellite uplink would allow us to control the ROV, or Rover, as Étienne called it, from right here in this building. It would be nice to have someone on the ground with a backup radio controller, but that's not a necessity. We drop the Rover, I'm just gonna' call it that, we drop it in the valley at night from the southwest, allowing her a good run up the valley and a soft rebound to help slow her down. Once she stops, the Operator will signal for the airbags to deflate and to start her moving towards the bunker. Our objective will be to get her to the southeast wall before sunrise. That will give us infrared and standard photography. We can keep the Rover on point until she's discovered by a patrol, or until the sun's apex is high enough to reveal her position, depending on the threat level."

"And then what," the chief asked?

"And then we blow her up! That leaves no real usable evidence, and if need be, our American friends here can release a cover story saying an old TV satellite got bumped out of orbit and is expected to burn up in the atmosphere. If any debris should survive, experts believe it will crash in the Persian Region or something like that."

The unnamed soldier, for whatever reason, seemed compelled to challenge Cleo. "What in God's name makes you think you can build an ROV capable of completing this mission in short order when they," he pointed an accusing finger at the Americans in the room, "can't build a reliable ROV with billions of dollars to waste and years of testing?"

Cleo sighed. She was long used to challenges from the by-the-book types and began patiently. "We would not be building something for space exploration. Which means, we don't have a twenty-four-hour time delay to manage. And we don't need to write a self-autonomy program, or a recharge program, or deal with data housekeeping, or upload schedules, or temperature differential, or a million other details. Our Rover won't be much more advanced than the radio-controlled toys they sell at the Camden Markets. The difference," she emphasized, "is that our Rover will be streaming live data via her satellite uplink, and we will be controlling her from here. By the way, our American friends should be very proud of the phenomenal success of *Spirit and Opportunity*. Do not however, make the mistake of comparing the Mars Pathfinder projects with our simplified needs. Compared to the Mars Rovers, our girl will be an ugly, brainless automaton, and nothing more."

"Bullocks!" The soldier said, getting up and stomping out of the room. His associate did not move but gave some silent signal to Sir Richard.

"Let's take a short break," Sir Richard said. "And I need the room."

He didn't have to tell her twice. Cleo was the first one to get out. In the hall she walked the length of the corridor to the windows facing the Thames. She had made this little excursion more than once over the last forty-eight hours. Whenever frustration set in, she needed to move to clear her head. "A change is as good as a rest," she told the planning team, during their marathon. She always found a little fresh air helpful when trying to think, but with security so tight, she had to make do with a few paces along the corridor. Still, the view of the river was clear and mesmerizing. Cleo liked that. She had always found the proximity to the water soothing, and the sight of the morning river traffic was heartening to watch.

"Whenever I stand here," said Tori, "I imagine what it must have been like when the world crossed paths in London."

Cleo had assumed Tori was still in the room with her father and the second unidentified soldier. She chanced a quick look at Tori then back down the hall. At the other end, Bo was swapping stories with her fellow Marine, while the rest of the team had disappeared.

Assured they were alone, Cleo smiled at Tori's whimsy. "Look there, isn't that the West Indies Packet just back from Jamaica and full of sugar?"

"What?" Tori said, looking up and down the Thames.

"And that one," Cleo added. "Isn't that a Brigantine, maybe six weeks out of Cape Town and loaded with diamonds and iron ore?"

Tori smiled at her, now getting the game. Playing along, she added, "and there are the oarsmen, waiting to take their fares up river, and that looks like a man-o-war getting underway. I wonder where she's headed?"

Watching Tori at play was like watching the world light up. Breaking the spell, the door to the Plantagenet Room opened, and the rest of the team began streaming in, with Cleo and Tori bring up the rear. Returning to the podium, Cleo took time to sip the fresh water Siobhan had placed on the shelf. Everyone was looking at her, leaving no time to wonder what had transpired in her absence.

"Operation Three," she began. "Otter!" Starting where she had left off, and watching the reaction of the room, she introduced her last option. "This idea is a little riskier than the others, but it has the advantage of reducing the amount of time a Rover would need to be in position. And, it would put a backup operator on site in case we have any hiccups with the satellite uplink. This plan does draw from the original idea to send Agent Commanda and myself into Tehran under the flag of the Six Nations of the Iroquois Confederacy, which, I would remind everyone, will absolutely require the approval of the Grand Council." Cleo had pronounced it *ear-o-kwa* in the Canadian fashion and not *ear-o-kway* as New Yorkers often did. "The only real difference with this plan is that we will fly in, or rather, fly ourselves into Iran. Once in the area of Q'on, we will release a mini-UAV. This UAV would not need the equipment that the Rover would require because the uplink and all the COM gear would be carried on board the aircraft."

"What type of military aircraft do you think the Iranians are going to let you fly into their airspace?" the Marine Major wanted to know.

"Well, that's the key, isn't it? The most suitable aircraft I could think of that would handle the loads we need, be slow enough to launch the surveillance portion of the operation, and be no threat to the Iranians is the DHC-3."

"Oo-rah!" the major called-out. "Lady, you sure have some balls!"

Mike Perkins, ignoring Major Butterworth's outburst, had to ask, "you want to fly a Gooney Bird into Iran?"

Before she could answer, the Marine Corps Major corrected him. "I don't think she's talking about an R4D, Mike." The R4D was the US Navy and Marine Corps variant of the Douglas Aircraft DC-3. "I think the Captain here is referring to a DeHavilland aircraft, a single engine, naturally aspirated piston airplane. If I remember correctly?"

About half of the room turned to look at to the Marine Major with confusion, when Tori asked, "What's the problem with that particular aircraft?"

"It's a relic, and that's just for starters. They haven't even built them in fifty years!"

"Thirty-five years," Cleo said, correcting him. "They stopped building them thirty-five years ago, and that was only because Hawker-Sidley, DeHavilland's parent company at that time, imagined they were destined to be the next Boeing and stopped taking orders."

This time Tori, who couldn't hide her concern, asked "Is there no other aircraft you might consider?"

"I did start by looking at the DeHavilland Caribou and Buffalo, but both were simply overkill. Plus those birds are in such high demand now; I very much doubt we could pry one loose from the UN. The Beaver was my next choice, but she just hasn't got the legs to take us over the Pole." This information drew more blank faces from across the room. Even the tech twins looked lost. "Think of it like this: a DHC-2 Beaver would be equivalent to a Jeep, while the Dash 3 Otter is the aerial version of the classic deuce-and-a-half." The deuce-and-a-half, or the military 2½ ton truck, had seen service in every theater of war for eighty-odd years. They were recognizable as the canvas covered, open troop carriers, featured in every Hollywood war movie ever made.

Cleo turned to the twins and asked them to bring up the specs for the DHC-3. Moments later another page from *Jane's Defense* popped onto the screen. "This, ladies and gentlemen, is the DeHavilland of Canada Single Engine Otter. It has one supercharged piston engine capable of generating six hundred brake horsepower. It's un-pressurized, with a service ceiling of 18,600 feet above sea level. The load capacity is 5,000 pounds after full fuel and crew." Cleo pointed to the detailed drawing of the fuselage. "And, right here in the baggage compartment, is a circular drop door."

"It's not in the drawing," Bo pointed out.

"That's the best part," Cleo said, explaining, "this information comes from *Jane's Defense* website and can be found in every aircraft book and digest they sell, and every online subscription they have. If the Iranians are curious and go looking for military-style features, they won't find this. It's not there."

"And where would we even find this airplane in this day and age?" the major asked, adding, "and what if it doesn't have the belly port you're talking about."

"Of the seven hundred or so built, all had this drop door, and as for finding one, I'm sure Étienne can find one if you guys can't."

"Us?" Mike Perkins asked. "A Piper Caravan I can do, or even Cessna Citation, but an Otter? I have no idea where we would find something like that."

"From what I could source, you have several hundred just sitting in that boneyard you operate near Pima, Arizona. We're going to have to make some modifications, and Agent Commanda will have to take some flying lessons, but finding a DeHavilland Otter is the easiest part of this plan."

Mike was hesitant to interrupt again, "Even if we could find this plane, and modify it, and get my agent trained in anything like a reasonable time frame, how on earth do you plan to stop the Iranians from inspecting it much less get permission to fly in their airspace?"

"They are going to want to do more than inspect it," the Marine Major added. "They will want to put an Air Force liaisons officer on board, most likely an Iranian Air Force pilot. How would you get around that, without getting shot down, or killing the liaison?"

"Slow down, I've thought about all of that. First, I do know we'll need to have a liaison officer on board, and yes, I know he will be a pilot so there's no conning him, and there's no avoiding an inspection either. So, the simple answer is we don't." Cleo turned to the tech twins, "Guys, can you expand the three-view, put up an interior layout, and draw in the things I need to add?" When they both nodded, she turned her attention to the others. "The Otter was designed to be operated by one pilot from the left seat, here," she pointed to the captain's seat on the plan diagram. "This is the observer's seat on the right, and where the liaisons officer will want to sit. These rows of boxes represent passenger seats that run the length of the cabin, which we will have replaced with extended-range fuel tanks, survival gear, and the like. This, this space, is the baggage compartment, which also contains the batteries and an avionics rack."

"What are the lines in front of the baggage compartment and behind the pilots' seats?" Tori asked.

"One of our secret weapons. Standard utility-grade bulkheads, and before you ask," she said to the room in general, "let me explain the advantage. This bulkhead, or wall, behind the pilots' seats protects the pilots from shifting cargo. It also severely limits the pilot's view of the main cabin." On the screen, Nici and Guy had added bright yellow sight lines to mark the area of the passenger cabin visible from the co-pilot's chair. "One of the modifications will be to convert the cargo compartment into a lavatory. That gives us a good reason to put a door on the rear bulkhead and keep the use of the drop door from the liaison pilot's obscured view."

"I thought you said the aircraft batteries and avionics were all in there?" the major asked.

"Yes, sir! It's going to be one tight, hot, smelly little space." By that point, the tech twins had added a cartoon-like depiction of a floor-mounted holding tank, with a toilet on top. A stick figure was on the throne, balancing a car battery on its lap and gasping for breath. Cleo shook her head. "I think that kind of explains it, and should be enough to limit the time anyone is willing to spend in there."

"Just how big is this drop door of yours?" the major asked. "I assume it was originally designed for photo recon?"

"That was the primary use. It's twenty-seven inches in diameter."

Once again, Rod Nelligan wanted to clarify a few points. "Let me see if I understand what you're now suggesting? You plan to shove a wee UAV up the shitter, then, when yer in the area, pop open the bay door and fly the thing by remote control?"

Cleo nodded.

Rod shook his head. "And how do you plan to fly the plane and fly the UAV and keep the JAFO busy while yer doin' it?"

She smiled, appreciating the details. "First, for the leg of the flight where we complete the surveillance operation, Agent Commanda will fly the plane, while I fly the UAV. She will be in the pilot's seat on the left and I will be in the lavatory. The UAV will not be hidden behind the door panel as much as it will be part of the panel. That way, if we are forced down for inspection after the operation is over, it will just look like the access panel to the holding tank fell off." Smiling at the irony of it, Cleo added wryly, "things like that happen to old airplanes that haven't been made in fifty years!"

"Where would you get the UAV?" Sir Richard asked, ignoring the joke.

"We'll have to build it, but again I think we can get everything we need off the shelf. If we get into trouble, the Japanese have a very slick mini-UAV they're developing for law enforcement. There are also several top-notch American companies working on minis for the US military."

"That's not your first choice?" Sir Richard asked.

"No sir! Not unless you're throwing money away." Cleo looked around the room. Everyone seemed confused by the plan. "Okay, let's just walk through this. We get an Otter and kit her out for an around the world promotional tour, or an air race like the *Arc-en-ciel*, something along that line. Next, we start the tour, with some hoopla, on our home reserve, a Mohawk Reserve, marking the beginning of the first circumpolar navigation by an aboriginal flight team. Which is why the Otter fits so much better than something like the Cessna. We also promote the fact that we have no intention of visiting any of the 'evil' Western nations that have kept us subjugated over the last five hundred years, and make a big thing of it in the Middle East."

"We could leak your militia service record, including the POW time in Israel," Tori said, thinking aloud, "Sorry."

"No worries. That would actually be helpful." Turning to Nici, she directed, "please put up the Operation Three flight plan and the World Aeronautics Chart we marked up. Here we go. We take off from Ahkwesáhsne, which as you know, is sandwiched in-between New York State, Ontario, and Quebec. From there we fly north, over the Pole, stopping at Iqaluit and the Canadian Forces station at Alert. Étienne, we would need you to clear our way with National Defense Headquarters and with both the Norwegians and the Danes. After Alert, it's just a short hop to Norway and down into Western Russia to visit Star City."

This time Tori spotted a problem, "the times listed beside the destinations. I take it they are not local times?"

"No Ma'am. That column is flight duration but don't worry, those numbers will change, once the actual winds and weather are calculated in."

"Fourteen point five hours?" Tori read off the flight times with dismay. "Twelve point seven-five hours, I expect these will be grueling flights. How will you manage?"

"That's half of the reason I want to visit Star City. One, it will be a very necessary resting point, and a location that all pilots would naturally want to visit. Second, we can generate some attention for our tour, attention that I am hoping *Al Jazeera* will pick up and rebroadcast, or at least show to the Iranians. As a benefit, Star City is home to a huge contingent of Americans, Canadians, and Europeans involved in the space program, which would provide us an added layer of security or obscurity." Cleo, almost dry-mouthed, stopped for another sip of water before continuing, "From this point, it's just one more fuel stop, and then on to Tehran. At which time, we show our respects to our oppressed cousins in the East, throw on Hijabs, shake hands with the women, and bow our heads at the men, then fly off to some tightly scheduled event in the United Arab Emirates. You would have to set something up for us in Dubai," Cleo added, almost apologetically. "The operation must be executed during our departure flight. As soon as we are off the ground, I will become ill, forcing Agent Commanda to take control of the aircraft. We will have already let it slip that she's a low-time pilot. That should be more than enough to keep the liaison officer in his seat." Cleo stopped, taking a minute to review the images on the screen.

Rod Nelligan, always the stickler for details, took her pause as invitation to ask, "Where do you plan to hide the radio controller for the wee plane and how will you fuel it and start her up if she's hidden in the tank?"

Cleo loved the way he worked through a plan, always the flight engineer; he needed to hear the mechanical side of things. "Even as slow as ninety knots, which is the speed Agent Commanda will be taught to fly the Otter, we will still only have a limited window of opportunity. Most probably less than ten minutes until range from the target becomes a problem. That means fuelling and starting complications must be eliminated, and it also means we only need enough power to keep our little bird in the air for about ten, maybe fifteen minutes." Cleo could see no one was following. "All we need is a small electric motor and a high-yield battery to power the mini-UAV. We can build that using a few cell phone batteries and a cordless drill. We will also need three radio-controlled servos and a lightweight surveillance camera and transmitter-receiver. The radio controller will be stripped down to look like a normal three-channel intercom box. The uplink and control program can be installed on a laptop which would serve as my personal computer and would uplink via some sort of ubiquitous port, like a headset plug-in."

Everyone sat silently.

"Major," Cleo said to the Marine officer, "I can see the steam rising. Why don't you start first?"

"I was just thinking, you said the door panel will be part of the UAV. Do you mean like a lifting body?"

"Yes. The idea is to keep it simple. We'll need to work through the aerodynamics, but something like a little flying saucer or an oversized VOR antenna would be ideal."

"I assume you plan to destroy the UAV much like the Rover?"

"Yes, sir. That's the plan."

"How much RDX would you need to blow something like that?"

Cleo looked to the chief to back her up. "I'm not the expert, but for the size and weight, I think we could forget the C-4 altogether and just use a length of primer cord."

The chief was nodding.

"You're really willing to do this?" Tori asked.

Cleo nodded, adding "there are some conditions."

"All right, we can talk about those later," she said, before turning to Bo, "and you, Agent Commanda. Are you willing to volunteer?"

"I always wanted to visit Dubai," Bo answered simply.

"One more thing," Sir Richard asked. "Do you have an escape plan in case the operation does not go well?"

"If we keep the operation to the exit side of the visit, we will be in the air and on an approved flight plan during the data acquisition phase. If things go belly-up then, well, we will place the liaison officer under our guardianship, and try to scud run our way out. Where we run to will depend on where we are when things go bad. I'm assuming we can head for Afghanistan, or Iraq, for NATO cover." Cleo had been pointing to the neighboring countries on the map and turned back to address the room, asking, "perhaps our American cousins can find some new equipment they just have to test along the eastern border of Saudi Arabia? If however, we are nabbed on the ground, all bets are off, including any action your three nations may feel compelled to provide." She directed this to Sir Richard, Mike Perkins, and Étienne Ste. Hubert. "And I want your word on that, all three of you."

"Why would we not want to be rescued?" Bo asked, on the edge of a pout.

"Any help from our 'oppressors' would undermine our position and give the Iranians an excuse to dig deeper. Once done, there is little chance of convincing them we're not spies. Eventually they will find out that I served in the Canadian Forces, and that you were a US Marine who is now with the FBI. In time, they will figure out the airplane too. So, it's very important that we give them no reason to poke around. If we are taken, we will stick to our cover and limit all communications to Mohawk. And, we will either negotiate our own way out or wait for the international community and media pressure to *embarrass* them for abducting us poor, mistreated Red Indians."

"Wow," Mike Perkins commented. "In all the years of planning covert operations, I have never been asked by the parties involved *not* to rescue them. Some are warned not to expect it but really, if things goes south, what does it matter who rescues you?"

Cleo sighed. Would North Americans ever really understand the concept of sovereign Indian Nations within *their* borders? "Mike, if we do this, it has to be with the blessing of the Grand Council. We will *not* be traveling as Americans or Canadians. We will be Mohawk warriors, albeit contrary warriors, but Mohawks just the same. Having you or Canada or even the Brits here, stand-up for us, would tell the world that the Six Nations are still just children needing your protection. It would dishonor all First Nations and make us look like pawns. Don't take our pride away, especially when it may be all we have to work with. If we are nabbed and charged with espionage, we must stand as Mohawks, and nothing more."

After the last of the questions were answered, Sir Richard thanked Cleo for the briefing, and left the room. Rod, the Marine Major, and the twins left for another meeting, one in which she was sure the chief had arranged to critique the technical aspects of her plan. Cleo, checking the wall clock at the back of the room, realized she had been at it for over thirty-six hours, and needed food and sleep and probably not in that order. Tori had left the room right behind her father, ordering her team to follow. She and Bo were alone. It was the first time in more than a dozen years.

"I'm sorry about the other night," Cleo said. "I had no right to say anything in front of Tori or Parminder."

"Well . . . look who's actually apologizing?"

"Oh, come on Bo," Cleo pleaded wearily. "Let's not do this. We may have to work together and we're going to need to get along. Hell, we'll need to support each other if we expect any chance of succeeding." She walked over from where she was standing and plopped herself down in the large upholstered chair next to her cousin, asking, "How have you been, dear queen Boudicca?"

"I am well, good queen Cleopatra!" Bo responded, kicking off their childhood game, as she always had. "Shall we attack the Romans today?"

"Why the *frack* not," she said, before remembering how the game was played. "Today is a good day to die!" They both chuckled, then broke out in laughter. Cleo's stomach chose that moment to rumble loudly, "Do you know where the canteen is? I guess I really could use some food."

Bo popped up from her seat. "No, but I'm sure we can find it. What's the worst that can happen? We get lost and end up in the brig?"

"You think they have one?" Cleo asked, following Bo from the room.

"Why not? They have one over at our embassy."

"Your embassy? Oh, you mean the American Embassy. I bet they even serve steak and eggs for breakfast over there."

"Is that what you're craving, a grand slam?"

"More like comfort food, but our kind of comfort food. You know?"

Bo nodded. They found the canteen without upsetting security. "Why don't you take a seat and I'll see what they have."

Cleo, too tired to fight, especially with Bo, agreed and found an empty four-place table by the window. It wasn't quite noon yet, so the traffic was still light. Cleo was so absorbed gazing out over the Thames, she didn't see Siobhan until she slid down in the seat beside her.

"That was so exciting," she said in her enthusiastic Irish lilt. "I've never seen anything like it. It's all they're talking about in the Tank!"

The "Tank" Cleo had learned, was slang for the SOE's operations centre. Looking at the young woman, and trying to understand what she was saying, she asked, "What's up?"

"Sir Richard's turning this place upside down! He's demanding to know why the analysts and photo boys couldn't do in thirty-six weeks, what you did in thirty-six hours!"

Cleo looked at the young woman, hearing her tone, but missing the point. "I knew he wasn't happy. I guess there's no point in hanging around for lunch."

"Captain Cleo," Siobhan said, clearly overwhelmed, "did yah' no hear me? C is so pleased he's beside himself. Literally! That man—the one that left the briefing—the one who was so rude to yeah. He's the bloke in charge down there and he's mad as a hatter. I've never seen Sir Richard so pleased. He says it's all because of you, for getting that pompous arse off 'is back!"

"Von," Bo called to Siobhan. She was walking to the table, carrying a tray with two plates. "Join us for lunch."

Siobhan, in her enthusiasm, beamed with pleasure at Bo's invitation. "Just let me go and grab a wee plate," she said, almost running, ". . . right back."

Both Cleo and Bo smiled at her energy. "Oh, to be twenty again," Bo said, unloading the canteen tray. She put one plate in front of Cleo and the other on the table across from her before sitting down.

Cleo looked suspiciously at the plate she'd been served. Not able to hide her admiration, she had to ask, "how'd you manage this?"

"I have my ways," Bo said, without explaining more.

They were both quick to dig into their meal. Before they could make much progress, Siobhan was back and Tori had walked in too.

"There you are," Tori said to Cleo, deciding at the last moment to acknowledge Bo as well. "How lovely to see you together," she said, before noticing their plates. "What in bleeding hell are you two eating?"

Cleo just smiled, leaving the explanations for Bo.

"Curve Lake Steaks and creamed corn!" Bo said, as if further explanation were unnecessary.

Tori looked at her with bewilderment, but it was Siobhan, in her youthful exuberance who asked, "What steak? That looks like bologna, what's been in the fryer?"

"You are correct, Miss O'Regan," Bo confirmed. "A Curve Lake Steak, as we like to call it, is nothing more than fried bologna. The only thing this meal is missing is some fly bread and hot maple syrup."

"Oh yeah," Cleo said. "Remember the fly bread Ishtah used to make us, but she used to serve it with corn syrup. I loved it like that too."

"Me three!" Bo agreed, automatically slipping into the old language the two had created as kids.

Turning her attention to Tori, Cleo decided to explain their odd choice of meal. "It's just comfort food for us. Trust me, when it comes to food, it doesn't take a whole lot to keep us happy."

Tori smiled at her. "I'm delighted to hear you say that. I also want to tell you that Sir Richard is very impressed with your operational brief."

Cleo interrupted her, too tired to care. It wasn't as if she hadn't expected it. How many times had she been challenged to come up with something completely "outside the box," only to have it rejected for that very reason? "It's okay, Tori. I know you can't use anything I came up with, but I appreciate being given the chance. It was fun to stretch the old brain matter again."

Tori considered her for the longest time. "I don't think you understand. Sir Richard wants detailed planning to begin on all three operations and he wants you along this afternoon, just in case the Joint Intelligence Committee or the PM has questions."

"He liked it? I don't understand?" She was clearly confused by the situation.

Bo punched her arm in salute, "Squirrel, you did it!"

She was still confused when Siobhan started raining happy tears. It hadn't even occurred to her that the team was probably just as tired as she was. Still trying to process the unexpected outcome, she probed shyly, "So, someone wants to ask me questions?"

"Perhaps," Tori said, "but first I think we will start with a shower, and some caffeine. Perhaps some energy drinks?"

Without another word, Siobhan lit off for the kitchen and was back with three cans of Red Bull in record time. "I've your suit and ablution kit in the ladies," Siobhan explained. "Whenever you're ready."

Finishing the bologna and corn, Cleo accepted the Red Bull Siobhan had shaken and poured in a glass. She pushed her chair back, looking back and forth between the three women. "Okay, I know I'm beyond beat, but I have now eaten comfort food, and my brain is being caffeinated as we speak. So, will someone please tell me what's going on?"

"They liked your plans, all of your plans," Tori explained gently. "Now there are many, many more questions that need to be answered, but first we must take our options to the Prime Minister and the JIC for approval to proceed. Sir Richard will meet with them at fourteen hundred, and you must be there in case they have a question he cannot answer. Do you understand what I'm saying?"

Cleo, now overwhelmed but completely cognizant, asked, "He liked them all? How is that possible?"

"That's our Squirrel, scores a Hat Trick!" Bo was genuinely happy for her cousin.

Tori looked at her watch. "We haven't much time. Siobhan, if you're finished, let's get Captain Deseronto downstairs to shower and change."

"I didn't bring anything to change into. What . . ."

Tori, reaching over and touching Cleo's hand, halted her questions. "I've taken care of everything. Now please follow Siobhan. Bo and I will catch you up afterwards. I promise!"

Getting up with a nod, Cleo stopped, turning to Bo first, "I really am sorry about the other night. What you do with your life is none of my business."

"Relax . . . I was asking for it. I didn't like what you said, but it was true. So thanks for that. Besides, now I get to call you Squirrel for good. Think of it as penance."

Cleo simply groaned as answer, before following after Siobhan. They marched down two flights of stairs, and followed a windowless corridor to enter a door marked Ladies. Once inside, she saw that it wasn't just a washroom, but a locker room with showers and a sauna.

"I've got yer stuff in here," Siobhan said, opening a louvered door to a rather large locker. She reached in, removing a set of towels and Cleo's ablution kit.

Inside, Cleo could see a suit she didn't recognize, along with other new items. "Whose stuff is this?"

"It's yours," Siobhan said, her confusion evident.

Pulling the suit out of the locker, without removing it from the hanger, she recognized the label as one from Parminder's custom collection. Hanging it back up, she took a seat on the nearby bench and stripped for her shower. Ten minutes later, wrapped in a towel, she made her way back to the locker. Now pulling everything out, she couldn't help notice that along with the suit, everything with the exception of her shoes, looked brand spanking new.

"Do you like them?" Siobhan asked, pointing to the new undergarments. "Bo picked everything out. She said we couldn't go through yer stuff at the hotel. That it was better to just pick-up the things you like, so I only grabbed your shoes and bath kit."

Cleo smiled at the young woman. "That was very nice. Thank you for respecting my privacy, and thank Bo for me, too." Looking over the new clothes, she asked, "Whose idea was it to order a new suit? It looks expensive."

"That was all Tori," Siobhan said. "She even picked it up herself!"

The comment caught Cleo by surprise. Having Tori buy the suit seemed a non-starter for Siobhan, but picking it up personally was something unexpected. "Siobhan, I really want to thank you for taking such good care of me these last few days."

Siobhan blushed before turning to let her dress. Five minutes later they were on the elevator and on their way to Tori's office. Then, after making sure she wasn't needed for anything else, the Irish junior headed back to the Tank, leaving her boss and Cleo completely alone for the first time since Heathrow.

Looking around the comfortable space, Cleo acknowledged her admiration. The office was not what she expected, but it was Tori all over. The pictures on the wall were an eclectic mix of wood block and engraved prints depicting historic London. Many portrayed scenes from the chaos of the docklands, historic markets, and military square-riggers. It was the very game they had played earlier in the day.

"Wow!" Cleo said.

"Wow, yourself." Tori answered.

Caught off guard with the compliment, she probed, "I understand, I have you to thank for the new duds?"

Tori smiled, getting up from behind her desk, and inviting Cleo to take in the view of the Thames from her window. "I asked Parminder if you had anything with you, suitable for a high-level meeting. She suggested the suit. I hope you don't mind?"

"Mind?" her astonishment clear. "I love Parminder's stuff. I just can't afford to buy them all that often. Thank you."

"After I saw how lovely you looked in that cocktail dress the other evening, I was quite sure a new suit from Parminder was just the ticket."

"What if I hadn't figured things out?" Cleo asked, still somewhat stunned.

Tori smiled at her, taking a small gift box from the top drawer of her desk. "From the moment we met, I knew that possibility couldn't exist," Handing over the gift box, she added, "I have this for you."

Cleo almost didn't want to open the box. She wasn't used to anyone believing in her, and had forgotten how exciting and nerve wracking it was to have someone, especially a certain someone, give you a gift. Not knowing what to expect, she took the box and opened it gingerly. Inside, wrapped in tissue paper, was a kind of purple-blue scarf. "Nice colors," was all Cleo said as she pulled it open.

Tori groaned, then shaking her head, smiled explaining, "I was warned that you might not know what it was. Here," she ordered, taking it from Cleo. "Let me show you." Moving closely, Tori started wrapping the shawl around Cleo's shoulders and under her lapels. "It's called a *Jalalma*. Women from India wear them as an indication of high social rank."

"I thought maybe it was a *Pajmena?*" she offered, slightly tripping on the pronunciation. It was the only frilly shawl thing she knew the name of, even if she wasn't sure what it was for.

Running her hands around Cleo's shoulders, Tori fussed with the scarf, moving closer with each adjustment.

Frozen in place, Cleo couldn't even bring herself to look at Tori, then reddened when she realized she had unconsciously placed her hands on Tori's waist. Sensing Tori had stopped fussing, she tried to think. *Say something! Anything! Good God woman, she's going to think you're an idiot!*

"Will you not let me see how you look?" Tori asked with such warmth, Cleo couldn't help but raise her head. "You are beautiful."

"No," she whispered, shaking her head. She had no reference to work from. In all her life, no one had ever called her beautiful.

Tori's hands moved from where they had been resting on her Cleo's shoulders, to her face. "You're beautiful to me," she said, pulling her gently closer.

Cleo had almost forgotten what it was like to be kissed, really kissed, pulled tight, held tenderly, and wonderfully, perfectly kissed.

At that precise moment, the extension on Tori's desk rang and both women jumped at the interruption. Gently letting go, Tori moved to answer the phone. The conversation was short and brief. Hanging up the handset, she turned to Cleo, "They're ready. Are you?"

Wanting to say more, wanting to kiss more, Cleo retreated to the safety of military decorum, "Yes, Ma'am." Taking in Tori's smile, she relaxed enough to say the only thing that didn't scare the daylights out of her, "Thank you."

Chapter Five

Cleo sat in a worn-out lawn chair holding a cold soda can against her forehead.

Rod Nelligan, who was reading something on his BlackBerry, looked over with concern. "This bloody heat," he said. "How's our resident snow walker holding up?"

Lowering the pop can, Cleo sat back in her chair. The spring weather in Arizona was the hottest on record. In an effort to cool off, she had unzipped her flight suit to her waist, pulling the top half off, and tying it around her hips using the sleeves. The well-worn jumper was patched in all the places that could catch and rip on the forty-year-old C-130 Lockheed Hercules she had flown for the Canadian Forces.

Under it, she was wearing a very dirty, very sweaty, yellow T-shirt that read Go Army across the front. Forced, just the previous day, to pick up some new Tees to bolster her limited wardrobe, she stopped at the PX and grabbed a half-dozen T-shirts, sports bras, and gitch. She and Rod had already spent several days combing through the "bone yard" the US Air Force operated. They had been trying to cobble a complete aircraft together from numerous divorced parts. Cleo's research had been right about the number of old cargo planes in stock. The US military still had over two hundred Otters on the books, but when they actually started inspecting what was available, they were hard pressed to find a fully assembled aircraft. It took three days for Cleo, Rod, and the two mechanics assigned by the Base Commander, to search the entire inventory.

The aircraft they wanted was at Davis-Monthan but not, as they had hoped, in one piece. Accepting the situation, they came up with a plan to find the best pieces and cobble them together. While Rod Nelligan, in his old Royal Navy coveralls, took their young Airman mechanic and started searching for a prospective powerplant, Cleo began inspecting airframes. An aircraft, from a maintenance perspective, is considered the marriage of three distinct parts: engine, airframe, and propeller.

The propeller, they knew, was available from the overhaul shop and was certified and ready to install. Searching for a suitable airframe, Cleo had taken the senior mechanic with her. She was sure they had been assigned as watchers only. To her surprise, the morning they began the airframe hunt, her mechanic showed up in an open Humvee, loaded with toolboxes, an aircraft tow bar and a portable air compressor. If she found what she was looking for, he told her, he was damn well gonna' get it!

A week after arriving, their little team was taking a break from the rigors of marrying the large radial engine and airframe when Mike Perkins called, ordering them to stand down. He had found a DeHavilland Otter, fully assembled and in pristine condition, only a few miles away.

As it turned out, the Pima Air Museum, housed on the opposite side of the airfield, had completed 98% of the major restoration of a US Army U-1A for their Vietnam collection. All they would need to finish was the application of vinyl tail numbers. With the white base paint finished and the aircraft certified airworthy, the team would still need to install the modifications specific to the operation. It was a huge break, compared to the herculean task they had been facing. Mike Perkins ordered them to report immediately. He wanted them to grab their prize before the museum boys could change their minds.

Bear, their grizzly Senior Master Sergeant, insisted he could get them across the field faster than calling for the assigned car and driver. Cleo, preferring to move out immediately, agreed and the four of them piled into the open Humvee. Instead of leaving the base and driving completely around the restricted area, Bear radioed the tower, receiving permission to drive across the operational runway, and directly to the airside entrance of the museum.

What a picture they must have made, walking into the open hangar, with Cleo in her grease-streaked flight suit tied around her waist, and the chief in his old Royal Navy khaki dungarees. At least their American Airmen were somewhat squared away, in summer-weight, sweat-soaked BDUs.

Bear made the introductions to the museum president before being led to a pristine, all white and unmarked, DeHavilland Otter.

"Wow!" was the first thing out of Cleo's mouth, and the comment made the museum president laugh.

"I couldn't have said it better myself."

Rod Nelligan, always the gentleman when it came to another man's aircraft, asked for permission to remove the engine cowls for a better look. "My, she's a pretty lass," he said. "Would you mind, if I take a peek under the bonnet?"

"I thought you'd never ask."

While they headed forward, Bear and Cleo did a walk-around. The rear cargo doors were propped open on both sides, with a simple two-step pipe ladder snapped into place on the port egress. Cleo was the first to climb aboard, not remembering the rule that "first in gets their ass checked out," until it was too late. *Oh well, if Senior Master Sergeant grizzly bear hasn't checked my ass out yet, he might as well do it now.*

Once on board, the first thing they both noticed was the interior insulated panels, or curtains as they were called, had yet to be installed. That was a bonus. It gave them complete access to inspect the fuselage interior. The important thing was to check the quality of the work. Generally, the restoration of aircraft by museum volunteers came in two flavors: top dog and the dog's breakfast. This one, both Bear and Cleo were sure, had been completed by competent and most probably retired American military aircraft professionals. For all intent, this was a brand-new, zero hour, Otter. By the time the other men joined them, both Cleo and Bear were face down on the cabin floor with their heads in the baggage compartment.

"Dare I ask what you two are doing? The museum president asked, looking curiously at the pair.

Bear gave him a look. "We're just trying to get the hatch open."

"The photo hatch? It's screwed in place from the outside," he explained, offering to get a screwdriver.

Cleo could hear Rod swear under his breath.

She ignored his expletive. This was a complication, and nothing more. They would have to fabricate a way of opening the hatch from the inside, while still having it look like a regular access panel. Cleo jumped down from the chest-high cargo door and crawled under the tail. The round panel was dead center and easy to access with a dozen tri-wind screws holding it in place. Cleo ran her fingers around the edges to make sure it wasn't painted-in. Pleased with the clean installation, she started removing the screws. Each was spring loaded, making it a quick job. A minute later she had the panel off and found herself starring at Rod Nelligan, who was crouched in the baggage compartment, trying to gauge for himself, just how small the space was.

Parked on his haunches and looking down between his knees and grinning, he said, "Cleopatra, my wee lass, I'm starting to think you know what you're doing."

She smiled back at him, replacing the panel and screwing it back in place. For the next hour, Cleo performed run-ups and system tests with Bear on board, while Rod reviewed all the documentation needed to prove the Aircraft safe to receive a civil registration. Rod didn't mention the registration would come from Canada and not the US. When the issue first came up, everyone assumed it was just another one of Cleo's *things!* What she actually intended was to add a second layer of obscurity.

Every country with any aviation program, had long ago adopted the UN standard of assigning each aircraft an alphabetical call sign, with the exception of one nation, the USA. In the pioneering days of Aviation, during the first rush to Standardization, the League of Nations used the French and British flight rules as a platform for all other nations to follow. All others, except the USA, which had already established a tail number system, and saw no need to comply with the new "alphabet soup." American legislators did make one exception and standardized the leading "N" letter, to signify a National registry. With most of the planet already using the Eurocentric letter system, the US remains the only nation to use "N" numbers. Even the most experienced air traffic controllers and customs people mix up the letters that distinguish each countries registration. No one, however, confuses a US aircraft with one from another country. Cleo had argued successfully that the more confusion or obfuscation surrounding the team, the more opportunities the team would have to exploit.

Building Materials Warehouse
Mirdamad Construction
Tehran, Islamic Republic of Iran

Hasid watched as several men unloaded a shipment of ceramic tiles. Once the first two skids were out of the way, they were clear to unload his shipment of American cigarettes. Hasid quickly counted the cases on the skid to be sure all of the shipment had made it. Carefully cutting the plastic shrink wrap away from the four-by-nine stack of cardboard boxes, he tossed the plastic to the side, before opening the closest box. Inside, was the first twelve of 432 cartons of filtered cigarettes. Before turning the shipment over to his men for local distribution, he emptied one box, tossing three cartons to each man. "There is more to come my friends. Now, stash those away and get these out today."

"What about the phones and computers?" one of the helpers asked, his tone none too friendly.

"All in good time, brother. All in good time."

The hostile man was not placated by Hasid's reassurances. "My contacts are becoming restless. They are asking about the women too!"

Hasid patted the man's shoulder, "We are building an enterprise my friend. It will take time to secure our supply chain. Our commander has worked hard to put everything in place. Are you not happy here?" he prodded. "Have you not been reunited with your family. Are they not well cared for? Are your sons not in school? Are you unhappy, brother?"

Embarrassed by the gentle rebuff, the man lowered his head. "No, Sergeant!"

"My brother, you must not worry so much," he counselled the man, before turning to the others. "These last few months have been difficult for us all, but we have made a commitment to this new life. The problems at home may be difficult to ignore, but we must remember, Only Allah is Victorious!"

Restricted Access Hangar
309 AMARG
USAFB Davis-Monthan
Tucson, Arizona

"Phone," the base-assigned airman yelled from inside the Otter. The young mechanic and Rod Nelligan were in the middle of installing the release mechanism for the photo hatch cover. They had finished all the modifications for the aircraft with the exception of installing the custom-built lavatory unit. That was sitting on a pallet waiting beside the airplane.

The tiny custom galley, with its five-gallon fresh water tank, had been mounted against the starboard side of the passenger cabin, running its length from behind the first passenger seat to the rear door. Cleo had wanted the same sort of setup on the port side for the auxiliary fuel cells. Instead of choosing one large collapsible tank, that they would be forced to crawl over, she had ordered three, sixty-six gallon barrel-shaped collapsible fuel bags, and connected each one to the fuel tanks under the floor. One of the things Cleo wanted to add was a set of fold-down bunks or litters on each side of the cabin, but when the original equipment from a medical evacuation Otter was delivered, Cleo changed her mind. The original cots installed into a pole mechanism that required permanent mounting. They did not fold, and worse, looked like hell. While they all agreed that the "utility" look of the aircraft interior was to be maintained, the army green canvas stretchers were just too much.

"Captain," Bear said, hanging up the telephone, "that was Base Ops. They say a Marine code-three just came in on the mail plane."

Cleo was not used to the old American manner of guarding the rank of officers in open communications by assigning a number code. She had to count-up to get to three. *Lieutenant . . . Captain . . . then, that would make the code-three a Major.* A Marine Major could only be Butterworth. He had been in on the planning since Cleo's first briefing, taking the point for the Americans. She had been waiting for him to send her the final design for the UAV.

"I guess we better pick him up," she lamented, not welcoming the interruption in their busy day.

"We could let him to cool his jets?"

Cleo appreciated the offer. It was rare for a man like Bear to respect an individual as opposed to just the rank. She knew she had earned his respect over the last two weeks. She had always believed that officers should work just as hard as their subordinates should, if not harder. She had worked side by side with the crew, getting just as tired and dirty as everyone else did.

"No point." She was clearly frustrated by the interruption. "Let's go see what's so important they had to send a code-three all this way." They were amiably silent, as they drove to Base Ops, in the open Humvee. Bear had learned early on that Cleo had no patience for small talk. When they pulled up in front of Base Ops, she still had her head down reading through her notes.

"You got family in the Corps?"

"What?" Shielding the sun from her eyes, she immediately recognized Bo. Bo was decked out in a brand-new United States Marine Corps uniform and sporting a shiny new pair of railroad tracks.

Cleo ordered him to keep his seat behind the wheel. Climbing out of the Humvee, she greeted the Marine officer.

"*Captain* Commanda?"

Bo looked at Cleo with what seemed like disappointment or irritation. While Bo was the perfect picture of a female Marine officer in her Service As, Cleo's appearance was more akin to an orphaned mechanic. Wearing one of her old Canadian flight suits, tied around her waist, plus a dirty Aim High— USAF T-shirt, with no headdress, rank, or service insignia, she was clearly a mess. Cleo introduced her to the Senior Master Sergeant as she loaded Bo's suitcase and two duffle bags into the back of the open Humvee, before asking, "Ops said there was a code-three waiting for us. Is Major Butterworth with you?"

"A code-three is a Captain! Second Lieutenant—Lieutenant—Captain." Bo informed her, adding, "We don't use NATO jargon around here."

Cleo climbed into the back seat of the Humvee, suggesting that Bo keep a hold of the large cardboard mailing tube she was carrying. After a short drive across base, they pulled into the hangar parking spot. Bear jumped out of the Humvee, without waiting for orders, and hauled Bo's entire kit to their secure work area.

"He should have saluted me," was the first thing out of Bo's mouth.

"There's no saluting airside," Cleo explained. "It's too dangerous. As a matter of fact, you need to remove your cover," she added, pointing to the female officer's headdress Bo was wearing. "Before we go in there, why don't you tell me what in seven hells is going on?"

"Sir Richard called us back to active duty!" It was clear from her proud stance that Bo Commanda thought this was a wonderful thing. Brushing off the new captain's bars on her shoulders, she was beaming with pride.

Gods save us, Cleo begged under her breath. To her, the call to active duty meant their commitment by reputation and responsibility now included the Official Secrets Act in three countries. There was no point in mentioning that part to Bo. She was too busy admiring her new rank. At least she hadn't pinned on her, as yet un-earned, wings of gold.

"So they promoted you from Lance Corporal to Captain?"

"Well actually," Bo said with a little disappointment. "I would have thought Major more appropriate, what with all my experience. I'm just hoping they'll promote us properly after we get back."

"Promote us properly?" Cleo asked, dreading whatever Bo was hinting at.

"They promoted you too." she hurriedly added, as if she didn't think that was important. "You are now a Lieutenant Colonel!" She said, proudly pronouncing the rank in the American and French fashion of *lew-tenent* and not *left-tenant* as was still the practice in the UK and the Commonwealth.

"Not in the Marines though. You get that, right? You're only a light Colonel in the Canadian Forces," she explained, making sure Cleo knew she didn't consider the two equal. "Tori will tell you everything when we get to Syracuse. The Grand Council wants to meet us before they give their blessing."

The Haudenosaunee Grand Council of Chiefs was the equivalent of a federal government for the Six Nation of the Iroquois Confederacy. The council hall or Great Longhouse was located on the tiny Onondaga Indian Reservation near the upstate New York city of Syracuse. As many as fifty chiefs would gather to debate issues and find solutions for the whole of the longhouse people regardless of which side of the US–Canada border their territory was found. "I thought Mike and Étienne were meeting with them?"

"Oh yeah," Bo said, not exactly sounding like a Marine Corps officer. "The Council also met with Albert but they want to meet the 'fly girls' too."

"*Fly girls,* Geez!" Cleo groaned. She couldn't help herself. "And who the *frack* is Albert?"

"Our new Crew Chief! Geezus, Cleo. Get with the program! The Council just wants to meet the *guys* on the team."

The Six Nations was a matriarchal society, led by a number of clan mothers. Back in the day, the clan matrons were responsible for everything from land management, agriculture, housing, and the health and welfare of the people. The professions of teaching, art, and medicine, were performed by both men and women, but politics, that was considered the type of work that attracted *abuse*, and therefore far too lowly a vocation for women who held the sole right to vote. There were exceptions, with one applying to any man or woman who crossed over the gender line, demonstrating a willingness to give up the privileges of their birthright, for the responsibilities of the opposite sex. It was rare, not to mention a practice that had fallen out of favor with many Mohawk men since first contact with Europeans and their patrilineal dogma. As a matter of guidance for the parents and family, old time medicine people would test youngsters at four years of age, to determine the role they were born for. Cleo's and Bo's grandfather, Joe Commanda, had insisted on providing this test for his two eldest granddaughters.

For their ceremony, as it was commonly referred to, both the four-year-old Cleo and the four-year-old Bo had been told that they would be shown two toys, but could only keep one. They were not to pay any attention to their parents and could choose only the toy they truly wanted to keep. Bo, had then been offered a big toy canoe and paddle, or a life-size porcelain doll that her mother had especially ordered from England. It was only a moment before the doll was brushed aside for the mini birch bark canoe. Cleo's test had been much the same. She was offered an Easy Bake Oven or a Radio Flyer Wagon. It hadn't taken more than a second before Cleo had the little red wagon out the door. Together, she and Bo had loaded up the canoe and headed for the wading pool in Winchester Park, leaving Joe Commanda to face the irate wives of his twin sons.

While not all warrior societies remembered that ceremony, and regardless of whether they were seen as men or women, Cleo and Bo would now go before the Grand Council as military officers, and Sir Richard, it seemed, wanted them to be given the highest regard possible. Cleo wasn't sure how she felt about this. She wasn't happy with the idea of an instant promotion, although a jump up the ladder of two rungs was not unheard of, but Bo's jump of what, nine rungs, just didn't happen in this day and age. She shrugged it off. If Bo wanted to play officer and gentlewoman, Cleo was not going to get in her way.

Security and Intelligence Service
Vauxhall Cross
London, United Kingdom

The team had gathered in the Tank for an update on Operation Polar Bear. The name "Polar Bear" had been selected at random from a secure list of over a millions names. Even Allan Bashir, the more "reflective" member of the team, had smiled at the irony of it, while Guy and Nici launched into their very own special version of Alanis Morissette's "Ironic."

Tori shook her head at the tech twins, ordering everyone to settle down.

Over the conference call audio unit, Rod announced his presence for the morning briefing. The office in the AMARG hangar, among other things, had a secure telephone line. Rod Nelligan had watched the security boys sweep the room for listening devices, but was sure they had probably placed more than they removed. It didn't really matter, both Mike Perkins, who was in New York state, and Étienne, his favorite Habitant were on the call too.

"Report!" Tori ordered to the assembled team and bodiless voices of Rod Nelligan, Étienne Ste. Hubert, and Mike Perkins. As was protocol, Allan Bashir was the first to comment.

"I've been working with Section Nine to expand the functionality of the navigation unit for the plane." Unlike the others, Allan had been a fan of the Otter from day one. He had seen them in operation in India performing Search and Rescue duties after severe floods had ripped through the Bangladesh region. Instead of being limited to airport use, the pilots from the Indian Air Force simply landed their SAR Otters on the muddy dirt roads of communities in need. "Cleo had a very difficult time making "Nine" understand that there was no need to tamper with the software. She asked them to create a black box of sorts. She wanted the ability to manipulate the analogue instrument inputs, and feed the changes back to the instrument display in the cockpit, using her laptop.

"What about the radios?" Tori asked. She had attended a technical briefing on the *changer*. The point was to allow Cleo to manipulate the pilots' heading and altitude display. Nothing more.

"That's done, and we sent the switches off to Arizona." Allan reported.

"We just got them," Rod's disjointed voice confirmed. "We also received some jump lights?"

"Excellent," Allan replied. "Section Nine thought you might benefit from some sort of warning system in the cabin. The lights function like normal signals for parachute jumping, but this set will also switch to green if Cleo cuts the radios from the laptop."

"What benefit does that provide?" Tori asked. "If she is stowed away in the lavatory?"

"Actually, mum," Allan explained, "it will give the pilot and the crew chief a heads up, allowing them time to distract the liaison pilot before he notices a problem."

"Speaking of which," Mike Perkins' voice piped in, "I have just the man for your team. He's a Pave Hawk Crew Chief, and he's a Mohawk from the Grand River Reservation in Ontario." Mike made the same mistake most North Americans did. Indian lands in the United States were listed as *Reservations* while the lands assigned to aboriginal people in Canada were called *Reserves*.

"Excellent," Tori said, asking, "Will you send a copy of his service record to the chief?

"Not a problem," Mike answered. "Actually, I just e-mailed a copy to you; I think you'll be impressed with Sergeant Mackenzie."

"Wonderful," Tori added. Cleo had originally wanted Chief Nelligan along for the ride, but it hadn't taken much to rule him out. Between Rod's age and the fact that there was no hiding his Scottish heritage, they just couldn't fit him into the cover story. If they wanted a mechanic on board, someone from the Six Nations was needed. Tori turned her attention to Darcy Gerrard, asking for his report.

"I am bowled over by the dedication these two officers have demonstrated," Darcy began. "I have been learning more about the 'warrior culture' of these people. I've completed a lengthy report for all concerned, including my recommendation that we consider recruiting from this group in the future." Quickly moving on to his primary concern, "As for whatever issues which may have existed between them, they have successfully set them aside. However, in a hostage situation, that underlying tension could be exploited."

Tori wanted to hear more on that subject, but would wait until she reviewed Dr. Gerrard's report. There was no point in sharing their dirty laundry with the Americans. "Nici, Guy," Tori said, moving on, "how is the UAV shaping up?"

"We received the Marine radar antenna from Kelvin Hughes yesterday," Nici answered.

"It's a two meter S-band antenna," Guy said, adding, "just the ticket. The boys in Nine are starting the design of the fiberglass skin that will give it a Canard look and feel. When Nine is done, it should simply look like a marine antenna adapted for aviation use."

"Major?" Tori asked; keen to hear the Marine Major's take on the antenna Cleo had suggested they adapt to use as the main wing for the mini-UAV. The plan was to mount the antenna array upside down to the exterior cover of the photo hatch. The thin rectangular array would be skinned and shaped like an airfoil. It would still be a strange sight, but the weather radar they were installing would have a feature for marine navigation suitable for use by seaplane pilots. Kelvin Hughes, a British defense contractor, was a builder of marine navigation systems and ship bridge controls. As part of the cover workup, they had agreed to add the modified antenna to their website as an example of their custom marine products for the commercial market.

Major Butterworth, who had joined them at Vauxhall for the meeting, leaned back in his chair shaking his head. "I can't believe I'm going to say this but I think this can work. We're still having problems with the two resulting angles-of-attack, but Captain Deseronto and I have come up with several alternatives."

"Lieutenant Colonel Deseronto!" Tori corrected. "She has been promoted to a rank commensurate with her experience and current responsibilities."

"Here, here!" Butterworth gave a cheer. "Now, we still have a number of issues to solve, but the computer model flies like a dream. If your guys in Section Nine continue working as they have, I am absolutely sure we'll have a winner from both the surveillance side and the aesthetic."

Tori nodded her head in appreciation. The Marine Major had proven to be more help than hindrance. He and the tech twins were working hard with Section Nine, or MI9 as they had once been designated. Even their leader, the second unidentified soldier from Cleo's briefing, had gotten on board, going to Kelvin Hughes to personally request the antenna.

Before Tori would sum up and give the team their marching orders, she wanted to hear from Étienne. They had basically taken the three proposed operations and begun detailed planning. The Rover operation was handed over to the Canadians and their design team had acquired most of the materials needed. Building a basic rover was easy. Building one that could survive the drop from altitude, even with the NASA airbags, would be an accomplishment. To beef up the police rover, an Argo, a two-person tracked all-terrain vehicle, would replace the existing undercarriage. The operational team had actually acquired four of the agile little Argos. Two would serve in the airdrop trials, with the third reserved as a backup for the *go* unit.

"Étienne, how are your people doing?"

"The optical package is . . . *mis en place?*"

"*Integrated?* she offered, as a possible translation.

"*Oui*, yes," he corrected, adding, "the jimmy and camera 'ave arrived, the roll cage is complete and waiting to . . . *integrate.*"

Across the conference table, Butterworth mouthed "Jimmy?" to Tori.

Reaching quickly to the conference phone, she hit the mute button before explaining, "Canadian slang for a Signalman. Étienne sometimes gets English a wee bit mangled. I believe he's referring to the communications uplink package."

"Ah," Butterworth nodded, "a signals *package* not a signal*man*. Got it!"

Releasing the mute, she prompted Étienne, "and the starting issues you reported on earlier?"

"They are replacing the carburetor with fuel injection and electric starting, electronic starter," he corrected. "Still, they wish to start the Rover before it leaves the plane."

"Colonel Ste. Hubert, its Major Butterworth here. May I ask if your guys have considered replacing the Argos gas engine with an electric motor. That could alleviate the starting issues," he suggested. "If power is an issue, I would consider using AMGs, gel batteries. I understand they can be oriented in any direction, so tumbling down a canyon should be easy enough."

Étienne was quiet for a moment, "we 'ave an extra Argo. I can 'ave them do it. It's a very good idea. I 'ave scheduled the drop test for the fifteen but for the gas Argo. Do we go still?"

"Yes," Tori answered. "Étienne, please continue on the current schedule. Can you work on an electric motorized version simultaneously?"

"*Oui*, but I don't know how long my people will need. I will let you know, but we only 'ave one test airbag."

"I can take care of that," Mike's voice cut in on the conference phone. "JPL has promised me the second airbag system within six weeks. They just can't pull them together any faster."

"Very well," Tori said, halting the discussion. "Étienne, we will proceed with the drop test using whichever Rover is ready, but I want you to continue with both versions. And, Étienne, I will join you in Trenton for the test."

While the Canadians were continuing with Operation Two, the Americans were continuing with Operation One: UAV. This plan was by far the easiest from the equipment side, but the most difficult from an operational standpoint. Working with the computer model the tech twins had created, USAF pilots had been flying a simulated mission for days without success. Just as Deseronto and Butterworth had guessed, the valley was too small to allow the forty-eight-foot wingspan any maneuverability. Even their best pilot, who had demonstrated his ability to navigate the remote recon aircraft in the tight space of the valley, had failed to avoid detection by a simulated Surface to Air Missile. They hadn't called it a bust just yet, but had pretty much ruled Surveillance by Unmanned Aeronautical reconnaissance Vehicle the absolute last resort.

When the meeting was officially over, everyone headed back to his or her workstations. Once Siobhan had escorted the American Marine out of the room, Tori announced the Tank clear to those still on the conference call.

"Still on the line, Chief?"

"Still here, Lass."

Technically, Tori Braithwaite was Rod Nelligan's superior officer, but she had never stood on ceremony with the chief. Uncle Roddy, had been at her father's side when she was born, and had stayed there all through the difficult days following Lady Caroline's slow death from the complications of an emergency Caesarean section. It had been Rod Nelligan who had taken baby Tori in his arms to a reluctant Richard.

"You've every right to grieve. No man will criticize you for that, but no matter how cruel your pain, this little lass needs you."

Richard had wanted to blame the child for his wife's death, but once Rod had placed the baby in his arms, he had to let that assumption pass. Baby Tori had her Mother's eyes and the recognition caused Richard to breakdown. Rod, having grown up with five sisters, knew the value of a good cry and left the father and daughter team to grieve privately. It had been a turning point for the young sub-lieutenant. From that day forward, other than when he was on active duty on board a ship, Richard Braithwaite insisted his daughter be at his side, and Rod Nelligan, then a lowly Petty Officer 2nd Class, had vowed to make it happen.

"Chief. Now that we have heard Mr. Perkins report on the team's progress, perhaps you would honor us with a little reality?"

"She's a bloody fine little plane, and our girl, well, they're a perfect pair. She flies her like they're old mates." Continuing for several minutes, Nelligan covered the technical issues they had resolved and listed those still needing solutions. Less than three weeks had passed since he and Cleo had arrived in Arizona, and their resolved list was fast outpacing the outstanding issues.

Unbelievably, it looked like Cleo's outlandish plan had a chance of succeeding. The weak points that Mike had waxed over related to the amount of flight training the team was getting, or in this case, wasn't. On the same day Bo Commanda arrived in Arizona, a flight instructor, complete with a brand-spanking-new Cessna 172 Skyhawk, joined the team. While his ID listed him as a Civilian Contractor for the FBI, it was apparent the man was *Company* through and through. The Base Commander couldn't prohibit the little civilian training aircraft from landing, but so many restrictions were placed on flight clearances that Bo wasn't getting the flight time Cleo had established as the minimum needed before deployment.

"What we need to do is move them to a remote training base," Tori announced. "If the Americans cannot accommodate us then I suggest we find a site in Canada. How far can she fly without a co-pilot?"

"Cleo or the airplane?" Rod asked. "If you're asking after Cleo, I wouldn't put a limit on her; as for the little Otter, with the extended rage tanks, count on 1,800 miles a day depending on the weather."

"Weather? Surely that's not a concern this time of year?" Tori asked with surprise.

"Not here, Lass," Rod answered, explaining, "but once she gets up north. Both the Arctic and the North Atlantic are unpredictable this time of year, and the aircraft has neither de-icing equipment nor cabin oxygen. She can neither climb over a storm, nor brazen it out if the dew point falls low enough to ice her up."

Tori stood, leaning on the table towards the conference phone, ordering, "Uncle Roddy, have them ready to move out at first light."

"That's no' doable, Lass. The airfield is on stand-down until thirteen hundred local. Besides, Cleo has requested a compass swing before we go anywhere. We could finish up in the morning and ship out at zero six hundred Zulu?" Rod was the type of man who planned best on his feet. Tori and the team at Vauxhall could hear him pacing as he began to consider the outstanding issues. "What about the American pilot and the little Cessna?"

"You tell us. Just what kind of man is this . . . Calvin?" Tori paused trying to recall the name Mike Perkins had mentioned.

"A good man, that one. *Company* would be my bet. If you're asking for my opinion, Calvin will do what he thinks is best for the success of the operation, and nothing less."

"Very well, call Mike Perkins. If he can't find a more suitable location for the team, I'm sure Étienne can find us a secure spot somewhere in Canada."

"That should be easy enough, three-quarters of that bloody country is uninhabited. We'll be ready," he assured her, chuckling politely. "One suggestion, if I may. Consider upgrading the accommodations. I don't think our girl has had any real rest since she landed at Heathrow. With all the young reservists coming and going here, no one's getting much sleep at all, not to mention this heat. It's a wee bit much for our resident snow walker."

Leaning closer to the conference call unit, brow lined, Tori questioned him, "I'm a little concerned that we are preparing someone for a desert operation who is waning from the Arizona heat?"

Rod chortled across the secure transatlantic line. "Lady Victoria! You should know better," he said in his thick brogue. "Maybe our girl doesn't enjoy the frying pan, but she can't wait to tackle the fire. A wee respite is all she needs."

Once Rod had signed off, Tori headed upstairs to her father's office. She had over twenty operational groups or Sections in various stages of readiness, from initial planning, operational go, or on stand-down. Cleo's team had been designated Section 28T. The "T" designation for *temporary* meant they would be disbanded after completion of the primary objective or failure of the operation.

"If this succeeds, and it looks like it may," Sir Richard asked, "will you consider making this a permanent asset?"

"We've had good success with other integrated teams, but this one is a bit different, don't you think?"

Sir Richard laughed inwardly at the situation, "I would not want to have to meet the Grand Council of the Iroquois for every little operational detail."

"Not much different than having to report to the JIC, or worse, hand-hold the Canadians through these things," she smiled, before asking pointedly. "Is that why you've been keeping such focus on this particular Section? Worried about all the different political toes I may have to step on?"

"Not so much. The SOE is your house, but I am interested in how our girl does, and how this plays out. If you disband twenty-eight, Section Nine have requested she be sequestered to their engineering team. What do you think of Agent Commanda? Would you consider having her join the team full-time?"

She seemed to consider the question at length, before offering, "I agree that Deseronto is an asset we should hold on to. Perhaps she could find a place at Nine when our needs wane, but what would I do with Commanda?"

"I believe they make a unique team, and Commanda is a trained investigator . . ."

"Is there something *else* you're not telling me?"

"Just a thought," he said, before standing and leading her to the door. "Think about it," was all he said as she left his office.

Think about it? It's all I've bloody done! Could this new section actually have a mandate beyond the current crisis? Her father was right, both Cleo and Bo had unique language skills, military training, and one hell of a personal cover story, but was it right to exploit their ethnicity for the gains of their nations. If only it were as simple as that. Both women were loyal compatriots, but their loyalty followed quite separate routes. Then there were the personal issues, both between the two women, and Tori as well. *Do I have issues with them?* Tori and Bo had dated a few times, had fun, and ended up in bed, twice. Once Bo was introduced to the team, their *fun* came to an abrupt halt. Tori had advised her immediately that fraternization within the SOE was frowned upon, and could undermine her authority. Bo hadn't seemed to care one way or the other. Of course, this was all BC, Before Cleo. *Cleopatra! Bloody hell, what do I do about you? She is a professional. I can count on Cleo Deseronto to maintain a professional relationship. And if that's not what I want, I must break my own rule, bleeding hell . . .*

Chapter Six

ATA Tire Company Airfield (Private)
South Florida
United States of America

The American Tractor and Aviation Tire Company had once belonged to Howard Hughes. Hughes had purchased the failing company during the depression when it was still American Tractor Tire and expanded the business model to include tires for airplanes. The decision to focus on aviation instead of the lucrative automotive sector had been a smart move. When the war broke out in Europe, ATA Tire was the only company tooled up to serve that industry, becoming the defacto leader in the field.

They had moved from the base in Arizona to the ATA field nine days earlier. Bo and her flight instructor had flown the Cessna 172, while Cleo and Rod had flown the little Otter, with everyone's gear and the extra equipment on board. Now working out of the single office in the airfield's sole hangar, Rod joined Cleo at the picnic table, sitting in the shade. It was still early by Florida standards and quite comfortable compared to the heat they had endured in Arizona. While the mechanics Mike Perkins assigned, had yet to arrive, Cleo was already hard at work. Rod watched her for several minutes, not wanting to interrupt her deep concentration. Instead, he kept his focus on the pine groves that surrounded the airfield, stretching for a few hundred feet, before quickly transforming into full-fledged Everglades.

On their first day in Florida, the airfield manager had come by and spotted Cleo and Rod at the outside table. "As long as yah' don't have any food out here you should be okay," he said, explaining that he was always shooing gaiters off the field.

"Gaiters!" The chief was stunned. "Alligators? You must be joking, lad!"

"Nope. Bold as brass," the manager informed him. "Ain't nothing for 'em to wander up here." With that said, he brought a loaded shotgun out of his truck and handed it over to Rod. "Best keep it out here, for when you need it."

The twelve gauge Winchester now rested, as it had every day since, on the center of the picnic table with the business end pointing in the direction of the glades. Cleo was flipping through a book of Norval Morrisseau's paintings. It had been suggested that she consider an aboriginal scene for the fuselage. The idea was to make it appear both unique and promotional. It had already been decided that the flag, or actually, the wampum belt of the Six Nations of the Iroquois Confederacy be displayed prominently on the tail, with little Mohawk flags painted on each of the pilot's door, next to Cleo's and Bo's names.

94

Paint was not the right word for what they were doing. The Otter was painted a glossy white. All that was left to add were the vinyl decals for the tail numbers. Now a large mural of some type was to be included with the names on the doors, the flags, and the wampum belt, all of which were part of the custom vinyl work still outstanding.

Cleo had left Bo in charge of the aesthetics of the operation, not expecting her enthusiasm. Just that morning, Bo had given her a copy of the final artwork for the custom flights suits and the Morrisseau book with sticky notes on several pages.

"What have you got there, lass?" Rod asked. He was curious to see just what had her so engrossed that she hadn't noticed the alligator lying just inside the tree line.

Cleo looked up to say hi and saw what the chief was focusing on, "she's harmless. At least for now. She's waiting for Kaminski. He throws her a breakfast burrito every morning."

As if on cue, Scott Kaminski, one of two CIA-supplied mechanics, barreled down the service road and tossed something in a MacDonald's wrapper out his truck window.

"That daft prick," Rod blurted, unable to hide his shock.

"For Christ sakes, Ski!" It was Scott's boss, the senior mechanic assigned to the team, "one day that little bastard's gonna' get tired of waiting for you and eat a VIP!"

Scott Kaminski reminded Cleo of a young, arrogant Bo Commanda. "That gator loves me," he said, as explanation for his stupidity. "Sides, she knows I'm the boss!"

"Yah, and one day she's gonna' know what *the boss* tastes like too!"

Cleo enjoyed listening to these two go on. Rod had already accused them of acting like an old married couple. Once Rod had parked his old creaking bones on the bench, Cleo showed him the ideas Bo had come up with. She was doing a good job. Both their heads were buried in the Morrisseau book when they heard the sound of a Cessna nearing the field.

"She was out early," Rod commented.

"She's trying to kick the nausea. I told her the only way was to get out as much as possible and force her body to acclimate."

Rod looked at the woman who had once saved his best friend's life and perhaps his professional reputation. "That's a wee bit harsh, don't yeah think?"

Cleo looked at him. "I was ten-times worse. *Trust me.* It's the only way." She went on to tell Rod just how many times she had thrown up during her basic flight training at Portage La Prairie. They had almost failed her, but she wouldn't give up, and by midcourse she had it under control and had proven herself capable. She assured him that Bo would break that barrier very soon. Besides, there was no time to find a replacement, and more importantly, Bo wasn't giving up either.

The Cessna Skyhawk taxied to the parking area, then swung around into an auxiliary aircraft parking spot, before starting the shutdown sequence. Terry Calvin, the Instructor Pilot the CIA had provided, popped open the co-pilot's door and climbed out. Even in the early morning, you could see that he had been sweating buckets. His flight suit, also old military issue, was completely soaked across his back.

Both Cleo and Rod turned to him for an update when he joined them at the picnic table.

"Better," Terry said, "much better. She's still fighting the nausea but that will pass. I think it's time to move her up." During his forty-odd years of service, Terry had flown everything from B-52s to A-10 Warthogs. Cleo wasn't happy about the prospect of handing the controls of her baby over to Bo but Terry was right; they didn't have much time and Bo would need all the flight training she could get.

Cleo exhaled slowly, "how many hours has she got?"

Terry looked at his clipboard, consulting his notes. "With yesterday's cross-country, that makes just over twenty-two, total."

She seemed to take a long time to think, before turning to Rod, "Can we finish everything on time, if Terry has her up every morning?"

Rod understood that she was referring to the Otter and not their student pilot. "We're almost done lass. Everything left to install has been weighed, and will go in today. That leaves only the vinyl skin left to cut and lay."

"Okay," Cleo said, understanding the need to get Bo in the Otter and familiar with the much larger aircraft. The one great advantage any pilot would have when transitioning to the big cargo plane, from the little Cessna, was the "StoL" characteristics of the Otter. The wing design actually slowed the much heavier Otter down to the same speeds for landing and takeoff as the Cessna Skyhawk Bo was learning to fly. It was still going to take work, but the plan wasn't for her to become a fully qualified pilot, but to teach Bo enough to fulfill the needs of the operation. Her one real flight would be the takeoff and departure from Tehran. After the release of the mini-UAV, Cleo would sub back in and land the plane in Dubai. "Let's get her in the Otter every morning. Early!" Cleo ordered. "It's important to concentrate on GPS navigation, takeoff and climb to altitude, and course corrections. How's she doing with everything else?"

Terry nodded. "Not bad. She's doing well with her cross-countries but that's dual." Dual flight was an important division for logging hours. Solo meant the pilot had flown the aircraft alone, while time logged under the "dual" heading said the hours accumulated had been with an instructor pilot in the next seat.

"I know what you're getting at. You can send her out on solo cross-countries starting this afternoon." Then, just to be sure there was no misunderstanding, she added, "in the Cessna! No solos in the Otter." She had to check her watch for the time in London. It was close to eight a.m. in South Florida and they had planned to have the UAV uplink test that morning. "Chief, when are we expecting the package?"

Rod Nelligan repeated the same instinctive move, checking his watch before answering, "Mike gave me his word that we'd have everything before zero eight hundred."

Cleo nodded, motioning for Bo to join them at the picnic table. She had just finished tying the Cessna down, and retrieving her charts and all the assorted flight and safety gear pilots carry.

Bo Commanda sat down next to the chief and dropped her gear on the table. "Did Ally-the-Gator get her burrito this morning?"

"Do not tell me you're encouraging Kaminski's behavior?" Cleo challenged.

"What's wrong with it?"

"What's wrong," Terry interjected, "is that an alligator will, very quickly, adjust to being fed. When we wrap up here and Kaminski goes home, she'll go looking for someone else to feed her. She'll follow the waterways and open drainage ditches, even roaming through backyards."

Bo still didn't get it. "What's the harm in letting a little gator in your pool?"

Cleo had to use an example from home. "It would be like feeding a bear."

"Who would be dumb enough to feed a bear?" Bo said, almost shocked by the comparison. "Start feeding a bear and he'll start eating your garbage, followed by your truck, and finish up by eating your tuque . . . while you're still wearing it!" The comparison troubled Bo, "are they really that bold?"

That's when the chief decided to get his two cents in. "Look at that bloody yod! She's still keeping an eye out. I ought to feed her that daft punter!"

The sound of a heavy helicopter approaching the small private field halted any plans to orchestrate Scott Kaminski's demise. A Black Hawk crossed the field and hovered in front of the hangar, forcing everyone seated at the picnic table to scramble to keep papers and charts from being blown away. Without shutting down the twin turbines or stopping the blades, a large crate and several boxes were unloaded, along with two people in BDUs. The two uniformed passengers had not done any of the unloading, which implied they were officers. As soon as the crew was back aboard, the sleek military helicopter went light on the skids, making a slow hovering turn, and accelerated into an easy ascent.

Cleo was on her way to help the officers escorting the test equipment when she realized she knew the pair. Butterworth, she would recognize anywhere, between his height and the MARPAT camouflage, the man always looked like he had just stepped off a Marine Corps recruiting poster. She was not, however, acquainted with the camouflage pattern of the second officer, but only needed a minute to realize it was Tori. That was a surprise.

Before she could greet anyone, Scott Kaminski raced by, driving a forklift and scooped up the large shipping crate and accompanying gear.

They all watched as he reversed course and sped off in the direction of the Otter. The package they had just received contained the new version of the mini-UAV, the black box uplink, and the special laptop computer with its built-in backup controller. When the first design proved to be too hard to fly, Butterworth had spent hours on *Jane's Database* searching for a similar antenna. Having no luck in the marine database, he switched to the aviation digest and found the specs for an old combo aircraft antenna that actually looked like an upside down airplane or a very large hood ornament from some 1950s Detroit gas guzzler. Cleo had only read the design data, and was looking forward to seeing it fly.

Butterworth, halted the prerequisite three paces before Cleo, and saluted crisply before extending his hand and congratulating her on the promotion. Once done, he dismissed himself, heading off to join the chief, and the mechanics, in the hangar.

Tori, after ordering "Stand Easy," in response to Cleo Deseronto's military posture, was all smiles too. Congratulating her on the promotion was the first order of business. Unlike the dirty old coveralls and unadorned flight suits the team was wearing, Braithwaite and Butterworth were in "proper" uniforms. At the sight of the full Colonel rank insignia Tori was sporting, Cleo had instinctively popped to Attention. Before either could say anymore, Bo joined them, giving Tori a slaphappy greeting, and injecting herself between the pair, before dragging Tori off to meet Ally-the-Gator.

Cleo watched them walk towards the side of the hangar and felt a small pang to see Bo's shameless flirting. She had not been surprised to see Major Butterworth in uniform but Tori was a surprise. *She looks amazing in uniform.* It was good to see her, especially here. They had a week to practice the drop and uplink maneuver. *A week to get it right, or is it the week with Tori that I'm really thinking about?* Turning her attention to the only thing she had any control over, she headed towards the aircraft and the assortment of equipment still laid out for installation.

There really wasn't that much left to do, but the items sitting beside the aircraft were all appreciably large, including the new tires for the landing gear. The ATA Tire company had generously supplied the airfield, hangar, office, and a new set of oversized Tundra Tires. The oversized tires, provided extra surface traction for Arctic conditions and had quite unexpectedly displayed the same ability in the desert. The extra surface area and reduced pressure from the added size, would help keep the big mains on the surface of both snow and sand. The boys had just started to get the little Otter up on jack stands when Cleo joined them. Major Butterworth had the new crate open, and was carefully unpacking the UAV. They had renamed it a satellite-controlled Unmanned Aeronautical reconnaissance Vehicle, sUAV, or son of a UAV, as Butterworth was calling it. Cleo knew guys always thought things like that were funny. Regardless of what they called it, she couldn't help but think of all aircraft, even Sonny here, as female, in the same way sailors have always applied the female gender to their ships.

With the sUAV out of the crate, Major Butterworth demonstrated how the photo hatch cover, which looked to be riveted to the rest of the sUAV, would simply fall away the moment it was released.

Cleo and Rod were very impressed with the design. The MI9 team and the US Marine Major had obviously invested a lot of time and effort getting it right. It took less than five minutes to snap the sUAV into place. Once there, it really did look like an antenna. Even Cleo was somewhat shocked to see how suitable it was. If she didn't know better, she too would have thought it was a standard modification, and having a *belonging* look was the key to getting away with this. With the sUAV squared away, Cleo and Butterworth installed the avionics upgrades, including the black box and several other final additions, while

Rod and the company mechanics swapped out the tires and started laying the exterior vinyl artwork. It was almost suppertime when they towed the Otter out of the hangar.

Cleo, with Major Butterworth in the co-pilot's seat, started the Otter for a test flight and taxied the length of the field, making sure the new equipment hadn't screwed up the center of gravity. She had calculated out all the changes to the Weight and Balance, just as the mechanics had done for the maintenance logs. Everything looked good on paper, and now felt good in operation. The Otter was as stable and docile as ever. *Good,* Cleo thought. *Now, all we need to do is demonstrate that our little Son of an UAV can do the job.*

Chapter Seven

VAGA Office of Counter-Intelligence
Ministry of Intelligence and National Security
Tehran, Islamic Republic of Iran

Major Suyfias showed the young Armored officer and demolitions expert out, expressing again, his condolences for the loss of two members of his team. Returning to his desk, after closing and locking the door, he removed a dossier from the top drawer. The file tab read MOSADDEGH, Hasid. The first page contained a summary of the entire Intelligence file, beginning with personal data, and military service. The major had already reviewed the file in detail. Hasid, while an enterprising young man, had failed to show much initiative in the Iraqi Army until the very last days of the war. It was then that the young armorer took command of a broken, officer less, light mechanized troop and started stashing weapons and armaments in buried caches, and organizing his tattered comrades into what had quickly become a future resistance cell operating as a black-market enterprise. As much as be didn't like the enterprising Iraqi, Hasid was in a position to help him tremendously. While Suyfias had failed to climb the ladder to the upper-echelon of the Intelligence corps, he had become known as the "go-to" man for everything a highly placed official might desire. That included everything and anything not readily available in Tehran, and not officially sanctioned by the Sazmane Basij-e Mostaz'afin. The Basij were the keepers of morals and charged with several internal duties, including the suppression of dissident gatherings. Suyfias stuffed the file back in his desk. He couldn't fault the young Iraqi. Hasid, as promised, had provided the location of every weapons cache he had created, along with detailed instruction explaining how he had rigged his homemade detonators. The demolitions expert, who had just briefed him, made it clear the accident was the fault of the soldiers charged with digging out the buried munitions. The recovery team had already opened four of the five caches Hasid had mapped out. One was already empty, as had been suspected. Having had no problems opening and retrieving the next three sites had lead the men to a false sense of security. Tired from a long day of travel and digging through frozen soil, not to mention preoccupied with the risks of operating beyond the Iranian border, had made the soldiers inattentive to the task at hand. Using pickaxes, instead of shovels, they hurried to clear the top few feet of hard-packed earth before beginning a more careful excise. That was all it took. Regardless of what the careless digger had hit, it not only exploded but began a chain reaction, igniting all of the armaments in the stockpile. Two of the young Officer's men were dead and several others injured. Suyfias felt bad for the young Army officer. The young man's career would suffer for this. He had so wanted to blame things on the Iraqi sergeant but had to admit, grudgingly, that the Mosaddegh had done no wrong.

Retrieving Hasid's file again, he carefully added the report and photographs from the recovery team, then placed everything under lock and key. He stood, checking his uniform, and making sure his appearance was up to snuff. Next stop, lunch with a certain high-ranking General. It was time to let the General know he had made a trustworthy connection, one who had the means to procure specialized commodities, commodities he knew the General desperately craved.

Fort Lauderdale, Florida
United States of America

Always unsteady on a social footing, Cleo rarely felt like she fit in anywhere. The military, at least, had a structure that seemed older than time and while archaic, had a feel of familiarity for her. Bo had been the one real exception. As kids, they had been more than friends, they were sisters, or more like twins, ensconced in their own little world. Born only a day apart, they had shared everything from their first birthday cake to their first crush. Now they were back in each other's company and interested in the same woman. Or were they?

When Tori and Butterworth arrived, she didn't really know what to think. Bo had flirted shamelessly to the point that Cleo just couldn't watch anymore. Instead, she concentrated all her efforts on the first stage of testing for the sUAV. She and Butterworth spent the morning in the hangar, with the Otter jacked up on a tail-stand, holding her straight and level. They repeated the remote and manual release procedures until they were both satisfied that it would release cleanly, regardless of which method they employed. When they finally came up for air, Rod called them to join the team for lunch.

The takeout Kaminski laid out on the picnic table consisted of crab cakes, hotdogs, fries, and coleslaw that looked suspiciously like it had been prepared in a blender. Everyone dug-in, too hungry to care. Warily, Cleo noted that two members of the group, Bo and Tori, were absent. She wanted to scream, laugh, or just plain run. *Talk about a helix wrapped around an inclined plane! Frack, now I've got run-away-itice!* She needed to talk to Tori but had no idea what to say. When it came to sharing her feelings, she was ill-equipped. Her hesitation grew more from lack of reference than any trauma she may have suffered. If the military ever released a manual detailing the procedures for communicating your emotions, Cleo would be a master, but without any idea how to begin, she usually didn't. When it came to attraction, she had always waited to be asked, never taking the risk of indicating her interest first, much less anything as forward as asking someone out. Tori had been the exception and Cleo wasn't sure why. Was it just the circumstances, the stress of being locked up at Heathrow with nothing to lose? *I like her but is pursuing her appropriate? Appropriate? What am I, the squadron protocol officer?* Choking down a dry crab cake with a cold soda, she walked the length of the apron, trying to sort her priorities. *It doesn't really matter if I like her, or even if she's interested in me. What I need to do is talk to Bo first. Forgiveness has to include Respect.*

After a long hot afternoon flight-testing the sUAV, and the Otter, Cleo, Butterworth, and the chief were driven to their Fort Lauderdale hotel. Cleo went straight to Bo's room, wanting to talk with her before she could disappear again. Bo opened her door then walked away, leaving it wide open. "Not you too?"

Cleo grabbed the door before the automatic closer could push it shut in her face. "What's wrong?" she asked, following Bo into the room. Bo pulled out a chair from the small table, so Cleo grabbed the other, sitting down across from her.

"I know what you want, Squirrel," There was no joy in her expression. She slouched in her chair, playing with her flight suit zipper. "She's all yours!"

"I'm sorry?"

"Look, I know you like her. So let me make this clear—where I'm concerned—she's a free agent."

Cleo tried to comprehend what Bo had just said. Nothing Bo ever told her was straight-up, there was always more to it. "I'm sorry, Bo. I didn't realize you two were serious."

"Geezus, Squirrel! I just told you! There's nothing going on between us!"

Cleo nodded. While wary of Bo's mood, she was never good at letting sleeping dogs lie, "Do you love her?"

"Oh Geez, you dumb ass!" Bo roared her frustration. "She's not into me. She wants you, you dumb shit!" Bo dumped the books and flight gear from her bag on the table and started sorting everything. When she was finally satisfied, she looked back at Cleo. "Why are you still here?"

"Because I came to talk to you about how you feel, not to ask your permission to ask her out. Although . . . I do feel like I should ask!"

Bo was leaning back in her chair. Her arms crossed over her chest. It was easy to see she was spoiling for a fight, but like everything Bo did, it was more complicated than just throwing a few punches. She bored her eyes into Cleo, but couldn't conceal a lopsided grin. "You're an ass, you know?"

"Yeah, but I'm a polite ass!" she said, grinning back at her cousin and oldest friend in the world. "Bo, I'm so sorry. I thought there was something but I didn't know you were so serious. I'll back-off. Scouts honor," she said, rendering a perfect Boy Scout salute.

"Nah . . ." Bo shook her head. "It's not like that. We did go out but only a few times. We had fun but we never clicked. I mean, she's hot and everything, but let me be honest here, she is a bit of a know-it-all. Now that I think about it, it might be fun watching you two bore each other to death."

"Bo . . ."

"No really, Squirrel. There's nothing between her *ladyshit* and me. So you're free and clear to ask her out."

"Really? Then why are you calling her a shit?"

Bo was grinning, "I was just making fun of her title. All that royal business gives me hives."

"You and my mother!"

"Oh fuck," Bo practically snorted her laughter. "Do you remember that big fucking *fleur-de-lis* your old lady had hanging off the balcony?"

Cleo was laughing too. Getting up from the table, she grabbed two bottles of water from the bar fridge and handed one to Bo. "Gods, I was sooooo humiliated. First, we spend half the day in the school auditorium watching the Queen dismantle the BNA on live TV, and Trudeau grinning his six-off, like it was some sort of reparation for the *Conquest of New France* . . ."

"Hey, I thought you liked Trudeau?

"I like all the Trudeaus. I just didn't share Pierre's vision of Canada as a French Republic.

"You would have preferred we remain a colony?"

"Don't be a goof," Cleo said, pulling Bo's Pilot's Log Book out from the pile in front of her. "I just think Confederation was a better deal under the BNA, at least for the First Nations, and ironically, Quebecers as well."

"I do like the three-founding nation's idea better than ten equal provinces. That equal states thing works in the good old U-S-of-A, but not up in Igloo-land!" Bo stopped suddenly, looking to Cleo with wide eyes, "Holy crap! You've got me talking politics! What's next . . . I'll start watching the Queen's speech on Christmas day?"

"Very funny!" Cleo finished checking Bo's logbook, "You know, you're doing very well. Have you thought about finishing your training, and adding those *wings-of-gold* to that spiffy Marine uniform?"

"Yeah," Bo took the logbook back from Cleo, starting to fill in the day's entry. "Mike says he'll have me on the first conversion course once we're back. Now, I have all this paperwork to do and you have a girl to ask out."

"Woman, Bo-Bo. I'm pretty sure she's a woman."

RCAF Station Mountainview (Closed)
Near Picton, Ontario
Canada

Tori had flown American Airlines from Miami to Toronto and then drove herself to CFB Trenton, where she met with the Rover team. The ROV operation had now been officially named Spirit Bear. The team included both civilian and military engineers and technicians, some of whom Cleo had selected personally. Following her original recommendations, they had purchased four Argos from the manufacturer and had built a custom safety cage to protect the rovers' electronics and communication equipment. Tori had arrived in time to witness the first full test of the rover and delivery system. An RCAF C-130 Hercules crew had been practicing the drop of the NASA Airbags with a simulated load. Now, for their dress rehearsal, they would drop the rover into a quarry and attempt to establish a satellite connection.

Standing on an outcropping less than a kilometer from the target, Tori was shocked to see the number of times the airbags bounced and how many bags broke during the run down the quarry and rebound back. The real surprise came when the airbags deflated. That was the first indication that the control team had successfully established an uplink with the rover.

Using binoculars, Tori watched the rover resting upside down with its six wheels and rubber tracks in the air. Cleo had warned her, but promised it would not be a big deal to correct the rover's attitude. Before she could ask how, one of the support bars from the roll cage snapped down, slapping the ground much in the way a whale might slap the ocean surface for leverage in a roll. The action caused the rover to rock heavily back and forth. A second slap of the cage arm pushed the rocking past the point of equilibrium, causing it to tip then roll, finally landing with a thud on its tracks.

A roar of cheers went up from the engineers. The rover was down, linked up, and on her feet, but would she start? As the minutes passed, Tori knew they had problems. Étienne called her to the command trailer so she could see the data streaming from the satellite uplink. The surveillance package was up and running, with several monitors displaying images from the quarry. While the images were amazing, the rover wasn't moving and the data monitors dedicated to engine operation all sat blank.

Leaving Étienne to sort out the Argo team, Tori joined the technicians experimenting with the surveillance package. Taking a seat with the team, she asked the leading technician, "Tell me about the capabilities you've cobbled together?"

She and the tech had not been introduced, and she was pleased to see him check her visitor's badge before answering. The red and white security stripe immediately signaled her VIP status and her all-access clearance. "Yes Ma'am. Like you said, we cobbled together a full setup using existing equipment, all controlled with an onboard laptop. That," he said, pointing to a monitor, "is a view from the laptop's exterior camera."

"I'm surprised it survived the drop?"

"That was easier than we thought," he explained. "When we started researching the specs, we found we already had these super tough laptops for use in tanks and APCs. We just pulled four from supply and started adding optics and controllers using the existing USB and Bluetooth connectivity."

Nodding toward the monitor, she asked, "Why bother using the onboard camera?" As if to demonstrate her point, the technician sitting next to him, moved the joystick and rotated the view of one of the accessory cameras.

Actually, Ma'am, the plan we received from *your* engineer instructed us to use available equipment first. We sort of took that to heart, so when we started building the package we decided to use the onboard camera because it was already there and working," adding almost defensibly, "It's a ten-megapixel processor. That's twice what your engineer wanted for the forward view!"

Tori smiled at his description of Cleo Deseronto as *her* engineer. "I'm glad it worked so well." Then something else occurred to her. "Tell me, is the microphone still working on the laptop?"

"Of course, but . . ."

"If we can't see what's wrong with the engine perhaps we can hear it?"

He smiled at the idea and turned to the technician in the seat beside him. The young soldier began typing earnestly, calling up several windows and entering commands. A moment later, he nodded to Tori for permission to proceed.

"Nice and loud then," she ordered, "send it to all speakers." They listened for a moment, hearing nothing. Tori was about to ask them to check the connection when the sound of the starter cranking ripped through the command trailer.

Now they had something other than blank instruments to concentrate on, a clatter of suggestions rippled through the room. The addition of sound did not alter the mood of the powerplant team. Étienne put his hand on the shoulder of the technician who was trying desperately to get the little engine to turn over. Halting the man's efforts, he suggested, "It is *flooded?*" At the tech's silent nod, he ordered the electric Argo be rolled out and swapped with the gas Argo, now sitting dead in the quarry.

As orders were relayed and the technicians sprang back to work, Tori left the confines of the trailer, heading for a large granite outcrop a hundred feet away. She had bad news to deliver and might as well take a few minutes to enjoy the countryside first.

After a quick call with Mike Perkins to confirm the timetable for delivery of more air bags, she called her father's direct line.

"Good news from Camp X?" he asked, jokingly using the name of the secret training base the SOE had operated in Canada during the Second World War.

"I'm afraid we're a good hundred kilometers from *the farm,* and success." Moving right to the issues, she explained, "Étienne's team has made progress and the drop was a success in measures. The comm link and surveillance package are operational and in good order. That data is being forwarded to section nine as we speak. The hitch came when it was time to crank-up the motor. The jostling she took on landing dumped most of her petrol and flooded the carburetor. Once they switch out the petrol undercarriage for the new electric Argo, testing will continue without a hitch, but . . ." Tori listened to silence from the secure connection to Vauxhall, knowing her father was looking through the initial reports streaming into Section Nine.

"What happened to replacing the carburetor with electric fuel injection?"

"I'm still waiting to hear why they dropped Argo One instead of Two, but the outcome remains the same. JPL still needs six weeks to deliver the second airbag system. Which leaves us to drop an untested Rover in six weeks or test again, then wait an additional six weeks for a third delivery system."

"Your gut take on this?" he asked.

Tori liked that most about working for her father. He believed instincts were a crucial part of the job and never shied away from letting her follow a line of her choosing. "No go! We must have a successful test before we deploy. JPL's delivery schedule is set in stone. As much as Mike would like to pop solutions out of his hat, the systems must still be built and that takes time." Tori sighed, taking a moment to consider the countryside around her. "Did I ever thank you for the summers in France?"

"Whatever made you think of that?"

"At Oxford, we had a copy of *Cartier's Journals.* I never could have read them if I hadn't spent those summers with Genny. It has given me a unique perspective on this country, but I never truly understood his descriptivism until just now. Can you imagine?" she asked, "I'm sitting on a slab of granite larger than Uncle Roddy's flat. Rugged does not describe it, but Godless, that I cannot see."

"I take it the mosquitoes are not out?"

She chuckled, "Yes, that's it, just add the mossies' to the mix and God just up and quits!"

"I'm not sure that's what Cartier meant when he said the place was *untouched by God*. I wonder what our Cleopatra would make of his musing on Terra Nova?"

Tori didn't know which surprised her more, the instant rush of heat she felt at the mention of Cleo's name, or the fact that her father had referred to her as *our* Cleopatra. *Is that how I want it?* "Actually, she has plenty a comment. Evidently RMC has a copy that's even older than the one I read at Oxford. She did laugh about his continuous carping about the bloody mosquitoes." She realized, almost too late, that she was waxing on about Cleo. There was no hiding her enthusiasm, but that didn't mean it was time to fess up to dear old dad.

As if sensing her sudden discomfort, he changed the subject. "Has Étienne arranged your transport?"

"It's all taken care of."

A Bombardier Challenger had been laid on to ferry Capt.(N) Braithwaite RN, to Fort Drum, not because of her rank but because it was available. The Canadians actually had six of them sitting on the ramp in Ottawa. Étienne believed that a quick hop in the Challenger would draw less attention than flying Tori to New York in the rear seat of a Royal Canadian Air Force F-18. When he bent the rules to send Tori in the Challenger, he assumed that the average American was unaware that the jet belonged to a special fleet dedicated to serving the Prime Minister of Canada and select members of the Privy Council. The US military knew better.

The 174th Fighter Wing NYANG base ops was expecting Tori, or more correctly, some Brit officer, but when she landed at Syracuse, the status of a Challenger jet, with the official seal of Canada's House of Parliament, forced heads to turn. Phone calls were immediately made, and the Garrison Commander ordered that the "foreign officers" be moved from temporary quarters to the VIP residence.

A decade earlier, the LeRay Mansion and adjoining estate lands had been turned over to the Army to manage. In return, the housing officer had updated the property and turned the actual estate house into luxury accommodations for visiting generals and dignitaries. It had never occurred to anyone that three senior officers and two enlisted men, even the most senior of enlisted men, would be considered VIPs.

Fort Drum had been designated Operation Polar Bears, "Go, No-Go," point. Tori had wanted the team to take a few days rest while she decided which operation should proceed. She had to choose between sending Cleo's crew to Iran, or waiting six to twelve weeks for another shot at dropping the rover. She didn't need three days to make her decision, it had been made for her. Not when the rover wouldn't start, but when technicians couldn't come together to find a solution. They lacked the technical leadership the Otter team had with Deseronto and Butterworth, and that made all the difference.

Weeks before she set the deadline, she learned that Mike Perkins was planning a small reception for the Otter team during their stop at Fort Drum. Mike, like her, wanted to grant the team a little R&R before they kicked-off. It had been Siobhan's job to arrange to have everyone's mess uniforms available. That had been easy to arrange for Rod and Albert. It was as simple as sending someone to Albert's quarters at Fort Rucker and Rod's flat in London. Bo was a snap too, since she had just been issued new uniforms, including a crisply tailored mess uniform of the United States Marine Corps.

Cleo however, was a problem. No one had a clue where her uniforms were stored or what condition they were in. The best thing to do was have Étienne send over a couple of different sizes and a full set of accoutrements from brass buttons to miniature medals and pilots wings. What they received from the quartermaster's store was a kit. All the pieces of the uniform, cut from the various material sections for the included pattern, but requiring a tailor to measure and sew everything together. Tory was not thrilled with the news, taking the complete kit to the only person who could finish the garment without laying an eye on Cleo.

Parminder was not surprised to see Tori enter her shop but was thrown by this newest commission. "Why on earth does Cleo require a uniform? She's retired! Isn't she?" Parminder asked defensively, suspicious of Tori Waite's continued involvement in Cleo's life.

Tori had vetted the clothing designer back when she was preparing to bring Cleo into the operation and initial surveillance had suggested the two were lovers. There was no need to "read" her in, but Parminder did deserve some sort of explanation.

"The Canadian Space Agency has invited Cleo and Bo to attend a formal dinner in Star City," adding, "you know what an enthusiast Cleo is. Since Bo will be attending in her American Marine uniform, it only seemed proper that Cleo wear hers as well."

For Parminder, who really didn't know what she thought of "Tori Waite, from the Foreign and Commonwealth Office," that was as good an explanation as any. And true to form, Parminder had Cleo's mess uniform finished, pressed, and packed for her in twenty-four hours, including adding the three wide gold bars of an Air Force Wing Commander, which Parminder knew very well, Cleo was not.

The formal mess dinner would be held in the ornate period dining room of the VIP residence. The sheer number of vehicles swarming around the LeRay Mansion clearly illustrated that several groups were scrambling to accommodate the last minute VIPs. A number of young service men and women, dressed in woodland camouflage, met her at the staff car, collecting the garment bags she had brought for the team. Once Tori had been relieved of her luggage, she was taken on a short tour of the mansion. In the dining room, the Chef, who had just arrived from the Officers Club, had several questions regarding Cleo's and Bo's food issues. Once armed with the information he needed, he was off to finalize the menu and to order fresh rations, while the housekeeper went over the seating arrangement for dinner.

"Admiral," she began respectfully, "with your permission, I would like to put you at the far end and the General at this one."

"Perhaps," Tori said, to the very professional housekeeper, "you should call me Captain. The Admiral bit is probably just a mash up with your American ranks."

The housekeeper or, Household Supervisor, had years of experience and had met many general officers. The difference between a British Navy Captain and an American one-star Admiral was only one rank, but the protocol for seating officers formally, was all that concerned her, now suggesting they seat the officers and ranks at opposite ends of the table, culminating with the most junior of each meeting in the center. As there were to be Senior NCOs dining-in, she suggested that the Commanding General would host the officers with him seated at one end while the Division Command Sergeant Major, as host for the NCOs, would sit opposite him at the other end of the formal table. Tori agreed, shrugging off her impatience with the necessities of military etiquette.

While she waited for the Otter team to arrive, she sat down with her laptop and started hammering out a formal report. If the powers that be wanted an immediate kick-off, they had one choice and it meant risking Cleo and her team. Risking human assets was part and parcel of her job but risking Cleo felt different. *I cannot let this change the way I make my decisions!*

Before Tori could order the operation to proceed, they still needed authorization from the Six Nations. Mike Perkins and Rubert Commanda, Bo's dad, had set the groundwork for acceptance but only Cleo could close the deal. The team could proceed without it, but it would require changes to their cover story. There was absolutely nothing else she could do now but wait to hear how things went with the Grand Chiefs before announcing her decision, Operation Polar Bear, in one guise or another, was now a "Go."

Haudenosaunee Grand Council of Chiefs
Onondaga Territory
Six Nations of the Iroquois Confederacy

Mike Perkins had asked Cleo for a big favor; two actually. He wanted Cleo to fly to Hancock International Airport north of Syracuse, drop Chief Nelligan off and pick up her new Crew Chief, Albert Mackenzie. Mike also had the new flight suits and a number of "gifts" they would present to the Council. Once they were ready to go, he wanted her to fly the Otter and her team, to the Great Longhouse for presentation to the chiefs. The problem was that the small reservation had no airfield, not even a grass strip. What Mike wanted was for them to land on the lacrosse field behind the Recreation Center, making a big show of their nimble little plane, and the *all* Mohawk Air Team.

Cleo spent a lot of time going over a topographical chart for the area. The field behind the Rec Center was not ideal, but with the right winds, she was sure she could get the Otter in. Getting her out though, was another thing. The flight manual called for an eight hundred and eighty-foot takeoff roll. That was eighty feet too long. Cleo finally gave in but with one caveat; if the winds did not work with the orientation of the field, she would land on Gibson Road or Martin Lane. While the FAA could not punish her for landing in Six Nations territory, they could bust her for taxiing across a state highway. If she was going to risk her plane and crew for this stunt, she was going to make sure Mike and his people worked the system first. She would have a good idea of the landing situation before taking off from Syracuse, but just in case, Bo had a satellite phone with her and would call to insure the New York State Troopers were ready to stop traffic.

The team was now dressed in the new custom flight suits created for the expedition. The purplish-blue color was representative of wampum beads. After inspecting and prepping the Otter, they took to the pilots lounge and waited for the order to move out. Cleo, stretching out in a big pullout recliner, was almost asleep when the call came. She woke Bo, and signaled to Albert Mackenzie, who had been diligently reviewing the flight manuals, before completing a final walk-around. They had already re-fueled the aircraft, checked the weather, and filed a flight plan hours ago. Now that the flight to Onondaga Territory was a go, they had to hustle. Once airborne, the flight would take less than nine minutes enroute.

The Otter, with its astonishing artwork, sat proudly on the General Aviation parking ramp south of Runway 10/28. Of all the artwork that Bo had shown Cleo and Rod Nelligan, only Morrisseau's painting *Great Voyage* came close to what would suitably define them. The problem; Norval Morrisseau was an Ojibwe Indian and not a member of a Longhouse Nation. That would be like hanging a picture of the Spanish Armada in a Royal Navy ship. Cleo asked Étienne to track down an Oneida artist she knew from the University of Toronto. Two hours later, she had a phone number in her hands and less than four hours after that she was looking at a color sketch sent via e-mail. Sinclair had stuck to the woodland style of the Morrisseau painting but had cut the number of colors in half. The new design featured an oblong circle representing creation, with horizontal lines pulled externally from the circle on the left and right sides, and running the length of the fuselage. Inside the circle, two bears and a wolf, representing the clans of the three crewmembers, were paddling a canoe. A crow, poised on the canoe's bowsprit and facing backwards, represented the always-present Trickster. That was a little joke Sinclair had added, reminding Cleo and the team, that nothing is ever as it appears.

In the twenty or so hours tied down at Landmark Aviation, the Otter attracted a number of camera-toting aviation enthusiasts, or "Plane-spotters," as the chief had labeled them.

With the aircraft running and the pre-taxi checklist complete, Cleo called Ground Control for taxi instruction, then listened as Bo read her the updated weather briefing. Nearing the active runway, she called for the takeoff checklist, making sure Bo first sent a text message to Mike, giving him a ten minute heads-up. At the threshold, Cleo held the toe brakes before flipping the yoke to the co-pilots side, "You have control."

At first Bo seemed wide-eyed, but once her hands were on the controls, a grin spread across her face. "I have control," she acknowledged.

The confirmation was standard procedure whenever primary operation of the aircraft changed from one pilot to the other. Bo eased off the brakes, then pushed the throttle and prop levers to the wall. The light winds made it easier to control the Otter on the takeoff roll, still, Bo man-handled her until the tail popped up, and forward visibility was restored. Now able to see the centerline, Bo let out a breath and relaxed her hold on the controls.

Once airborne, the Otter was tame and enjoyable to fly. Bo leveled the aircraft off and turned south for the short flight. Overhead Onondaga Territory, Cleo talked Bo through a descent into the pattern, leveling out at one thousand feet above the ground. With the winds from the north, she prepared for a landing that would run northeast along the length of field. On their first go around, she asked Bo to follow the State Road, Tully Valley northeast so she could get a closer look at the lacrosse field. Nothing would be worse than to set up for a final approach only to notice an obstruction at the last minute. That's when she saw the line of cars parked on the shoulders of the highway for close to a mile in each direction. The parking lot and the rear terrace too, were packed to overflowing with people. Over the intercom, she commented to her crew, "get a load of the crowd down there."

Bo turned to look out Cleo's window, only to find a hand turning her head forward. "Fly the plane," Cleo ordered. "Always fly the plane first! I'll take control now," she said and accepted the control yoke as Bo swung it back.

"You have control," Bo acknowledged properly.

Cleo started a standard fifteen degree turn to the left, while calling for the Pre-landing checklist.

On the flight north from Florida, Bo had gotten her first real crack at flying as Cleo's co-pilot. Cleo had lots of experience with two-pilot operations, and had seen high-time pilots fight for control. For that reason, she had also asked Terry Calvin to introduce Bo to Crew Resource Management. The idea was to clearly divide the duties each pilot would undertake and instill a positive mechanism for managing risks with procedure. Bo was adapting quickly to Cleo's style of operation. Moreover, Cleo, for her part, had no problem handing over the controls to her, and would do so whenever there were non-flying details that required her attention. She didn't have to. She had met a lot of captains who bullied the co-joes and hogged all the flight time for themselves. With more than 14,000 hours flying multi-engine transports, Cleo could handle the Otter without thinking. What she did do was give Bo, and soon Albert too, every opportunity to fly.

Bo had the Flight Manual open to the pre-landing checklist, waiting while Cleo completed the turn to the downwind leg of the landing pattern. "Mixture?"

"Full rich," Cleo said. It still felt strange to have only one engine to think about.

"Prop?"

"Full RPM."

"Throttle?"

Cleo adjusted the throttle, slowing the airspeed to seventy knots. "Throttle set." She thought it important to be clear on what changes she made, not just what she had checked. "You can take a look now."

They were almost abeam the field and Bo craned her neck to see the crowd below them. "Holy Shit!" she shouted, calling to Albert, "are you seeing this?"

His voice over the intercom sounded steady and even. "There's more on the road, too."

"All right, guys, back to work. Let's have a sterile flight deck. Albert, time to buckle up." She rolled the Otter into a turn for the base leg and reduced the throttle again to slow the airplane to sixty knots. "Let's make this look good. Flaps to Landing," Cleo ordered, before continuing with the pre-landing checklist. She rolled the Otter on to final, preparing to land directly ahead while Bo pumped the wing flaps down. Now only a thousand feet short of the field and three hundred feet above the ground and descending, Cleo reduced their airspeed to the absolute slowest the Otter could fly at, and let gravity pull the plane to the ground. With one eye on the field ahead, she asked Bo, "What do you feel?"

"Like I'm being *pulled* to the ground . . ." then suddenly understanding, enthused, "by the seat of my pants! Now I get it. I can feel it in my ass . . . by the seat of my pants, cool!"

The wheels of the Otter touched the dry grass field just one hundred and fifty feet inside the tree line. Cleo cut the throttle to idle, and pulled back hard on the yoke in an effort to slash the forward velocity, before trying the brakes. With little cargo on board, she was able to slow the plane before the end of the main field and swing it back around for the short taxi to the patio area where the dignitaries were waiting.

As they taxied, Albert popped and locked open the rear doors, and Bo joined him in the cabin. As soon as Cleo halted the Otter, Bo and Albert jumped out opposite doors and took up position to block anyone from getting too close while the prop was still spinning. Once the engine shut down and the prop stopped, Bo and Albert chalked the main landing gear while Cleo locked the controls in place, and climbed down from the pilot's door.

Cleo, Bo, and Albert stood side by side in front of the cooling DeHavilland Otter and waited for the crowd to move towards them. The Mohawk Warrior Society was responsible for security, and had maintained a safety perimeter for them. With the Otter now parked and ready for inspection, Rubert Commanda, Bo's dad, invited everyone to approach the team. Bo, it turned out, was just as surprised by his involvement as Cleo was. It made sense. While Mike Perkins might be able to represent them in the "closed" Council house, he certainly made for a suspicious public affairs representative.

With the meet and greet started, introductions were made, T-shirts and coffee mugs were handed out, and copies of Cleo's book were signed and given away. Once the grand feast began, a group of men started to set up in a circle and the water drum was tuned for play. That's when Mike Perkins grabbed the team. He led them to a meeting room, where the Grand Chief of the Six Nations and a chief from each of the Mohawk, Onondaga, and Oneida Nations were waiting.

Sitting down with the chiefs was more about respect than negotiating. Cleo was sure whatever terms might be asked of them, Mike was already in agreement. A lot of responsibility came with their endorsement, and she knew they would need to balance that in some way. She came prepared for this, providing digital copies of all the artwork and promotional materials that had been created for the team. The only thing she could not give them were the rights to her book. Her contract was too tight for that, but they would receive the preferred wholesale rate from the publisher. She then offered one more thing, even surprising herself. She would create a small book on the Woodland Longhouse, which she suggested could be printed by Iroquois Reprints and sold exclusively by the Six Nations.

The promotional rights, and the proposed special edition book, turned out to be far more than the chiefs were expecting, except for one. His son was in a third-year apprentice aviation maintenance engineer, and he wanted him on the team.

Cleo's stomach rolled at the upset to their plans but looked to Albert, explaining, "Albert's our Crew Chief. We will only take on a second mechanic *if* he is pleased with the young man and the other parties involved agree." It was a tough stand to take; one she knew was undefendable. If Mike said they had to take the kid, then they had to take the kid. Even so, she wasn't going to be intimidated by this chief. This was a test of her resolve and nothing more. Cleo asked if the boy was at Onondaga and could meet with Albert. He was.

In less than five minutes, Albert had the kid sussed out, reporting, "He's okay. Wet behind the ears but I can use him."

Cleo was on the patio talking with a group of teens when Albert gave her his assessment. Mike had already taken her aside and suggested she accept the request. She scanned the crowd for the chief in question. When she caught his attention, she signaled her agreement, and that was it. The Haudenosaunee Grand Council of Chiefs had given their blessing. With just the formal dinner scheduled that evening at Fort Drum, they were good to go. Tomorrow, they would officially start their transpolar tour with a visit to three prominent Mohawk Reserves, before taking off for Iqaluit on Frobisher Bay. *Transpolar Tour!* Cleo had to silence that little joking voice in her head that kept calling this operation the *bipolar* tour!

LeRay Mansion
Fort Drum, New York
United States of America

Cleo stood dead numb in the center of the luxury bathroom of the VIP Quarters. Eight hours ago, she had done the difficult, landing at Onondaga. Three hours ago, she was the guest of honor at a dinner with respected colleagues. And, two minutes ago, she had been ready to take on the world. *What am I now*, she asked herself unkindly? Unable to stand and refusing to drop to the floor, she sat on the edge of the bathtub, resting her head in her hands. Her face and skin felt like fire and some sort of shame or loathing had started to shred its way into her gut. At first, she imagined she would vomit, but no such expulsion would release what she was feeling.

Tori Braithwaite, the woman she knew would change her life, was currently in Bo's arms and by now probably in Bo's bed.

She hated herself for not knowing better. After all, she was well aware that the two had been sleeping together in London, but Tori had told her that it had been a mistake and was long over. Why would she lie about it? Nothing could be more painful for Cleo than something that made no sense. Rubbing her burning temples, she pushed herself off the tub, and staggered to the bed. When she woke up, three hours later, she was red-eyed and the blouse and skirt of her uniform were a completely wrinkled mess. She stripped off her mess kit and headed for a hot shower. She knew she needed to sleep. The first leg of tomorrow's flight schedule would take them to St. Catherine's Airport, to clear Canada Customs, then on to the Six Nations of the Grand River near Brantford. That visit would require another off-airport landing but this time on the local speedway. From there, they would stop at Bo's and Cleo's home reserve of Tyendinaga, and finally, fly to Ahkwesáhsne for presentation to the Mohawk Nation Council of Chiefs.

It would be a busy and demanding day. Cleo stepped into the hot streaming shower and rested her raised arms and forehead against the tile wall. *It didn't matter*, she told herself. *It just didn't matter.* The only thing she needed to think about was this operation. It was going to hurt, she acknowledge. *Well frack that!* What was that compared to how important this was. Besides, the Agencies involved had all agreed that she could keep the Otter when everything was over. Of course, getting caught and shot for espionage would make that a moot point. *Frack that too!* Cleo told herself. *When it's all over and done with, I will head for South America like I originally planned. I will start the research for my next book and to hell with Tori Braithwaite and the horse she rode in on!*

Chapter Eight

Cold Spring Longhouse
Mohawk Nation, Council of Chiefs
Ahkwesáhsne, Mohawk Territory
Six Nations of the Iroquois Confederacy

The arrival of the Transpolar Air Team was just as big a deal at Ahkwesáhsne as it had been the day before at the Great Longhouse in Onondaga Territory. The team began as they had on the three previous stopovers, with a gift giving of T-shirts, posters of their aircraft artwork, and signed copies of Cleo's books. The first volume of her series, *100 Mile House, Native North America* was well known on the Reserve and available from the bookstore, but the second volume, *The Persian East* had yet to be released. Those who took an interest accepted the book thoughtfully.

As before, the drummers assembled, with singers and dancers joining them. Soon the heartbeat of Mother Earth was heard as the afternoon became a time of dance and celebration. In the morning, they would depart in earnest for Operation Polar Bear. Until then, it was a time to relax and enjoy the medicine of the drum.

With Mike Perkins, Major Butterworth, and the MI6 members, on their way back to London, Cleo was starting to relax. She had not spoken to Tori before they left and had kept her distance from Bo. Although avoiding Bo was limited to emotional contact. Cleo was just going to have to deal with Bo being physically in her space. Her, and the kid they had been saddled with, Cyril something-or-other. She had to check the crew manifest to find his last name. Johnson. At least Mr. Johnson had arrived and was kitted out as required, including the rush order flight suit to match the rest of the crew. Mike had given her his word on the kid. If Cyril Johnson, who wasn't "read-in," turned out to be too much of a pain in the ass, it would only take one call and he would be on the next plane back to the States. Mike had done one more thing for Cleo; he had sent her the open mesh litters she had wanted for the Otter.

The mesh fold-down litters or aircraft bunks they received had been pulled from an old US Navy P3 Orion. She had received two of them, each comprised of a simple aluminum tube frame with widely spaced yellow webbing straps. The hinges were designed to be positioned along the cabin wall anywhere a structural rib could be found. Originally, Cleo wanted to install two litters over the auxiliary fuel bags and another above the galley on the opposite

114

side of the little cabin. The idea was to have them folded-up when not in use, but provide three bunks when they needed to rest.

A note had been included with the bunks, scrawled in Bear's handwriting: "You'll only get two of these in the old girl, but if you find a way to make it work, I'll send you another."

Bear was right. She and Albert had only been able to install one bunk on each side of the plane. Anymore and the headspace around the crew seats would be compromised. *Oh well,* Cleo thought, *if we ever really need to sleep on the plane, she and Albert could grab the bunks and leave Bo and Cyril to fight for the floor.* What Cleo really believed was the bunks would make the long flights much more comfortable for everyone. It would give the crew somewhere to move, stretch out, or rest other than the utility-grade cabin seats. When she learned that Albert had his Private Pilot's License; she was even more relieved to get the bunks in. In good weather, she could probably get away with letting Bo and Albert fly the plane if she needed an hour of rest.

The evening feast and storytelling from the Elders turned out to be the perfect tonic for Cleo's troubled spirits. The weather was ideal as well. They had gathered around a large open fire under a starlit night. It amazed Cleo that the night sky here, so close to Montreal, could still be so bright. Bo found her exactly where she had spent the entire evening, stretched out on an old blanket, by the dying embers of the fire.

Bo collapsed on the blanket beside her cousin. "Ready to head back to the hotel?" she asked, reminding Cleo quite unnecessarily, that they had a big day ahead.

The last thing Cleo Deseronto wanted was to leave this place. The singing and storytelling were soothing medicine. She lowered her eyes from the night sky to see that the "boys," Albert and Cyril, were waiting for her as well. With a sigh, she dragged herself up, only then realizing how much the night air had grown cold. Cleo let out a shiver, and said her good-byes, before heading to the waiting van.

They did have a big day ahead of them. The flight to Iqaluit on Frobisher Bay, depending on the winds, could take more than ten hours. Cleo had taken the time while they were in Florida to complete all of the flight planning, with only the weather data to be added. She had even completed the flight planning for the segment of the transpolar tour that they would never complete, solely for the purpose of their cover. This night had been food for the spirit. Tomorrow would take them 1300 miles due north towards the Arctic Circle and ultimately set the tone for the long hours of flying that lay ahead.

Iqaluit Airport
Iqaluit, Nunavut Territory
Canada

The flight to Frobisher Bay, with the constant headwinds, had taken almost two hours longer than planned. The rising heat from the Boreal forest of Northern Quebec had provided non-stop turbulence. Cleo had tried several altitudes to get them above the unstable air mass without luck. By the time they reached Nunavut, the constant bucking and pounding had taken a toll on the crew.

Cleo and Albert had the flying stamina needed to endure the conditions, but Bo and Cyril were forced to tolerate the ride.

Cyril was the first to buckle. His pride had kept him from telling Albert that he was airsick. By the time Albert noticed, the kid was well beyond a fix of motion sickness medication. Albert grabbed him, pulling Cyril to the lavatory just in time. He left the boy there to clean himself up while he reported to Cleo. They both agreed that rest was all Cyril needed, and maybe the Dramamine they carried for motion sickness. Albert folded down the bunk over the fuel cells and laid out Cyril's sleeping bag and pillow. Cleo had insisted they all have a "sleep set" on board. Between the small custom galley, the three sixty-six gallon fuel bags and all the survival and promotional gear they now had in the aircraft, moving around was extremely difficult.

It shocked and pleased Cleo to see just how fast Albert could get around when she called for help with Bo. She had been fussing with a chart when she realized Bo was suddenly silent. It was easy to see she was struggling. Over the years, she had noticed an interesting phenomenon while flying in bad weather. If the passengers and crewmembers, even people with the weakest of stomachs, could keep things down, the flight always improved. However, if just one person were to vomit, a cascade failure begins wherein everyone, including some of the more hardy members of the crew, succumb to nausea.

Cleo barely had the airsickness bag open for Bo before Albert was there to haul her from the co-pilot's seat. He pulled her out and got her to the lavatory with seconds to spare. He then went through the same exercise of folding down a cot and getting her set up. Once Bo was comfortable, Albert leaned into the flight deck, checking on his captain. She was fine, even with her Cojo out of business.

"Why don't you grab us some pops and come sit up here?"

Albert pulled two Pepsi Colas from the built-in cooler and slid into the right pilot's seat, taking the time to do up the seat belt, and attach the emergency equipment tether. The tether ran to the first aid kit mounted on the bulkhead behind him. The idea was if they were in an accident and unable to move, he could simply pull the tether strap to access their store of emergency supplies, a satellite phone, and a Personal Locator Beacon. If they were down the Emergency Locator Transmitter would tell Search and Rescue "where" they were, but the SAT Phone would allow them to tell SAR "how" they were.

Cleo and Albert sat in silence for some time while they drank their sodas and followed the GPS route north. Drinking the pop was more about propelling gas than curbing their thirst, and both ended up laughing at their cacophony of resulting burps. It might have sounded rude to anyone else, but with the smell of vomit still lingering in the cabin, it was a lifesaver for the two experienced flyers.

"By the way, thanks," Albert said.

"Thanks for what?"

"For letting me take part. I think I had forgotten the medicine of the drum."

"It's hard, walking between two worlds." She watched him for a long moment. "Tell me, are they going to send you back to Afghanistan after this?"

"Eventually," he answered honestly. "They offered Warrant Officer Candidate and Flight School, if we pull this off. I don't mind going back though," he said, then thought to add, "I just wonder if we're helping."

"It's the question we all ask. Does our life make a difference for the people? Do you think what you're doing is helping the Afghanis?"

"Not always," he admitted, "but some days . . . when you get to see the kids, boys playing in the streets, girls going to school . . . that's when you know it's worth it."

She smiled, liking this soldier, and even understanding why he had chosen the US Army instead of the heading north. Back in the day, the only thing that the Canadian Army was into was peacekeeping. If you wanted more excitement, you had to consider military service in the US. She had chosen the Canadian Militia simply as a part-time job, until she could afford university, but her peacekeeping experience had changed her opinion about the opportunities a military career might offer north of the border.

Cleo flew for another hour before asking Albert if he would like to take over. She needed to visit the lavatory and wanted to check on the two sleeping beauties in the cabin. She flipped the yoke over while Albert held the unlock button down. "You have control."

"I have control," he acknowledged, before making a slight trim adjustment.

She sat for a few minutes watching Albert fly the Otter. He was well trained, displaying none of the bad habits she had noticed with other low-time pilots. Confident that *her* Otter was in good hands, she made her way down the center of the cabin. Both Bo and Cyril were sound asleep. There was no point in waking them now. They really had nothing to do and would only end up sick again, and a second bout with nothing on their stomachs, would be much harder to recover from. The trick, she knew from experience, was to get them eating the minute they were up. Nothing fancy; some saltines and a carbonated soda would do the trick. Albert must have been thinking the same thing, when he helped them into their bunks. A box of crackers sat under the bungee strap that ran the length of the galley backsplash. Cleo liked that. He not only knew how to think ahead, but also knew better than to bother her with the details.

Forty minutes out from Iqaluit Airport, Albert went back and woke Bo and Cyril. He had to help each from their bunk and got both of them strapped in their seats. With that done, he folded up the bunks and handed them each a little bowl of saltines and green grapes, with an unopened can of soda balanced on top. Neither Bo nor Cyril looked as if they wanted anything but almost immediately started munching, ever so delicately, on the crackers. Cleo smiled at that. She had been sick more than a few times in her flying career, and knew how wonderful a dry cracker could taste.

Albert had the cabin battened down for landing and was back in the co-pilot's seat just as she started a straight-in approach to the single runway airport.

Above the rugged Frobisher Bay landscape, there was no missing the airport, with the Nunavut capital standing proudly off the starboard quarter. The bright orange terminal building stood out for miles. That, and the fact that Frobisher Bay seemed to run like an index finger, leading all the way to the threshold of Runway three-five.

Bo's voice over the intercom surprised Albert and Cleo. "Is that a submarine?" she asked, in amazement.

"One of two," Albert informed her. There were other watercraft of varying sizes anchored in the bay, including a Canada Steamship Lines freighter, a Coast Guard icebreaker, and a three-mast square-rigger.

Cyril, a little on the giddy side, laughed at the mention of the Coast Guard sailing an icebreaker in June, until Albert suggested he take a look at the stony beach. Icebergs, the size of minivans, had been pushed ashore at high tide. There were so many, the beach looked more like a parking lot than a summer coastline. The airport was just as surprising. Cleo received her clearance to land third, after a BAe 142 from the United Arab Emirates, and a Swedish Air Force F16. Iqaluit, was a busy place. When the wheels of the Otter touched the runway, both Albert and Cleo let out a sigh of relief.

The ramp was littered with DeHavilland Dash 8s and Twin Otters. Two ski-fitted Boeing 737s, were being unloaded, while passengers heading to more remote communities boarded Otters, just like theirs, but still painted in the old Wardair livery.

Ground handlers marshaled them into a parking spot across from the First Air hangar, where a handful of people waited for them. Cleo noted their landing time for the logbooks: 21:48, or 9:48 p.m. Summer in the Arctic Circle meant the sun shone twenty-fours a day. The Inuit people, having long adapted to the endless days of summer, coped by simply keeping busy at all hours. Having completed their first long leg with the aircraft operating perfectly, all they needed to start the next leg was about a hundred and twenty gallons of Avgas and eight hours sleep.

Canadian Forces Station Alert
Nunavut Territory

The Canadian Forces Station on Baffin Island was the northernmost airfield in the world. The flight to Alert had taken under nine hours, thanks in part to a trailing crosswind from the southwest. Cleo was tempted to simply refuel and push on to Norway. The next leg of the trip to Svalbard would only take six hours with the current winds. With twenty-four hours of daylight, it wasn't like they would have to face a night landing at a strange airport. Svalbard was almost as far north as CFS Alert was. It was simply on the downhill side of the Arctic Circle from a North American point of view. The only thing that stopped her was the "know" factor.

Here at Alert, she knew what to expect as far as food and accommodation went. Once they passed the North Pole and entered Norway, they would have to deal with the unknowns, like the condition of their accommodations and if the Avgas they requisitioned was available. Better to bunk down here for the night and deal with the Svalbardians bright and early the next day.

The schedule called for a four a.m. departure. In the Met Office, she took notes on the weather anticipated for the next twenty-four hours. She didn't really have to write much down. The outlook was CavOK, or Ceiling and visibility Okay, for the entire trip. With the winds also working in their favor, she decided to push a little farther southeast towards Moscow. The new flight plan called for their departure from Alert with a direct course to Ivalo, Finland. The original flight, planned to take only six hours, would now stretch into another twelve-hour back-breaker. It would also shorten the next leg to Moscow, by five hours. The updated seven-hour flight would be a real treat for the team. Besides, when it came to the Russians, it always paid to be extra prepared.

In the aircraft, Cleo surprised everyone when she invited Bo to take the left seat. "You might as well get used to flying from the captain's chair. It'll be up to you to take off and set course from Tehran, so we might as well practice that."

Albert had already started teaching Cyril some of the duties expected of him as a crewmember, and stood blocking the cargo door while explaining the importance of not bringing oily rags into the cabin.

Once the two juniors were properly schooled, Cleo got on the departure frequency and asked for their flight clearance. That took longer than expected. It turned out that the Norwegians had planned a link-up for some photos alongside one of their retired DeHavilland Search and Rescue Otters. Cleo offered to meet them in the air and follow them for an aerial photo shoot. Photos of the Norwegian and Iroquois Otters flying together over the breathtaking fiords was exactly the type of attention that would aid their cover.

With their Departure Clearance finally granted, Cleo gave Bo the signal to start her takeoff roll from the hard-packed gravel strip. Within seconds, even with full fuel, the little Otter sprang into the air. Acting as co-pilot, Cleo read the takeoff, climb, and cruise checklists for Bo. The sky conditions were much more favorable than the previous day, allowing Bo to cruise the Otter comfortably at 9,000 feet Above Sea Level. Cleo let her continue to fly for three hours before taking over. She stayed in the co-pilot's seat, ordering Albert to replace Bo in the captain's seat. It was important that her crew get all the experience they could. Albert wasn't expected to perform flight duties during the operation but a little extra experience would only help.

Bo made it clear she didn't want to rest, but had to acknowledge Cleo's experience on the matter. Three hours was a long time to fly without an autopilot to ease the duties, and flying a cargo plane was a physically demanding job. Like Albert, Bo would get to pilot the Otter more and more, working toward building her stamina.

Cleo sat quietly letting Albert fly the plane. She smiled knowing Bo had the flying bug. There was nothing like it, she admitted to herself. *Maybe now, she won't give me so much grief about my time "just flying around."*

In the cabin, Bo helped Cyril at the small galley, pulling lunch together. Cleo had eaten before she replaced Bo, leaving Bo and Cyril to feed themselves and prepare something for Albert. When it was finally Bo's turn to fly again, Albert had to wake her up. Flying an airplane, Bo admitted, while climbing into the right seat, was harder than it looked. Bo was just buckling up when a Royal

Norwegian Air Force F-16 went streaking by their port side. A crackle came over the HF radio announcing, "*Velkommen*, DeHavilland Otter! Bravo One"

"Bravo One. *Takk du*," Cleo replied. "This is Charlie-Golf-Foxtrot-Alpha-Bravo, request joining instructions." C-GFAB, the Otter's Registration number, was required use in all radio communications. The F-16 however, as a military aircraft, would only be required to use a number assigned by the home squadron.

"Foxtrot-Alpha-Bravo," A Norwegian accented voice said, truncating the long call number down to the last three letters, "Turn left heading zero-three-zero. Descend and maintain five-thousand, five-hundred. Flight group 'Charlie' three-zero nautical miles. Bravo One."

"Bravo One," Cleo said in reply, repeating her orders while banking the Otter left and starting a five-hundred-foot-per-minute descent. The descent would take seven minutes before they could hook-up. When they leveled off, Cleo called for everyone to watch for the traffic, before she spotted a Twin Otter, and a single like theirs, just ten miles ahead and a thousand feet below. "Bravo One. Foxtrot-Alpha-Bravo. We have the traffic in sight. Request permission to join from the south?"

They received a new heading and a frequency change. After the welcomes and introductions, not to mention a lot of hand waving at the windows, they were assigned a heading to maintain, while the Norwegian Otter formed up on them. The chase plane, the Twin engine Otter, set them up for several shots in formation over and around the spectacular Norwegian coastline.

Cleo made a mental note to ask Rod Nelligan if they could get a few copies from the shoot. A photo like that would look great framed and hanging in her office. Of course, that would require actually having an office at some point. That usually followed having a job, a home, a life, and perhaps someone to share it with. Someone who matters! *I let myself believe she could care for me, that I could matter to someone like her. Cleo could hear her father's cruel reminders of her place in the world. "You think some white woman will see you as her equal? You're nothing but a dirty half breed. Go ahead . . . you can fuck all the white women you want, but mark my words, when the time comes to choose, they'll never choose you."*

Chapter Nine

Star City Cosmodrome
Russian Federation

Cleo was both amazed and disappointed with Star City. The assortment of various buildings established the facility as the largest complex of its type in the world. There was also a certain spotless but impoverished look about the place. On the drive from the Airport to crew quarters, she couldn't help but compare the worn suburban feel of the place to Toronto's Regent Park, the government housing project both she and Bo had grown up in. The squat two- and three-story buildings housing the Russian administrative offices and design bureaus looked dirty and mean, while the tall apartment blocks were something right out of the Jane-Finch corridor. She shook it off. It was still Star City. This was still the place that launched the likes of Yuri Gagarin and Valentina Tereshkova, and Cleo Deseronto was determined to drink it all in.

Star City was more than their current stop and a place she had always wanted to visit. It was their Hold point while they waited to receive permission to enter Iran. The Iranian government had already granted them permission to transition Iranian airspace and even approving one landing at Tehran and one takeoff. The unresolved issue stemmed from where they would pick up the liaison officer and where he was to be deplaned. As expected, the Iranians wanted a liaison officer aboard; they just did not want him out of the country. Cleo had offered to fly a published commercial route into Tehran, but that still left the issue of where the liaison officer would get off the plane, before crossing the border into the United Arab Emirates. Tehran was obviously more concerned with losing an officer than having the team running around the country unescorted. That was the silver lining, the team was not being considered any kind of threat if the Iranians greatest concern was not supervising them but losing control of their asset.

Sitting in her room, Cleo sat staring at her laptop screen. She was required to file a short Status Report every day. Before she left London, Tori gave her a simple code to use in her reports. She would ostensibly be providing the team's publicist with updates on their progress to promote the tour. Ever since Cleo discovered Tori and Bo were still . . . *Still what?* After the formal dinner with the Fort Drum brass, the senior American officers departed en mass while the sergeant majors joined Rod and Albert in the Library where the smoking lamp was lit. Rod had a case of Cuban Bolivar cigars he had carried from London, and had little difficulty convincing the other senior enlisted men to join him. Cleo had been on her way up to the guest rooms with Tori and Bo when the chief's voice rattled the window panes, calling out in his best parade square roar; "Deseronto, Front and Center."

Tori and Bo laughed. With a gentle pat on the arm, Tori warned her not to keep the chief waiting. Cleo reported to the library, interested to see what all the fuss was about? The fuss, it turned out, was her. The Garrison Sergeant-Major, just having learned that Cleo had served in the ranks as a peace-keeper, before becoming an officer, thought she should join them as an honorary NCO. It was a high compliment, one Cleo did not want to insult. While she could get away with skipping the drink offer with the "flying duty" excuse, she could hardly turn down a real Cuban Bolivar.

Smoking a cigar was one of the very rare indulgences she allowed herself. Truth be told, the last time she could remember indulging, was more than ten years ago, on a holiday to Cuba with Samantha. By the time she had smoked her way through an inch of her Bolivar, she had heard a number of stories about everything from Iraq, to Afghanistan. Of course, Rod Nelligan couldn't keep from relating the story of a night, several million years ago, when a spunky little Trooper crawled into a top secret test-platform of a Sea King, and rigged a homemade detonator to several pounds of C-4.

She always admired the way the chief told the story. In her version, she was the idiot who didn't know enough to get back in the truck and mind her own business. She had been there to take pictures, not to perform first aid, not to drag bodies from a minefield, and definitely not to rig a smashed-up helicopter to blow. To the joy and laughter of the senior NCOs she explained her heroism as a combination of poor military discipline and the foolhardiness of youth.

After thanking the group for the invitation to join the brains behind the brass, she left the old boys to their brandy and headed back upstairs. She had almost reached the landing when Bo left her room and knocked on Tori's door. Cleo had actually smiled at that, and then froze in place, watching Tori pull Bo into her room and into her arms. During their time in Florida, she and Tori had spent most of their waking hours together. After long walks on the beach every night, Cleo would retire alone and in-love. The alone part had been her idea too. Gosa, she chided herself. She was so confident of her feelings that she had been the one to ask Tori to go slow. She didn't want to rush anything. *Instead of waiting, like someone who actually cared, you happily substituted Bo in my place. Or, was I just the substitute?* Cleo asked herself unkindly, before settling down to file her report.

To:	Anne Waite, Waite Public Relations
From:	Cleo Deseronto, Transpolar Air Team
The team has arrived in Moscow without incident. Total flight time of 12 hours and 43 minutes. As a friendship gesture, Air Traffic Control re-routed us from Domodedovo Airport to Chkalovsky Aerodrome in Star City. This evening we were welcomed by a home-style meal with Colonel Hatfield and staff. We have been provided wonderful crew quarters at the Cosmonaut training center and look forward to tomorrows scheduled tour.	

Cleo sent the e-mail. It contained none of the personal codes they had devised in Florida to let Tori know how much she was missed. It did conform to the format she had been taught. The message was simple. Moscow Center re-routed them from their intended destination to a Russian military airfield. They had not checked into their hotel as planned but were staying in crew quarters at the Cosmodrome and had been assigned an escort. The Otter was now in the hands of the Russia Air Force and there was nothing Cleo, nor the Head of the International Space Agency, could do about it.

With that sent, she checked the schedule for the next day and shut down her computer. There was no point letting Tori or Bo get to her. It was just that she couldn't understand the motivation. She was committed to the operation. She certainly didn't need Tori to push her "duty" button, so why the subterfuge? She had to hand it to Tori for convincing her of her affection so completely. They had even sat on the beach one night, talking earnestly about Cleo relocating to London, just to be near Tori. That was the kind of thing that really hurt. Even if Tori and Bo hadn't actually spent the night together, and she was sure they had, why all the secrecy and why all the sneaking around? If it was something else completely, why not simply say so.

Cleo popped open her laptop again and hit the power switch. While the Internet connection was being established, she opened her e-mail program and typed a quick note to a Gmail account Tori had set up just for Cleo to use. The message text was simple: I know about you and Boudicca. You had my devotion from the moment we met. Why betray me? She read and re-read those three little sentences over and over again. Devotion wasn't the right word but she still had to be careful about what open text she sent. No doubt the Russians were reading everything they sent, received, and surfed whenever they were online. *Well, this should really give the FSB Analysts on the USA, and the Canada desk, something to talk about!*

Azadi Coffee House
Tehran, Islamic Republic of Iran

Hasid sat at an outside table, under a long canvas awning, casually surveying the street. He had learned early on that Major Suyfias preferred to meet indoors, where he would have more control of the environment. To that end, Suyfias was always careful to arrive first and reconnoiter the area ahead of time. This time Hasid had chosen the site, and time of the emergency meeting, aiming at upsetting the apple cart. Suyfias, so far, had played the noble officer, simply following orders. What his boss wanted, or who Hasid guessed was the boss of his boss, was a little play thing. While Hasid and his associates were not adverse to supplying some such merchandise, this was one request he had intended to ignore. That is, until he received word that a very special package was about to fall into his hands. Not wanting to burn his current business interests, he was sure the best way to proceed was to combine the request from home with his current focus.

Watching Major Suyfias make his way to the outdoor table was well worth arriving two hours early. Hasid stood to welcome the major. "Asalaam Alaykum."

"Wa 'Alaykum Asalaam." The men did not embrace, and the major, was clearly uncomfortable with their lack of cover. "Perhaps we will go inside." It wasn't a suggestion, nevertheless Hasid did not move.

"There has been a spill of sorts, inside. The owner will not seat anyone until he has everything repaired!" He watched as the major clearly wrestled with the situation. It was well worth the two hundred American dollars he had paid the café owner to keep the inside room closed.

Finally conceding the situation, and clearly under some sort of time constraint, Major Suyfias sat heavily, demanding, "What is so urgent I must meet you like this? Have you found a boy?"

"I think perhaps, but it is complicated. The people who supply such things have no wish for money. They have asked that in exchange for what you request, we will deliver to them, two women." Hasid watched as Suyfias considered this new complication.

"Women have little value to me, but I am uncomfortable with the idea of abducting Iranians for such use."

"Fortunately, that will not be necessary. The women my contacts are looking for, are from America, and should arrive here within days."

That information surprised the major from the Intelligence Corps. "I know nothing of Americans arriving. There are no applications from the American Embassy," he stated accusingly.

"My apologies, brother. They are from America but do not travel as such. They are Amerindians from a place near Montreal."

Suyfias eyed him suspiciously. "I have read the file. These people are nothing to you. Why do you want them?"

"Not me!" Hasid explained, hands raised in surrender. "These men, who trade in such things, have asked that I provide the Amerindian Women in exchange for a boy."

"Two women for one boy?"

Hasid nodded, "It seems a fair trade."

"What about the other two? The major asked.

"There is one man with them. I believe he is their captain, perhaps the women are his wives?" Hasid suggested lightly. "If I understand anything about these people, it is that they are enlightened about such things."

Suyfias ignored the comment, curious to know how a mid-level criminal of Hasid's ilk had come upon such information. "How did you learn about these Amerindians?"

"Ah, again, it was the men who collect and supply such things. They brought this to my attention. They say they also have a market for the man, if we were to take the entire family?"

"Actually, they are traveling with a fourth member, a boy. Did you not hear about this?"

"A boy?" Hasid did not mask his surprise. He had received a coded message ordering the immediate capture of the three-member crew from an Amerindian Flight team, who were expected to arrive within the next two days. He had received a complicated plan to move his detainees out of Iran once captured, but Hasid had vetoed that, sending an update that explained how he would infiltrate the team and accompany them to their next port of call. His next communique warned that handover could not be made at the next stop, asking if he could stick with the team until Mumbai. When he replied that he could, he was sure getting on board was as simple as convincing Major Suyfias that the team held some special value to him and him alone.

Temporarily contemplative, the major studied Hasid carefully. "Perhaps this opportunity can benefit us both. Detaining them is simple work but how do you plan to deliver them to your contacts? You must have a plan?"

Hasid nodded his confirmation. "With your approval, I was thinking I should be attached to the liaison pilot's detail. Perhaps as an interpreter? I do know some English and my French is very good."

"And?" the major prompted him impatiently.

"And, I would accompany them until their next stop, which is Dubai. My contacts will arrange for the Amerindians to be 'collected' while in transit to their hotel."

Suyfias nodded, appreciating the simplicity of the plan, and thankful the abduction would take place outside of Iranian jurisdiction. "Very well. I will arrange for you, and I, to join the liaison officer. We will fly with these Amerindians to Dubai, where you and your contacts will take the three adults. I will take the boy and return to Tehran with him."

"Why bring him back?" Hasid was confused.

"I do not know if he is young enough to serve the needs of my superior, but I will offer him first. I'm sure it will only be a matter of time before I am asked to find another. When that day arrives, we will call on your Russian friends to pay their debt."

"How did you know my suppliers are Russian?" Hasid was genuinely surprised.

The major's smile was anything but benign. Sergeant Mosaddegh, it is my business to know everything. And I assure you, I do."

Hasid nodded his head respectfully, while fuming inside. Whoever had informed his superiors of the Amerindians had failed to mention a child was travelling with them. Normally, it wouldn't have made a difference, but now? The distasteful request from Suyfias to find a young plaything for one of his superiors, was not something he actually intended to do. If the Amerindians had a child with them, there was no way he could let Suyfias, or any of his ilk, within a mile of the group. Turning suspected Terrorists over to the Mossad was one thing. Letting some sick fucker take their child, was something completely different.

Chapter Ten

Victoria Embankment
London, United Kingdom

The Victoria Embankment was one of the places Sir Richard preferred on cold and rainy days. The rain had a way of driving the punters away. Nevertheless, it was more than the isolation he enjoyed. For him, standing in the rain overlooking the Thames made London plain again. Plain, simple, and lovable, and not at all like the complicated tapestry of lies and deceptions that every operation seemed to require. Days like this always made him long for his Navy years. As a helicopter pilot and squadron commander, he had enjoyed the straightforward objectives of an operation. They were predictable; fly from here to there, rescue some people and fly back, or, fly from here to there, kill some people and fly back. It was all straightforward.

The Intelligence Service by contrast was complicated, not by choice but by the sheer nature of the business. Once upon a time, intelligence gathering was considered a "very good game of chess." That had changed long ago. Today the players changed sides at will, and entire Nations changed teams so often, even the simplest bits of intelligence were broken down and compartmentalized to such a degree that it was often impossible to collate data into something usable.

Today had been a bit more like old times. Sir Richard had churned enough disinformation with real intelligence to inspire his FSB colleague to use his alliances to get Cleo's team back into the air. The Russian Federations top man in London was also a Federal Security Bureau agent. As successor to the KGB, the FSB had been playing catch-up and was busy collecting favors. Sir Richard knew he didn't have much to offer the FSB man but the current age of churn could be used to the team's benefit. With little to no intel to bargain with, the trick was to keep the Russians thinking you knew much more. The real point of contention was his belief that the Russians did know a lot more about what was going on in Iran than they were willing to share. For this move, the chessboard would have to be discarded altogether, for an entirely different sort of game. This one was straight out of the American playbook, and could easily be turned against them. That was always the best way to play the Russians. Let them think your plans have gone to sod, and only they can help, if they choose. To aid with the discussion, the Americans had given MI6 a copy of a historical trade document between Czarist Russia and a very young USA. Among several "gifts" listed, was a one-thousand-man-strong Regiment of Mohawk Warriors.

The FSB man could care less about any incident that did or did not happen during the time of Imperial Russia.

Sir Richard also had a long list of antiquities the Six Nations alleged were held in the vaults of the St. Petersburg museum. The Air Tour team, Sir Richard explained, was more than a promotional stunt; it aimed to highlight the suffering the Longhouse Nations had endured under their colonial subjugators.

This didn't bother the FSB man either. Even if the savages were to stir up trouble, the World Court had never given them a platform. The situation did have the makings of a media circus though, something Moscow would prefer he avoid. The thought that Russia had once traded wheat for slave-soldiers would raise questions; there would be media requests for information and possible academic research applications. Having Russia linked to those who profited from the slave trade was no threat, but learning that the savages preferred dogging the Americans, now that was worth a little hospitality.

Sir Richard hinted that the Six Nations of the Iroquois had already reached an understanding with the UK and were willing to forget Russia's indiscretions too, if only they could help smooth the way for the Air Team.

The FSB man wasn't a fool. You didn't get to the top echelon of any security service by being stupid. Having Sir Richard reach out over something so insignificant set off all sorts of warning bells. While the allegations could play out poorly in the international press, public image was not his concern. Over the years, the Russians, under every guise of government, had been accused of one atrocity after another. Slave traders and grave robbers though, that would be new. Maybe it was better to let sleeping dogs lie. Better to keep the savages happy with Russia, and one more angry thorn in the American backside. Better yet, having Sir Richard owe him would be a real feather in his cap! Whatever the game, he decided; the best way to win was to play. The FSB man snapped open his cell phone and speed dialed a number while they continued walking. In Russian, he ordered that the "team of savages" be given all possible assistance in getting back on their way, including all the necessary clearances. That was all it took. He snapped his phone closed and smiled, reminding Sir Richard of his new debt, before walking away.

Within two hours, Cleo's team would have everything they needed to get into Iran and with luck, Sir Richard thought, he would have his daughter back in London before anything else could go wrong. What could go wrong? That was the real question that had him puttering about in the afternoon rain.

Spotting his car and driver, he headed to where they were waiting. The rain had soaked the collar of his overcoat and shirt, sending cold shivers down his spine. He had sent his daughter into harm's way on more than once occasion, but this felt different. This time he had sent her after Cleo Deseronto. Cleo had saved his life, been his friend, and more than that, she had never asked for a thing in return. He didn't want to lose her, but he would gladly do so if it meant saving his daughter. Instead, the needs of the operation and the Western world, had put them both in harm's way. He knew he was risking them both, but worse was the knowledge that he had pushed them together. *And for what? To displace Bo Commanda from Victoria's life?* Sir Richard shook his overcoat off before stepping into the staff car. He had pushed them together and had no idea why. *Instinct? The needs of the service, of the country? And when they figure that out, and they will, will I lose them both?*

Vehicle Simulator Building
Yuri A. Gagarin State Scientific Cosmonaut Training Center
Moscow oblast of Shchyolkovo, Russia

Their tour guide for the day was Nicky Thibeau, a French Canadian astronaut trainee, who had jumped at the chance to show her Mohawk neighbors around the simulator room. As they moved from station to station, Nicky, who had mastered the Russian language, would converse with the technicians for permission to climb aboard, or to answer some questions from the team.

She had started trying to explain the often complicated answers in her much weaker English until Cleo suggested she explain the tough stuff in French and let her do the translation to English. They were making their way through the MIR Space Station mock-up when one of the technicians started to laugh. He had been in the middle of a long explanation in Russian when he realized that they were double translating into English. Switching to English, he revealed an accent straight from London's East End.

"MIR you might know is not an acronym, but the Russian word for Peace." The young engineer turned out to be from the European Space Agency. He offered to assist Nicky with the rest of the tour and introduced himself to the team, shaking hands with Cleo first.

That surprised Cleo. Most men assumed Albert would be the guy in charge. She had a second shock when she took his outstretched hand and realized he was palming something to her. She finished the introductions, waiting until it would look natural to stuff her hand in her pocket to hide the secret note until later, when she could find a discrete place to read it. She had to wait almost two hours. When lunchtime rolled around, Nicky took them to the cafeteria with the other trainee astronauts and cosmonauts. That's when she headed for the women's washroom. With both Bo and Nicky trailing her, she was forced to sequester herself in a stall. She looked around carefully but couldn't detect any surveillance devices, which didn't mean they weren't there, just that she couldn't find any. She zipped down her flight suit and sat gingerly on the toilet, careful to keep the top of her uniform jumper from dragging on the floor.

While sitting and fussing to keep her flight suit from falling, she pulled out the note and read it: *Old friend from CBC Radio's French-language station is in town for an interview.* The Canadian Broadcasting Corporation operated several TV networks and radio stations in both official languages in Canada and all around the francophone world. The note also warned *TC Inspectors enroute. Expected tomorrow!* That simply meant the cavalry had been called in to deal with the Russians. She expected Étienne would be sent to clear up the delays they were facing, and it made sense he would pose as a Transport Canada Inspector. The CBC interview however didn't make any sense at all. Maybe MI6 was planning to use media attention to grease the Russian wheels.

She crumpled up the note and flushed it. *So Mr. EastEnders is MI6. Good to know.* Cleo washed up, joining the other two women as they headed into lunch.

While the cafeteria-style lunchroom was an ordinary example of utility, the food was surprisingly good and hardy. After the gruel they had been served at breakfast, the team had no problem cleaning their plates. When Cleo asked if the guys could have seconds, a large and threatening woman stomped out of the kitchen, as if insulted by the very prospect that she had failed to stuff one of her charges. Then she saw Cyril and laughed, shaking her bear-size head at him. Albert, with a little encouragement, followed Cyril to the servery and was rewarded with a second full lunch. They both grinned sheepishly, as they sat back down, to a round of applause.

Smiling, Bo warned, "You guys better eat everything or you know who's gonna be back!"

Nicky, missing the joke, corrected her gently, "Actually, they should leave one bite on the plate to demonstrate they can eat possibly no more. It will be a grand compliment!"

Cleo agreed, knowing the two crewmen could easily pack away the extra helping, and more. Albert, she could see. He was carrying more than two hundred pounds of pure muscle. Cyril, on the other hand, couldn't weigh more than a hundred and ten pounds, soaking wet!

Once they had finished eating, and the team got up to leave, the big boss of the kitchen marched out to see how *her* boys had done. Their plates were practically licked clean with the exception of the last bite they had left. Nicky had been right when she said it would be a compliment. The Kitchen boss squeezed Albert first with a huge bear hug, before turning to Cyril, who already looked frightened. She must have assumed that he was worried she would be mad and laugh at his expression. She scooped him up into a hug, squishing his head into her ample breasts. Cyril squirmed to escape her huge arms, managing to turn beet red in the process, which only made her laugh even more.

Everyone laughed good-heartedly as they made their way from the cafeteria to the waiting van. For the afternoon, they were going to experience being suited up for an External Vehicular Activity, or what the media liked to call a spacewalk. Cleo was so excited about the unique opportunity, she had almost forgotten about the note from MI6. Once they were out of the van and walking to the EVA Building, Cleo launched into a casual discussion with Bo. "CBC Radio is sending a *French* journalist to interview the team."

Bo didn't seem to catch the warning word "French," so Cleo repeated herself. "She's from the *French* language side and probably won't speak English." Bo caught it that time.

The French warning could only mean that MI6 was sending someone they knew, someone posing as a CBC reporter. This could be a warning that Tori was on her way. She couldn't guess what Tori wanted now, but it looked like she needed to avoid speaking English for her cover to work. Cleo wondered if maybe Tori couldn't pull-off an American-style accent. It was almost a joke in the American intelligence community; if you couldn't hide your American ethnicity then disguise yourself as a French Canadian Journalist.

Cleo's heart quavered, as the only fluent French speaker on the team, she would have to talk to Tori. *Looks like the Honorable Viscountess Dufferin wants to*

---

push me into a corner. Maybe I'll suggest Bo play the '66 Muhammad Ali vs. Chuvalo fight, and let her see what happens when you frack with one of us. We don't step back, ever!

International Media Center
Yuri A. Gagarin State Scientific Cosmonaut Training Center
Moscow oblast of Shchyolkovo

The Transpolar Air Team had been sequestered to the green room of Star City's new media facility, while Tori set up in the studio. The media specialists on-hand wanted to tape the interview and re-cut portions for a press release on Russian state television. Tori had tried to put them off, explaining that her interview would be in French. They could care less, as the tape would be dubbed into Russian anyway. Renée Rochette, Tori's current cover, acquiesced. The last thing she wanted to do was draw attention to her visit.

Tori watched carefully as the team entered the studio. Bo, who appeared to have been warned, was the first to approach her.

"Renée," Bo called out to her. *". . . une grande fan!"*

Bo, Tori noted, was as much a risk taker as Cleo, but lacked the forbearance she had learned to expect from her cousin. Bracing herself for the coming storm, Tori introduced herself in French, then waited for someone to translate.

Cleo introduced Bo, Albert, and Cyril to *Renée*, before introducing herself. She didn't offer her hand, and even though Tori pretended not to notice, it worried her. She had received the Gmail note from Cleo. It was the only time Cleo had used the account, and the note she sent hit an unexpected nerve. How was she going to pull this off? Cleo was keeping her distance. At least she wasn't blatant about her hostility. That was no surprise; she knew she could count on Cleo to put duty first. If she needed to act out some stoic Indian cliché to feel safe, then Tori was determined to let her have her way. *Until we can sort this daft bullocks, or I thrash the living daylights out of Bo Commanda!*

For the next half hour chairs were set up, then moved, then moved again. The lights were switched this way, then back, and several checks were made of the individual microphone packs and the overhead boom. Finally, they were seated and the interview began.

Renée introduced herself and her Radio Canada program then recited some of the details from the team's promotional brochure as a segue to her first question, namely, why a Mohawk team?

Cleo translated the question for the team, making no effort to answer it herself.

Momentarily surprised, Tori was visible relieved when Albert took the lead. He talked about the Six Nations being a sovereign state, recognized by the United Nations. He was articulate and charming, displaying all the oratory skills of a great longhouse chief. Tori appreciated Albert's effort. Rod Nelligan had described him as a "bloody good bloke in a storm" adding, "that one will protect our fearless leader with his life." By fearless leader, Tori knew Rod was referring to Cleo. His assessment was spot on. Albert, instinctively aware of Cleo's discomfort, had immediately taken an active role. Tori was pleased to see how well Cleo was protected, and shattered to think that Cleo felt she needed to be protected from her.

They spent another forty minutes going through the list of questions she had put together on the flight from London. Once they were done, the media guys wanted to shoot some additional footage and had the team line-up to show off their flight suits and a World Aeronautical Chart, which had been marked out with their polar navigation route, including the highlighted section from Tyendinaga, Mohawk Territory, to the Moscow oblast of Star City.

With Cleo keeping her distance, the only thing Tori could think to do was simply ask her out. She knew it was unfair to ask. Cleo would feel compelled to accept for duty sake. *"Magnifique interview!"* Tori said. Her heart was in her throat when she asked, *"Dîner avec moi? Oui?"*

Cleo nodded, accepting a business card for a taxi service.

Tori, reassuringly explained that the she could expense the cab ride, and suggested a restaurant where they would dine. Cleo wrote down the name and address of the restaurant phonetically, to be sure she could repeat it correctly later. Tori watched her do it, knowing there was little risk of her being side-tracked to some Bedouin strip club, not with her MI6 driver at the wheel.

Alexander Garden
Red Square, Moscow

The Training Center's Public Information Officer had drawn up a schedule for the team. He had been good enough to show it to Tori when they met on her arrival. The schedule called for an hour of personal time before Nicky Thibeau was to escort the team on a walking tour of Red Square and the adjoining area. Tori hadn't set a time for supper, assuming Cleo would leave when the others did. She wasn't meeting Cleo at a restaurant but had instructed her driver to deliver her to Alexander Garden. Not wanting to miss her, or upsetting her any more than she was, Tori had gone straight to the formal parkette and took her time reconnoitering the area for any undercover FSB agents. She was pretty certain the area was clear, but decided to stick to her cover anyway. *Who's to say we don't know each other from Canada?* While most of Europe imagined all Canadians knew each other, the Russians, much more familiar with the difficult logistics of such a large territory, would know better. Meeting Cleo like this was a risk but she couldn't stop herself. When Cleo's taxi pulled into view, Tori was still examining her motivation for rushing to Moscow. She caught herself jogging but didn't stop. She wanted to be the first thing Cleo saw when she stepped out of the cab.

While Tori addressed the driver, Cleo climbed out and stood without expression, looking very much like an officer waiting for orders. *"Tu êtes ici! Bienvenue,"* Tori said brightly before acknowledging Cleo's attitude. She did not appear at all pleased. "Don't you have a hug for me?"

Cleo stood stone cold still. Tori scolded herself silently, remembering clearly the warning Darcy Gerrard had given her. Cleo Deseronto was a survivor in all aspect, except one. Darcy believed that personal betrayal was her Achilles' Heel. Once it was personal, he predicted, Cleo would morph into her stoic Indian persona. As he explained it, she always maintained at least two options for every situation. The first was usually the customary "by-the-book" approach, which he attributed largely to Cleo's upbringing and military experience. When that failed, she knew Cleo would unconsciously revert to her fallback, her gut, and Tori was counting on that.

Moving as close as she dared, she suggested they tour the formal garden. Taking Cleo's arm, and gently leading the way, Tori was in agony by her physical rebuff. Every night for their week in Florida, they had walked, hand in hand along Fort Lauderdale beach, talking and getting to know one another. And, in all those walks, and all their talks, she had never seen Cleo like this. She had a good idea what had happened to upset her, but was shocked to realize how long Cleo had waited to say something. How could all the trust she had built be destroyed so quickly? How many times had she tried to tell herself she didn't care, and how many times had she been forced to admit that she did? She cared about Cleo, she wanted Cleo, and everything and everyone seemed to be working against that. Tori was even suspicious of her father's motivation. Why had he never introduced them? After all, he'd had almost twenty years to do so. Then there was the suggestion to get Cleo emotionally hooked when it was clear she was already committed to the operation.

"I think I know why you're hurt," Tori said quietly. "I want to—I need to—explain what happened. Then, if you're still certain . . ." her voice trailed off when she looked into Cleo's eyes.

"I saw you," Cleo said, barely above a whisper.

After the mess dinner at the LeRay Mansion, Bo had come to Tori's room, ostensibly to ask something. When Tori had suggested they discuss whatever issues she had over breakfast, Bo had tried to give her a hug. When she resisted, Bo had pulled her closer and kissed her, kicking the door closed as she did. Tori hated the fact that Bo truly imagined that everything between her and Cleo was simply an act. *Perhaps in the beginning*, she admitted to herself. That day in the office, what was that? At the time, it felt a wee bit hook-line-and-sinker but that had changed. How that had changed. She hadn't planned on kissing Cleo, but then she hadn't planned on the way it would make her feel, when Cleo rested those shaking hands on her waist. It was gentle and familiar, much like something she might have done a million times with Samantha Stewart, her dead lover, and that had angered Tori.

Tori had been overwhelmed by jealousy. Kissing Cleo had come from some unchecked desire to hurt her, *just like old times, is it?* Clearly demonstrating that she, Victoria Braithwaite, was not a casual replacement. *Well, that did not go as planned!* Not only was Cleo a great kisser, but there was something else. Something in her kiss, in her embrace, that was clearly new and not about old ghosts at all. In the moment, Cleo asked for nothing, in a manner that was simply genuine and not the act of a woman seeking a substitute lover. Since then, they had shared their innermost thoughts and desires. The long talks they enjoyed while in Florida had opened Tori's heart to considerations she had long ago abandoned.

Tori Braithwaite had the type of confidence that drew men and women to her like moths to a flame. When it came to it, Tori could "pull" with the best of them. That, however, had never satisfied her. She couldn't help but acknowledge the fact that very few men or women were actually interested in her; that is, interested in the plain old Tori who read history at Oxford, and dreamed of living on the Thames, in a converted canal boat. How was it that Cleo had taken an interest in her? The women who flocked to her were needy, often looking for a partner who could fix them or fill some unnamed void. Cleo, it turned out, was quite the opposite.

"Bo came to my room," she began. "I did not invite her. I should have come to you immediately, but I assumed you were still taking libations with the gents." When there was no response from Cleo, Tori pressed on. "Bleeding hell, Cleopatra! Bo made a pass at me and I sent her off, quite chastised, for it!"

Cleo sat down on the edge of one of the formal tulip planters, keeping her head down. "Now you're just being mean."

Tori's desperation was more than audible, "I would not have . . ."

Cleo cut her off gently. A measure of warmth had returned to her voice, though her body language remained cold. "Please stop calling me Cleopatra, you know I hate that. Now tell me why Bo thinks you two are still an item?"

Tori sat down beside her, taking Cleo's hand in her own. "I was dishonest with her when it came to my feelings for you; I thought well, it's early days yet, no sense in ruffling Bo too much." She groaned to think of how casual she had been with Bo Commanda. "I have now made it clear that my interests, my feelings, are for you. Which is something I will not put at risk," she could feel Cleo's muscles start to relax and the hand she was holding closing gently around her own.

"When we had our stopover at Alert, I caught her and Cyril drinking in the Junior Ranks Mess. After I handed Mr. Oblivious over to Albert for a little men's medicine, I took Bo for a walk in the cold air, intending to read her the riot act. Instead, what I got was a whole lot of Tori in my face." Cleo paused, visibly uncomfortable. "Tori, Bo said your father put you up to this, up to . . . me. And that you . . ." She wouldn't continue and Tori couldn't decide where to start.

"Let's walk a bit, shall we?" They started back silently, but Cleo didn't drop her hand. Tori took that as a positive sign, while trying to think of a way to explain the situation. "Uncle Rod once told me that my dad was sure I would fall for you, and, as a precaution, he refused to be the one to introduce us. As for my father, he once described you as one part philosopher, one part visionary, one part adventurer, and not a single part conventional. All of which sounded quite intriguing to me."

"Is that true?" Cleo asked. Her tone still reserved.

Tori stopped her, turning Cleo in her arms. "If nothing else, it appears that my father knows his daughter very well."

As if by some act of a forgiving God, Cleo slipped her arms around Tori's waist. "I felt humiliated," she said plainly. "I understand your dad not wanting you involved with someone like me, but I don't understand the suggestion to get closer, or why Bo knew about it?"

Tori could plainly see the hurt on her face, not anger, not accusation, not even distrust, just hurt; and it was tearing her apart. She couldn't hold back the tears that had welled up, and closed her eyes only to open them when Cleo began to kiss an errant tear away.

"The Cabala," Cleo explained gently, "says *God counts the tears of women.*"

Tori smiled, "Hebrew mysticism? Only you!" she shook her head, overwhelmed with relief, almost adding *I love you.* Instead, and barely above a whisper, she asked, "Come back to my hotel?"

Cleo, who was already holding on to Tori as close as public decorum permitted, pulled her closer, before whispering, "Yes."

Chkalovsky Aerodrome
Star City

The team had just gotten out of the Hydro Lab when they told Cleo the Inspectors from Transport Canada had arrived. They had been given the rare privilege, just the day before, of being fitted out in EVA suits, but the real bonus came when they were taken into the pool to experience the microgravity environment. The circular pool was more than fifty feet wide and at least twenty deep. A mock-up of the original Zvezda, or primary module for the International Space Station, was installed dead center. The team, decked out in space suits, were lowered into the pool on an open elevator platform with safety divers alongside. The feeling of being immersed reminded Cleo of wearing her old hip waters to pick wild rice and cranberries. The sensation of something cold pressing against her extremities, while remaining warm and dry was familiar and incongruous at the same time.

Each team member was assigned a safety diver and an EVA Controller, a trainee cosmonaut in this case, to advise them over their helmet intercom. Fully submerged, the green tinge of the water was undetectable, while the Russian lab was breathtaking even if it wasn't the real thing. Cleo looked around the pool to see Cyril not far from her. His diver was in the middle of turning him upside down and giving him a little spin. Everyone was having fun with Cyril. Cleo was amazed at how well the kid took the constant razzing.

Even yesterday, when they were being fitted with the practice EVA suits, the Russian Technicians had teased the kid about being too small for a space suit for a "real man," and that they would have to find one for a girl. Cyril, took it all in stride, even suggesting they look for one with pink command stripes. Everywhere they went, the kid had people in stitches, often unintentionally. It was good for their cover, but still, at home she would have advised the guys to KIO, or knock-it-off, as it were. Here though, she had to hope that Cyril understood he was receiving the experience of a lifetime. While the Hydro Lab was now part of the public tour, this opportunity to play baby astronauts was not. She shrugged off her concerns for her junior spaceman. She would leave Cyril's mental well-being to Albert. This morning was all about being an Astronaut or Cosmonaut depending on your viewpoint, and she wasn't going to let anyone, or anything, ruin that experience.

After only an hour in the Hydro Lab, the entire team had come out soaked with sweat. Cleo had just gotten out of the shower and into her flight suit when Nicky walked into the women's change room. Working in space, Cleo had to admit, would be just as physically demanding as any work she had ever done here on Mother Earth. The shower, and the sheer excitement of the experience, was all that was keeping her moving. They were expecting tomorrow's promised departure clearance in the early morning, but hoped for another delay, allowing them to play baby astronauts for one more day. When Nicky told her she was wanted at the airfield, the reality of their visit came rushing in. She grabbed her gear, and headed for the waiting car. Nicky gave the driver instructions in Russian and then, promising to keep the team entertained, offered her farewell.

When the car pulled into a spot at Chkalovsky Aerodrome, Cleo could see Étienne and Rod Nelligan talking with two Russian Air Force officers. Tori had warned her the night before about Rod and Étienne. They would be posing as Inspectors from Transport Canada, who had been dispatched to ensure the highly modified aircraft had not caused the Russian authorities any problems. Later she would learn that Rod had hinted to the Russian officers, that high-ranking politicians back home had taken an interest in the team's success.

Cleo introduced herself to the waiting officers in French, and Étienne shook her hand, explaining that the Russians knew some English and his companion spoke both English and Russian but none, except him, knew French. Switching to English, the junior of the two Russians took the lead, explaining that they would ensure her aircraft was safe to fly, and provide any maintenance work she deemed necessary. According to the Russian lieutenant, they had yet to inspect the aircraft and wanted to know what systems required attention.

Rod Nelligan, who had introduced himself as Rob McDougall, suggested she find something for them to do. "It's a generous offer missy. I would suggest you take these gents up on it."

Under pressure, it took Cleo's brain a few seconds to click to the fact that Rod wanted the Russians working on the Otter. "She could use her first oil change?" she offered. "I wasn't planning to do it until she hit the fifty-hour mark, but I think it would be better to get it done here instead of waiting until Dubai. We could also inspect all the new belts and hoses?"

"And perhaps," the lieutenant said, "we should put good Russian tires on airplane. Better than Canadian donut, no?"

Cleo laughed and shook her head. "You know us Canadians, can't be without our donuts!" It was an embarrassing fact that Canada had more Donut Shops per capita than any other country in the world. There was no explaining the Canadian perchance for Tim Horton's coffee.

"Well then," Rod smiled, "Shall we get started?" Turning to the Russian officers, he suggested, "Perhaps I'll have a quick inspection of the aircraft while my French compatriot makes sure missy's logbooks are all in order." The officers all agreed. And while the senior of the two Russians headed for an office complex next to the hangar, the lieutenant led Cleo inside to the guarded aircraft. She couldn't wait to hear why they were suddenly inviting the Russians to examine the aircraft but knew she would have to be patient and play along.

In the hangar, all of their survival gear lay open on the floor, along with boxes of promotional items. When they got closer to the Otter it became clear that they had taken her apart. Not completely, but her panels had all been removed and greasy handprints everywhere attested to the quality of the work. Either the Russians had yet to discover the surveillance package or didn't care.

Judging by the mess they had made, they had been too busy taking things apart, to actually open their eyes, and look at what they were doing. Cleo was angry. Her Otter was a mess inside and out. She started to say something when Rod signaled her silence with just the slightest tilt of his head.

Curbing her tone, Cleo said simply, "I think she needs a bath."

The lieutenant, for his part, either didn't notice how upset Cleo was, or had no idea what had happened.

Cleo may not have been familiar with the Russian military, but she did know pilots. And any pilot who found his or her aircraft looking like this would have blown a fuse. *If this was Trenton, the squadron Chief Warrant Officer would have everyone below the rank of Sergeant down doing push-ups, and everybody else running for cover.* Cleo stood dead still. She didn't know what to say much less what to do. Her first instinct was to pull off every panel and make sure everything was okay. That's when Rod put a hand on her shoulder and suggested she call for Albert's help. This was going to be a long afternoon.

Four hours later, Cleo, Albert, and Cyril were sitting with a handful of *Serzhánts* and their *Praporshchik*, eating a boxed dinner of greasy sausage, boiled potato, and some sort of unidentifiable vegetable, none of the team would eat. That had been very amusing for the Russian mechanics, who not only laughed about it, but also asked for their helpings. Earlier, the lieutenant had extended Cleo the privilege of being able to put his men to work. She wasn't sure who was more surprised when she ordered them to clean up their mess, and made a big deal of challenging their professionalism as aircraftsmen. There had been some grumbling and a few insults, but she hadn't embarrassed them so much that they didn't want to prove they could do a better job. By eight p.m. local time, they had the Otter tight and shiny again. The engine had been inspected and the oil changed, all the panels removed, cleaned and re-installed. Now, with everything back in order, Albert organized their gear and promo items, and began stowing everything in its rightful place. That's when the lieutenant handed Cleo a sheet of paper printed in Russian on one side, with the English translation on the other.

"You have been cleared for your flight to Tehran. Perhaps I take you to Metrological Office?" he suggested, a huge smile transforming his hawkish features.

"Now?" Cleo asked. "Why not wait till morning?" Then she saw what he hadn't said. The Arrival Clearance for Tehran read 08:00 Zulu. If they were to have any chance of making the morning arrival slot, and if the flight time stayed under the planned eleven hours, they only had three hours to get ready and go. Then she read the second requirement. They were to enter Iranian Airspace on a three hundred and sixty degree Bearing from the IKA Beacon, at an altitude of 17,000 feet. Cleo, much to the confusion of every Russian within five hundred feet, let fly with a torrent of every superlative sci-fi writers had ever invented.

"Missy," Rod called, walking over to join Cleo and the Russian lieutenant, "what seems to be the problem?"

"Forgive me, Inspector, but this clearance calls for our departure within the next few hours. That we can do, but we can't fly at the assigned altitude. We don't have oxygen on board, and without it I can't fly above 10,000 feet for more than twenty minutes."

"How high must you fly and how long?" the Russian lieutenant asked, pointing to the clearance form in her hand.

"Seventeen thousand feet for the entire flight. The plane can do it, but the crew certainly can't." It wasn't a complaint, just a statement of fact. They had considered putting a system in at Davis-Monthan but had dismissed the plan with an eye for keeping the aircraft weight to a minimum. To transition the Alborz Mountain Range, she had flight planned to follow Highway 59 south from the Chaloos estuary on the Caspian Sea, until overhead the village of Maydanak, then GPS direct to Tehran Mehrabad International Airport. It was a lot more work considering just how unpredictable mountain flying could be, but it did eliminate the need for O_2.

"My general," the lieutenant said, referring to the other officer they had met, "has ordered that we give all that is necessary. I will find oxygen for you." And with that he went after one of the sergeants, and disappeared out a side door.

Rod watched him leave before explaining, "C had a word with a certain Russian friend at home. They are now just as invested as we are."

Cleo nodded, letting Rod continue.

"I'll keep an eye on these lads here, while you get your weather briefing, and collect your crew. The equipment they use isn't fancy, but I bet they'll bring you the best they have."

"I'm fine with that. I'd prefer an old-fashioned manual system anyway. My problem is a night flight, for twelve hours, when I haven't slept and neither of my co-pilots has any night flying experience."

"Buck up," Rod offered. "If ever I knew a little filly who could run all night, I know it to be you. Besides, I've a little gift for you, and the Frenchman has brought you several splendid items your Mohawk Elders sent along."

Ten minutes later, the side door to the hangar banged open, and the lieutenant walked back in. Based on the size of his grin, he had been successful. As he joined Cleo and Rod, one of the sergeants wheeled a heavy Belarus tractor through the main door with an equipment trailer in tow. He pulled up very grandly in front of the Otter and waved to Cleo. She and Rod accompanied the lieutenant over to the wagon and inspected the chosen equipment. Cleo was blown away. She had no idea who Sir Richard's friend in London might be but these guys in Moscow were not afraid to do their best.

The system they had was basically four individual O_2 setups. Each had a regulator and altimeter and the mask she had seen used by crews of the big Antonov cargo planes. There was a microphone cord with each mask but she was sure they wouldn't be compatible, until the big sergeant pulled four sets of patch cords from his pocket, announcing with delight, "David Clark!"

David Clark was the premium American manufacturer of aviation headsets and audio accessories for airplanes and helicopters, and was recognizable worldwide by the olive drab color of the ear cups. Cleo had never met a pilot who didn't own at least one David Clark headset. She smiled and thanked him. The helmets and masks would get uncomfortable but they were well designed. The instruction labels were in Russian only. With no need to comply with NATO standards, nothing was in English, but everything was definitely new.

"Wow," was all Cleo could think to say.

Rod, speaking Russian, suggested that he, Albert, and the sergeants get the new equipment on board and calibrated while the lieutenant took Cyril back to their quarters and got Cleo to the Meteorological Office. It was agreed. The lieutenant drove Cyril back to the technicians' barracks with instructions to pack Albert's kit and have Bo pull Cleo's gear together while she got a weather briefing.

While the guys had been billeted on the main floor, Cleo and Bo were upstairs in the restricted access female quarters. Cleo had just returned from the Met office when she heard Bo's voice through the second-floor fire door. She was arguing with someone, and her angry shouts could be heard the entire length of the corridor. Cleo found the door to her room partially open and walked in to find Bo fighting with Tori.

"Mademoiselle Rochette!" Cleo said with surprise. "What's the problem?"

"I was just trying to explain the need to depart immediately to your insensitive co-pilot!" Tori said to Cleo in English, with the unmistakeably posh accent of a Québécois academic. "I wanted to pack your things. I thought you would be pleased with the assistance."

Cleo turned to the fuming Bo, "Are you packed?"

"I'm not going," She hissed through clenched teeth. Crossing her arms, she squared off for a fight.

Tori was about to say something more when Cleo stopped her. "Renée, perhaps you could check on Cyril for me, and make sure he gets Albert's kit packed neatly?"

Tori hesitated before quietly ducking out. Cleo closed the door in silence, before turning to Bo, "What's this about? I haven't got time for bullshit so just give it, straight-up, now!" When Bo hesitated, she pushed her again, her voice barely above whisper, "What the *frack* has you so pissed you're willing to throw your career away? And don't think you can crawl back to the Bureau of Indian Affairs without anyone noticing. Not with the *Company* you've been keeping."

"Well that's the fucking problem, isn't it?" Bo challenged, still too loud for Cleo's comfort. "It seems we've both been fucking the company. How do you feel about that dear Queen Cleopatra?"

This was bound to happen, and it was always bound to happen at the worst possible moment. Cleo had been honest when she told Bo there was no time to beat around the bush.

"Bo," she started, stopped, and then pushed past her discomfort, knowing honesty was her only recourse. "I don't know how you feel about her. Two weeks ago you said it was just a fun little romp and nothing more. Did you mislead me?"

"I don't give a rat's ass about her," Bo said, betraying her emotions. "I was just worried about her taking advantage of you."

She didn't buy the sudden concern for a minute, but was truly sorry to see Bo so hurt. If Bo had feelings for Tori, she was denying them to everyone, including herself. "I love her," Cleo admitted quietly. "Listen, I know you think she's playing me, but that's something I'm willing to risk. Can't you just let this be, without blowing everything apart?"

Bo stared hard for a long moment before dropping her arms. "I know you think I like her, but that's not it. When she told me about being sent to you, I blew a gasket." Bo closed her eyes and exhaled. "Back when Sam got sick, I pretended I didn't know anything about it, so I wouldn't have to visit, but that didn't stop Gran from calling me every week, keeping me posted, asking me to help. I guess I've been feeling like a piece of shit ever since Sam died. What kind of Faith Keeper does that make me?"

"The human kind," she said without judgment. "Boudicca, you are who you are. And I have always loved you for it, you *fracking* pain in the ass! Now would you like to pack your things? We have a flight to catch."

Bo Commanda smiled her most mischievous smile, "I happen to know for a fact that they won't leave without us. You're not mad?"

"Not as long as you refrain from sleeping with my girlfriend."

Bo, heading for the door began singing, "Squirrel's got a girlfriend. Squirrel's got a girlfriend!"

Cleo shook her head but had to laugh; Bo just had to get away with something. She looked around the room to see that Tori had indeed packed most of her things. She checked the drawers and wardrobe for any stray items and had just started zipping things up when she heard Tori behind her. "Everything is good, yes?"

"Squared away nicely," Cleo said, reaching out to her. "I'm going to miss you."

"Not half as much as I will miss you," Tori whispered, pulling Cleo as closely as she could.

The depth of Tori's emotion both surprised Cleo and assuaged any doubts she still had. "When I get home, will you be there to meet me?"

"I'll stand in the middle of the bloody runway and wave you in myself!" Tori whispered between kisses. "I promise you. I'll be waiting."

Chapter Eleven

17,000 feet above the Caspian Sea
Ten Miles Northeast of Dehgâh Point
Islamic Republic of Iran

The Transpolar Air Team was flying in circles, literally. They had reached the southern coast of the Caspian Sea at altitude, on the proscribed bearing, and well before the cut-off time. For their trouble they had been vectored back and forth, given altitude changes up and down, and were in the umpteenth turn of their assigned hold. Cleo had just requested clearance to enter Iranian airspace again and had again been assigned a Hold. She had been flying for fourteen hours now and had just lost her last ounce of patience. If they weren't cleared within the next few minutes, they would lose their landing slot and have to divert to Baku in Azerbaijan.

Cleo was just about to tell Air Traffic Control that she was diverting when something occurred to her. She flipped the switch on her oxygen mask from Transmit to Intercom. "Albert, I need you up here." Bo was surprised but unclipped her seatbelt and microphone cord and let Albert take her place. Once he was settled, she ordered him to take over communications with ATC. Albert understood immediately, asking for a little coaching on the proper procedure.

"Tehran Center," Albert said over the radio. "This is Charlie-Golf-Foxtrot-Alpha-Bravo."

"Charlie-Golf-Foxtrot-Alpha-Bravo. Tehran Center."

Cleo nodded, encouraging Albert to continue, "Tehran Center, Charlie-Golf-Foxtrot-Alpha-Bravo, is a DeHavilland Otter. Request immediate clearance for Mehrabad International Airport. We are pre-cleared and fourteen hours out of Moscow. We must land now or divert."

"Golf-Foxtrot-Alpha-Bravo. Tehran Center. You are cleared to enter Iranian Airspace. Maintain one-seven-thousand feet. Report crossing the coastline on heading one-five-zero."

Albert was stunned at the sudden change, but read back the clearance as Cleo instructed.

Immediately relieved, Cleo called to Bo over the intercom, "It looks like they were just frackin' us around. You might as well pull out our Hijabs now."

Sounding tinny and faraway over the intercom, Bo's reply was laced in hostility, "This is bullshit!"

"Affirmative on the Bravo Sierra," Cleo said evenly, "but we all expected this type of thing coming in. Now that we're in, we need to concentrate on getting through the next couple of days without any more problems. With any luck, we won't have to marry Cyril off just to get out of the country."

"I don't wanna get married!" Cyril wailed over the intercom. "No one said anything about me getting married!"

"Don't worry," Albert assured him. "That's only as a last resort. You know, in case we get into trouble and need your wife to sneak us out."

"Besides," Bo chimed in. "You already met her Mom, remember? She was the kitchen lady in the Star City cafeteria!"

While Cyril moaned in panic, the rest of the crew had a good laugh. "Don't worry Cyril," Cleo consoled him gently. "I would prefer to sell you to a rich Persian Princess. I think you'd make a wonderful harem boy!"

That made them all laugh and had the effect of evaporating the tension that had been building in the little Otter for the last several hours. Cleo checked their altitude and looked to Albert. "Report passing the coastline."

Albert nodded and called for the control center.

Tehran responded with a course change and step-down instructions. While Albert read back the instructions, Cleo turned the Otter right, for the new heading.

"Aren't they a little premature with the descent clearance?" Albert asked. He had every right to be concerned. They had yet to cross the Alborz Mountain range. Their 17,000-foot cruising height would take them safely across, but any reduction in altitude now could still spell disaster.

"Pilot's Discretion. That was the key to the clearance," Cleo answered, explaining, "Even though we are on an instrument flight plan, with the weather being so great, the controllers are reducing their workload by making us responsible for a safe descent. If it was night or the weather was a factor, they would never have given us the option."

"The differences between Instrument and Visual Flight Rules seem very confusing."

"Don't worry, by the time you get to Instrument Ground School this will all be second nature for you. Actually, you'll probably have more night and instrument flight hours logged than most of your instructors."

Albert doubted that but before he could ask more, Bo chimed in.

"Where the hell are we? I thought this was supposed to be some sort of desert country. Everything I see is green. Look at those fields down there. What do you think they're growing, Opium?"

Cleo shook her head. She had purposely avoided telling the crew anything about the Persian region just to learn their reaction. While much of the lands south of the Alborz Mountains were arid, the lush northern region was a startling green oasis of forest, farms, and orchards. "What you're looking at are family farms. They grow everything from wheat and barley, to pistachios and saffron. Higher up the mountains they grow orchard fruits and mountain coffee, even a little tobacco."

The northern region of Iran ranked among the most breathtaking she had ever seen. "It sort of reminds me of flying home from Manitoulin Island. You know what the Bruce is like in early summer, everything's a lush green, and Georgian Bay . . . well the water is so clear, you can see to the bottom of the lake. It's all this mass of granite in undulations of every color imaginable.

It's like nothing I've ever seen. You can't look at something like that and not immediately recognize that you're looking back in time. It's just one of those places man couldn't change."

"Squirrel!" Bo said, "I had no idea?"

"Oh come on, have you never been inspired by the Pacha Mama?" Cleo asked, referring to Mother Earth using the Maya name.

"I have!" Cyril surprised everyone with his confession. "Last summer, we had a sweat lodge down by the lake. It was so sweet! When I came out, I felt awesome, the moon was full and you could practically see across Lake Ontario." Barely taking a breath in his rush to tell the story, he waxed on, "There was this line of lake freighters heading for the Canal, and the women hand drummers had come to protect us and play. It was way awesome! I think I'll always remember it."

"The perfect moment," Albert said, seriously.

"Congratulations, Cyril" Cleo piped in. "You've experienced something many people wish for all their life." The crew became introspective, watching the landscape slip beneath them. From the air, the Alborz Mountain range appeared mostly untouched by progress. Heading south, the odd village was visible, seen nestled in the valley below them. There was only one road in sight, a skinny, winding, highway that connected north and south. They had just passed the imaginary halfway point for the mountain crossing when the visual differences between the two sides became noticeable. While several rivers flowed south towards Tehran, the range itself lacked the moisture needed to combat the direct effect of full-time summer sun.

Immersed in the joy of mountain flying, Cleo waited another ten minutes before starting a gradual step-down descent. Once they hit ten thousand feet, the team could ditch the oxygen masks they had endured for the last fourteen hours and breathe in the fresh mountain air.

"Holy shit!" It was Bo, who as usual, had drawn on all the oratory skills of a fifteen-year-old.

"Could you be a little more descriptive?" Cleo asked.

Bo had moved from her cabin seat, to stand at the pilot's bulkhead, for a better view forward. "That can't be Tehran?" she said incredulously. "It's so big. I didn't expect that."

"Fourteen million people call Tehran home. Surprised?"

"Hell yes! I mean, I don't know what I was expecting. Maybe some Persian village like in your book."

"You read my book?"

"Actually, I just looked at the pictures, but I did read all the captions!"

Cleo shook her head. "Well, that's something," she acknowledged with some admiration. Bo could make flipping through your work sound like she had devoted her entire graduate thesis to the subject.

Fajr Ashian Hangar
Mehr Abad Airport, Tehran

The team expected to be met by government officials when they landed but the fifty or so people, and TV crew, were far more than had anticipated. None of their other stops, with the exception of the Six Nations, had garnered much attention. Cleo pulled the Otter into a tie-down spot, before starting the shut-down checklist. She wanted to go over their rules of engagement one more time.

"Listen up! This is one of the few places where what we do will count as much as what we say. Let's keep in mind that the culture here is far different than what we have learned to expect from the west. So let's go over the SOPs one more time. Cyril?"

"I'm always first through the door or the first to be presented," he said, adding, "and I won't talk, and I will shake hands."

"Bo?"

"I've got it. I'm second on everything. I won't let anyone know I speak Farsi. And I keep this stupid thing on my head, and I don't shake hands, right?"

"You've got it, and it's called the hijab. As for you Mr. Wolf Clan," Cleo said, looking to Albert in the co-pilot's seat, "you are now the defacto spokes-man for the team, but some protocols will remain. You enter a room before me, and make the introductions and take handshakes and questions. Try not to defer to me in public unless necessary. Any questions?"

They all moaned, signaling their combined readiness. That was all she need-ed to hear. She had taken them through her expectations several times. Ac-knowledging their preparedness, Cleo retarded the throttle and fuel mixture levers. In response, the engine coughed, suddenly starved for fuel and stopped.

Bo and Cyril, who were now standing by the rear cargo doors removed their headsets, popped the door open and jumped out. Cyril chalked the main wheels in place while Bo snapped the tube stairs into the doorway. Albert was the next out of the aircraft. He had the Remove-Before-Flight flag for the pitot tube and a safety harness for the propeller. Cleo, the last to climb down from the Otter, was now sporting her white hijab with the bottom tucked neatly under the collar of her flight suit. Done helping Albert with the tie-down ropes, she remembered the gifts that had been stored behind her seat, and climbed back aboard. Cyril was already stacking their personal luggage by the door, when Bo began loading it all onto a luggage cart that had just been wheeled over for them. When Cleo emerged with the gift items, Albert already had the rest of the team lined up.

The first to approach were customs officials, who made a good show of checking their bags and the aircraft. A few photos were taken when Albert handed over their Six Nations passports for inspection. The yellow cover of the passports always attracted attention, and an unnamed Iranian authority made sure the team, and the TV crew, knew that this was the "first" time citizens from the Six Nations of the Iroquois Confederacy had come to visit Iran. Cleo had her doubts about that, but who was she to argue. If *Al Jazee-ra* wanted to report this as some sort of diplomatic mission, all the better. Introductions began, and Cleo could detect some relief when Albert stepped forward as the team's spokesman. She couldn't help but smile. Here they were in one of the oldest cities in the world, in big, modern, fourteen-million-strong Tehran, and everything was going as planned.

It was exactly twelve noon local time. They had made their landing slot, after a twelve-hour flight and two hours of being screwed around, with only minutes to spare. As exhausted as she was, she knew they still had a long day ahead of them. During the overnight flight, she had been able to sub Bo and Albert out of the right seat, and allow them time to sleep. Other than a quick trip to the lavatory, she hadn't been out of her seat the entire flight, and every muscle in her body was working hard to remind her of that fact. From experience, she knew what to expect and had already choked down a couple of Tylenol. That would help some, but what she really needed was breakfast and a nap. *Oh well, I'll rest when I'm dead.*

Once Customs Officials stamped their passports, they we're directed to join the *Al Jazeera* TV crew, which had set up an interview area, just inside the open doors of the hangar. They proposed shooting the interview with the aircraft in the background. Cleo liked the idea and agreed to have the Otter towed over.

Much to everyone's surprise, the reporter from *Al Jazeera* was a woman. She introduced herself impatiently to the team, then pulled Albert aside to discuss the interview. Albert stopped her in her tracks, explaining that he wasn't the captain, Cleo was. Everyone could plainly see that she was surprised by this information, and for a moment almost seemed unsure how to proceed.

Cleo stepped forward, politely adding, "I'm the expedition leader, Ma'am. Mr. Mackenzie is our Crew Chief, and spokesman. We believe in respecting the ways of our hosts. If it would be easier to interview just Albert, please do so with my respect."

The reporter, in her perfect American-accented English, studied Cleo for some time. "Are you the writer?"

"Yes Ma'am."

She took a minute to consider that, before clearly deciding, "I will interview him first and then you. You will sit with the crew for his interview?"

"Of course. My team is honored to participate." That answer made no inroads in placating the woman. Whatever it was that Cleo had said or done, the reporter was already offended. *And we just met!* It didn't really surprise her. It has been an ongoing theme in her life. People either loved or hated Cleo and usually made that leap within seconds of meeting her. All in all, it took another thirty minutes for the TV crew to finish setting up for the interview. Albert was placed in a chair with the team behind, and the reporter across from him. The Otter now sat just outside the open hangar doors and right behind Albert and the team.

With the stunning artwork on the old-fashioned aircraft and the team all decked out in matching flight suits, Cleo had to admit the effect, even on TV, would be dramatic. The interview went pretty much as expected. Albert handled all the questions regarding the Six Nations extremely well, even explaining the different rights and privileges enjoyed by men and women. When the "why" question came he, as usual, was well prepared, impressing Cleo with the depth of his oration.

"Why take this old airplane and why fly around the world? For what purpose?" the reporter asked him.

"When you learned that a group from the Six Nations of the Iroquois Confederacy would visit your great land, did you know who we were, or did you have to pull out the history books? Most of the world has been taught that we, the people of the First Nations of North America, are either extinct or were assimilated long ago. Neither is true. We are the survivors of the largest genocide mankind has ever known. We are still here. We have survived, and we are our own people, entitled to the same rights as any other sovereign nation. Our purpose as a flight team is to simply let the world know: we are still here. We are strong and proud, and we remember and continue to live by the teachings and beliefs of our ancestors."

Cleo marveled at how easily Albert fell into his role as spokesman. While she never adhered to the idea that leaders were born, she couldn't help but believe that the best leaders are not made but forged by their experiences. One day, she hoped, Albert would take his place among the great chiefs of the Mohawk longhouse. Right now, though, they were all tired and could use some rest. One more interview, a little hand shaking, and they would be on their way to the hotel and hopefully a quiet afternoon.

Taking the chair Albert had just vacated, Cleo waited patiently while the TV crew bustled about. Finally, the reporter resumed her place across from her and the lights were switched on again. Last minute checks were made for the sound, and then each of the crewmembers reported ready. "Are you ready?" the reporter asked.

Sitting up straight, she took a deep breath, "Ready when you are."

The reporter looked at her subject for a long moment before launching into an attack on Cleo's backward view of modern-day Iran. Cleo, a little caught off guard, let the woman continue with her scathing assault. When she finally finished, Cleo couldn't help but give her a hard time. "Was that a question or just your personal opinion on something you know nothing about?"

That seemed to stop her for a second. When she recovered, it was with the "Do you deny" type of pre-suppositions Cleo hated so much. Tired and irritated, she almost laughed out loud at the complete lack of comprehension the reported displayed.

"Have you even seen my books?" she asked, continuing before the reporter could cut her off. "My books are about the art of human shelter. If I'm guilty of anything, it's my complete joy of the art form and envy of the artists. Any distain I have conveyed would be for the West, and their constant need to destroy anything and everything they did not invent, can't control, won't make money from, or couldn't hope to replicate." Cleo then asked Bo to bring over a copy of her second book. Bo was way ahead of her and had already pulled one from each series out of the two boxes they had. Cleo opened *Volume One: Native North America.*

"In this chapter, I discuss the Plains Bison Lodge, or what the average person would call a Teepee." Cleo opened the book to the title page photo and held it for both the reporter and the camera to see. "This chapter discusses the design characteristics of the plains teepee, the materials it is made with, its versatility and mobility, and the actual application of modern engineering principles to explain why this is such an amazing form of shelter. Nowhere in this book or any other, do I comment on the culture of my Brothers and Sisters of the Sioux Nations. Likewise, neither do I comment on the culture or modernity of the Iranian people, when I detailed the stone and adobe shelters of Persian vernacular." To accentuate the point, Cleo opened the second book to a page with an architectural drawing of an indoor cooking pit. "Look at this. This is brilliant engineering! No. It's better than that. This is art! Five thousand-year-old Persian art, made for and by the people." Cleo could have gone on for hours without interruption, but saw the reporter raise her hand for the TV crew.

The interview was over, or at least that's what Cleo thought. *Guess I screwed up any chance I had of generating book sales!* The reported offered her crew a break. Once they wondered off, she accepted the two volumes Cleo offered her. The look on her face, while she skimmed though each, said everything. Whoever had briefed her for this interview had described Cleo's work quite differently.

"I must apologize. This is not what I was told to expect. To be honest, my past experience with Western women has been quite negative."

"Well, maybe that's the problem," Cleo said kindly, explaining, "we are not Westerners. We just live there. I could spend hour after hour talking about the similarities of our two cultures. And I'm referring to both modern and historic similarities, but most people assume that because our lands are currently colonized, that we have been assimilated. Nothing could be further from the truth. For example, do you know that we are not Christians? We practiced and maintained our own spiritual beliefs long before and since European contact.

"Another thing most people don't know, especially Westerners, is that millions of aboriginal men and women were sold into slavery in an effort to profit from both the acquisition of our land and the disposition of our people. Since our *discovery* by European nations, we have known genocide, slavery, and forced relocations. We have experienced the theft of our children, and had Western religions forced upon us. Our children were beaten for speaking their own language, and our Elders incarcerated for preserving our culture." Cleo paused, trying to determine if she had persuaded the reporter or simply delayed the debate.

"Perhaps we might start again?" the reporter suggested.

Cleo smiled and agreed. The interview, the second time through, went without a hitch. There were still a number of questions involving Western issues, but much more thoughtfully formed, and with a light on art and culture from the aboriginal viewpoint.

Chapter Twelve

This presentation was supposed to be just a simple repeat of Cleo's regular slide show, but for some reason she was nervous, really nervous. The interview at the airport had started off with serious misconceptions and she couldn't help but worry how things would go today. The Salar Street Bookstore had been open for less than a year but had already earned a reputation as the place for information on Persian culture and history in Farsi, as well as English and French. Many had accused the store and its manager of being pro-Western but nothing could be farther from the truth. What they were was pro-education, and nothing more, and the store had become an extension of that desire.

Cleo was set up in the small gallery space, waiting quietly, and honestly wondering if anyone would show up. Salar Street wasn't the largest bookshop in Iran but it did stock a wonderful collection of books on Persian history, and it hosted English-language classes. It was the primary reason the boutique shop had been selected. Cleo kicked herself for not bringing Bo along. At least she could speak Farsi. Her ultimate fear was that readers would see her work as a commentary on Iranian life by an outsider much as the reporter had assumed. She shook it off as the manager joined her in the small gallery.

"There is a line to pay for your book. Perhaps you will wait until everyone is seated?"

"Everyone?" Cleo asked, stunned by the surprise. "Yes, absolutely, why don't you tell me when to start?"

The manager agreed and returned to the store. Twenty minutes later she led over a dozen souls into the room. Cleo went through her slide show pretty much as she did anywhere, with the addition of asking if everyone was comfortable with English, or French. She apologized for not knowing the Farsi language. Surprisingly, everyone was comfortable with English and only needed her to explain a few concepts in more basic terms, which the resident English teacher could then translate. Everyone seemed pleased with her talk, but the Q&A always told the true tale of her success or failure. To her surprise, the questions were plenty and thoughtful, and stretched the session into a full two hours. More amazing was the fact that everyone had purchased a copy of her book, and most had bought both volumes and waited patiently for her to sign them. Cleo was more than honored. The small group had been gracious and interesting, and the session underscored for her just how out of touch the Iranian government was with its own people.

Laleh International Hotel
Laleh Park, Tehran

Bo had the key card out, and opened the door to the room she and Cleo were sharing. She headed straight for the bathroom while Cleo fell back on the first double bed. "I can't believe how tired I am," she said, not wanting to move but knowing she still had a lot of work to do.

Tonight she wanted to go over the flight plan again and review it with Bo. Tomorrow they would fly out of Tehran heading south to Dubai. They still hadn't been told if they would have a liaison pilot on board and if he would need to be dropped somewhere other than their intended destination. She would have given anything to be able to review the operational plan for tomorrow with the team, but there was no way for them to know whether it was safe to do so or not.

They had already spent several hours reviewing each vital step. Cyril, for his part had no idea why they were going to act out their little pantomime, but had simply accepted his assigned duties without question. One thing Cleo always insisted on in every op plan was a secondary on all positions. What that really meant was each person would need to know their job inside out, plus the job of another crewmember. That way every part of a plan would remain doable even if one member of the crew were compromised. This plan could be completed with only two team members, but would flow better with everyone's participation.

She was still brooding over certain details when Bo walked into the room. "Come on sleepyhead. You promised to go over the flight plan with me." Bo offered her hand, pulling Cleo to a sitting position.

"Okay," she yawned, pulling out the chart and the flight planning forms from her flight bag. "While we're at it, we should take a look at our actual fuel consumption and compare it to the flight manual."

"I've kept a record of our power settings for each leg of the flight," Bo said. "I think we have enough information now to make an accurate comparison. It's all in a spreadsheet on the laptop."

"Nice work!" Joining Bo at the small table, she slid into the chair and sighed. "It's too bad we can't get a forecast now. It could save us some time in the morning."

"We can. I'm connected, just pulling up the AirNav page now."

"Will wonders never cease?" Cleo asked absently. "This hotel has open Wi-Fi, but we couldn't get connected in New York State."

"It's quite a place, isn't it? I mean, it's not at all what I expected. I know I'm rambling, I see the look you're giving me, but I'm really seeing a side of the Middle East that I didn't know existed." She held up her hand like a cop signaling a stop. "You were right about this being a good place with good people. Did you see the look on the Imam's face when Albert presented him with the medicine bundle?"

Cleo smiled at the thought. "He looked so proud. He was beaming, though I think he's going to spend a lot of time trying to understand the significance of the gift."

"Are you kidding? After you gave them the teachings of the pipe and explained that it was the role of women to form a protective circle around the men . . . well, that just blew them away!"

"I thought they were just relieved that they hadn't been asked to smoke with us women! Can you believe the Elders made us pipe carriers for this trip?"

"Made you a pipe carrier, you mean. You earned it. On the other hand, the jackets are a total bonus. Can you believe it? I would never have received a coat like this," Bo said, referring to the buckskin jackets they had all been presented with. The jackets had been purchased "off the rack," but the women had custom beaded them in the clan motif of each member. Cleo's featured a medicine bear and a woodland floral pattern. Albert's jacket depicted the wolf, while Cyril's had a turtle. Bo's jacket was the only one that hadn't been decorated with her clan denomination. Instead, hers featured the same flower motif as the others but her animal was an eagle. While the eagle featured predominantly with most First Nations, The Mohawks only recognized three clans: Turtle, Wolf, and Bear. Bo, not completely oblivious to the slight transgression, was honored beyond words.

Cleo looked at the buckskin jacket Bo was modeling with interest, secretly wondering if the eagle was actually a crow. "Hey, have you ever heard the Haisla story about the crow?"

"Oh God no!" Bo pleaded. "Please, not some native parable."

"It's cute!" Cleo protested, undeterred. "One day, a crow was hanging out in the village, listening to the old women talk, when he heard one say, 'You'll never go hungry if you sit in a canoe.' Well the crow, who was always hungry, remembered seeing an old half-rotten boat down by the beach. So he flies straight to the canoe and sits himself down and waits, and waits, and waits, until he's so weak he can hardly move. That's when someone comes along and asks him why he's sitting there. Crow explains by repeating the proverb he had heard, and much to his shame learns what she truly meant was, if you got your tail out of the house and into your canoe, you could spend your days fishing and would never starve."

Bo had hung the buckskin jacket over the back of one of the chairs and sat down across from Cleo. "Poor little crow, lives his whole life just for fun. I can see how going out fishing everyday would put a real damper on life."

"That's because you don't like fish, you weirdo."

"I can't help it," Bo whined. "Fish taste fishy!"

Cleo shook her head. "What's the forecast calling for?"

Bo navigated around the laptop screen, reading bits and pieces, "Oh here it is. Winds from the West, at five knots, ten miles visibility in haze and improving as the day continues. It looks CavOK for the trip to Dubai."

"Excellent," Cleo said through a stifled yawn.

"Go grab your shower and get in bed." Bo ordered. "I can finish up the flight plan and customs notification. I'll call for a wakeup time and let the guys know when to be ready."

Cleo nodded, too tired to object. Tomorrow, she needed to run the op without a hitch and that meant getting sleep now. Normally she would have obsessed a little more, but tonight she was just too tired.

Fajr Ashian Hangar
Mehr Abad Airport, Tehran

Everybody has their own morning routine. Cleo, for example, preferred to wake up slowly and spend a few minutes getting the day sorted in her brain before putting her feet on the floor. Bo, on the other hand, still shot out of bed like some boot camp recruit. In response, Cleo threw her pillow at her rumpus cousin and rolled over. "Have you no respect for the workings of a peaceful mind?"

"C'mon Squirrel," Bo said, with excitement in her voice. "Move your ass. We've got a big day ahead and I'm in the mood for a Grand Slam!"

Cleo groaned, "Good luck finding a Denny's here." She swung her legs out from under the bedding and sat up on the edge of the hotel bed. "Uhhhh," was about the only thing she managed to say before Bo bounced down beside her, with the laptop in hand. She was already connected to the weather information site.

"Look! The weather's perfect for our entire flight. We even have a nice little tail wind too!"

She groaned again. "Winds aloft?"

Bo pulled up a second page. "I knew you would ask, and yes I updated the flight plan with the new winds. It should knock ten minutes off our enroute time."

They had planned this little farce in case their room was bugged. Now that T-minus-zero had arrived, she was thinking that between her headache and her aching back, the circumstances were just a little too close to reality. "You've done an excellent job, Bo. Are you up to flying this leg?" she asked before adding, just to make sure *everyone* understood what she meant, "Pilot-in-Command."

"Really? Are you kidding? You bet! I'm so ready. I promise you will not be disappointed." She bounced up from the bed, simultaneously shutting down the laptop and putting her flight gear away. "Let's get some grub. I know you're feeling rough, but I think some food in your belly will help. Now go do something with that porcupine hairdo of yours."

Cleo nodded, slipping from the bed, "Okay, give me ten."

It actually took them fifteen minutes to get ready. Cleo had insisted they drag their bags and flight gear along. She didn't want to waste time going back to the room for their stuff. In preparation for the day, she had stuffed her flight suit with cash, the credit card the CIA had provided, and her toothbrush and toothpaste. It was just one of Cleo's odd things. No matter how dirty a job got, or how horrible the field conditions might get, she could handle anything but a dirty face or scummy teeth. Even on survival courses, you could count on Cleo having a toothbrush and toothpaste stuffed in some pocket. Bo offered assurances as they finished packing, "Don't worry Squirrel, we have plenty of time to eat breakfast, get you cleaned up and shiny, and still be at the airport before seven o'clock."

When they arrived at the Fajr Ashian hangar, Cleo wasn't surprised to see a small group waiting for them, but was bothered to see how many were in uniform. She handed her chart case to Bo, before ordering her and Albert to see to the liaison officer, and the departure clearance. Turning to Cyril, she explained that the other two would act as captain and co-pilot for this flight, leaving the crew chief duties for them to complete. She wanted to get their gear loaded and complete the walk-around while Albert and Bo dealt with the paperwork.

They were halfway out the door when Cleo stopped, turning back toward the desk, she called to Bo. "You're going to need this." She pulled the credit card from the breast pocket of her flight suit. "Try not to let then overcharge us," she said, but didn't really care what they were charged for fuel and ramp fees, just as long as they were allowed to pay the bill and leave.

Out on the ramp, she helped Cyril load the aircraft. The important thing was to load everything exactly as they had practiced in Florida and during their enroute stopovers. For that reason, she kept hold of the laptop, and was now loading it safely into its galley slot so Albert would know exactly where to find it when the time came. The last pre-flight detail would be the installation of the propeller on the mini-UAV. The prop, a nine-inch plastic piece, had cost less than two US dollars, and had been purchased right out of a Model Aircraft store in London. They had actually purchased a bag of five hundred plastic props. Openly carrying a large number was a simple smokescreen. The large toy propellers were marked as commemorative souvenirs, and handed out as a set, with a balsa model plane and rubber bands. All of which and been heavily depleted during their school visits. One of the advantages of carrying so much "junk," was all the "junk" investigators would have to figure out. And whether it made sense or not, most investigators leaned towards things making sense. Carrying souvenirs for kids, was easier to believe than imagining how a toy prop could be part of some nefarious objective. The truth was, any inspector, with some technical knowledge and a little savvy could put the prop and the sUAV together. They had to hope their little diversion would provide the extra buffer they needed.

With the prop explained, creating an effortless means to install one was next. To quickly connect the propeller, a custom prop shaft was designed to install without tools. While the small shaft was less than two inches long, the custom-machined process meant they couldn't have a large number to pass off as souvenirs. Instead, each team member had received one of the small titanium connectors and had snapped them to their dog tag chain.

Étienne had presented the team with Canadian-style tags that would identify them as members of the Six Nations. They had all agreed that the Canadian design was distinct enough that very few people would associate them with the military and especially not the British or American military. Other than on Canadian peacekeepers and gung-ho thirteen-year-old cadets, Cleo had only seen them used once in a movie, the first segment of the X-Men franchise.

At the time, she was surprised that the producers had the forethought to use Canadian dog tags on Wolverine, but imagined American audiences would not be amused. Sure enough, by the sequel of X-Men, the scene where

Wolverine finds his old dog tags at the secret base in Canada had been re-shot with a standard set of American military tags.

In reality, the team didn't need dog tags, but Cleo didn't like the idea of everyone carrying the prop shaft loose, much less leaving the keys for the locked Winchesters lying around. She had insisted that every crewmember have a full set of keys, including the prop shaft that hung on a little retainer, making it appear decorative. If questioned, they would all explain that the little split shaft pendant was a talisman, used during the Sunrise Ceremony. So far no one had taken an interest in the tags, or the keys, or any of their specialized gear.

She had to admit surprise too that neither the Russians nor the Iranians had made any fuss over the firearms they were carrying. The Winchesters, four of them, were listed on the equipment manifest under survival equipment. There had been a number of suggestions on how to hide some weapons on board, but Cleo had vetoed that idea. If they were going to carry anything, it would be out in the open, for everyone to see.

The choice of the carbines had been Albert's and Cleo's to make. Both knew the stout Winchesters would take down an aggressive polar bear as easily as any liaison pilot. While the carbine, a shorter, lighter version of a standard hunting rifle, lacked the muzzle velocity of their long gun big brothers, it made a perfect up-close-and-personal firearm, and a good choice in a cramped space like the cabin of an airplane. With luck, they would never need to pull them from their mounts. The four carbines had been locked and secured in plain sight against the rear bulkhead, with two on each side of the lavatory door. All four security locks were keyed alike, and everyone had a key. An ammo can had been painted to match the galley, and was hard mounted, preventing anyone from removing it from the plane. The key that unlocked the Winchesters would also unlock the ammunition, giving the entire crew access at all times.

As part of the Otter's Standard Operating Procedures, which Cleo insisted be printed and attached to each passenger safety card, they agreed that the steel ammunition container would remain unlocked during every flight. None of them had actually fired the carbines, but that was a non-issue with this crew. They were all experienced riflemen, having learned to shoot as children. With the exception of Cyril, each also held a number of military marksmanship awards to prove their skill. To ensure Cyril was up to the challenge, Albert had spent time drilling him on the use and safety skills needed. He was more than confident that the kid could handle himself if trouble should come calling. "Trouble" however, was something neither Cleo nor Albert wanted to see. Not the trouble, they could handle that, but putting the kid in a position where he might have to pull the trigger on another human being. Cyril hadn't signed up for that, and they were determined he never would.

Cleo had just finished her walk-around and was climbing up the cargo ladder when she noticed Cyril unlocking the ammunition as per SOPs. "Are the Winchesters loaded?" Cleo asked. That was not SOP but a precaution for this leg of the trip.

"Yep," Cyril confirmed. "Five rounds each. Should I leave them unlocked?"

"No. Lock them up until we take off," she ordered then thought to add, "Cyril, you have been really great about not asking questions, but if there's anything you want to know, now may not be the time, but feel free to ask."

He was pensive for a minute, "how come no one ever talks to me about the trip after India. Are you going to send me home?"

Cleo gave him the only answer she could. "You are an excellent Maintenance Engineer and crew member, and I'm glad we have you aboard." She held back from saying more. There was no way of knowing if the aircraft had been bugged and even a hint that they didn't plan to continue on to India after Dubai would raise red flags in all the wrong places.

She looked around the small cabin. Everything looked to be in order. The Winchesters were loaded and locked. The ammo can was closed and unlocked. The laptop was in its case and stowed in the galley. The headsets had been switched around with the aircraft spare hanging above the co-pilot's seat. Cleo's headset now hung over the headrest of the rearmost cabin seat. Now all that was left to do was to attach the plastic prop to the sUAV. They wouldn't risk doing that until the absolute last minute. Ostensibly, Albert would snap in the little prop, when he made his final walk-around. If something happened to prevent Albert from installing the prop, they all had a backup prop in their flight suits and could complete the installation. Failure to install the prop would not spell complete catastrophe, there was a chance that Butterworth could glide the sUAV onto the target, but that was definitely a long shot.

Cleo and Cyril were standing outside the aircraft by the open cargo doors when Bo and Albert arrived with the liaison pilot and customs officers. One of the customs officers climbed aboard the Otter and poked around the galley and their personal luggage. When he finally climbed down he asked each a few questions in Farsi which none of them answered. Cleo thought it was interesting to see that the liaison officer had not offered to translate. The customs officer handed Albert their passports and shook his hand before heading back to the hangar. The two other official-looking men that had followed the customs officer to the plane remained. She looked to Bo and Albert for some explanation, but got nothing. She wasn't sure how to proceed but did the only thing she knew and took command. "Which of you gentlemen is our liaison officer?"

There was an awkward pause until one of the officials, the only one in civilian clothing, stepped forward. "May I introduce Major Yosef Suyfias. Major Suyfias has been chosen to serve as liaison officer for your flight."

"Excellent!" Cleo said, now turning to the speaker and the third unidentified soldier. "Thank you gentlemen for seeing us off, for your own safety, I must now ask you to return to the hangar, while we perform our engine run-up."

No one moved. The civilian official, who had been doing all the talking, seemed almost apologetic and uncertain about what to do next. One thing was certain, the spokesman was low man on the totem pole and obviously unwilling to put a foot, or in this case, a word wrong. Cleo groaned inwardly. There was always some fracking stupid thing. "What's the problem?"

There was a little shuffling and a few words shared in Farsi but no one spoke. Cleo turned her back to the two officials, zeroing in on the liaison officer. "Major Suyfias, this is my aircraft. If you have a problem, I need to hear it now!" It was an order, and Cleo delivered it in clear military fashion, which was their only common ground. In reaction, he turned his attention from Cleo to Mr. Low Man on the Totem Pole, who appeared to be translating Cleo's question.

Cleo looked at the major with just the slightest hint of distrust. "You can't speak English?" dumbfounded, she turned to Low Man. "Somebody better tell me what's going on right this minute, or I swear I will have the biggest *gorram chen-wa* hissy fit anyone has ever seen!"

The ferocity of Cleo's words shocked Bo, but it was Albert who figured out that Cleo had just put the Iranian officers on the carpet, and finally fessed up. "They want all of these gentlemen to accompany us."

"What? No! We haven't enough room and it will put us over weight." That wasn't quite true, they had plenty of load left before they hit Gross Weight, but they were definitely short on space. They had only planned for one extra passenger, and unless she put them in the overhead bunks, which was illegal during takeoff and landing, she just didn't have the seats for them all.

Bo instinctively moved closer too Cleo, but kept her voice loud enough for the Iranians to hear. "Albert explained that we only have five seats, but they won't let us depart, not without the liaison pilot and an interpreter. We tried to explain that we need to meet with our sponsor today, and that arriving tomorrow would mean the loss of our funding, but," she said, "they say their hands are tied."

"We have to fly with the major and *one* interpreter, singular, is that right?" Cleo asked. Bo nodded and Albert asked the men for confirmation that only two of them were needed for the trip. The interpreter nodded, explaining the situation to the second soldier. The second man simply smiled, shook Albert's hand again, and headed for the hangar.

"That still leaves us one passenger too many." Bo believed.

"Oh yeh of little faith! It looks like I'll be riding side saddle." That confused Bo, but not the guys. They were familiar with the term. "It means, I get to sit in the lavatory, which is listed as a passenger seat on the Airworthiness Certificate. "Albert," Cleo said turning to her crew chief. "Do we have another headset?"

"Only the helmets with the microphone in the O$_2$ masks," he explained apologetically.

Cleo thought about that for a second, a little supplemental oxygen certainly wouldn't hurt her headache. "All right, Cyril, please get the major and his translator aboard, and see that they are comfortable. The translator can sit in a forward passenger seat and give him my headset. Then set up one of the Russian O$_2$ systems in the Lav for me," she smiled at him before continuing to spit out orders. "Bo! Once Albert has finished his safety check, you can start her up and flip the Avionics Master switch to ON for him to test the comms." In an unusual show of respect, Cleo snapped to attention and rendered a parade-perfect salute, which Bo returned before thinking, "Climb aboard Captain. This is your flight to command." Quickly turning her attention to her next priority, Cleo ordered, "Albert, time for your final walk-around. Okay people, we are good to go!" Making a spinning motion with her right index finger, she gave the word to climb aboard. "Let's move."

Before anyone could board, the liaison pilot halted their progress, demanding to know why Cleo wasn't going to be flying. Cleo looked him straight in the face, saying plainly, "I have my period," then turned and walked away. Keeping a serious look pasted across her face, she couldn't wait for Bo to tell her how the interpreter had explained that. *To hell with feigning sickness, you can eat my hormones you arrogant ass.*

Cyril had jumped aboard and switched the headsets into the appropriate places, then offered his hand to help the interpreter aboard. Bo was in next, and Cleo laughed to herself when she realized the major hadn't bothered to avert his eyes on that scene. The rule of first-in-gets-their-ass-checked-out seemed to be universal. Major Suyfias, was stalling. Hovering at the boarding ladder, he appeared to be more interested in what Albert was doing than climbing aboard. Albert had already made his way around the plane and was farting with the rudder trim tab. Cleo stepped into the line of sight between the major and the big crew chief. The major acquiesced, climbing aboard without comment. Before following him into the Otter, Cleo watched as Albert snapped the plastic propeller into the fake antennae.

Climbing aboard next, she stowed the pipe ladder Albert handed up. He then pushed himself up with his back to the cabin, much as you would when getting out of a swimming pool, then swung his feet up and in, closing the cargo doors shut. Once they were buttoned up, Albert made sure the passenger cabin was squared away. With that done, Cleo waited for the engine to start then pulled on the helmet and tried the mask, calling for a check of the intercom. She squatted down on the brushed aluminum toilet seat and gave her standard pre-flight briefing with a few caveats.

First she asked the interpreter, who finally introduced himself as Hasid, to translate everything that was said, including all communications with Air Traffic Control. She warned that ATC communications would require him to be patient and wait until Bo was finished responding before trying to translate everything for the major. English is the international language of aviation, and even here, in the heart of the East, that standard still ruled. It was also the reason Cleo was sure Major Suyfias understood everything being said. Even as an Iranian military pilot, you just couldn't fly anywhere without being able to communicate in English with Air Traffic Control. She set worry aside, continuing her pre-flight briefing with a reminder to everyone that Bo was pilot-in-command for this leg of the trip and that meant her word was law. Everyone with the exception of Albert and Cyril were to remain seated with their seatbelts fastened at all times. Because a portion of their flight would take them out over the Persian Gulf, they were to don their "Mae West" lifejackets now, and keep them on for the entire flight. Smoking was not permitted, and finally, anyone wanting something from the galley should simply ask Albert or Cyril.

She let Hasid translate then asked for questions. There were none. The liaison officer had already donned the Mae West that had been sitting on the co-pilot's seat, but Cyril wasn't sure what to do with Hasid. They only had five life vests with them.

"Cyril, please offer Hasid a floater suit. He only has to pull it up halfway. You can tie the top half around his waist using the sleeves." She stuck her head around the lavatory bulkhead to get a look at how that went over. To her surprise, Hasid seemed to be pleased with the offer of the full floatation suit over the rubber keyhole life vest. Cleo couldn't blame him. Even un-inflated, the Mae West was restrictive, confining, and hot. "All right Boudicca," Cleo said over the intercom. "Wind up the rubber band, the Transpolar Air Tour is good to go!"

Bo released the brakes and inched the throttle forward until the Otter started to roll. She taxied to the run-up area, swinging the tail-dragger back and forth in an "S" pattern to give her some forward visibility. While she went through the run-up checklist, Albert handed out bottles of water. When the liaison officer waved off the offer, Albert simply reached past him and slipped the bottle into the cup holder mounted on the co-pilot's door. When they were in Florida, Albert had picked up four plastic cup holders at the local Pep Boys. Everyone had teased Albert and Cleo about adding the small detail. A cup holder didn't sound as silly now, with the cabin temperature already climbing above one hundred degrees.

Both Albert and Cleo knew the importance of comfort and being able to work hands-free if a situation should arise. There was no cup holder in the lavatory. It just hadn't occurred to either of them to install one there. Cleo took a long drink from the ice-cold water, then pinned the bottle between her feet.

Back in the passenger cabin, Albert finished handing out water bottles, then casually handed Cleo the laptop in its zipper case. She unzipped and discarded the canvas cover and set the laptop in an opening in the avionics rack that had been specifically left for this purpose. She pulled out the patch cables that had been taped behind the Black Box and connected them to her notebook, before hitting the power button. Waiting for the computer to boot, she listened over the intercom, as Bo was receiving their departure clearance. A minute later, Bo released the brakes and taxied to the active runway. At 07:31, local time, the DeHavilland Otter lifted off from Mehrabad Airport and started the long trek south.

Taking a peek back out in the cabin, it was clear it would be less suspicious if she kept the lavatory door open instead of closing herself in. With the Russian helmet and O_2 mask on, no one would even know she was talking. Besides, she had both Albert and Cyril to run interference between the front and rear of the small aircraft. Cyril was in the forward passenger seat beside the interpreter. The two of them were flipping through a copy of Cleo's book. Both men had pushed one of their headset ear cups back so they could talk without jamming up the intercom.

Once they were off the ground, Albert positioned himself in the narrow aisle between the extended range fuel bags and the galley. If anyone wanted to reach Cleo, they would have to go straight through Albert.

It was time. Cleo stretched up and disconnected her communications cable from the No. 1 port and plugged into the No. 2 comm port. She was surprised that no one had noticed or asked why the lavatory had two communication ports. When she pushed the plug into the second port, the cabin Paratrooper Jump lights turned red. That would tell the crew she was live with MI6 and to cover for her. She peeked out around the lav bulkhead again. No one seemed to have noticed the jump lights come on. Thankfully, it was a very sunny day and the sheer brightness made the red light barely noticeable. Cleo pulled the laptop from the rack and set it on her knees. Opening a DOS window, she typed: CD SQUIRREL\SQUIRREL\PRELAUNCH\DIAG LOAD.

Several control windows popped open then minimized as the program spun to life. A moment later she heard a familiar voice over the helmet speakers. "Momma Squirrel, this is Big Dog." Major Butterworth's smooth New England accent was unmistakable.

"Big Dog, Momma Squirrel. We read you five by five." Cleo replied. She hadn't chosen the call signs and had groaned when the whole animal thing came up. Even that had been a headache. They had wanted to avoid any of the names that DeHavilland and similar aircraft manufactures used. That did cause some problems, what with DeHavilland already using most of the woodland creature names in common use. *With all animals to choose from, I still end up with Squirrel. At least no one's calling me Momma Beaver or Big Buffalo,* Cleo thought. With the sUAV now nicknamed the Flying Squirrel, Cleo ended up with Momma Squirrel. Butterworth, who would pilot the sUAV, was Big Dog, and Tori, as operational controller, had been assigned Mother Hen.

"Momma Squirrel, this is Mother Hen, you're streaming live data five by five. We read all diagnostics green. Verify?"

"Affirmative," Cleo replied, welcoming the sound of Tori's voice. "On course one-niner-zero, at eight thousand, five hundred, Request Calisto . . . five degrees."

Tori ordered her to stand by while they ran the course correction through the simulator. A code word had been assigned for each direction of possible course changes: Up, down, left and right. Calisto, Jupiter's fourth-primary moon, was used to indicate a change to the right or starboard side of the airplane. Tori's voice was crystal clear over the satellite uplink. "Momma Squirrel, Calisto approved. Big Dog requests second Calisto at Release minus ten."

Cleo, checking the countdown timer, agreeing with Butterworth. Two small changes in the aircraft direction would be less noticeable than one big change. On the laptop screen, she watched, as the changes to the flight instruments were input from somewhere in Vauxhall. Bo would now find she was five degrees off-course from her assigned heading and would need to make a small five degree correction. From where the liaison officer was sitting, the change would appear to be nothing more than a simple heading adjustment.

With two windows open on the laptop, she was monitoring the status of the flying squirrel. At the moment, all of her navigation and photo acquisition programming was being downloaded. They had added that precaution for the sake of the crew. If they had been caught with the surveillance package on board, the hard drive would be void of any data indicating a mission or target. The secondary window showed that the download was complete and the files were unpacking. The countdown clock displayed twenty-one minutes to the five mile target range. The target circle was actually shaped like a bowl. The farther they released the sUAV from the target, the higher they would need to be.

The sUAV had a 1:2 glide ratio; for every 1,000 feet of altitude above ground, the Flying Squirrel could glide 2,000 feet in distance without the use of power. At their current altitude, it would glide a mile and a half before the engine switch was remotely engaged, leaving enough power to fly up to five miles or fifteen minutes. That's all they had; fifteen minutes of guaranteed flight time. If they couldn't get close enough, they wouldn't have the range to complete the operation. Everything depended on Bo getting the Otter as close to the target as possible.

"Momma Squirrel," Tori's voice called over Cleo's helmet speaker. "Oberon reports three Pax on board. Confirm?"

"Negative, Mother Hen. Two Pax on board, just the horse and the horse's mouth."

There was a long delay before Tori's voice was heard again. "Momma Squirrel, Mother Hen. Say initials Pax One and Two."

"Pax One . . . Alpha Sierra, is a Code-Three. Pax Two . . . Hotel, no last initial," Cleo said, while checking the cabin to be sure all was in order. The countdown timer now read Time to Release: sixteen minutes. "Mother Hen, this is Momma Squirrel. Is there a problem?"

"Affirmative, Momma Squirrel." Tori answered. "Pax Three was your liaison pilot. Pax Two is as yet unknown. Pax One is Charlie India. Risk Level: Extremely High."

Pax was an old airline abbreviation for passenger, and was used throughout the aviation world, but that wasn't what concerned Cleo. The CI code, read phonetically as Charlie India meant the major, sitting beside Bo, was not a pilot at all but a military officer from Iran's counter-intelligence service. Was someone on to them, or were the Iranians just being extra cautious? Cleo looked over the flight instruments displayed on her laptop. Bo was on course and everything looked good. She closed her eyes and exhaled heavily behind the O$_2$ mask. *Now we have to figure out if Major Suyfias, and chatty-Cathy Hasid are armed, and if my crew is compromised? Some days, I just love this job.*

"Mother Hen," Cleo called to the team at Vauxhall. "Expediting immediate ATC climb to 13,500 feet ASL. Does Pax one speak English?"

"Momma Squirrel. This is Big Dog. Stand by your climb."

"Momma Squirrel, Mother Hen. Affirmative! Pax One is fluent in English."

Cleo swore to herself as she listened to the rest of Tori's report on the Iranian counter-intelligence officer. Once quickly briefed, and with Butterworth's approval to climb, she pulled off her oxygen mask and helmet, and called to Albert. He leaned into the lavatory door and lowered his head close to Cleo's. "The major is Iranian counter-intelligence and he speaks English. Mother Hen thinks he may try to order us down for an *Inspection* before we leave Iran."

There was no need to explain the obvious to Albert. He knew better than most that the photo port would be conspicuously empty when they landed. "I want you to suggest to Bo that we climb to 13,500 feet—say it's too turbulent at this altitude for me. Tell them I'm sick or something. Then get you, Bo and Major phony-baloney on oxygen. That will give you a reason to crawl around the pilot's seats and try and figure out if he's carrying a weapon."

"You're thinking an ankle-holster?" Albert asked.

Cleo nodded, and then looked at the laptop. "We are Release minus twelve. Get her to climb, and be ready to take out that SOB!"

Albert nodded and turned back to the cabin. His "off" intercom discussion with the team's leader had caught everyone's attention. Albert reached into several of the galley drawers and turning back to Cleo, handed her two Tylenol, and a barf bag. She swallowed the tablets while everyone watched, then pulled the helmet and mask back on, and appeared to play with the mixture level on the O_2 controller. Albert made his way up the narrow aisle and stuck his head in the flight deck door. Over the intercom he said, for everyone to hear, "Bo, she's pretty sick. Any chance we can climb to thirteen thousand, five hundred? It's legal if we don't keep it up for more than thirty minutes, but I'll set up the O_2 as well."

"You think a few extra thousand feet will make a difference?" she asked.

"Yeah," Albert confirmed before adding, "at least until the motion sickness pills kick-in."

Major Suyfias had been watching the two of them intently, and asked something that Hasid translated. "What did you give her for the sickness?" It was a challenge and not a friendly question. Albert was caught for a second, but Bo chimed in with the name of the only nausea medication she knew of.

"Gravol." Bo said. "She takes Gravol for nausea. I prefer the Dramamine myself."

The two Iranians went back and forth over that one, giving Bo the opportunity to request the altitude change, and start her climb before the liaison officer could protest. Taking her hands off the control yoke, just long enough to pull off her headset, she replaced it with the Russian flight helmet and mask. Albert had already set the mixture to twenty percent and had switched her microphone cords.

With Bo's hands back on the controls and her attention on flying, Albert got the co-pilot's position set up including crawling half under the seat to secure the O_2 bottle. He showed the major how the system worked, and joked that it was probably the exact same setup as the Iranian Air Force used. When he finally tucked the bottle behind the seat, he reset the flow meter to ten percent O_2 hoping it would make the gun-toting spook sleepy. Contrary to Cleo's order, he then placed Hasid on the last O_2 bottle. Both he and Cyril were young enough that twenty minutes above 10,000 feet would have little effect. But setting both of their passenger oxygen levels at ten percent would slow down their reaction time, especially now that he knew Major Suyfias was armed. Albert took his headset off and rubbed his ears, then motioned for Cyril to do the same. He suggested Cyril plant himself in the rear passenger seat, and be ready to grab their Winchesters.

Wide-eyed, Cyril got up from his seat and moved to the rear of the cabin. Albert planted himself, tree-like, in the doorway of the flight deck.

At the moment he had his back turned, ostensibly to supervise Cyril, but he was actually waiting to signal Cleo.

When she looked up to check on things, he gave her a thumbs up. To Hasid, sitting in the passenger seat beside him, it would look like he wanted Cleo to know they were climbing. To Cleo, it confirmed that the major from Iranian Intelligence had a firearm on her airplane. She swore to herself, and was again relieved that the mask hid any expression on her face. "Mother Hen, this is Momma Squirrel. We confirm Pax One is packing minimum one heater."

She thought about the code she had just created, but knew Major Butterworth, or any of the Americans in the room, would translate the code to mean a semi-automatic pistol. Cleo could feel the aircraft leveling off, and knew Bo had reached altitude. Vauxhall had already added another five degree Calisto correction to keep Bo on the operational course, and ATC had yet to notice, or at least mention it. That was how it was supposed to work. In four minutes they would release the Flying Squirrel, and then bring Bo back on course.

"Time to Release, three minutes." Cleo could hardly breathe, and made a silent prayer, thanking the Creator for protecting her crew. On the small laptop screen she could monitor both the readiness of the sUAV and the flight instruments. Bo was right on course, with heading and altitude. The actual track line was ten degrees west of their reported position. Perfect . . . so far. Everything was nominal, including the pre-flight diagnostics for the Flying Squirrel.

At Release minus two minutes, Cleo had to force herself to breathe, turning her attentions temporarily to Cyril, who was carefully watching their passengers. Hasid, looked funny. The orange floater suit gave the impression he was wearing ski pants, while his upper torso was draped in a cheap summer suit jacket that had to be two sizes too large. *What does that make you?*

"Release minus one minute," a nameless voice chimed in from Vauxhall.

Albert was on the long headphone cord and could move around the crowded cabin without limitation. Once Cyril had moved back to the aft passenger seat, Albert had planted himself beside Hasid, blocking the pilot's bulkhead door.

Now sitting in the single rear seat, Cyril, without anyone noticing, unlocked the mounting clamps on two of the Winchesters. With his arm behind him, he casually swung one of the carbines from its position behind his seat, into the doorway of the lavatory. Cleo now had one of the Winchesters at her side, while a second stood behind Cyril's seat. They were ready. As if she could read minds, Tori's voice rang in over the satellite uplink. "Momma squirrel, Mother Hen. Requests Go status?"

There were only two code words assigned to the operation's go/no-go status "Ariel." Cleo said. That meant the operation, from the Otter's perspective, was a go.

Tori ran the countdown for the drop. "Release minus five . . . four . . . three . . . Release servo answering, all systems green, Flying Squirrel away."

Cleo felt a slight rumbling under her feet and a pop, as the sUAV fell away from the Otter's tail. "Momma Squirrel here, we have separation."

Major Butterworth's voice was next. "Separation is clean, inversion sequence complete. Squirrel is on target and in range."

Yes! Cleo had been worried about the funny little maneuver that was required to set the sUAV upright in flight, from its upside down mounting position on the belly of the plane.

Tori's voice came over the satellite uplink. "Momma Squirrel, this is Mother Hen. Ariel, Ariel. Squirrel is away cleanly. Suggest Ganymede ten."

Cleo hadn't realized it until she exhaled, but she had been hanging onto the fore stock of the hidden Winchester with a white-knuckled death grip. She eased her hand from the weapon and took a deep breath. The mission wasn't a success, not yet. Ariel repeated three times would indicate their success, but the Otter and her crew, had done their part. All that was left now was to get away with it. "Mother Hen, Momma Squirrel. Request Ganymede in two steps." Cleo was asking Tori to start correcting the heading error in the instruments with two small changes. Almost immediately, the first five-degree input changed the instrument display and she could feel Bo making the tiny correction to the left.

Cleo poked her head around the lavatory bulkhead. It looked like Hasid was almost asleep. She couldn't see what condition the major was in, but had to assume he was alert. With her attention back on the laptop, she clicked open the navigation page. The page displayed the flight progress for the Flying Squirrel. Cleo had every faith in the Marine Corps pilot and a million concerns with their little creation.

Tori's voice pulled her back, "Momma Squirrel, Mother Hen. We are ready to send the second Ganymede for course reacquisition."

"Mother Hen, Momma Squirrel. Wilco." Cleo answered, indicating their "willingness to comply" then thought to ask. "Do we have special instructions for Pax handling?"

"Stand by one," Tori ordered.

There was nothing she could do now but wait.

The release point had been perfect, putting the Squirrel three miles north and 13,500 feet above the target. That would allow the major to glide the Squirrel, with the power off, for more than two-and-a-half miles. The tail wind had also pushed the little sUAV even farther. Butterworth had just powered the electric motor on, and was skirting the elevation at five hundred feet above the ground. Cleo couldn't believe how much more refined the sUAVs software had become, since she last witnessed the practice run. The terrain data looked good, and she suspected that Guy and Nici had spent every waking moment on it. If the data they were collecting was as good as the GUI, Butterworth would have no problems completing the operation successfully.

The Flying Squirrel reached the valley wall and started her descent for the short river run. Approaching from the north, she cleared the horseshoe end of the valley with a hundred feet to spare, and then dived down another hundred feet below the canyon rim. Major Butterworth had used eight of the precious fifteen minutes of operating time getting to the target. The seven minutes remaining was enough for three possible passes, providing the Squirrel went without detection. Back at Vauxhall, Cleo knew they would have a number of data screens displayed including the satellite surveillance of the area. They would have a bird's eye view of the operation, while she would have to watch over their little squirrel from the pilot's perspective, and without the added big brother view from space.

The Squirrel made its first successful pass of the valley. Butterworth, who had to be loving this, used a chandelle maneuver to bring her around quickly, before dropping his altitude by another fifty feet. By now, the analysts at Vauxhall would be ripping through the data for targets of opportunity. Cleo could see the interrogation details being transmitted via the satellite uplink from the Otter. The Squirrel was honing in on the hidden facility and she couldn't believe the amount of data pouring in.

At the end of the second run, Major Butterworth used another chandelle to turn the squirrel around for her third run, and almost hit the narrow canyon wall as the sUAV circled back and leveled out.

Cleo inhaled sharply and forced herself to breathe. Without even realizing it, she had been holding her breath again. The squirrel descended another hundred feet, skimming the ground. With a target in its sight, and capturing detailed data as fast as the microprocessors would allow. She watched as Major Butterworth piloted the sUAV into a tight steep turn and dove for the valley floor. At what looked like inches, on the little laptop screen, he leveled the sUAV out for one last fast pass. This one would be up close and personal. Again masses of data streamed through the satellite uplink, then suddenly nothing. For a second Cleo froze, actually thinking something had gone wrong, then remembered. Squirrel was dead! And to think, destroying the poor little thing had been her idea.

A long sigh of relief involuntarily escaped from Cleo's mouth. Thankfully, the indiscretion was camouflaged within the privacy of the O_2 mask. She was about to pull it and the helmet off, when she remembered she hadn't received instructions for dealing with their two passengers. She waited until the last data file on her computer was uploaded then transmitted, "Mother Hen, this is Momma Squirrel, my sympathies on your recent loss."

"Momma Squirrel, Mother Hen. Ariel, Ariel, Ariel." That was it. After nine weeks of planning and preparing, and ten minutes of holding her breath, their little flying Squirrel had succeeded. Now they just had to get out of Dodge. "Stand by for Pax op."

Cleo didn't have to wait long for instructions on how Vauxhall wanted to handle their Iranian passengers. "Momma Squirrel, Mother Hen. Ready to copy?" The question was more of a "prepare yourself" request than an order to write stuff down.

"Affirmative."

"Pax Two," Tori began, "is a criminal with several outstanding warrants. He is considered very dangerous. Pax One is *company* but would appear to be freelancing. The plan is to force you down, somewhere in the south. You and the crew are to be traded. For what, we're not yet certain."

Cleo swore under her mask for the umpteenth time. "Advise our response level?" She was asking how far they were authorized to go in diverting their imminent capture. The long pause that followed warned of complications. There was also the team's ability to defend any action they might take, while they were still in Iranian airspace.

"Oberon advises Pax Two may be dropped anywhere convenient. Request Pax One be delivered to port of destination. Baggage handler will retrieve on landing. Response level green is authorized in handling of both Pax One and Two. This link will remain open until threat is eliminated."

"Understand Level GREEN all Pax? Pax One to baggage and Pax Two express departure?" Cleo had been keeping an eye on Hasid ever since Tori had warned her of the possible hijack. Since the two men had left their pilot, hijacker number three, back in Tehran, they were obviously confident they could intimidate one of the women pilots into obeying their orders.

"Momma Squirrel, Mother Hen. Affirmative! Extreme measures are authorized. Proceed with caution."

"Don't worry Mother Hen. I have four friends named Winchester and they're ready to lend a hand." Cleo answered with some bravado, then advised Tori that she would be off the frequency for some time. There was no point in trying to guess how long it would be until she could make her next report. They hadn't counted on maintaining the uplink for the entire transition to Iran's southern border but having it now was a huge bonus. Cleo reached above the avionics rank, switched her headset cord to the number one comm and pressed a hidden button. It allowed her to transmit directly to Bo without anyone connected to the intercom listening in. Unfortunately, there was no way for Bo to respond that wouldn't be heard by everyone on board. Cleo crossed her fingers hoping Bo remembered that important little detail.

"Bo, listen up, Do Not Reply! If you're receiving me, slowly reach up with your right hand and fuss with your helmet." Cleo stuck her head around the bulkhead. She could just see Bo's right side and watched as Bo's arm came up. "Good work. Now listen. The Officer beside you is a scumbag and he's armed. When you say it's time for the oxygen masks to come off, Albert will take him out. All I need you to do is wait until Albert asks you to descend, then get ATC clearance and go. When you're ready, and only when you're ready, order the oxygen turned off and masks and helmets removed. Expect a scuffle while Albert takes him out. Your only job is to fly the plane! Got it, fly the plane!" Bo's arm came up again, even before Cleo could ask for the signal. It was a lot to ask from a pilot with only fifty hours of flying time.

Before she took her O_2 mask off, Cleo took one long last look at Hasid. He looked like he was asleep but he might just be playing possum. She pulled her mask off, removing the helmet and stepped through the low lavatory doorway, to stand hunched beside Cyril. Hasid still hadn't moved, and Cleo continued to watch him as Albert stepped over to her side. She put her head next to his ear and gave him the update. She wanted him to order Bo to descend, then help with removing the bulky equipment from the cockpit. At his first opportunity, Albert was to get the good major in a chokehold, then drag him, as fast as possible, from the co-pilot's seat and into the cabin, where they could restrain both men.

"Risky," was Albert's only reply.

"We're code green if necessary. If you have to, shove the bastard out the co-pilot's door."

Albert nodded and headed forward, sticking his head into the tiny flight deck. Over the intercom, he advised Bo that Cleo had come off oxygen and wanted her to descend back to flight planned altitude. Bo nodded her head in compliance, telling Major Suyfias in English that he and Hasid could remove their masks and helmets and put the headsets back on. She then made the call to ATC to advise them of her altitude change. They grumbled about it, but had no reason to object. Cleo, still watching Hasid carefully, squeezed Cyril's arm and pulled his Winchester out from behind his seat and handed it to him. She then pulled her own Winchester out from its hiding spot in the lav. From where both she and Cyril were standing, there was a good chance they would hit one of the auxiliary fuel bags, or worse, hit the pilot's bulkhead and shoot a round into Bo. Someone had to get closer to cover Hasid, before Albert moved in. Cyril must have been thinking the same thing and made a move to crawl up over the fuel bags. He was carefully lowering the bunk over the sleeping Hasid while Cleo made her way to the empty seat beside him.

Suddenly, everyone heard Major Suyfias shouting from the co-pilot's seat. Hasid was instantly awake and pulled a Tokarev from a hidden holster, swinging it around wildly, trying to gauge the situation. Albert was still trying to pull Major Suyfias into the cabin when Suyfias started kicking. He got his foot planted on the center console of the control yoke and kicked it forward, forcing the Otter into a power dive. Bo couldn't fight the strength of his legs but knew enough to retard the throttle.

Hasid stood and pointed the pistol at Albert's head. Cleo was about to pull the trigger on Hasid when he suddenly crumpled to the floor. Cyril, having the same intuitive understanding of the situation, had hit Hasid with the butt of his rifle. Cleo followed his example and spun her Winchester around, cracking the major in the head. With all resistance suddenly gone, Albert, with Suyfias still in his headlock, fell backward into the cabin aisle, taking Cleo with them. As soon as they hit the floor, Albert flipped the dead weight off and struggled to stand back up, pulling Cleo up next.

Her first instinct was to rush forward and take control of the aircraft. Sensing the dive under control, she left the recovery of the airplane's attitude to Bo, keeping her focus on their passengers instead.

Albert took Cyril's Winchester, and sent him looking for something to restrain the men with, while he carefully searched the Iranians. Between them, they had three semi-automatic pistols, two very mean-looking folding knives, and one garrote. More alarming was the stash he found in Hasid's jacket, including two vials of Ketamine and several syringes.

Cyril wanted to know if they were planning on drugging them or cutting their throats. It was a fair question, but a question that would never be answered.

Cleo grabbed the spare headset hanging over Hasid's seat and pulled it on. "Bo," she called over the intercom. "Is everything Okay?"

"I'm fine and we're back at altitude. Can I take this stupid thing off now?" she asked, waving at to her O$_2$ mask and helmet.

"One minute and I'll come give you a hand." Turning her attention to Cyril, she found he was having a hard time finding something to secure the men with. "Try the first aid kit. I'm pretty sure I put a roll of hockey tape in there." He turned and pulled the first aid kit from its cubby, unzipping it on the small counter. Sure enough, there were two rolls of white hockey tape. Cleo and Bo had always been extremely sensitive to medical tapes and bandages, and had discovered years ago, that the adhesive used on fabric hockey tape, wasn't near-ly as irritating. Ever since, they had always kept a few rolls on hand.

The guys pulled Hasid back into his seat and bound his hands, before fastening his seatbelt. Albert pulled the O_2 mask and helmet off Hasid and checked his pulse. With the flight helmet protecting his head, Cyril had been forced to strike Hasid in the back of the neck. Albert looked from Hasid to Cleo and nodded, "He'll live."

With Hasid secured, Albert and Cyril managed to lift Major Suyfias out of the aisle and into the other forward seat. While the guys were trying to tape his hands, he started to moan, then wrestle, but stopped abruptly when Cleo shoved the barrel of her carbine in his mouth. Albert finished securing the major, then took Cleo's Winchester, allowing her to go forward and join Bo. Sliding into the co-pilot's chair, it was immediately evident that Bo was in control. She had managed to remove her mask and helmet, and had pulled her headset back on. Cleo plugged into the intercom and looked over to see how the pilot-in-command was doing.

"You okay?"

"Sweet Baby Jesus! I almost pissed my pants back there . . . holy crap! I had no idea this flying shit could be so much fun!"

Cleo smiled at her, "My dear cousin Boudicca, you ain't seen nothin' yet."

Albert's voice came ringing over the intercom, singing the words to the old B.T.O. hit of the same name. They all started laughing and joined in for a round of the chorus. The excitement hadn't ebbed when they ran out of words. Undeterred, Albert launched into "Takin' Care of Business." It felt like a huge weight had just been lifted off the crew. Even Cyril was relieved and excited and he didn't have a clue what was going on.

"You guys are frackin' amazing!" Cleo said with real pride. She checked her watch: 08:40 Tehran local time. She changed the output on the instrument panel in front of her to show the moving map display. They were on course and just south of Khoneyn, but they were still two hundred and fifteen naut-ical miles short of the coast. That put a damper on her mood for a minute. She pulled out the Flight Manual and turned to the Power Schedule. "Ready to pick up the pace?" she asked Bo.

"I've been ready all morning, this sloshing around at ninety knots is killing me."

"Well then, let's get ready to blow the fuel consumption through the roof," Cleo offered with a grin, "Mixture Full Rich. Prop, thirty-five inches. And for the Throttle . . . set it at twenty-two hundred and fifty rpm."

"Roger," Bo said, repeating her orders and making the control changes, "thirty-five inches manifold pressure, and twenty-two, fifty on the power. Inci-dentally how much extra fuel are we about to burn?"

"Too much to keep it up all the way to Dubai. Would you believe triple? We're now burning an extra thirty gallons per hour, but with the tail wind it should give us a ground speed of around two hundred knots."

Bo whistled. "It's still going to take how long to get out of no woman's land?" she asked, then started playing with to GPS program to calculate the enroute time to the Persian Gulf. While she fussed with the program, Cleo pulled out her old reliable Jeppeson E3 circular slide rule and calculated the time using the distance and ground speed.

"One hour and twenty-five minutes." Cleo announced, before taking a suspicious look behind her. Albert, as usual, had everything in order.

"I don't know which is harder to believe," Bo asked. "That you actually still use that wiz wheel thing or that you're faster than the computer."

Cleo laughed, "Ah, the old ways were the best, weren't they?"

Bo flipped the intercom switch on the panel from ALL to PILOTS and signaled back towards the cabin. "How are the guys?"

"Cyril's in his bunk reading one of those Russian comic books he bought in Moscow, and Albert's . . . Albert! He's sitting shotgun from the rear seat. Are you okay for a bit? We may still have an uplink, and it might soothe a few nerves if we report in."

Bo nodded. "Send her a kiss for me."

Cleo snapped the seatbelt open, and leaving her headset on, unplugged the cord and made her way down the narrow aisle and into the lavatory. One of the guys had cleared away the O_2 setup including the mask and helmet. Her water bottle was in the cup holder by the rear cabin seat and the laptop, still running, was sitting open in its cubbyhole. Cleo plugged her headset into the number two-intercom and called the operations center. "Oberon, this is Momma Squirrel."

The time following her call seemed to indicate that the uplink was lost. She was about to try once more when Tori's jubilant voice broke out. "Momma Squirrel, Mother Hen. Ariel, Ariel, Ariel. I can't say it enough! We are delighted. Can you report your situation?"

"We are seventy-five minutes from X-ray. We have the baggage packed for delivery. We'll make our first drop right after X-ray, probably four to five miles out. I want to be outside the red zone but still close enough to attract local fishing boats." X-ray was the code for the Persian Gulf, or rather the point over the Persian Gulf where they would cross out of Iranian airspace, and into International territory.

"Understood." Tori replied simply. "Say intended altitude?"

"Ten to twenty feet, unless you're ordering something higher?"

"Negative. Altitude is your discretion. Oberon seconds the drop-off plan but advises caution on the altitude. Cleopatra," Tori cautioned, her unease clear over the sat link, "don't take any risks. Remember, he was planning to ransom you off to the highest bidder."

"Understood! Should we sever the uplink?"

"Negative. Oberon is on standby. Remember you have Friendlys waiting at X-ray."

Cleo's own concern matched Tori's. As perfect as the Otter was, she wasn't built for speed. Even blowing the doors off at two hundred miles per hour, they were still a long way from safety. They needed to make the coastline before they could begin to relax. The Friendlys Tori had mentioned, were a flight of two USAF fighters out of Saudi Arabia. The American jets would be on station in seventy minutes. Until then, the team was alone. So far, they had handled everything thrown their way, but that didn't mean they could relax just yet. They were still in Iran. They had just participated in a covert surveillance operation and were therefore guilty of espionage.

"Momma Squirrel," Tori said. "Report Pax Two drop concluded."

"Mother Hen, Momma Squirrel, Wilco and Thanks." Cleo, waiting to be sure Tori didn't have anything else for them, sat quietly before pulling the laptop out of its space in the avionics rack, and closing the DOS windows. Once done she slipped it back in place for safe keeping before turning her attention back to the situation at hand. Setting the countdown timer on her wristwatch to seventy minutes, she pressed the start button then checked the cabin again. *Only seventy minutes to go. For the next hour and ten minutes, we are spies guilty of espionage, fleeing the jurisdiction of the host nation. Maybe I should have taken Mike Perkins up on the offer of a Cessna Citation. We would still be spies in a foreign land but at least we would be flying a lot faster than this damned puddle jumper can move!*

Security and Intelligence Service
Vauxhall Cross
London, United Kingdom

The Tank, with its extensive multi-media setup had been used as the control center for the operation, with one exception. Major Butterworth had been sequestered to the Tutor Room. They weren't excluding him, just protecting his attention from the gaggle of analysts gathered together. When Butterworth finally joined the others, cheers went up from everyone. Even though it was five in the morning, someone had managed to find and crack open a bottle of Champagne. Butterworth, all grins, accepted his improvised grog served in a teacup.

All around, the analysts were wild with the data that had been streaming in from Cleo's laptop. Image files too large for quick transmission had been buffered via the custom-built computer. The high-speed digital camera on the flying squirrel had captured ten-megapixel shots of the bunker from several heights. The true stroke of luck came when they realized the hangar-style loading doors were wide open. Some of the pictures were so detailed you could read the labels on the shipping cartons in the receiving bay.

Rod Nelligan sidled up beside Tori and tipped his cup to hers. "So, what do yah think of our lass now?"

Tori smiled at him, content with all the bustle and excitement around her. "I think she is positively mad! And I adore her for it."

Rod chinked his cup again. "Here's to their safe return."

"Hail Mary. Uncle Rod. Hail Bloody Mary!"

"And to all of our good Queens, before and since!"

Chapter Thirteen

Iranian Airspace, Khuzestan Province
22 Nautical Miles from the Persian Gulf
Islamic Republic of Iran

If Bo Commanda thought the surveillance portion of the operation was exciting, she really hadn't seen anything yet. Cleo climbed back into the co-pilot's
seat. She had just finished a complete inspection of the cabin. Not that Albert
would allow anything on *his* aircraft to be out of place. It was just that she
wanted to be extra sure everything was secure and strapped down nice and
tight. Things were complicated enough without risking injuries to the crew, or
their passengers, from shifting cargo or bodies.

Once she was confident that all was secure, she plugged her headset in,
and pulled on her seatbelt and shoulder harness. Bo had offered to switch
seats with her, but it really didn't make a difference. She could fly comfortably
from either the left or right side. At the moment, that wasn't even an issue. Bo
was still in command and doing a fine job. They were cruising at top speed,
sitting together silently for more than thirty minutes, completely engrossed in
the view. "Bo, ask Tehran Center for two-thousand five-hundred. If they ask
why, tell them we would like to take snapshots of the beautiful coastal waters."

"You don't expect me to say that, 'snapshots of the beautiful coastal waters' do you?" Bo asked with exaggerated disgust.

"As a matter of fact I do. Come on. We're just over a half hour from the
border and it will take you fourteen minutes to descend."

"Just watch me," Bo warned mischievously. "I'll show you how to descend
in twelve seconds flat."

"Yah, yah, Chuck Yeager. Just fly the plane and save the fun stuff for later."

"You're killing me with the boring!"

"Just give me a nice five-hundred-foot-per-minute descent." Cleo was smiling. "Oh, by the way, how low do you think you can fly this thing before hitting
the water?"

"What cha' mean?"

"I'm asking if you can keep her straight and level at, oh say twenty-five feet?"

"Oh, I like the sound of this! What have you got planned?"

"Nothing too tough. Oberon is suggesting we drop Hasid off at point X-ray."

"Drop him off?" Bo asked. It took her a moment to put it all together.
"Holy shit! Are you serious? That seems a bit extreme, even to me!"

Before Cleo could respond or even think about her feelings on the subject, Albert's voice chimed in over the intercom. "You're not gonna' believe this! Hasid, here, just offered me ten grand US for the two of you. He wants to buy you guys! Evidently, you two would make quite a pair of exotic savage women, and worth a lot of bucks on the open market."

Bo was enjoying herself way too much, "Hey Cyril. What do you think of that?"

Cleo glanced back into the cabin. She had asked the guys to prepare Hasid for his departure. She hadn't really planned on dumping him in the Gulf, but the attempted bribery pissed her off. With her head craned around, she could now see how agitated Cyril was getting. She knew full well how volatile a seventeen-year-old could be. "You okay, Cyril?"

"Me?" the kid asked. He was practically hopping with aggression.

"Cyril, put your headset on Mister Ten Grand for a minute, please." She normally didn't include words like please with an order, but she was treading lightly, not wanting Cyril to go off prematurely.

The kid pulled his headset off, then got in Hasid's face, yelling loud enough to be heard over the drone of the engine, "Our women are the granddaughters of Sky Woman. THEY ARE NOT FOR SALE!"

Cleo and Bo smiled at each other. Their young crewman didn't just know the stories of the people, he was ready to honor them. Cleo turned to look at Hasid who was still strapped into the forward port seat. From her place in the co-pilot's chair to Hasid, was less than four feet. If she stretched out, she could just reach his scrawny little neck. "Hasid," Cleo shouted over the intercom. "Can you hear me?"

Hasid nodded his head but kept his gaze down.

"Look at me!" she demanded, waiting until he looked up before giving her verdict. "Have you any idea how much trouble you're in?" He nodded again, as she continued to question him. "What do you think is going to happen to you now?"

"I will pay you not to turn me in," he begged. "Please. I have money."

Cleo actually felt bad for the bastard. "We're not going to turn you in. I was planning to just land on the south end of Highway Four-four and let you out, but the drugs and the bribery blew that chance. Under the laws of the Six Nations, my cousin and I can challenge you to run the gauntlet, but I'm going to give you a choice. You can keep that very expensive floatation suit, and we will drop you off near the coast, or I will arrange for you to run the gauntlet as soon as we reach the Emirates. Which do you choose?"

"How will you land?"

"I don't think you understand. We will not be landing. You are free to get out anytime you like, but if you're planning on surviving, a low level jump into the water is your best bet."

"Then I want the gauntlet," Hasid said, almost panicking before asking, "What is the gauntlet?"

A radio call from Tehran Center diverted Cleo's attention for a minute. By the time she turned back to Hasid, Cyril had explained the challenge with great enthusiasm. Hasid however was not moved. "I will gladly face a few women with sticks. What harm can they do?"

"Man," Albert piped in. "You have no idea what a few dozen angry women can do. No one makes it through the gauntlet alive, at least not without losing his balls. I mean that literally, not to mention getting their heads bashed in! If the women in the UAE are a tenth as angry as our women, you won't make it a foot past the start line." Albert grabbed Hasid by the shoulder and gave him a shake. "Man, these women are offering you your life back. All you have to do is go for a little swim. I'll make sure you're safe. Trust me; I've jumped out of planes and into the water more than a dozen times."

Hasid, still begging, had tears rolling down his cheeks. "Why do you follow these two? They are mere women!" He pleaded with Albert while everyone listened.

"In our culture, women are recognized as creators right here on Earth. They are the keepers of the past and the seers of the future. We men are the protectors of the present," Albert explained, kneeling down beside Hasid. "You see, one cannot exist without the other. Take the jump, man. These women don't want to kill you, but they will. They're Mohawk women. They have no fear!"

Hasid tried once more. Begging, he seemed desperate to wordlessly convey something, finally, in defeat he said, "I have a family."

Cleo shook her head. "I'm running out of patience. If you're getting out, you have to get ready now. If you don't, you will run the gauntlet and I promise you, you will die!" She had no intention of making him run the gauntlet. While she was sure she could find a few dozen angry women and kids, she couldn't ask them or anyone else, to beat a man to death. In reality, it wasn't just a beating. The man being challenged had a chance to survive, but only if he was very strong and extremely aggressive.

The gauntlet was considered a warrior's test. Two rows of women and children armed with sticks and stones would be assembled. The start and finish line would be clearly marked, leaving the challenger a clear path to freedom. All any challenger had to do was get from the start line and to the finish while twenty or thirty women got their licks in. While Cleo didn't think anyone had run the gauntlet in several hundred years, she had no qualms about bringing the "old medicine" back. Finally, Hasid caved and the guys started getting him zipped up for the jump.

As they did, Tehran Center called their tail number, demanding answers, "You are not following your flight plan. Why have you not turned for your destination?"

Cleo turned back in her seat and held up her hand to let Bo know she would handle the radio. "Tehran Center," she responded, in her best airline pilot's voice, "this is Charlie-Golf-Foxtrot-Alpha-Bravo. We are on assigned course and altitude. We are in compliance with our flight plan."

"Negative!" The area controller said. "You must turn to heading three-three-zero, and descent to one thousand, five hundred. Now!"

"Tehran Center, Foxtrot-Alpha-Bravo. A three-three-zero heading is in the opposite direction of Dubai. Please explain your request." While her voice remained professional, Cleo was entitled to demand answers. She had filed a Visual flight plan for a trans-border crossing, and according to aviation law, she could refuse orders from ATC if they were considered erroneous or a danger to the aircraft or crew.

"Negative, Foxtrot-Alpha-Bravo. Your flight plan is cleared for off-airport landing, two miles north of Bandar-e Khomeynī."

Using a tone preferred by miffed airline captains, she announced impatiently, "Tehran Center, stand by."

"That must be where they were going to force us down," Bo offered over the intercom. "What do we do now?"

With so much attention focused on Hasid, Cleo had lost track of their flight time. Her watch showed they had four minutes to go. The view through the forward windscreen made it clear they had reached the coast. "How many more minutes to X-ray?"

"Almost there," Bo said. "The flight computer says we're two minutes out."

Cleo thought for a minute then ordered, "Push the nose down, Bo. Take her down to the deck. Full power."

"How fast do you want to go?" Bo asked, knowing a full-power dive could tear an aircraft apart.

"Just try to keep the wings from falling off," she replied, adding with seriousness, "Take her to the Red Line Bo, the Red Line, and no farther!" She reached to the stack of Nav/Coms and turned the Transponder dial, from the position and altitude reporting, to just position reporting only. She didn't know how low they would need to get before area radar would lose them, but there was no need to let Tehran voluntarily know just how low they were going. "Tehran Center, Foxtrot-Alpha-Bravo. We request you close out our flight plan at this time. We will file a new flight plan with Dubai Flight Service," she said reasonably, watching as Bo dived the Otter towards the Persian Gulf.

Bo had been running the big radial engine hard and well past the Yellow line on the airspeed indicator. They were nearing the water fast. One look at Bo was all she needed to see. "Start to level off. Aim for two hundred feet." Two hundred feet sounded like a lot of room, but for a low-time pilot trying to hang on at two hundred miles per hour, two hundred feet could be lost or gained without batting an eye.

"Foxtrot-Alpha-Bravo, Tehran Center. You are not authorized to amend your flight plan. Turn right heading three-three-zero. You are to divert to Ahvāz and file a new flight plan from there."

"One minute to X-ray." Bo said. There was fear in her voice as she fought to level the plane.

"Understood," Cleo acknowledging her cousin's report, "Go back and get on the SAT Phone. Tell Oberon we're on the deck and running hard. "Bad boy number one must be more important than we thought. I'm guessing we'll have Iranian F-4s on our ass any second."

"Shit!" was all Bo had managed before ATC came back over the radio, demanding they comply with the order to change course.

Cleo turned to Bo, "I have control," she confirmed, accepting command as Bo swung the control yoke over. Bo immediately unbuckled, then remembering her headset, unplugged it and barreled her way back through the cabin.

"Tehran Center," Cleo said, still keeping her tone professional, "This is Foxtrot-Alpha-Bravo. We are now diverting to Ahvāz as ordered. Can you repeat the altitude?"

"Foxtrot-Alpha-Bravo!" the flustered area controller came back, "You must turn heading three-three-zero. Altitude, one thousand, five hundred feet. You are not reporting your altitude. Reset your transponder for altitude reporting."

Bingo, Cleo thought. If they wanted her transponder turned back on, she was probably below area radar. The transponder, when turned on, would transmit the aircraft's position and altitude, letting anyone with the right receiver know where they were and how high. "Tehran Center, Um, sorry but it's turned on. Let me play with it for a minute." Cleo reached over and turned the Transponder to Off, "Tehran Center, Foxtrot-Alpha-Bravo, squawking twelve-hundred. Have you got our transponder signal now?"

"Negative," a very agitated voice responded. "Negative, Foxtrot-Alpha-Bravo. Say heading and altitude?"

"We're just rolling onto three-three-zero at one thousand feet. Should we climb?" She asked while lowering the nose of the Otter and edging her down to fifty feet above the water. They were seconds to X-ray, and she wanted to get rid of Hasid as soon as they hit international waters, but couldn't just dump the bastard at their current speed. For some inexplicable reason, the thought of killing the man, by dumping him out of a perfectly good airplane, was even less appealing than beating him to death. To drop him safely, the aircraft would need to be low and slow. And that would only happen if they had air cover from the Americans. Without it, she was sure the Iranians would ignore their three-mile sovereign limit, and go after them out over international waters. Hopefully, they were buying the misdirection and more importantly, she was counting on the Yanks to be on-station and on time.

"Foxtrot-Alpha-Bravo. Tehran Center. Climb to two thousand feet and squawk one-two-zero-one." 1200 was the usual number assigned to aircraft on VFR flight plans. The 1201, she guessed, was an effort to readily separate her from other air traffic, and generate a solid radar target.

"Roger, Tehran Center. Foxtrot-Alpha-Bravo, leaving 1,000 for 2,000 feet and squawking one-two-zero-one." Cleo's eyes flashed across the instrument panel. At fifty feet above the water there was no room for errors. "Albert, what's the word from Oberon."

"Stand by, Colonel!" Albert called back. That caught her attention for a second. It wasn't like Albert to get flustered. Cleo let it go. They were all a little pumped.

"Foxtrot-Alpha-Bravo, Tehran Center. What is you altitude? Foxtrot-Alpha-Bravo, Tehran Center. Foxtrot-Alpha-Bravo, this is Tehran Center. Respond!"

Cleo ignored the air traffic controller, turning the radio volume down, when Bo's voice broke over the intercom. "They're on station. They want our coordinates?"

"Latitude, two-niner point niner-three. Longitude, four-niner point niner-two-six. Heading southwest," Cleo replied before calling to Albert, "Get the doors open. We're on target. I want to drop him as close in as possible."

"Can we slow . . ."

BOOM!

Two F-4 Phantoms in desert camouflage buzzed them from both sides, rocking the little Otter in a rain of turbulence. Streaking forward from each side of the Otter, the F-4s sucked up sea water and spewed it out their exhaust burners creating the illusion of a parting sea. Cleo hung onto the buffeting flight controls, spinning the trim wheel nose-up to assist her strained muscles. If the Iranian pilots thought they could intimidate her, they were mistaken. She'd had fighter pilots pull this stunt before. The last time this happened, she'd been flying a Hercules over the Baffin Bay, and the fighters had been Danes. *Jet jocks—same bat moves, same bat channel.*

Cleo could see the pair of fighters burning hard turns in the distance. According to international law, the fighters were required to pull alongside, and indicate the direction they wanted her to turn. Then, if she refused to comply and only then, they were legally authorized to force the aircraft down or open fire. The Otter had reached point X-ray. Technically they were outside Iranian airspace, but she was absolutely sure the fighter pilots didn't give a rat's ass about "technically."

Sure enough, one F-4 buzzed them again, before the other tried to pull alongside. The pilot, anonymous behind his helmet's sun visor, signaled for Cleo to turn the Otter around. Clearly they could care less that the Otter had passed the three mile Iranian sovereign limit.

Cleo rocked the wings of the Otter back and forth to indicate that she understood the pilot's order and would comply. Even as she signaled her understanding, she made small heading changes as if confused as to which way to go and kept slowing the plane more and more. As she suspected, the F-4 had to move off after the initial contact, not being able to slow enough to stay alongside the Otter. Cleo inched the throttle and prop levers back again, slowing the aircraft even more. She thought about adding flaps but that would give away her strategy. She wanted to be too slow to communicate with, not purposefully slowing to avoid contact. Cleo was betting their lives that the pilot who made first contact would want to try again, worried that he hadn't been clear with his signal.

Sure enough, the F-4 eased in along her port side again, buffeting badly, trying to keep the jet in the sky at the low airspeed. He signaled Cleo frantically, as he slowly slipped past. She smiled and pointed past him, watching as he turned his head just in time to see a USAF F-16 glide into place on his port wing. What a sight they must have made from the high-altitude perspective of the wingmen for the two air force flights. The Otter on the right, being outpaced by a Vietnam-era relic like the F-4, which in turn was being outpaced by the modern but also soon to be obsolete F-16.

The Otter crew watched as the F-4 pulled-up, regrouped with his wingman, and turned tail for home. The F-16 gave them a friendly wing rock then climbed out with full afterburners. All through the aircraft, hoots and hollers went up for the timely intervention of the United States Air Force. With the immediate threat over, Cleo gave them a few minutes to blow off steam before calling for them to knock it off, "All right people, time to K-I-O! Are we ready to drop Hasid off?"

Albert had spent several minutes coaching Hasid on how to protect himself during the fall and once in the water. He now threw the handguns, garrote, and horse tranquilizers out the open cargo door. He also tossed-out the knife they pulled from Major Suyfias but put Hasid's in the lower leg pocket of the floater suit.

"What about the money?" Albert asked Cleo over the intercom. Hasid was carrying more than ten thousand American dollars.

"Give it back," Cleo answered. "We're not thieves," she said, then thought of something else. "Wait, take five hundred and sixty bucks for the cost of the floatation suit," she said, adding defensively. "Those things are expensive!"

"He only has hundreds in greenbacks," Albert answered.

"Fine," Cleo said, turning the aircraft south-southwest and keeping the Iranian coast off her port side. "Give him a compass and one of the flare guns too. That odda' add up to six hundred dollars."

"Sounds good."

She edged the throttle and prop levels back again. To give Hasid the best chance of survival, she was slowing the Otter to Vmc, the minimum controllable airspeed for the aircraft.

Over the years, coast guard swimmers from around the world had made the exact same jump. Everyone from the Norwegians to the Australians had used the Otter for Search and Rescue, and some still did. Tori had warned her about being too soft on a man who had attempted to abduct them, or worse, had tried to bribe her crew and sell her and Bo into slavery. But she couldn't just kill him and she couldn't say why. As the Otter skimmed over the surface, Cleo briefed her team, "Okay guys, we are at minimum airspeed, and as low as I can go. Do this safely. I don't want anyone hurt. Understood?" she asked, waiting until each of them reported their ready status over the intercom. "Get Hasid set up in the door, and put a headset on him."

Albert took Cyril's and popped it on Hasid. "The boss wants a word."

"Hasid," Cleo voice was clear and level over the intercom. Flying from the co-pilot's seat, the Otter skimmed above the surface of the Gulf. "You probably think I'm trying to kill you, but I'm actually trying to save your life. There are some people, very high up, who have noticed you and not in a good way. Once you're in the water, swim south for the island of Kharg. Be careful and good luck," she said, giving Albert the "go" signal.

"Remember," he advised, Hasid, "keep your arms and ankles crossed, and remember to breathe out as you descend in the water. You don't want air bubbles blowin' your brain up." Albert pulled the headset off and handed it back to Cyril, who was standing in the aisle holding his Winchester in case a little persuasion was needed.

Whatever Hasid was or might be, a fool he wasn't. The second Albert released his grip, the man moved to the open cargo doors and stepped out. Cleo couldn't fly the plane and watch what was going on. She was relying on the crew's feedback. Once Hasid was out, and in an effort to give Albert a better view behind the plane, Cleo steered the Otter through a series of left and right turns, while ramping up the air speed and starting an easy climb back to attitude.

"I got him!" Cyril yelled. He was watching out the starboard windows and spotted the floater suit a quarter-mile back. When the aircraft turned left again, Bo was ready with the binoculars. They didn't have a long-strap to tether her, so Albert wrapped a seatbelt around one hand and clamped his other arm around Bo's waist. She leaned out just in time to spot Hasid. He was waving vigorously, according to Cyril's running commentary. Cleo rocked the wings back and forth as a sort of wave, then put the Otter back on course for Dubai.

"Okay, Albert, pull Bo in and get the cabin battened down, and unload the Winchesters."

"How about I unload all but one? At least until we touchdown in friendly territory."

"Good call," she acknowledged, as Bo climbed into the left seat. She started to say something then realized she hadn't plugged in her headset cord. With that done, she put her seatbelt on and sat quietly for a while. The deep blues and emerald greens of the Persian Gulf were spectacular. There really was no better view in an airplane than from the captain's seat.

"I owe you an apology," Bo said simply.

Cleo looked at her cousin, waiting for more.

"This *just flying around shit* is a lot more exciting than I ever imagined! Now I understand why you spent twenty years doing it."

"To be fair, there weren't many days like this, but . . . there were a few," a wry smile spread across her round face.

"Well that's something! That really is."

Security Intelligence Service
Vauxhall Cross
London, United Kingdom

Rod Nelligan walked into the Tank and nodded to Tori. That was the signal she had been waiting for. Their people were ready for the team's arrival in Dubai, and were in place to "receive" the special package. Major Yosef Suyfias wasn't the highest-ranking intelligence officer they had ever nabbed, but he was corrupt, and that made him unpredictable. His involvement with Hasid's little abduction plan proved that. The team's flight plan changes must have come from Suyfias or one of his men. Hasid, regardless of his talents, or chutzpah, couldn't have pulled that off. Now, the order to scramble a flight of F-4s . . . that must have come from someone much farther up the food chain. Besides, it had happened too fast. From the time that Air Traffic Control ordered the team to change course, to the moment the Otter had been engaged, had taken less than four minutes. That was three minutes too fast for the closest squadron to respond. To react that quickly, the Iranians must have been in the air and on-station. Like the Americans, could the Iranians have planned the engagement ahead of time? Tori turned her attention back to the senior photo analyst, who was presenting a list of items that had so far been identified, from the pass of the receiving bay and exposed bunker.

The day had been a wonderful success. The team had delivered the surveillance package, which had yielded unimagined results. They had thwarted a hijack attempt, captured a corrupt intelligence operative, and dispatched a wanted criminal. The Americans too, were beside themselves. For the price of an old airplane, they had the intelligence they needed to prove the Iranians had begun a nuclear program, and they had even gotten a chance to show off. That was a lot of action for the London early morning. Tori wondered if the public would ever truly understand all that went onto gathering even the simplest piece of information. How many good men and women had risked their lives today, and for what? So the world could confront Iran's out-of-touch government with proof of their duplicity.

The team was clear of Iranian airspace, but were still four hundred miles from Dubai. The attention and mood at Vauxhall had gone from jovial to manic with all the information that needed to be sorted, catalogued, and analyzed. It was barely 6:30 a.m. in London, but Tori was already exhausted. It would take Cleo's team three more hours to reach the United Arab Emirates, and the entire flight would be with the coast of Iran constantly in sight. It was troubling. The farther the team got from Iran the more she worried about them, or more pointedly, Cleo. This had been, or was, depending on your viewpoint, one of the most unorthodox operations she had ever participated in, and yet the results were outstanding. It had been Rod Nelligan who suggested they bring Cleo Deseronto in on the operation, back when the Americans had shown up with her cousin Boudicca in tow. The idea to "utilize" the neutrality of the Six Nations had come from the Americans, but in a very different guise. It had been Rod who insisted Cleo be brought in, and Rod who persuaded C to give her the go to plan something outside the box. On days like these, she really appreciated the tough Scotsman.

As soon as the analyst finished his briefing, Tori got up from her chair and joined Rod next to one of the large monitors. "Uncle Rod!"

Turning to her, he removed his reading glasses, "Victoria, what can I do for you?"

"Take me to breakfast. Some place where we can talk."

Rod Nelligan regarded his goddaughter with warmth, "Aye Lass, let's go have a cup with yer' Uncle Will."

Tori walked, holding Rod's arm, from HQ to their favorite pub, just across the street.

Arch 73 of the Albert Embankment had been the home of the Loyal Archer since 1988. The place didn't open until eight, but the owner was a friend, and had frequently served Rod and Tori an early breakfast, after many a long night. With the dining room all to themselves, Rod escorted her to the table closest the kitchen. There was no point in making Will Green, the proprietor and cook, walk farther than necessary.

Will and Rod had been mates since their Navy recruit school days, and Rod, with a number of other "Chiefs," had come together as investors in the public house. Acquaintances had called them mad when they announced the location, steps from the Vauxhall Cross tube station. Only weeks after the property purchase closed, the UK government announced the location for a new Head Quarters for the Security Services. Interestingly enough, the new location just happened to be the vacant lot across from Arch 73. It would be a long haul before the new building opened, but they kept the place going by catering to everyone, from construction workers, to wankers from the local estates. Over the years, the Lambeth neighborhood had changed too. Today the Arches of the Albert Embankment housed several gay clubs and a huge motorcycle dealership. The Loyal Archer had changed too. The lunch and after-work crowd were mostly MI6, but as the pub emptied of government types, the dinner crowd would move in and was fast becoming a solid cross section of the new gay scene.

William Green hadn't been bothered by it. While he couldn't quite relate to his new customers, generally, they were better behaved than their straight Happy Hour counterparts, and definitely more profitable. Will's solution was simple; hire someone to manage the pub in the evening, someone who could cater to the changing clientele, while he contentedly ruled over the kitchen. Preferring to cook anyway, he found the arrangement quite pleasing, and his investors found it very profitable.

Tori sat down with a thud and exhaled heavily. Will Green was about to set a coffee mug in front of her but instead pulled it away. "You've had too much already," he said, turning to Rod for confirmation. Tori Braithwaite may have lost her mother at birth, but she had gained an entire division of Petty Officers as caregivers, with Will Green serving as chief cook and bottle washer. "I'm gonna put the kettle on and make you a cuppa'. And don't tell me you're not hungry. While I'm at it, I'll poach a few eggs."

Tori watched him disappear into the kitchen. Leaning heavily against the well-worn green leather booth, she was silent and withdrawn.

Noticing her solemn mood, Rod couldn't help but comment. "Maybe they didn't cover post-operation merriment at Oxford, but most people like to celebrate a success."

"Celebrate, Uncle Rod? They still have a three-hour flight ahead, not to mention the obstacles they will face flying home."

Studying her face with interest, he finally asked, "By obstacles, do you mean threading their way between Iraq and Saudi Arabia? Or are your concerns more singular?"

"You know something?" she accused him, desperate for the information he was holding back.

"Aye," he said. "But you're not going to like it."

Tori sat quietly waiting for her godfather to explain.

"They're planning to offer her a promotion and send her abroad immediately." The pained look on his face told Tori that he sincerely regretted having to tell her. "I'm sorry, lass . . ." Rod continued to apologize, attempting to soothe her with what he imagined was logical reasoning.

Tori however, began tuning out. Externally, she was too well trained and disciplined to allow her emotions to escape, but inside, inside felt like she'd just been kneed in the stomach. While Rod droned on, she began to lose the fight to control the pain. A clawing emotional torrent started ripping at her chest. She felt nauseas and her head began to spin.

". . . truthfully, I was surprised when you took up with the other one," he was saying, continuing without noticing her mood, or perhaps, with too much respect to let her know he wasn't fooled. "They want her back in Washington by Monday."

"What?" Tori asked confused. "I don't understand. Why would they send her to Washington? Who will fly the plane? I can't believe she would just up and leave it." Tori, in her confusion, ripped through a long list of questions, before she finally heard exactly what Rod had been saying. "What did you mean, when you said, I took up with the other one?"

He colored a little at the question. "I'm an old man, Victoria. I've spent most of my life married to duty and honor and I've been a lucky man. For my service I've been rewarded with a wonderful goddaughter," he explained in his marbley highland brogue. "Make no mistake, I love duty and honor, but perhaps she would have made a better mistress than wife. Lass, when you get to be my age, you start to question all the years you spent alone. I have always hoped it would be different for you. Your dad too! We all hoped you might take a fancy to someone. Someone we trusted would care for you properly." Rod half chortled as he commented, "I once even suggested that our Miss Cleopatra would be a suitable partner for you. I guess that might be why I was a wee bit taken aback when you took up with the other one, Miss Boudicca."

Tori, sitting across from him, rested her chin on her folded hands. Her head had stopped pounding and the ache in her chest was subsiding. "You don't think much of her? Boudicca, I mean."

Rod sighed, clearly not comfortable being on the hook. "Maybe this is a conversation for you and your dad?"

Tori, half smiling at him, and half grinning with childlike pleasure, announced, "Uncle Rod, I'm not involved with Agent Commanda."

Practically exploding with relief, but still terribly confused, he asked, "I don't understand. You seemed so shattered when I talked about her being recalled to America?"

Before she could explain, William burst through the kitchen door with a large serving tray. He set three teacups down, poached eggs and toast for Tori, plus fried eggs with kippers for him, and for Rod.

"Uncle Will, you're just in time," Tori said, as her other Godfather joined them. "I hope you won't be too shocked, but I wanted you both to know," she paused giving Will a moment settle in and pour the tea before announcing, "I've met someone, and I've asked her to move to London."

Both men shared a look, before Will Green spoke up. "Well thank bloody Christ! We were wondering when you might settle down."

Tori smiled at him. "Well, it's early days yet, but I'm pretty sure Uncle Rod approves."

"Uncle Rod approves? Approves of what?" Rod said, clearly demonstrating his confusion. "I have no bloody idea who it is. In Moscow, I was sure you . . ." Rod stopped talking. Tori watched, as his eyes grew bigger. "No?"

She nodded, a Cheshire grin spread across her face. Turning to Will, she explained eagerly, "her name is Cleo Deseronto, she's a pilot from Canada, and I think you'll be quite taken with her."

"Can you believe it Roddy?" Will said. "Our little girl's growing up! I can't wait to meet her. Oh," he said with excitement. "I've got to start planning your Hen party!" he announced with enthusiasm.

"Slow down Uncle Will," Tori warned. She was beaming now but still concerned with how her Uncle Rod was taking the news.

"Bloody hell, lass," Rod expelled the words like hot jet blast. "You always astonish me. A bloody bolt from the blue, without a doubt," he added, matching her grin with his own, "a bloody good one."

Dubai International Airport
United Arab Emirates

No one on board the little Otter was surprised when Dubai Tower ordered them to Hold on Taxiway Kilo, nor did the Ambulance surprise them. MI6 had advised them to expect the pickup of their liaison officer before reaching the General Aviation parking ramp. What they didn't expect was the Iranian Officer, who quietly boarded the aircraft with the ambulance attendants.

Once Major Suyfias was removed and the ambulance pulled away, the Iranian officer suggested that he switch seats with Cleo who still occupied the co-pilot's chair. "The customs officers will expect it," was all he said. When they finally parked, he got on the radio to the ground controller and requested officials expedite their customs clearance. Not only was customs willing to accommodate him, they had been informed by security that the second Iranian officer, listed on the flight plan, had fallen ill and had been taken to the airport infirmary immediately upon landing. Finally, the customs officer released the Iranian to join his flight, and stamped the team's passports, formally welcoming them to the United Arab Emirates.

Chapter Fourteen

Dubai, United Arab Emirates

Torontonians love to say there are only two seasons in Canada: winter and construction. A little winter would have made the mid-day drive with the heat, sun, and Dubai's continuous construction a little easier. As hungry as she was, Cleo was never good in the heat. When they arrived at their hotel, all she wanted to do was to head straight to her room and her bed, but found a small group of reporters waiting. The team did an impromptu interview and answered their questions. Most of the "reporters," it turned out, were journalism students from the local university. This didn't make them less insightful, just less pragmatic.

It was a nice change after some of the interviews she had endured on her book tour. On several stops, Cleo had been confronted by the people who held her responsible for Alberta's Tar Sands Oil Project, and several other Canadian misdeeds. Once she had even made the mistake of trying to explain why the annual Seal Hunt was essential to the Inuit peoples of the Arctic Council. It didn't matter that she believed all seal hunting should be off limits with the single exception of aboriginal subsistence hunters. The published interview called Cleo a hypocrite, painting her as a fossil-fuel-guzzling bomber pilot who, as a hobby, enjoyed clubbing baby seals over the head. It was a hard lesson for Cleo, one that still invoked sore feelings, and kept her vigilant with the press.

Finally done with the interviews, they headed for the hotel check-in and their rooms. It wasn't until they boarded the elevator, that the team was completely alone.

"Oo-rah!" Bo offered, in a giggly whisper.

The little cheer was followed by silence, and then stifled grins. "Hoo-ah, indeed," Albert concurred, while his restraint remained constant, his eyes where alight with amusement and something more, pride maybe. The operation was over. They had succeeded, and if Tori's enthusiasm was any indication, they had more than succeeded. Now all they had to do was keep up appearances for a few more days, then head home.

A new cover story had been planted online. Blogs were already speculating on whether the Transpolar Air Team had the financial backing to complete the entire tour. One of the journalism students in the lobby had asked who was backing them. Albert had made it sound like the Air Tour was being financed with bake sales and bingo games. That was bound to increase the speculation. Cleo's only concern now was how to tell Cyril they were turning around. Even that had been solved for her. The team received several messages when they checked in. One, it turned out, was from Cyril's dad. The kid wasn't in his own room five minutes before he came storming in to see Bo and Cleo.

"My dad says I have to come home!" he shouted, with all of the indignant outrage a teenager could foster. "I'm not going!" he said, still shouting before throwing himself in the only upholstered chair in the room.

Cleo and Bo looked at each other. The only thing Cleo wanted to do was call in her report to Vauxhall. She wasn't sure when she would get another chance to talk to Tori, even if the conversation would be all business. The operation might be over, but it was important to remain vigilant in case they were still under surveillance. When Bo failed to offer aid to Cyril, Cleo knew it was up to her. Maybe she'd get a chance to talk to Tori tomorrow.

She grabbed the hijab she had just pulled off and motioned to the kid. "C'mon Mr. Johnson, I feel like taking a walk, and you're just the man I need to escort me." When he didn't immediately get up, Cleo realized she might be forced to drag him out. There was no need. In the short time he had served as a member of her crew, he had learned the difference between orders and suggestions. It was clear the walk was no suggestion. "Bo, why don't you call the office and see if they have our updated itinerary yet."

* * *

It hadn't taken long to find a place to talk. Most of the techniques she had been taught to use in avoiding audio surveillance were null and void here. The lot next to their hotel, like every other lot in the city, was under construction. The ambient noise would be too much for any device designed to listen from a distance. They found an area in the plywood and chain link fence, where several smallish openings were cut out. The idea was to create safe places where a passerby could stop and watch the progress of the construction project.

Cyril Johnson may not have been read-in on the operation, but he had earned her trust, and that was all that really mattered when vetting a seventeen-year-old. He didn't need all the details, but she wanted to make sure he went home knowing as much as his father had been told. She didn't have to mention that he had gained the experience of actually being part of the team, and sticking with them until they were finished. And, whether they liked it or not, they were finished.

Dubai was the end of the road for the Transpolar Air Team. Cleo had thought repeatedly of continuing the route around the Poles. The biggest obstacle was the cost. Even the price of Avgas, at five dollars a gallon, was hard to swallow at twenty to thirty gallons per hour. And that was the price in North America and the Middle East. She expected it would double in places like Indonesia and Australia. She had estimated a fuel bill for the entire trip at more than 60,000 US dollars. She had actually crunched the numbers on such an excursion as part of the research for her book series. While Volume One had been quite a success for a non-fiction book, it was far too soon to gauge how Volume Two would do. If for no other reason than the timing, it was just not doable, at least not yet.

By the time Cyril and Cleo returned to the hotel, she found Bo had finished reporting in, taken a shower, and was now passed out on one of the beds. Very few people realized just how physically challenging flying could be. Bo had remained at the controls for almost all of the five-and-a-half hours it took to reach Dubai.

Cleo had already informed Cyril that he had the rest of the day off. She knew Albert was eager to see the sites, so she sent the boy off the join their crew chief, but not without a parting gift. She pulled an envelope from her flight bag and tossed it too him. Cyril tore into it, only to freeze when a stack of US twenties started spilling out.

"Don't worry," Cleo said, explaining, "I didn't rob a bank or anything. You earned it. Now go have some fun and don't spend it all in one place."

Smiling, he stuttered a flurry of indiscernible gratitudes, while making fast tracks for his room. It was only five grand. That was a lot less than what she wanted for him, but it was all Étienne could come up with. She also wanted him awarded the Meritorious Service Medal for Civilians. That too, Étienne said, was out of his hands but he would see the recommendation made it to the Governor General's office. Cyril Johnson might never know about it, but just being considered was indeed a testimony to his actions. She was sure the GG's committee would not consider him for such recognition. The simple fact was, the kid's performance was outstanding, especially considering that until thirty minutes ago, he had no idea what was going on. As soon as she was home, she intended to write a letter of recommendation for him.

She would do the same for any of them but truth be told, both Bo and Albert's "employers" would know more about their performance on this operation than she could ever put in writing. That was especially true with Boudicca. Mike Perkins had not only brought her into the operation, he had found the money to run it. It would be interesting to know what he thought of the results they had achieved. For now, that would have to wait. It didn't matter how anxious Cleo was, or how much she wanted to hear what Tori had to say, Bo was fast asleep and she didn't have the heart to wake her up. Instead she stripped out of her kit and headed for the shower. *That's probably for the best,* Cleo thought to herself. *When I get to talk to Tori, I don't want all of Vauxhall listening in. I just want a little alone time, even if we're 3,000 miles apart.*

General Aviation Ramp
Dubai International Airport

Cyril had gotten a little choked up when Cleo gave him a good-bye hug. They were standing in the portico of the Exxon General Aviation building. The van that had driven them from the hotel was waiting while Cyril and Bo said their farewells. The two had been ordered home immediately. Cyril by his father, and Bo too had fresh orders from the FBI. Their next stop was the main airport terminal. They would board a British Airways flight to London, then after being debriefed, Cyril would fly Air Canada to Toronto and Bo would fly military priority AA to Washington, DC.

Bo had been offered a promotion and an assignment with the Bureau of Indian Affairs. It was exactly the type of work she was after and the FBI had come through as promised. Cleo gave Special Agent Commanda a big hug good-bye.

Albert did the same, giving Bo a big hug before turning to Cyril for a handshake. The handshake offered, was a traditional warrior's clasp of the forearms, and caught the boy off guard. No one had ever considered him a warrior, especially not a real one like Albert. Cyril Johnson beamed with pride and new confidence, as he and Bo got back in the van, waving furiously as they pulled away.

With their co-pilot and loadmaster gone, Albert and Cleo walked quietly to the ramp and the waiting DeHavilland Otter. Technically, the Otter was all hers now, although MI6 and the CIA would still be picking up the fuel tab until they reached London. It was going to be a long haul back without the Joker and Bat Girl on board. Thankfully, Cleo and Albert had the same taste in music. He had rigged his iPod to one of the intercom channels. They could now blast away with the tunes while monitoring Air Traffic Control.

Today, they would fly to Amman, Jordan, and stop for the night. Tomorrow, weather permitting, they would skirt around the Mediterranean Sea, all the way to Athens. That flight-leg was three hundred miles shorter, but would require transitioning the airspace of several different nations. For today, they would head west from Dubai then turn northwest to transverse the entirety of Saudi Arabia for the kingdom of Jordan. The flight planning for the return trip was almost anticlimactic; they still had to be cautious, especially with Iran. If they strayed too far north they would enter Iraqi airspace, and too far west could put them in the Sinai region. Still, it was an easier flight than they had faced to date. The heat and the constant headwinds did wear on them, but they touched down in Amman just before sunset, and enjoyed supper in the hotel restaurant before heading to their rooms.

Security and Intelligence Service
Vauxhall Cross
London, United Kingdom

Darcy Gerrard was hovering outside the Lancaster Room. It might be quitting time in most London offices, but at MI6, many of the regional security teams were just getting started. The group covering South America was presently briefing C and his Section Commanders on Argentina's battered banking sector. Sir Richard, aware that Dr. Gerrard was waiting, moved the briefing to a quick conclusion. The minute the meeting broke-up, Darcy pushed in, shooing everyone from the room except for Tori and C. "Allan's picked up some chatter out of Jordan, and it has our girl all over it!"

"What?" Tori asked confused. For her, the Iranian Op was over. Getting Cleo and Albert home now was simply a lesson in basic cross-country navigation.

Rod Nelligan, who had followed Darcy into the office, seemed struck by the announcement too. "What would the Jordanians want with our people?"

The question seemed to double the strain on Darcy Gerrard's boyish face. "No one's interested in Mr. Mackenzie. At least they haven't mentioned him. It's Cleo Deseronto they want."

"Darcy," Tori ordered, pointing to a chair. "Sit down and tell us exactly who and what the threat is." She was trying to calm him down while keeping herself under control. "What new Intel have you uncovered? What could the Iranians be up to?"

"That's it," Darcy said, looking completely shattered. "It's not Iran. Or Jordan, or any other nation we might expect. Some of the channels are . . . American!" he strained in a hushed tone, that only served to reveal the depth of his shock.

"Who exactly wants her?" Sir Richard asked pointedly. "And why?"

As the in-house psychiatrist, it was Darcy Gerrard's job to evaluate both the mental state of operatives, as well as any threats to that mental state. Sir Richard was sure the man was feeling like he had let Deseronto down. He had evaluated and approved her participation in the mission, fully aware that she was still carrying the emotional scars from her last incarceration.

Bracing himself, Darcy practically whispered, "Mossad agents were supposed to grab her during the team's scheduled stop in Mumbai. We picked up heavy in-fighting between the Israeli Defense Force, Mossad, and some old CIA backchannels, when they realized, too late, that the team had turned around."

"By now," Rod, thinking out loud, speculated, "They'll have her new flight plan and know where she's headed."

"Where she is," Darcy said, correcting the chief. "According to my schedule, she and Sergeant Mackenzie have already landed. How do we know they haven't nabbed her already?"

Surprising everyone, Tori cut in, "I have a man covering them. Currently, they are both in the hotel dining room."

"I doubt very much that the Mossad, as bold as they are, will attempt to grab her in Jordan," Sir Richard pointed out. "Darcy, grab Allan and get everyone in the Tank working on this. Tell the twins to snatch anything of relevance they can mine from the IDF mainframe but not to go near the Mossad network, or Shin Bet, under any circumstances." He looked back and forth between Tori and Darcy to make sure they both understood. He let Darcy leave before turning all of his attention to Tori, "have your people dig up every shred of intelligence out there. We need to know who or what is truly behind this. While you work that side, Rod and I will try a little old-fashioned diplomacy." Standing, he turned for his office before asking, "Have you finished debriefing the other one?"

"The other one?" Tori asked, before realizing what he was saying. "You mean, of course, Special Agent Commanda? She is still being debriefed. The Americans are planning to fly her out by military transport later this evening. She however, has been encouraging the debriefing team to take their time, with an aim at missing her scheduled flight. She wants to fly commercial. Evidently it's more comfortable than sitting in webbing for seven hours!"

"That soon?" Sir Richard said, without commenting on the comfort jab. "I would have assumed she would want to enjoy a little holiday with you first."

"Perhaps," Rod interjected, clearing his throat diplomatically, "this would be a good time for you Victoria, to bring your father up to speed on your uh, situation?"

Tori colored slightly but understood exactly why Uncle Rod had chosen this precise time to bring the subject up. She closed her eyes for a millisecond to frame a reply. The worst part about telling her father something personal was that he almost always seemed to already know. By way of explanation Tori simply blurted, "I know it's near impossible for relationships to work in this job. All the same, I want the chance."

Sir Richard studied his daughter for a moment. This wasn't the first time she had gotten involved with someone. By all accounts, Tori had enjoyed more than her fair share of companions but never anyone serious. This however was different. Even though he had suggested it, it took Sir Richard a moment to realize that his daughter was referring to Cleo Deseronto and not Agent Commanda. He stood and walked the three steps to where his daughter was standing, and placed his heavy hands on her shoulders, "Why this one?"

"She fits me!"

That was not what he had expected to hear. Long ago, he had developed what her Petty Officer godfathers referred to as the Tori Interest Scale. Dad and the boys simply noted her enthusiasm for someone new then inverted that level. Thus, the more Tori talked about the new man or woman in her life, the shorter they expected the relationship to last. And so far, they had been dead right, every time. Sir Richard sighed to himself, *a simple three-word sentence*. Tori had never described anyone in this fashion.

"First, let's concentrate on getting her home. Then, I will decide if I should welcome her into the family, or wring her modest red neck." He squeezed Tori's shoulder, watching her turn for the Tank. It wouldn't take long for her to get everyone working and focused on finding the pertinent intelligence they would need. Once she was clear of the meeting room, he motioned for Rod to follow him. "I want you to get over to the US Embassy and talk to Mike Perkins. He gave me his word that no one would re-open this nonsense. If they want *Trooper* Deseronto now, it better be for a good reason!"

"Fair enough," Rod replied. "I take it you're off to meet with our Israeli counterpart then?"

Rod and Sir Richard had boarded the lift while they talked. The secure elevator opened at the car pool level, where a car and driver were waiting. "Ride with me, Chief."

Rod Nelligan walked around the waiting vehicle and climbed into the rear passenger seat. Sir Richard, already in the sedan, signaled the driver to pull out the moment the doors closed.

"First things first," Sir Richard ordered. "Take the *other one* into holding. If the Americans are involved with this, we may have to remind them that one does not abduct our people without consequence."

Rod's eyes widened. "Yeh' sure you want to take that road?"

"I am certain my daughter will survive the loss of one Lieutenant Colonel Deseronto, Royal Canadian Air Force, but I gave that girl my word and I will not back down. Not without a very good reason, or a direct order from our own superiors to do so." Sir Richard knew his language was harsh. There were often times when he was forced to adopt a *by-the-book* stance that clashed with Rod's world view. That was part of the job. What was good for the nation was not always best for the individuals involved. Frankly, intelligence work had a way of devouring the best and brightest.

"Good reason?" Rod asked quietly. "That girl saved our lives."

"I don't need to be reminded of that!" C snapped at his oldest friend.

"Maybe you should be." Rod Nelligan was truly annoyed. "If she hadn't, the last memory your Victoria would have of her lovin' father would have been a vid of some jihadists draggin' yer dead body through the streets of Beirut. Speaking of which," Rod said, aggressively pushing the point. "What is it that the Israeli's don't already know about that operation? Why do they want her back nineteen bloody years later?"

"If you are under the impression that I'm happy about this, you are mistaken."

"Good God, man! What if Caroline were here?" Rod asked referring to Tori's deceased mother. "How would you explain sacrificing your daughter's love interest?"

"The only thing her mother would be asking is what I did to turn her daughter into a lesbian!"

"Is that what's eating at you?" Rod exhaled bluntly. "Caroline would not have been surprised or upset. It runs in the family! She told you that on your first date! Tori's Aunt Clara is as lavender as they come. Bloody hell, Ritchie, you have a gay uncle. If that's your only complaint, then I think you've horribly underestimated your daughter, and her feelings."

The silence inside the sedan seemed to engulf them and the surrounding roadway. Rod Nelligan was Sir Richard's oldest and dearest friend. They had been mates since Richard's earliest days in the Navy, when he had been an uncomplicated, wet-behind-the-ears Midshipman.

Back then, plain and common Richard Braithwaite's only ambition was to one day command a squadron. Early on in his career, he had been "noticed" and his progress monitored. Rod Nelligan, as a Petty Officer attached to Aviation Academy of the Fleet Air Arm, noticed the brash young Richard Braithwaite too, and offered to mentor the promising young officer. In less time than it took most Navy pilots to reach the rank of lieutenant and earn a co-pilot's position, Richard had his command, a Sea King Squadron aboard HMS *Bulwark*.

The "Rusty B" as the crew affectionately referred to her, was the oldest of her Majesty's Aircraft Carriers, but that didn't matter a snick to Richard. It was his Squadron, and he was determined to put his stamp on it, from the very start. His first order of business was to name Rod Nelligan Squadron Chief Petty Officer, as well as retaining him in his previous capacity of Crew Chief on his helicopter.

With his new position, Rod was responsible for the health, welfare, and discipline of every NCO and Rating assigned to the squadron. It was unusual for the squadron chief to continue with flying duties once promoted, but Richard reasoned that if he and the squadron's Executive Officer could find time amongst their various administrative duties to fly, then Chief Nelligan would be an example to the ship's company of how it's done.

Two years later, when HMS *Bulwark* was laid-up for refit, Richard Braithwaite accidentally took the first tentative steps towards his new career. He was the junior-most officer to be accepted to the newly formed Defense Academy of the UK. The prestige of the school and the Master's Degree it offered quickly became renowned within the military and intelligence communities. One of Richard's classmates was head analyst at MI6, and it didn't take long for that organization to come to the same conclusion the Navy had reached. Richard Braithwaite was a man with a future. For the next eight years a battle was waged between the Navy and MI6 for him.

Cleo and Richard had met back when he was doing the job he loved most, flying a helicopter. He had been assigned to an advanced avionics testing group and had taken Rod Nelligan, as usual, along as his chief. His co-pilot had been assigned by the Commanding Officer of the test group. After the crash, many had hinted that those inside Richard's inner circle were untouchable. He had actually gained that reputation during the Falklands War during Operation Mikado.

Operation Mikado had been run up the ladder twice and had twice been shot down. Both versions had been too complex and convoluted in Richard's opinion, and he had said so when he proposed version three. It was simple: one helicopter, one aircrew, and one squad of Royal Marines or Special Air Service commandos. The operation would be strictly "off the reservation," with Richard and the SAS squad leader searching for and harassing targets of opportunity. Their ultimate target would be the five advanced fighter jets and Exocet missiles the Argentineans had purchased from the French government.

Many had assumed Operation Mikado had failed when the fighters and armaments were still intact at the end of the Falklands War. While the first two plans had called for incursion of the fighter base by force, the wholesale murder of the aircrews and the complete destruction of the Exocet missiles, Richard thought better. Choosing instead to infiltrate the base without being detected, locate the missiles, and then enter the failure codes. The codes had been quietly provided by the French manufacturer, who also happened to be a large British defense contractor. Once done, the Exocet Missiles would have the destructive force of a paperweight. The Argentineans had to choose between admitting a half-dozen SAS commandos had infiltrated a highly secure bunker guarded by four battalions of Marines, or maintain their pride and never mention the circumstances of the missile failure. In a nation where so much is placed on macho pride, it was no surprise that the French never received even the slightest hint of protest from Argentina.

Sir Richard's staff car pulled up in front of the US Embassy. Rod Nelligan was half out when he stopped and turned back to his old friend. "Your girl deserves better, Ritchie. They both do."

"I know that, and I want that too, for both of them." He sighed at the personal gravity of the situation. "I just wish life could be easier for her. Everything she does is already doubly scrutinized, because she's my daughter, and a Dufferin. A relationship, this relationship, could very well end her career."

"Things have changed, Ritchie. You know that. Besides, for better or for worse it's her choice." Rod offered, still half-in and half-out of the sedan. "Moreover, it's early days yet. Maybe we should concentrate on getting our wee Cleopatra home before we debate Tori's opportunities lost or found?"

Sir Richard nodded his agreement with Rod and watched the old Scotsman as he headed into the US Embassy. Now all he needed to do was uncover the real reason the Israelis wanted *Trooper* Deseronto.

Hotel Americana
Amman, Kingdom of Jordan

Tori had wanted to call Cleo as soon as she checked into the hotel, but too much was still unresolved. If she was going to rob Cleo of a night's rest, she would do so when she had something encouraging to report. When the hotel switchboard put her call through it was just past midnight local time, and she wasn't surprised to hear Cleo's sleep-ridden voice. "Sweetheart, I've woken you, I'm so sorry!" Tori said, over the long distance line. "I was eager for a little chin wag?"

Cleo groaned her reply.

Tori listened to the telltale sound of bed linen being tossed.

"I'm awake now," she announced. "Still want to, what did you say, wiggle-waggle?"

"Chin wag. It means to have a discussion, you silly goose," she explained, trying to sound light-hearted. "Although, once you're home, we can work on our waggle too."

Cleo stretched and tried to yawn silently. "Oh, now that sounds much more fun."

"I could spend all night talking about nothing at all, and enjoying it very much, but we have something more difficult to tackle."

"It's never simple, is it? So what's the problem now? Are the Yanks going to pull Albert too?"

"Not exactly," was all Tori could think to say. There was no real way to ease into things with Cleo. She had found it best to follow Rod's example, and simply drop the ball in her court and see what she came back with. "The Israelis would like to ask you a few questions." For a moment Tori could only hear static on the line.

"Did you say the Israelis? Wait, did Bo put you up to this?"

"Sweetheart," Tori almost wailed. "Please wake up. I need you to listen. We have a serious threat."

"I heard you," now very wake, Cleo voice was dead sober. "I was just hoping I misunderstood. Does anyone know why? I don't mean the reason they're giving everyone, but the real reason they want to *talk?* Again!"

Even over the long-distance phone line, Tori couldn't miss her emphasis. "We are working on that. Cleo, the entire team is on this. I promise you we will have answers soon."

"Answers are good," she said, trying to sound jovial. "You know, the Americans must have some idea what this is really all about. It's not the Wild, Wild East anymore. And it's certainly not like the Israelis to run around grabbing whomever they like. Well," Cleo chuckled lightly, "maybe they have grabbed a few people over the years, but I understand they were all very, very bad."

Tori wasn't surprised to hear her joke, and countered back, "what, like *Trooper* Deseronto? I understand she was very bad indeed."

"Oh!" Cleo sang out. "What did you call me the other day, a philistine?" The sound of her smile could be heard over the line. "Oh Tori, that poor little Trooper was nothing more than a thick-headed numbskull, with a foul mouth and a bad temper. I tell yah, she had the whole *gor'am* shootin' match goin' on!"

"I see," Tori said, following along, before asking "How is it I never hear you swear; at least not in English. What's that all about?"

"Originally I was just trying to promote multiculturalism by learning to cuss in several languages! Besides, I had to stop saying things like 'fuck' after the chief told me what it meant."

"I presume you're referring to our Chief Nelligan, and you're saying you were shocked to learn the meaning of the f-word at the tender age of . . ." Tori had to visually recall Cleo's service record. "At nineteen?"

"That is not what I meant, you *chen-wa!* I was referring to the Military Acronym: Forced Use of Carnal Knowledge!"

Tori was caught off guard by the revelation, "I had no idea my love. Is that why your profanities seem to be a bunch of made up words?"

"Exactly," she said with pride, "except I didn't make them up. I just borrowed them from sci-fi programs. That way I reduce the risk of insulting someone's culture or heritage, and the science fiction enthusiasts get a private little laugh from my military posture."

Tori sighed contentedly. "I can't decide if you're a psychological genius or a friggin' nutter?" The little laugh they both enjoyed flamed out when Tori turned the conversation back to the situation at hand. "I have approved an extraction plan that would pull you from the hotel before dawn. You will be flown by Jordanian military transport to RAF Cyprus. From there, getting you home, is simply an exercise in logistics." When Tori referred to home, she meant London, and presupposed that Cleo thought that way too. The long pause on the line forced her to wonder if she had supposed too much.

"I think I should stay. Whatever Mossad needs to know will not be answered if you smuggle me off. What's to say they won't just grab me in London?"

"They wouldn't dare!"

Cleo's chuckle was easy to hear. "Now you sound like a stuck-up Limey!"

Tori laughed too. She hated sounding like some posh knob. "So you want to run with this. Well then, I need to know what support you want and where?"

"Fair enough," she answered, thinking carefully about the situation. "Well, Intel would be the priority, starting with what they want or at least what they know. I also need a clear idea of what I can and can't discuss. Then I need one piece of Intel they don't have, it doesn't have to be real, you can make it up, but it does have to be plausible."

"I think I understand, you're after some sort of bargaining chip?" Tori asked.

"Actually, I was looking for a line I could plant that your team could follow, and hopefully follow back to whomever or whatever is actually behind this."

"Smart," Tori admitted, "but it will have to be something almost inconsequential. The Intel community is quite adept these days at routing out disinformation. I'll work on that. Anything else?"

After a pause, Cleo asked, "you won't let anyone take my airplane will you?" Her despair was evident in every syllable.

Tori might have laughed, if Cleo hadn't sounded so wretched. "Take your airplane! Good God, Cleo! I call to warn that a foreign intelligence service plans to take you into custody and your first concern is that sodding piece of tin?"

Laughing softly, she couldn't help but joke around. "Actually, my first concern was that you might do something hasty."

"What, like send in the Royal Marines?"

"Oh, wouldn't that be a headline. Royal Marines descend on the Hotel Americana."

"Not exactly the sort of low profile Op I prefer," Tori laughed too. The lightness Cleo brought to the conversation was a gift. As Rod Nelligan had described it, Cleo became this soothing bundle of light, at the very moment things seemed darkest. Tori prayed she could keep it up. If she let this play out, there was no telling how things would go. "Are you sure you don't want me to pull you out now? Sweetheart, really! This might not go well. Are you prepared for that?"

"I can't answer that, at least not honestly," Cleo said. "Only time will tell if I am prepared and what it is I need to be prepared for. I just think the important thing here would be to follow this through to the finish. If I don't do it now, I'm sure it'll just keep popping up again and again."

"That's a long stretch don't you think?"

"Could be, but without a better idea about what's going on, I think meeting them straight on is our best play. At least until you can come up with something better."

Tori sighed. Cleo was right. At the moment they had nothing better, and perhaps just going straight to the source was the best defense. "All right my love, we play this round your way, but you have to allow me to work the situation from this side. I will not sit on my hands. Is that understood?"

"Yes Ma'am," Cleo said with the enthusiasm of a first-year cadet. "Now, how about we leave the shop talk for my morning briefing? I assume you're planning to brief me in the blessed a.m.?"

"Of course, bright and early, say zero five hundred, your time? I know how exhausted you must be, but the Mossad can be quite bold. I would hate for them to *collect* you before we speak again."

Cleo groaned. "So, you are planning to speak to me again, even if I love my airplane?"

"Even if you love your airplane more than me!" She hadn't meant to say it. Tori wasn't ashamed to admit she was in love with Cleo, but this was hardly the time. Even if they had both discussed pursuing a relationship, neither had voiced their feelings, and she was suddenly distraught at the thought of Cleo's reaction.

She need not have worried. Cleo's voice was loud and clear, "I knew you were jealous of her! And to think, I just spent the last nine hours of flying time telling her that you were *numero uno*, and she'd just have to get used to being the only other thing in this world that I love."

It wasn't exactly a conventional espousal of love, but nothing Cleo did was conventional. Sitting in her Vauxhall office, the whole situation felt surreal. "Cleopatra," Tori said gently, "promise me you will take care, and I'll call back in five hours with everything we can scratch up."

They exchanged farewells and finally Tori laid the receiver down. Several minutes passed before she became aware that she had been sitting, just sitting, unfocused and lost. For the first time in her life, she felt overwhelmed. Tori had just met Cleo, but already she felt so much more than connected. She hadn't imagined it could be like that, and the sex had been a surprise too. Tori touched her fingertips to her lips without thinking. There was no forgetting the way Cleo's hands had seemed to glide over her skin, following lines of muscle and sinew, from knee to neck and back again. How those hands had caressed her every curve, holding her, encouraging her to slow, to breathe, to let go.

Tori slapped her hand on her desk, and stood up, as if trying to shake off the image of Cleo in her Moscow hotel room. Cleo had fallen asleep sprawled in the center of the bed. A bent knee and outstretched arm hinted that she had reached out for Tori. The bed linen had pooled on the floor with the exception of the top sheet, of which, only a small corner draped across Cleo's hip.

Tori paused for the longest time, transfixed by the tableau vivant. Dressed in a hotel robe, she stood, watching Cleo sleep, with only the Moscow night to illuminate the scene. With the robe pulled tight across her chest, Tori squeezed the collar closed against the cold night air. Watching Cleo sleep was like glimpsing into her soul. Awake, Cleo was fun and light, insightful and strong. Asleep, she was sensuous in a manner she had never encountered. Like her Clan's namesake, she slept like a bear, completely unthreatened by the world around her and oblivious to the cool temperature of the room. Her skin too, was like nothing Tori had ever felt. Her skin was smooth and soft but thick somehow, like some inexplicably exotic hide. The heat had been a surprise too. Cleo could somehow influence her body temperature. As some sort of response to the cool room, every inch of her skin seemed to heat up. Touching her was like reaching out to a warm fire but with no risk of being burnt.

Tori sat down beside her. Cleo, not completely asleep, offered a hand, inviting her back to bed. Taking her hand, she allowed Cleo to pull her into a comforting embrace. As Cleo pulled the top sheet up to cover her, Tori snuggled back. For the first time she understood what it meant to "fit" someone so perfectly. She was fascinated by their intellectual and emotional fit, but the physical sensation of skin-to-skin, head-to-foot, had been overwhelming.

"Mai Mai," Cleo murmured, her voice drifting from just behind her ear, "You're beautiful."

Tori, rolling in Cleo's arms, turned her face to her. A moan inadvertently escaping at the sensation of Cleo's arms and legs intertwining with her own. "Mai Mai? What does that mean?"

It was hard for Cleo to answer immediately. Tori had chosen that precise moment to wrap her long arms around her neck, pulling her into a deep languorous kiss. When she moved on to the hollow of her neck, Cleo began, haltingly, "Mai is Mandarin for sister, but if you double it, it means the woman in question is someone extraordinary. Someone intelligent and beautiful," she whispered, adding, "someone like you."

Tori responded to the compliment by deepening the kiss. The accompanying moan was simply non-verbal gratitude. Cleo's breathing hitched at the onslaught of sensation from Tori's attention. Pulling her closer, she slowly traced a line from Tori's hip to her face, before retracing the line with her lips.

Now in her office, alone and unfocused, Tori struggled for a solution. Today they had admitted their love, albeit, quite unconventionally. Nine days ago, they had made love for the first time. Seven days earlier, they had walked along Fort Lauderdale beach every evening, sharing their ideas, hopes, and hinting around at a joint future. After all the stories she had heard, from both Rod and her father, she felt as if she had known Cleo for years. That wasn't true though. What did she really know about Cleopatra Deseronto, RCAF (ret.)? They had met each other only sixty-seven days ago. Sixty-seven days. A linear measure, Cleo would point out. Something, she had suggested, the human spirit was powerless to comprehend. Human spirit, human heart, but what about the human world? From where she was sitting, there was never any escape from the reality of the world around them. Whispering, "Cleopatra. Please forgive me," Tori entered her password, to open a Top Secret file she was loath to read. It wasn't the contents she feared, but the thought of delving into Cleo's psyche. Cleo was slow to trust and had shared so much of her troubled past, in the name of full disclosure, already. When the full document opened, she groaned at the page count: Fifty-one pages. Dr. Darcy Gerrard had long ago learned to be precise in his professional communications. Tori had read his Operational Assessment, but sealed the complete study he had compiled on Cleo and Bo, unread. There was no need for anyone to access the sensitive details of the traumas each had endured, either in childhood, or as adults. Tori scrolled to the introductory paragraph and began to read. She had no choice. Either, examine every detail they had on Cleo, with a view to save her life and risking her trust, or respect her privacy and lose her anyway. Darcy had told her that Cleo didn't believe in the no-win scenario, and today, for Cleo's sake, she wouldn't either.

Chapter Fifteen

Amman International Airport
Amman, Kingdom of Jordan

Day 1, 06:00 UTC

Cleo spread out a blanket and sat down cross-legged, in the only shade to be found, under the wing of the Otter. At half past eight in the morning, it was already scorching hot. The temperature had surpassed her comfort zone and perfectly suited everything else whirling around in her head. Things were not shaping up the way she had hoped.

First had been the early morning briefing, which turned up a lot of speculation and nothing concrete, except for the deal Sir Richard had worked out. Based on Cleo's willingness to meet with the Israeli authorities, she was to fly directly to Haifa, where she would spend a few hours clarifying the information they had collated all those years ago. The Israelis had framed their request as a review of past incidents that could be considered Post Traumatic Stress Disorder.

During the six weeks she spent in the detention center, she had been isolated from the other inmates for her own protection. She knew the technique was designed to force a prisoner to bond with their interrogator. The emotional link would then become a carrot dangled to motivate the prisoner, or a lifeline offered with strings attached. Cleo laughed at the long parade of interrogators they had tried to "fit" her with. Whoever had been pulling the strings back then had failed to bond anyone, or thing, to her. She guessed then and still believed now, that the psychological model in use, couldn't be used with someone like her. *Is it being Native or is it just me? Gran always said I preferred my own company!*

After enduring six weeks of isolation and endless interrogations, her unknown captors had driven her to Ben Gurion airport, putting her on the first ElAl flight for Europe. Hours later, Cleo landed in Copenhagen wearing a combat uniform that looked bad, and smelled worse than your average hockey bag after a weekend tournament. Her distinctive blue United Nations beret and cap badge had been "lost," as had her ID, and dog tags. When she landed, all she had on her was a Canadian fifty-dollar bill she kept hidden in the tongue of her boot. Whoever had searched her things had missed the hidden pocket she had created the day they were issued. It wasn't anything she had been taught from her instructors; it was just instinct. Cleo may not have been university bound back then, but she had graduated from the hard streets of Toronto's Regent Park.

With the fifty-dollar bill now firmly stuffed in her pocket, the nineteen-year-old, exhausted and disoriented peacekeeper from Canada, disembarked the ElAl jet and began a slow, confusing search for assistance. Cleo had assumed that Danish Customs would detain her until the federal police could contact the Canadian Embassy. It wasn't until she approached the fourth or fifth official-looking person that she found someone who spoke enough English to understand her situation. She was also surprised to learn that she had already cleared customs without realizing it. The English-speaking Good Samaritan was a flight attendant with SAS, Scandinavia's national airline. He pointed out where in the concourse she could find a phone, and where she could exchange her money. Cleo thanked him and headed for the currency exchange first.

Back in the day, the Canadian dollar did not go far compared to most European currencies. For her trouble, Cleo's fifty bucks worked down to a measly nine Danish Kroner. Certainly not enough for a taxi cab to the embassy, wherever that might be. The next option was to call the embassy and report her situation. Her first attempt ended with a rude operator, who explained impatiently that the replacement of lost ID required twenty-four-hours' notice. She would also be required to pay a twenty-dollar replacement fee when the passport office reopened on the next business day. Cleo's second call was received by the same operator, who, obviously irritated by her inability to follow simple instructions, transferred her to an answering machine where a complaint could be left. Cleo rested her head against the acrylic partition that separated each phone box and pushed hard to hold back the tears. *Third time's a charm*, she told herself and redialed the number, now from memory.

By luck or fluke someone else answered, and not willing to risk the same misunderstanding, Cleo announced, "This is Captain Green, UNDOF Command. Put me through to the Military Attaché immediately."

The operator was respectful but unimpressed. "I don't believe he's available this afternoon, Ma'am. Would you like to try again tomorrow?"

"He better be available," Cleo warned, realizing that she'd be sleeping on a bench if she didn't break through this bureaucratic wall. "You tell him, we have a situation here. I'll hold," Cleo announced, and then added, "You tell him we are code word Valiant!"

The operator switched the call to hold without comment. Code words were assigned whenever an operation required compartmentalization or when the security clearance needed was higher than Top Secret. Cleo had no idea if there was, or had ever been, an operation named Valiant. It was just a name that popped into her head as she began her impromptu masquerade as a UN officer. She could only hope the officer on duty had too low a clearance to be briefed on code word operations or was too proud to admit he didn't have a clue what Valiant was. The gambit had all the makings of a complete disaster with a Court Marshal thrown in for fun.

Seconds later a male voice answered the phone, sounding like he had run some distance. "Lieutenant Semple, Sir! I mean Ma'am, Captain . . ."

"Semple," Cleo breathed a sigh of relief, a young wet-behind-the-ears junior officer made things easier. "I've got a young private who has been missing for months and has just resurfaced in Copenhagen. I need you to pick her up immediately."

"Wow, yes Sir. Ma'am, sorry," Lt. Semple apologized again. "I've never had an AWOL case before."

"She's not AWOL, Lieutenant," Cleo said a little too forcefully. "This soldier was kidnapped and has either been released or escaped. I need you to get to the Copenhagen Airport and pick her up before something else befalls her. Is that understood, Lieutenant?"

"Her? Yes Ma'am," Semple replied then seemed to change his mind. "What do I do with her once I pick her up? We haven't any female quarters here or anything like that."

"That's all right," Cleo assured him. "What I need you to do is pick her up, get her some ID and a travel advance, then put her on the next train to Germany. I want her on that train tonight, Mr. Semple. An SIU team is flying in from Trenton, and I want Trooper Deseronto there tomorrow morning, when they arrive."

"I understand Captain, but I think I should run this by my boss, Captain Hanson?" Semple said tentatively. "He's going to be back from leave tomorrow or maybe later tonight."

"For Christ sakes Semple, did you miss the part about this kid having been kidnapped? God knows what condition she's in, or exactly what they did to her." With as much force and military decorum as she could muster, she added. "You do whatever you want as far as your chain of command, but I'm ordering you to get her squared away immediately, and on that train tonight."

Wanting desperately to prove himself, Semple grabbed at the opportunity. "I've got a pen and paper Ma'am, ready to copy!"

After everything that had transpired, Cleo hadn't know where to go, or who could be trusted. In training, the instructors advised their recruits to turn themselves into the nearest command, but instinct had kicked in, and she still had no idea why she'd been grabbed. For that matter, she was sure it had happened with the oversight of her Command, the United Nations Disengagement Observer Force for the Golan Heights. How else could a team enter a secure military compound and remove her without anyone taking notice?

Cleo remembered falling asleep in her bunk in Syria and waking in a holding cell in Tel Aviv. Her grandfather had taught her that when you save a man's life, you share a debt of honor. Days before being nabbed, Cleo had helped to save two British Navy officers. Her gut had told her that those two could be trusted. Maybe not to tell her what was going on. Cleo was sure that was way beyond her pay grade and really didn't care. What she needed was someone to help her figure out what to do next.

Resting under the wing of the Otter, Cleo watched Albert make his way from the hangar to where she was camped out. "Have a seat," she ordered. Albert sat down, nodding his head toward the engine cowl she had removed.

"Find another problem?"

They had experienced a fuel pump failure during the start-up and were stuck AOG until a replacement could be installed. Of course, installing it would be an easy job for either of them. The real trick would be finding one. While there were still hundreds of DeHavilland Otters in operation all over the world, Cleo doubted there was a single one registered within five hundred miles, and was sure that was true for aircraft parts as well. After the failure, she had cancelled their flight plan, while Albert had gone to the Jet Center looking for help in locating a supplier with DeHavilland parts.

That had bothered Cleo. For some reason, she didn't like Albert's reaction to their breakdown. For that matter, she was suspicious of the fuel pump failure itself. Fuel pumps weren't known to fail unless they had seen unusually long and hard hours of use. It had bothered her enough, that once Albert was out of sight, she climbed back in to the aircraft and ran the pre-start checklist again. This time, without the cacophony of paperwork and radio communication, Cleo was able to listen to the Otter. *Come on girl. Tell me what's really wrong*, she whispered then flipped the pump switch. Nothing. Cleo cycled the switch. Still nothing.

It occurred to her that the Otter's big piston engine, compared to the turbines on the Hercules, had one feature that the C-130s powerplant lacked: an old-fashioned primer. Cleo pumped the primer handle five times, then pulled the handle from the pedestal, completely removing it before sticking her index finger into the empty sleeve. It was dry. She was tired, but knew she had to figure this out. The aircraft had been refueled yesterday when they landed. She had just re-checked the actual fuel levels for each tank, along with draining any water, and completing an *eyeball* check for quality, before attempting a start-up. So fuel couldn't be the problem. If the tanks were full, but the primer and the fuel pump failed to supply the engine, then there was something else going on.

Cleo opened the pilot's door and climbed out onto the engine cowl, unscrewing the fasteners holding the top of the big metal skins in place. Once done, she climbed back inside, shimmied her way through the cabin and jumped down onto the tarmac. Returning to the engine, she removing the engine cover from below. Once everything was open for inspection, it was easy to find the problem. The fuel pump hadn't failed; it was gone. And without the pump, the cut fuel line was literally hanging in the air. The pump had been removed and she doubted there was a mechanic within a thousand miles with a use for it.

"Did you find a spare?" Cleo asked, as Albert took a seat beside her.

"We lucked out. There's an aviation firm in Israel that supplies parts to the entire Middle East. They can have one here in two days. Or we can rig-up a by-pass, fly to Haifa, and install the replacement today." He was obviously pleased with the outcome of his search. Tipping his head towards the aircraft, he asked again, "Is there something else wrong?"

Cleo had thought about the strategy she should use but being direct was all she and Albert knew. It was their SOP. "The pump didn't fail. It was removed. Did you know about this?"

Albert looked as surprised by the revelation as she had been. She was sure he was hiding something but this wasn't it.

In response to her directness, he explained in a pensive tone, "I was given new orders last night."

"New orders?" Cleo had expected Mike Perkins would have asked him to keep an extra eye out, but delaying their departure didn't make sense. If he was trying to protect her from the Mossad, then sitting here and waiting for them to catch up, was a mistake. And forcing them to fly to Haifa for the replacement part was crazy too. Cleo had already agreed to meet the Israeli interview team today. Forcing her hand seemed a little over the top.

Albert was the key she needed to unlock the mystery, but how? He didn't seem willing to share what his new orders were, and she was reluctant to ask. "In this day, we all answer to more than one master. And we, First Nations people, have gotten pretty good at balancing all the differing demands heaped upon us. We have stayed loyal to our spirituality, whether that includes the Code of Handsome Lake, or not. We have remained loyal to the Mohawk Nation and the Six Nations, and we have served a host of colonizing nations with the same courage and loyalty for over four hundred years. It's worked out pretty well, except on those occasions when we have been ordered to serve the needs of one brother in opposition to another . . . that's when things get complicated."

Albert's head hung slightly. "Like the American Revolution? I know the Americans asked us to join their cause and were disappointed to find the Grand Council considered it dishonorable to interfere in a conflict between brothers."

"Exactly, and you know the *Yahn-keys* sure didn't take that very well."

"Yah," Albert said, the unfairness evident in his dark eyes. "When we were at Onondaga, I was really hit by the injustice of it. Their descendants had witnessed the wholesale destruction of the Five Nations of the Iroquois for choosing to remain neutral. The Onondaga must have been desperate to offer their loyalty to the Americans, hoping to avoid their fierce retribution. But look at that place now! For their loyalty, the Onondaga Nation has been stripped and starved down to what, a few thousand members and a shitty thirty-five-acre scrap of land. Where's the justice? Where's the respect?"

Cleo listened to him vent. It wasn't like she hadn't fumed over past and present injustices herself. She was pretty sure though, that whatever he had been ordered to do was the real cause of his current discomfort. Duty versus honor. It was the ultimate conundrum for the military mind.

"You know, with everything that's been going on and our hectic schedule, I missed out on some of your storytelling. Bo says you're the master, and I really missed something. Since we have time, why don't you tell me one now?" It was hardly what you would call cryptic, but they were too short on time for true subterfuge.

"A story, now?" Albert asked impatiently. He was just about to refuse when Cleo gave him a look, hoping to impart her strategy. She watched carefully as that revelation flashed quickly in his eyes, "any story?"

"Whatever you're up for," she suggested amiably. "Isn't there an old story about a bear and wolf? Those are always my favorite." It was a little too blatant, but she was getting restless and wanted answers. Albert, for his part, seemed to need a moment to actually decide how far he would go.

"Just a story?" he asked. It wasn't a real question. The man had his six in a crack, but he was still committed to the team. "Let me see, why don't I tell you about the wolf and the crows? That's a good one." He shifted slightly, getting into the role of storyteller, "Okay. So . . . two crows brought a message to a young wolf. It was an opportunity to prove himself, and being ambitious and competitive, he leaped at the chance.

"The crows told him of a medicine bear who lived deep in the woods. The bear's medicine was needed by a clan far from her territory. She was willing to help but had many enemies and would not travel alone. His challenge was simple, escort the bear to where she was needed and bring her home safely.

"Well, wolf was skeptical that such an outing would raise his status in the pack, but he joined the bear and began their trek. Bear wasn't fast like wolf, but as she ambled along, she would talk and teach. She would stop here and there to gather plants and roots, always taking the time to show him what she had found, explaining why and how she would use the medicine, even reminding him to thank the Pacha Mama for each gift.

"Before wolf realized, they reached the clan in need, and he was proud to help. By the time they began their journey home, he knew she had done much more than deliver her medicine. She had treated him as an equal, and insisted he be considered her colleague while they worked among those in need. At the start, the crows had ordered him to be respectful, as if that was something he would never have considered on his own. He had shown her respect but under-stood for the first time what it felt like when someone had earned his respect. As they ventured home, he could only hope he had earned her respect too.

"That's where his mind was at, when the crows joined him again. This time they came in the night, and sang a different song. They had lost their respect for the bear and her medicine, and no longer trusted her. They had a new chal-lenge for him and guaranteed his advancement in the pack.

"Wolf's new duty was to deliver the bear to a new den site. The crows warned him that she might want to return to her old territory and may fight, but returning her home, they said, was no longer an option. Once she was safe-ly delivered to her new den, he was then to take her medicine. This, they told him, would be a true test of how much he had learned. 'Take the medicine far out into the big water,' they ordered, 'and let it sink.' They didn't want anyone to find her medicine bundle ever again.

"Wolf wanted to refuse, but the crows warned that they were acting on or-ders from eagle himself. All night, he prayed for a way to complete his orders, earn the respect of his pack, and return the bear to her home. When grand-father began to rise, he was still without answer. He consoled himself with the knowledge that eagle was wise, and had a plan. The bear, he was sure, would be okay but her medicine . . . why dump it, he asked? They had laughed at his concern but finally explained that bear had made a great effort to collect her medicine bundle, so much so that they couldn't risk anyone else taking it. So the bear, for her own safety, was to be taken to her new den and her medicine bundle sunk in the big water. 'It's the only way,' the crows explained. Once the medicine was gone, they promised, he would be helped home by a hawk. The crows assured wolf, 'when all is as eagle wishes, you will be greatly respected.' All wolf could do was begin the day trusting that eagle had a plan that was best for everyone, even his friend the bear."

Even in the shade of the aircraft wing, the temperature had climbed above one hundred degrees. Albert signaled his need for a quick break, standing and heading for the Cargo door. Earlier, while Cleo finished with the paperwork for their departure, he had prepped the aircraft, including loading the tiny galley with ice. He grabbed two bottles of chilled water and headed back out.

Under the wing, Cleo was combing over a Michelin road map. She had taken a pencil and a flight ruler from her bag and was fussing with the protractor. Accepting the bottle of water he handed over, she turned the road map around to Albert's viewpoint. "I was thinking . . . if we clamped a hose pipe in place of the pump, we could get her flying. And, for safety, we could follow the highway from here all the way to Haifa. That way, if we get into any trouble, we can just land on the side of the road and wait for the Israeli Defense Force for rescue."

Albert looked at the map carefully. Cleo hadn't marked a route at all. Instead, she had scribbled a note: "Are we under audio surveillance?" He was caught off guard for a second then shook his head, saying, "Satellite, but no audio."

"What about the airplane?"

He hung his head slightly. "Our intercom is being monitored, but there aren't any bugs," he offered, adding. "I'm certain of that."

"All intercoms?" she asked somewhat cryptically.

He knew immediately what she was referring to and grinned. "Not that one, no."

Whether he realized it or not, Albert had just taken his first step down, what could be considered by some as a treasonous path. Cleo didn't like it. They had been given conflicting orders, and Albert's new directives didn't just put her in harm's way, it broke the deal the CIA and MI6 and made with her. What she needed to do was find a way they could both complete their assigned duties. There had to be a way to satisfy everyone and still keep her plane. "Okay," she said. "Let's go flying. I'll work up a new flight plan to Haifa that does indeed follow the highway while you see if you can scrounge up a high-temp hose and some clamps."

"Sounds good," Albert said, immediately climbing to his feet.

"And Albert, don't take no for an answer. If we're really stuck, just rent a car from them. We can pull a hose from the oil cooler and let the company pick up the repair tab."

Albert smiled and headed off in the direction of the maintenance hangar.

Cleo didn't waste any time, heading straight for the airplane. Once inside she climbed the isle to the flight deck and pulled the primary first aid kit down from the co-pilot's bulkhead. She opened the hard-sided case and removed the satellite phone, which was neatly packed between rows of pressure bandages. Within seconds of hitting the power switch, a full charge bar lit across the screen.

She headed back down the aisle to the lavatory. The uplink system used to maintain contact with Vauxhall was no longer completely intact. While they were enjoying the sights in Dubai the aircraft had been quietly stripped of her "spooky" components. The black box was gone and so was her special laptop, but the satellite setup was partially intact. All she needed to do, in theory, was to substitute the SAT Phone for the black box.

Cleo grabbed a headset, then thought better of it, instead pulling out her Russian helmet and mask, before sitting down on the lavatory bench. She ran a patch cord from the number two intercom plug, to the phone, then plugged her helmet and mask cables in. She watched as the number beside the satellite icon started to climb. Within seconds, there were enough green bars to light up Boston on St. Patty's Day.

Dialing a number by heart, she waited impatiently for an answer.

"Cleopatra!" Tori's tone seemed as much surprised as delighted. "I wasn't expecting you to call this morning. Are you all right?"

"I'm peachy, but we need to talk."

"C and I are just on our way to meet with your curious old friends."

As frustrating as the conversation was, Cleo knew it was just Tori's way of reminding her that the satellite connection was no longer secure. "Tori, we need to talk," she repeated. "Now, before your meeting!" All Cleo could hear was silence and forced herself not let her imagination run wild.

"Where are you?" Tori asked, in her tight controlled way.

"We're still at the jet center in Amman," she answered, carefully adopting a professional tone to hide her rising concern. "We are AOG and about to try a non-certified repair to put us back on schedule."

"I see," Tori said, but clearly had no idea what the problem was. "All right, give me twenty minutes Cleo. Twenty minutes. Do not leave off until I ring you back."

She agreed and disconnected the call, leaving the phone powered up and plugged in. For a brief moment, she let herself believe that Tori, and by extension Rod and Sir Richard were somehow involved with this. It had to be one hundred and ten degrees in the lav. More than any snow walker should ever endure. Pushing herself up to a hunched stance, she made her way to the cargo door and parked her six on the edge, letting her feet rest on the first rung of the pipe ladder. She was still sitting there twenty minutes later when Albert returned with a cardboard box of odds and ends.

"I've got four different fuel pipes, plus caps, clamps, Loctite and one of the guys lent me this funny little pipe bender," he said, holding up what looked like pliers bent into a happy face smile.

It took every ounce of energy Cleo could muster as she pushed herself down the last step and joined Albert beside the engine. They sorted the parts, and set up a small stepladder. Once Albert found a comfortable working height, Cleo turned for the blanket and tools she had pulled out earlier, and realized they were now sitting in the hot sun. She was about to drag everything back into the shade of the aircraft wing when an airport van pulled up beside the aircraft. The driver got out, opened the side door, and retrieved a medium size package marked AOG on every side. He looked around, presumably for the guy in charge then settled on Cleo. Walking over, he pulled an electronic signature pad out and handed it to her. She scribbled her name across the pad and returned the unit, in exchange for her aircraft-on-ground package.

Once the van pulled away, Cleo took the box over to the cargo door, and placed it on the aircraft floor. With the utility knife from the thigh pocket, she cut open the carton, and was surprised to find the black box MI9 had built. An invoice had been taped to the cover with her name in the customer box and a local address for the repair shop. The amount due was marked N/C, and a short reference note inside the Description of Work box included a previous invoice number. She had to look it over several times until she realized the previous invoice was actually a telephone number.

Climbing back into the Otter, she fished out the communications harness to reconnect the black box. She entered the number from the invoice on the Sat phone and pressed the call button.

It took longer than usual to establish a connection but once it picked up, Tori's worried voice was loud and clear, "Good God, Cleo. What's happened?"

"Are you at home, or are you using the neighbor's phone?" she asked cautiously. It wasn't even eight a.m. in London, and Tori had said that she and Sir Richard were heading to the Israeli Embassy. Was it possible to make it to Vauxhall Cross in fifteen minutes or had she opted for a secure line from Canada House or the US Embassy. There was no point in blurting everything out, if Tori was sitting next to the very people who had decided to change the rules after the game had been won.

Tori's voice was patient but concerned, "I'm at Vauxhall, sweetheart. I promise you, no one is listening in."

Cleo sucked in a deep breath. "Mai Mai. Something's going on here, and I don't think it has anything to do with the Israelis. If they're involved at all, it must be out of some necessity to assist the Americans."

"This is about your airplane breaking down?"

"Tori, the plane didn't break down. The fuel pump was removed and nothing else. It was probably taken by the same folks who had a little chat with Albert last night. He's been given new orders. He's to get me to Haifa, where a replacement part is supposed to be waiting. Then while I'm having my little talk with the Israelis, he is supposed to take off, fly the Otter out over the Mediterranean and dump her into the sea."

"Dump her? It? The aircraft you mean? That makes no sense. How would he hope to survive?"

"Trust me! Of all the things this little airplane can do, a jump and dump would be a walk in the park, especially for Albert. He's already done the jump thing a dozen times, and we have all the gear he needs. A US helicopter, probably a Navy Seahawk has been laid on to pull him from the drink. Do the Americans have any ships in the Mediterranean?"

"The US 4th Fleet," Tori confirmed. "They set sail from Italy last night for the Eastern Med." She sighed over the crisp digital signal. "You're sure about this? Albert came to you with his new orders?"

"Of course not! Albert didn't say anything about his orders. Trust me on that point. He's done nothing to betray his oath. I'm just hoping that we find another way for him to fulfill those orders. One where I don't get screwed from both ends!" Cleo's temper was rising, much like the stifling heat in the aircraft.

"Sweetheart, would you be bothered if I take your call into the Tank? I think, if I put you and the team together, we might have a chance. Other than that, I'm lost to even comprehend why this is happening, and what rationale is at work. I'm so sorry my love. You did not sign on for this."

"It's all right. Tori?" she had to ask. "They're not just going to interview me for a few hours are they?"

"Well, to be honest, that was the point of this morning's meeting. Rod and I have been combing through every piece of intelligence we can find that even remotely relates to you in an effort to understand what they could possibly want. I hope you're not offended?"

"Offended, that you had to dig through my dirty laundry, hell no. Find anything interesting?"

"You're hurt," Tori acknowledged gently.

"No, you had to do it and I'm glad you did. At least this way it saves me having to explain my fracked-up family." Cleo was quiet, and for a moment her confidence seemed to fail. "So, now that you've met the skeletons in my closet, still want to take me home?"

"Don't give up on me, Cleo. Please," Tori pleaded. "We will get the team on this right now, and as soon as Rod and father are back, I will insist they bring every pressure to bear, diplomatic or otherwise. I love you, and no matter what you have to do, and however long it takes to get you home, I will be waiting."

"You know, back in the day, the people didn't have a word for love," Cleo said quietly. "Instead, when you fell in love you would say, I respect you deeply."

"And that, my love, is exactly why I will be waiting. In a way," she admitted, as much to herself as Cleo, "I feel as if I've been waiting all my life for you. A few more days won't hurt a bit."

"And if the days turn into weeks or months, how could I expect you to wait?"

"Oh, my love, please! You must remind yourself that I'm here doing everything in my power to get you home."

"It's like medicine to hear you say that," she admitted quietly. "Tori, there's something else. Something I need you to remember."

"All right," she answered cautiously.

"I need you to always remember, the first rule of flying is love. It's something only the best pilots understand and I need you to remember it."

"I don't understand."

"Good," Cleo answered genuinely. "Let's hope you never do. Okay my love, hook me up with the team. It's time to get creative."

Embassy of Israel
London, United Kingdom

Sir Richard had expected to meet the Deputy Ambassador again, and if they were lucky, perhaps get a few words in with the Mossad Station Chief. Instead, he and Rod Nelligan, were escorted directly to the Ambassador's office. He was surprised to see the Americans were already there, but missing was Mike Perkins, and any Canadians. Major Butterworth, dashing in his perfectly tailored Marine Corps uniform, was escorting Hank Darien, and old time CIA handler whom C had thought dead or long retired.

With Rod Nelligan in tow, Sir Richard strode into the Ambassador's Office, halting the requisite three paces in front of an ornate Regency desk. "Your Excellency," Sir Richard said with respect, "It's good to meet again."

The warm reply he received betrayed the Ambassador's fondness for him, and her very French accent. Genevieve Schelling had grown up in two worlds, spending the school year with her mother in the South of France and her summers traipsing about the Middle East with her archaeologist father. She had learned the art of negotiation as a child, watching him reconcile the needs of scholars with local and national governments in Israel and several Arab nations. She had absorbed the cultures and languages of the region, and had been given the formal education needed to put her skills to use. "You, of course, Sir *Richard*, remember our American friends," she said, nodding to Hank Darien and Major Butterworth.

Butterworth, who stood to welcome the pair, remained standing while the Ambassador renewed her acquaintances. Hank hadn't bothered to get to his feet for the Brits but was forced to when the Ambassador stood. She walked around her desk to greet Sir Richard with an affectionate but formal embrace. "Welcome," she said warmly.

"Thank you, Madam Ambassador. I wish I could say our visit was social, unfortunately, I'm here with a problem."

The Ambassador strolled back behind her desk and took her seat. There was no way to not notice Genevieve Schelling. She was beautiful by any standard, and at fifty-eight she carried her looks with an ageless grace. "The major has just been briefing me on the success of your mission, or should I say the mission of the Red Indians?"

"Credit for inviting the Mohawk team goes to our American counterparts," he said, tipping his head towards Butterworth, "but the real credit goes to Lieutenant Colonel Deseronto and her crew."

"Captain Deseronto," Hank interrupted.

"No," Sir Richard said plainly. "The Canadians have confirmed her promotion, and I will not be surprised if they pin a few medals on her. I know we will." Turning his attention back to the Ambassador, he asked, "by the way, where are the Canadians?"

"I don't understand?" Ambassador Schelling asked.

"She and the crew are Canadians, and their government has been a partner in the operation from the start."

Hank was on his feet and spitting fire. "Like hell she is," the venom surprised everyone in the room, leaving them silenced by the sight of Hank whipping spittle from the corners of his mouth.

Rod Nelligan quietly stepped forward, "Gents, let's not go down that road again!" Turning to the Ambassador, he explained, "Mum, if I may . . . All four crew members were born in Canada but two are serving in the American Military. Mr. Darien seems to think that makes them Americans."

"Seems to think . . ." Hank interrupted, still on his feet and obviously irritated with Rod for raising the contentious issue of citizenship. "Seems to think . . . I God-damned seem to know they're Indians and that makes them Americans." The twang of his Texas accent was unmistakable.

Standing at the end of the Ambassador's desk, Hank looked like something out of a Western movie. His suit, while expensive, was Western cut with the shoulders in suede and boot-cut pants over flashy snakeskin boots. And while his tapered shirt looked Italian, he had finished off his ensemble with a bolero tie. All he was missing was the Stetson and both Rod and Sir Richard expected to find that sitting with the footman who had ushered them in. In sharp contrast to his handler, Major Butterworth looked more like an American movie star in his dashing Class A Marine Corps uniform.

Butterworth stood and interjected himself between the brewing groups. "Gentlemen, I think what Hank is trying to say is that the crew is representing . . ."

"Don't bloody well tell me what I'm trying to say," Hank hissed at Butterworth. "You God-damned fighter jocks think you know everything. Well get this kid, those fucking Indians are Americans, and I'm sick and tired of them hiding behind the Canadians every time we tell them to get off of their lazy drunken asses and stop crying about losing the war. Didn't they teach you *gyrines* anything at Annapolis?" Hank, a West Point ring knocker, added as insult.

Butterworth looked at Hank Darien, his superior, with complete distain. "Watch your language."

The Ambassador's sprawling office was silent. "Perhaps, we will reschedule for a time when the Canadian delegation may be present," she said, standing behind her desk, and signaling the end of their meeting.

Everyone immediately got to their feet. Sir Richard, following protocol, was about to acquiesce and reschedule when Rod Nelligan, sensing something more sinister afoot, took another step towards Genevieve Schelling.

"Your Excellency, I agree that the boys from Canada House should be here, but that doesn't change the urgency of the situation. You're about to pull our girl in for questioning and we can't understand why?" Rod practically begged, "Mum, she's done all of our nations a great service and done what none of our agencies, not ours, not theirs, not even the Mossad, could do. She and her crew have given us all the evidence we need to prove Iran has started a Nuclear Weapons program. You Madam, of all people, should understand the value of what we have received!"

Genevieve Schelling took Rod's open hands into hers, "These Indians, whomever they belong to, have done a great service for Israel," she said in her soft accented voice. "Believe me, I wish to reward them as well, but your compatriots have provided compelling evidence that Miss Deseronto, regardless of her rank or nationality, has established terrorist links to the Palestinians. You don't expect me to just ignore this threat because it is from someone in your favor?"

"Terrorist links?" Sir Richard asked. "What on earth . . ." he started to ask, then saw the menacing smile on Hank Darien's face.

"Well Ricky, my boy, I thought that would get your attention," Hank said, removing a CIA folder from his briefcase. "I was just about to show this to our Lady Ambassador when you arrived." The pleasure on his face was obvious. Something about putting Sir Richard in his place seemed to be part of Hank's jubilation.

Genevieve Schelling detested being called a Lady Ambassador almost as much as it bothered her to see Sir Richard addressed as Ricky. She accepted the file Hank handed over wordlessly. Inside were several reports and a stack of 8 x 10 photos. She started thumbing through the photos expecting Hank to present his report. When he simply returned to his seat, without further comment, she was forced to ask, "What am I looking at?"

Butterworth, moving to the Ambassador's side, offered a narrative on the photographs. "That's Colonel Deseronto. It's a recent shot," he said, and then added, "and that looks like Davis-Monthan Air Field?" he guessed, sounding a little confused. Turning to Hank he asked, "Did we have her under surveillance in Arizona?"

"Of course we did," Hank said, as if scolding a small child. "You don't take your eye off the ball just 'cause you're playing on home turf, kid!"

The Ambassador had just thumbed through a series of grainy black-and-white photos that didn't seem to show anything but Cleo with one airplane or another. The work pictures were followed by a series of shots of Cleo on a beach with another woman. These pictures seemed as ubiquitous as the first set, until she reached the last two. These showed the two women in a sensuous embrace.

Genevieve studied a photo of the two women standing side by side. Colonel Deseronto was wearing a one-piece bathing suit that looked akin to military issue. In one photo, she was cradling a rather large iguana for her companion to see. The other woman stood off from the Colonel, obviously repelled with the animal. She looked to be the same age as Cleo, but her bathing suit, sunglasses, and hat were the height of fashion, or had been a decade ago. "These photos are at least ten years old. Why are they relevant?"

Butterworth didn't know who the other woman was and asked Rod to fill in the blanks. Back on his feet, Rod Nelligan move around the Ambassador's desk, taking up station at her right side. "These are old snaps indeed," he said. "That young lady is Samantha Stewart. A professor . . ."

"Associate Professor," Hank interrupted.

"Associate Professor of Divinity at the University in Toronto," Rod continued, not letting Hank's interruption bother him. "She and our girl were domestic partners until three or four years ago."

"That's when her little lez-be friend disappeared from our radar," Hank interrupted with disgust.

"Jesus Christ, Hank!" This time it was Butterworth who lost his temper. "Samantha Stewart did not fall off the radar. She died of cancer!"

Ambassador Schelling put the file down, taking a deep breath before turning to Darien, "Proof of a Sapphic relationship is not proof of anything. Is this woman at risk of blackmail? Is this the issue?"

Rod answered before Hank could say anything. "She's out to her family, the military, and anyone who asks," he explained. "If you ask me, and you're the ones with the experience asking, she is no risk to anything. That wee lass is as loyal as they come!"

"Loyal my ass!" Hank howled. Blasting up from his seat, he pushed Butterworth aside, grabbed the stack of photos from the Ambassador and spread them out fan-like on her desk. "We know you had issues with her in the Golan. Now we find she's been consorting with some French cookie in Moscow. A cookie we suspect has Palestinian connections."

He found the photos he was looking for, pushing one forward for Schelling to see. The photo showed Cleo, with the Kremlin in the background, and the back of a blond woman. The two appeared to be in deep conversation. The second photo was from the same angle, but clearly showed the two women embracing, although Cleo's face portrayed little joy in the act.

Butterworth, who had moved over to Rod's side of the desk, craned his eyes to see the photo. Something seemed familiar but he couldn't put his finger on it. It wasn't until Hank slapped down the next shot down that the major put it all together, "Are you insane?" he called out to Darien, automatically bracing for Rod Nelligan's reaction.

"You bastard!" Rod shouted. For a moment it looked like the chief would go right over the Ambassador and beat the living daylights out of Hank. "How dare you! That's my goddaughter, you thick-headed . . ." Before he could say another word, several officers from the Ambassador's security detail barged into the room. The site of Butterworth holding Rod back right next to the Ambassador drew the security detail to the belief that she was in danger. It was pretty easy to surmise that the meeting was under video surveillance only. If they had been listening in, they would know it was Hank and not the Ambassador being threatened. They would never have suspected that Hank Darien had just signed his own death warrant.

Two security men grabbed Rod, and were helping Butterworth hold him back, when the Ambassador stood. "Please escort my guests to the reception hall. Sir *Richard* and I have much to discuss." Major Butterworth and Chief Nelligan, who was starting to calm down, complied immediately, following the security detail to the door. Hank however didn't move, stopping the security officers in their tracks. "Hank, please leave us," was all the Ambassador had to say. Hank didn't respond immediately but the security detail did.

Recognizing that he was about to be bodily removed, Hank Darien shook off the guards, and defiantly stormed out.

When the doors finally closed, Genevieve picked up a color photograph of Cleo and Tori arm in arm, and took a seat in the chair next to Sir Richard. "It has been a long time, *non?*"

"More than twenty years," he answered, adding with some guilt, "I called when I learned of your appointment."

She smiled at him. "I received your flowers. Irises not lilies, you remember. I was touched, *merci.*"

"Touched," he said, with a wry smile, "but not enough to call?"

"*Richard*, you and I know it wise to not open old ones."

"Old wounds," he corrected gently. "I had forgotten your mixed metaphors. Do you remember how you would have Tori laughing hysterically with your jests about English phrases?"

Genevieve Schelling smiled at the memory. "It would seem that our little girl is all grown up, and in love, if I am correct?"

"Very much, I'm afraid," Sir Richard, admitted.

"You do not approve?" Genevieve asked with concern. "Surely, in this day and age you cannot be upset? Perhaps you prefer she would fall in love with a handsome Prince, with title and lands?"

He smiled warmly at her concern. "You know better than that. I just hoped her life would be less complicated. Besides, her mother left her all the titles and lands she needs. She is now the The Right Honorable Viscountess Dufferin. Her Majesty made it official last year."

"And now you are a knight, and no longer a sailor."

"And you're the Ambassador for Israel. No longer a simple vintner."

Genevieve was quiet for a long moment. "Is it not ironic that we should travel apart for so long, and now we find one another once more? And my little Tori is grown and what, working for you?"

"Now she is. She came up through the ranks at MI5, when she wasn't serving with the Navy. She wanted to prove she wasn't riding on my coattails."

"And now?"

"And now, she runs the Special Operations Executive. It's a sort of think tank and command and control center we turn to when no one else can solve a given problem."

"Like proving the Iranians have a nuclear weapons program," she said with a smile.

"Like proving the Iranians have a nuclear weapons program," he repeated, smiling back.

"And this relationship with the Red Indian? This is the first woman in her life, perhaps?"

Sir Richard exhaled, revealing his discomfort. "No actually. There have been others. All of which have been quite insignificant, except for a recent indiscretion." Richard seemed reluctant to explain but continued at the Ambassador's urging. "Before this operation was even contemplated, she got involved with the other young woman on the crew."

"The woman from the American Marines?" Genevieve asked, with sincere surprise. "How could this come about, if it was before planning had begun?"

"Agent Commanda, now Captain Commanda, was here in London with the FBI and working on a task force, retrieving stolen artifacts."

"How does an agent of the FBI become a captain of Marines?"

"Something I've been asking myself? Miss Commanda was a private in the Marine Corps before she attended university. When the Americans came up with this plan, or at least the idea of sending someone with special status into Iran, they delivered the only Red Indian they had readily available."

"And they planned this mission and found the other one?"

"No, actually, it was Roddy's plan to bring the other one in. And it was Colonel Deseronto who planned the entire operation. She is quite an unconventional strategist, that one."

"*Richard*, I remember something about a Red Indian soldier," she said, reaching over to touch his arm. "Is this the one, the one who rescued you and our Roddy?"

"Yes. That's how we knew of her. Rod and I have kept in contact, and I followed her career over the years. She is a fine officer who wasted her time in loyal service to her country of choice, which in contrast to Hank's revisionist history, was Canada."

"An unconventional strategist, yes," she said, somehow distracted by the idea. "What is it the Americans say, outside thinking?"

"Outside the box," he answered. "They say her people actually have a term for it. They call her a Contrary Warrior!"

"Contrary Warrior?" she repeated, as if trying the term on for size. "Contrary lover, contrary soldier. Perhaps it is more suitable than we understand? She sounds of things my little bird would love."

"Genny, now that you know she's no threat, will you call off your people?"

Genevieve took Sir Richards hand in hers, and said with deep regret, "I cannot. I am so sorry, *Richard*. I love Tori and I wish her not to be hurt, but this is beyond my say. Why they wish to interrogate her again I do not know."

She was about to say more when Richard interrupted. "Again? So you know she was previously held and questioned by your government?" It was more accusation than a question and the implication clearly hurt the Ambassador.

She went to her desk and retrieved the dossier the Mossad had provided. Returning to sit down next to Sir Richard, she opened the file. "I only learned of this late yesterday," she explained, while turning to a specific page. "I have read the entire record. It is not the work of the Mossad. These pages—reports of her initial interrogations—where translated, very badly translated, into Hebrew. The original transcripts of the actual interrogations, and the Interrogation/Observation Reports, are all missing," she paused before handing the file to Sir Richard. "Racial profiling is not something we do, but this document assumes her racial proclivity is to other subjugated peoples."

"Subjugated?" Sir Richard questioned, his surprise evident as he scanned over a cover page which she translated for him. "It actually says that?" he asked, as he flipped through the report.

Genevieve nodded. "Have you ever heard my government refer to the Palestinians as subjugated?"

"It would never happen! Not even by mistake. It doesn't even sound very American, except for the racial profiling business."

"As for who is behind this, I believe the Americans are involved, and the Canadian government may be duplicitous."

"That makes sense," he said, thinking out loud. "She's never said anything about the experience to me, but Rod says she was kidnapped from her quarters in the Canadian compound. The next thing I remember was her showing up at the hospital in Germany about six weeks after the helicopter crash."

"She trusted you," Genevieve said. "This I understand, but then she told you nothing of what had happened?"

Sir Richard shook his head. "At the time, I was still flat out in my hospital bed, but Rod was ambulatory and spent most of his time with her."

"Still the Mother Hen, our Roddy, *Oui?*"

"He most certainly is with Victoria. If Deseronto told him anything that could help us now, Rod would have said so."

"Even if doing so would betray her confidence in him?"

"Yes," he answered without hesitation. "If anything, this relationship with Tori has made it personal for him. If he knew anything, he would have said so if not to Tori, then to me."

Genevieve took the dossier back and placed it on the side table. Turning back, she took his hand in hers again, watching his eyes intently. "You never call her by her Christian name. Why is this?"

"She's not Christian," he said, side-stepping her question. "She follows something called the teachings of Sky Woman and the Great Law or the Great Peace. I'm not sure which it is, but it's some sort of aboriginal spiritual belief. Secondly," he paused, letting out a long sigh, "Genny, I guess I'm just old fashioned. I keep thinking that she should have done the honorable thing and asked for permission before pursuing my daughter, or made some sort of archaic gesture!"

"Perhaps she did. Tori is a big girl and so is this Cleopatra. Perhaps she asked our Tori. Is this too much to imagine?"

He smiled slightly, giving in to her reasoning. "You always had a way of changing my perspective."

"Maybe there is a little *contrary warrior* in me too!" Smiling, she stood, and taking him by the hand, led him to the door. "Sir *Richard*," she said formally, while still holding his hand. "I must pick up the telephone now and upset many people, including General Robilard at the Canadian High Commission. And you must return to Vauxhall Cross." She raised her free hand and touched his face gently. "When I have answers, you will have answers. Please tell my Tori and Roddy too, I will not rest."

"Thank you," was all he could think to say, before impulsively kissing her cheek. Back in the grand foyer, Sir Richard found both Rod Nelligan and Major Butterworth waiting. "Where is he?"

"He took off, sir," Butterworth explained. "He's probably back at the Embassy by now."

"Walk with me, Major," was all Sir Richard said, before heading out the Embassy door. On the street he turned for Trafalgar Square, thinking he would head right for Canada House. Stopping, he turned to Rod, "Where does Robilard keep his office?"

Rodney had to work his brain to catch up with the conversation. "The High Commissioner? They moved him from Trafalgar Square to Mackenzie House about two years ago, but Étienne is still here." Rod tipped his head in the direction of Canada House.

Sir Richard stopped and turned back to the waiting staff car. "Chief, get on your mobile and tell Étienne we will pick him up. He can warn General Robilard that we are enroute to Mackenzie House for an emergency meeting." Turning his attention back to Butterworth, he asked simply, "In for a penny, in for a pound?"

"You know," Major Butterworth smiled broadly, "I just got that. In for a penny—in for a Pound Sterling! Aye, sir! You bet I'm in!"

Chapter Sixteen

Mackenzie House
Office of the Canadian High Commissioner to Great Britain
London, United Kingdom

Day 1, 07:30 UTC

Rod Nelligan sat in a "clean" office on a secure telephone line to the SOE Tank at Vauxhall. While Sir Richard had been escorted directly to General Robilard, the High Commissioner, Étienne immediately asked for a private office for the chief. The CSIS technicians had just swept the building for listening devices and other bugs that may have been planted. To their consternation, Étienne ordered them to sweep the small office again, and check the secure line before Rod got to work.

For an old guy, Rod Nelligan was quite tech savvy. For security reasons, Mackenzie House was a cellular dead zone, forcing Rod to physically plug his smart phone into one of the secure DSL lines, before connecting to the Tank.

Nici answered his call, immediately conferencing him into the working session.

"Chief," Tori began with a quick update. Letting him know, Cleo was on a secure line as well.

Sitting in the stifling heat of the grounded Otter, which was still parked on the ramp in Amman, Cleo told him that she was willing to fly to Haifa and turn herself in, but she was not willing to sacrifice her newly acquired DeHavilland Otter to do so. Instead of dumping the plane, they had worked out a plan wherein Albert would take off from Haifa as planned, but fly to RAF Cyprus instead. The Otter would be immediately towed into a hangar to remove it from satellites surveillance. At the same time, a Sea King helicopter would fly Albert, decked out in survival gear and carrying his kit, and a weighted bag containing the Otter's Emergency Locator Transmitter, out over the Mediterranean. Once they reached the target location, Albert would activate the ELT and jump into the sea.

At the moment, they were debating whether to also pull the aircraft transponder, and if Albert should have the Personal Locator Beacon on him or in the bag. After a few rounds of debate, it was Cleo who vetoed the idea. "We need to have a working transponder to even get out of Jordanian airspace. To pull it, and still make it usable, would require me and Albert to do a lot of wiring and connect a separate power supply. The easiest solution is to use it until Haifa. When Albert takes off for his jump and dump, we ask him to simply forget to turn it on. If ATC calls him on it, well, he'll just have to stall until he reaches Cypriote airspace. Of course, position reporting will be the least of our problems if the Otter is under satellite surveillance."

Rod agreed it was their only option at the moment. While Tori had already set the wheels in motion for the Sea King and aircraft handling on Cyprus, it was Rod who had all the connections to make things happen fast. With a brand-new BlackBerry in hand, Rod connected to his personal files at Vauxhall. "I might have a way to get your wee airplane off Cyprus without notice. The Turks are still flyin' these Otters for Search and Rescue. They're in and out of the Island all the time. Yes!" Rod said, over the secure line, while tabbing through his address book. "I have a few calls to make. What I'm thinking is we get the plane into the hangar for a few days. Then we have the Turks fly her out, as if she's a regular patrol aircraft. From the sight view of a satellite, she'll just be one more SAR Otter returning to Turkey."

Tori approved the plan knowing Rod had the connections to make it happen without a hassle. With that settled, Cleo calmed down about the fate of her airplane, and the team said their good-byes to her. What they needed now was Albert on the secure satellite connection.

It was time for Tori to give a direct order that would countermand any others SSG Mackenzie, US Army, may have been given. The objective was not to come down hard on Albert, but to insulate him from a charge of insubordination, or worse yet, allegations of treason. While the operation was over, the flight team was still on Temporary Duty to the SOE and under Tori's command. That meant her orders would technically countermand any he received from other sources. In the end though, the real decision to jump and dump or follow Tori's plan, came down to Albert.

Albert's voice cut in over the secure line, "Staff Sergeant Mackenzie, Ma'am!"

Sitting in the comfortable office in Mackenzie House, Rod tried not to think about the sheer will it would have taken Cleo to sit in the lavatory of the little plane for any length of time. The heat alone would have been unbearable, and the smell too. But it was the thought of the big crew chief scrunching down in the converted cargo hold that really bothered him. In the air, the cabin would be nice and level like an airliner, but sitting on the ground, with the tail sitting twenty degrees lower than the nose, the cabin aisle and the side facing toilet seat were steeply angled making even something as simple as sitting down a real challenge.

"Attention to orders," was the first thing he heard Captain(n) Braithwaite, RN say. "Staff Sergeant Mackenzie, as you are still under my command, ostensible until your return to America, I am going to give you a direct order."

"Yes, Ma'am!"

"You will continue your current post as Crew Chief for Lieutenant Colonel Deseronto, and assume the duties proscribed to the co-pilot and second-in-command, until the port of Haifa. On your arrival there, Colonel Deseronto will hand command of the flight to you, whereupon you will immediately depart Haifa for RAF Cyprus, by the fastest route possible." Tori's voice over the secure SAT Phone was crisply military. There would be no mistaking her orders for suggestions. "Once on the ground, an aircraft tug will meet you on the runway and tow you to a hangar. A Sea King helicopter will then collect you, your kit, and the weight bag Colonel Deseronto is preparing. The Sea King will fly you to any point you desire. While enroute to the coordinates you provide, you will don your sea survival gear. At your requested destination you will set off both your PLB, which you will retain for your own safety, and the ELT which you will then place in the weight bag and drop into the sea. Staff Sergeant Mackenzie, are my orders understood?"

Albert's voice rang back forcefully, "Yes Ma'am!"

Before Tori could say more, the chief chimed in, "My Lady," Rod Nelligan began formally, "I was wondering if it is at all necessary to dump our man here into the sea. Why not simply suit him up, rinse him down then deliver him to his friends directly? I suspect the SAR boys on Cyprus might be in closer range and would reach him long before the Yanks could dispatch a Sea Hawk."

"I'm not so sure about that, Chief," Albert's skepticism was crystal clear. "Those boys can really scramble."

Rod opened a map application on his BlackBerry, and navigated to the Mediterranean Sea. His app, actually created by Guy and Nici, allowed him to draw rough course lines and calculate distances. "Do we have a location on Albert's friends?"

"Are you thinking what I'm thinking," Tori asked?

Rod could hear her signal for Nici to bring up the live satellite feed for the Mediterranean.

"We have them," she said, referring to the US 4th Fleet. "Three hundred kilometers east of Malta, making fourteen knots. I'll have confirmation on the range for the helicopter in a moment, but I'm thinking the current position of the fleet would prohibit their assistance. Yes, I have it," Tori announced to the callers who were blind to the fresh information the team had popped up on the widescreen display. "The one-way limit for the Sea Hawk is five hundred, and ninety-two kilometers. That would put rescue out of range for at least another day or likely two if they continue to steam at their current rate."

"Albert," Rod asked. "When were your friends expecting you?"

"I thought it would be today. But when we found the fuel pump was missing, and couldn't be replaced for two or three days, I suspected the problem was intentional."

"That makes sense," Tori said almost absently. "Colonel Deseronto tells me you have rigged some sort of illegal bypass. Is it safe?"

"I would call it an uncertified modification," Albert said lightly. "And yes Ma'am, it will work. Plus the Colonel has planned an old-fashioned dead reckoning flight that follows the highway all the way from here to Haifa. If things go south, we'll just land on the highway and call for the cavalry. Frankly, I don't think you have to concern yourselves with that possibility. After Onondaga, I know the Colonel could land this little bird in Trafalgar Square!"

Rod couldn't help but imagine what that scene would look like. General Robilard would be so proud to have the little Otter sitting in front of Canada House while the Air Ministry would flip their wigs over the stunt.

"All right then," Tori said. "I'll leave you gents to discuss the technical aspect of the operation. Albert . . ." her silence carried her unexpressed worry.

"Trust me, Ma'am," Albert's reply was as solemn as any oath, "I understand."

Tori excused herself from the call and left Rod to fill in any blanks. "Well lad, I can't help but believe that the greatest sin of command is putting a man in the field with conflicting orders."

"Don't worry Chief, I'm working my way through this."

"Good man," the chief said sincerely. "Now listen carefully. I expect you to follow our courageous leaders' orders until Haifa. Once there, do as your conscience dictates. Despite the strongly worded orders to the contrary, no one here will think any less of you if you are compelled to follow any opposing instructions you may have received. Just remember what Lady Tori said. Your cavalry is out of range, so take your time. You don't want to tread water for days on end, do yeh' now?"

"Don't worry," Albert repeated. "I'll get Cleo to Haifa today, even if I have to push the airplane all the way. Should I assume that your friends are ready for my arrival?"

"Everything's in place lad. My best advice is to drop our girl, then run like the dickens, before someone decides to interview you as well." Rod, ever aware that Albert was sitting in a scorching aircraft, did not want to keep the young soldier on the line longer than necessary. What he did want was to make absolutely sure Albert was ready for whatever course of action he chose.

"Chief? If the fleet is so far out, how would an old Sea King be able to take me there?"

"They won't lad, at least not today, not with that distance. With your fleet so far out of range, what we would do is bring you in, then inform your friends that one of our SAR stations picked up your emergency signal and plucked you from the sea. From that point, we can play it by ear. My guess is, if they want you bad enough, they'll dispatch an aircraft to fetch you from Cyprus. If not, you'll be stuck enjoying the beach for three days, if you don't mind that sort of thing?"

"I could use a little R&R," Albert admitted, sighing heavily. "And it makes sense that the SAR helicopter would take me back to their base. In the real world they would probably want to investigate the crash too. You know, I can handle the swim, and if it comes to it, maybe even the two or three days in the water, but I think I like your idea better. Thanks, Chief. I owe you one."

"Don't mention it. Remember . . . Do what you think is right! You've earned our respect. You've nothing more to prove, so don't be putting yourself in harm's way for that wee piece of tin." Rod went over a few more details with Albert, including giving him a contact name in Haifa before ending the call. Sitting quietly in the private office at Mackenzie House, he tabbed through the "to do list" he had been accumulating during the conversation. Everything could wait until he was back at Vauxhall. Slipping out of the room, he found Sir Richard and Étienne just finishing with General Robilard. Butterworth, having reported the situation to his command, was waiting in the foyer as well.

The chief took one look at his boss and his favorite Frenchman, and knew by experience that things had gone badly. Knowing Sir Richard's habits, Rod knew better than to ask. Instead he turned to the Marine for an update. "Have you anything you can share with us?"

"Whatever Darien's up to, it's totally off the reservation, and completely unsanctioned. He managed to get Mike Perkins sent off to Baghdad on some emergency fact-finding mission. No one will say where that order came from, but the suspicion is that Hank somehow worked the system to get Mike out of the way.

Rod groaned at that. Whatever happened on the American side of things was just that—American and completely out of their hands.

"Mike Perkins has been recalled to London, but I couldn't get a commitment to pull Colonel Deseronto. Whatever's going on, it goes much higher than Hank Darien and one of his special projects. Someone wants to see this through, someone very high up!"

"What about our boy?" Chief Nelligan asked the Marine. "What about Mackenzie and the whole aircraft situation?"

"They don't care about him or the plane," Butterworth explained. "The order to dump-and-swim didn't come from Langley. They think it was just part of Darien's scheme. Maybe he thought he could use the loss of the aircraft against her? Psychologically, I mean."

Sir Richard nodded his head in agreement. "I'm certain Dr. Gerrard will agree. Let's be sure we get Mr. Mackenzie out of harm's way." Turning to Rod Nelligan, he ordered, "As soon as he touches down on Cyprus, have him brought here by the fastest means available."

Rod ran through the options in his head. "We've nothing in the med," he admitted, "nothing faster than a Sea King."

Without hesitation C turned to the only pilot in the group. "Are you up to a little training flight, Major? I understand you're current in the Harrier jump jet?"

Before he could answer, Rod jumped in, "Our fleet's Harriers are not equipped as those the major's been flying. I'm not so certain about the transition."

"Neither am I, but what about the training school birds? Those Harriers are fitted out just like our AV8 trainers."

The chief and Sir Richard shared a knowing smile. "Étienne?" Sir Richard asked. "How fast can you get the major out to the Fleet Air Arm?"

Étienne smiled back. "Perhaps the General's auto could be escorted quickly to the school?"

Rod slipped back into the office and grabbing the secure phone, called his contact at Scotland Yard. He needed to get Butterworth out to the Fleet Air school, and if Étienne was willing to send the US Marine in the General's limo, he would get the Met to provide the high-speed escort. Once done, Rod rejoined the group.

Étienne had just finished giving orders to a uniformed Mountie, who wordlessly escorted Major Butterworth to the rear courtyard, where the High Commissioner's limousine was waiting. Once done, Étienne Ste. Hubert, the CSIS Station Chief, walked his two old friends out to the waiting staff car, before returning to face General Robilard, the High Commissioner.

In the car, the chief sat quietly letting his old friend organize his thoughts. It was C's habit to think things through, and then pose questions or observations to the chief for critique. "He knows her," Sir Richard finally said. "What I mean is, they have actually met. He was on the interview team in Lahr."

"Lahr?" the chief repeated incredulously. "He was in Germany with us? When they debriefed her?"

Sir Richard nodded his head, absently watching the streets slip by. "Yes," he said turning his attention back to the conversation. "Back then *Colonel* Robilard led the interview team. He's the one who didn't believe her story and wanted to charge her with desertion."

"Bloody hell!" Rod exhaled.

"He also thinks she's a traitor for that business of exposing the French separatists at school. We knew it hurt her career but I had no idea the level of abhorrence they felt for her. Her last year at RMC must have been horrendous," Sir Richard said. "Evidently, that distaste remains to this day. And," he exhaled heavily, "he wanted to know if I was only defending her because of our one-time love interest, or were we still lovers?"

"Love interest?" Rod Nelligan practically spat the words across the car. "What bloody rubbish is that arse going on about?"

"It all goes back to her original capture and how the Israelis released her. ElAl would never confirm that she was on the flight from Tel Aviv and she didn't have any proof. At the time, and evidently to this day, Robilard believed she skipped out of Syria to meet one of us in Germany, then pulled her re-appearing act in Copenhagen, when she grew homesick or ran out of money. The investigation team backed Deseronto, based our statements, and the Flight Surgeon's report. Robilard however, has always disagreed. He was sure she had just buggered off to be with one of us." Sir Richard paused and sighed again. Practically whispering he added, "He actually referred to her as one of *those* people and a *fucking Indian*. It took every ounce of diplomacy and a few threats before Étienne successfully urged Robilard to accept a call from Ambassador Schelling. It pained me to hear Genevieve confess her country's duplicity in this. I did however enjoy the moment when she told Robilard that he was dead wrong about our girl. That her government had indeed taken *Trooper* Deseronto into custody then, and would do it again, most probably today."

"She actually admitted they were going to grab our girl?"

"Much more, actually. Her hands may be tied, but her mouth isn't. She's just as outraged as we are. She just disclosed her Mossad Chief's entire briefing. It seems that the Mossad was asked to grab both of our women officers after Tehran. That request came from the Americans while Operation Polar Bear was still in the work-up stage. Uncharacteristically, the Americans did not brief Israel on the operation. The Mossad had no idea why they were to wait until Dubai. Evidently, we were lucky they didn't kick-off while the operation was in progress."

"All this without a bloody word to us?" Rod was still incredulous.

"It would seem that our American friends have been doing a lot of things without our knowledge, and it doesn't end there," C announced with disgust. "I may have ordered a Mossad agent to his death."

"What! That wanker we had Cleo drop in the Persian Gulf?" the chief asked obviously maddened by the idea that their team had made such a colossal mistake. "Everything we had on him was solid?"

"A solid cover I'm afraid," Sir Richard admitted. "Genny's not too upset with us. She's blaming the Canadians and Americans for not communicating their intentions with the operational group. Evidently General Robilard knew all about the plan to pull the two women after Tehran."

The sedan drove in silence for several minutes while both men considered the implications. "Tell me Étienne did not know about this? He, of all people, should remember the sorry sight of our girl back in Germany."

"From what Genny has put together, and Robilard admitted, neither Étienne nor Mike Perkins had any idea what was to happen."

Rod Nelligan swore as the driver pulled the sedan into the car park. "What's Robilard doing now?"

"Calling the PMO, their PMO," he qualified. "To offer his resignation."

"The Prime Minister's Office! The bloody Prime Minister of Canada? That oilman? The only thing that yod hates more than women and Toronto are the Red Indians! Our girl doesn't stand a chance."

Sir Richard's voice, in comparison to the broiling chief, was deadpan flat. "Let's make sure someone is monitoring the CBC and the other Canadian news feeds today. If they announce the resignation or retirement of General Robilard from the Canadian High Commission, it will be a signal that we can count on the Canadians."

The sedan stopped, letting the two men exit directly in front of the door to the lifts.

Sir Richard's voice was quieter now. Disappointment, or his disenchantment with the subterfuge of his colleagues, had hurt him. "Étienne lost his composure when he realized that the High Commissioner was complicit in the plan to kidnap two of his citizens. Our old friend asked—no, he ordered—General Robilard to resign, and threatened to call the London reporter from the CBC. Evidently, he has her and her BBC colleagues, on speed dial."

"Will he do it? Robilard I mean. Will he resign?"

"Rod, you didn't see the look on the man's face when he realized that Hank Darien had used his own prejudices to dupe him into this . . . this business."

When the lift doors opened, both men stood motionless for a moment. An air of frustration clung to them. It wasn't until the doors started to close that either man moved. Rod reached out and tapped his hand on the door safety strip, then held it there until the doors opened fully.

Sir Richard stepped out of the lift, and turning to Rod, stopped him before he could exit. "Chief! Go make your calls. At least we can try to keep our boy out of this mess. And tell Tori to hold her horses. I will meet her and the team in about . . ." C looked at his watch, seeming to calculate the time he needed. "I'll be down for a brief at half past."

Rod hit the lift button for two floors lower and let the doors close. An impossible operation completed successfully, and instead of celebrating they had an international incident on their hands. At this moment, the chief did not envy the boss. Of course, it hadn't escaped his attention that he would now have to brief his goddaughter on the outcome of the morning's meeting.

C-GFAB, 7500 Feet ASL
Israeli–Jordanian Border

The airborne border crossing was as simple as switching from Jordanian Air Traffic Control to Israeli ATC. Both Cleo and Albert had been quiet since takeoff. They hadn't bothered with the music today. Not feeling much joy for the prospects ahead, they had flown in silence since takeoff. Albert was in the pilot's seat, and flying the plane. Over the past weeks Bo Commanda had spent several hours flying, while Albert had only flown a few, and all from the co-pilot's chair. Even if her Otter was destined to end up at the bottom of the Mediterranean, Cleo was still a commanding officer, with a duty to her crew. She was determined that Albert would be prepared, even if he chose to swim.

Leaning forward, she was craning her neck for the best view of the region, when Albert spoke, rousing her attention from the terrain below. "I'm really sorry about all of this."

"Don't!" she ordered, immediately regretting her tone. "This is not your responsibility Albert. Not in a million years. Whatever is going on here, started long ago."

Many people of European descent would think it rude to sit in brooding silence, but Albert and Cleo found small talk trying, and often invasive. Both were in the habit of keeping their mouths shut until they had something to say. Other people assumed this had more to do with their military training. The truth was much simpler. From example, they had both learned at an early age, that watching and listening garnered more information than running your mouth off. "Albert? Who taught you to speak Mohawk?"

"My Granny, mostly," he answered honestly. "Not right away, but when we started learning in school, she started to remember her talk and helped me with it. Of course, she cried a lot at first."

"Mine too," she admitted, clearly remembering the shame her grandmother had been taught. "My Auntie was taking Native Studies at Trent University and would play word games with us, getting me and Bo to act sentences out."

"We did that too," Albert confessed. "My Granny would act out different animals and we would have to guess the names. Or she would say the name of something, and we would race out into the woods and try and find what we thought she was asking for. I remember racing my sisters back to Granny in her lawn chair, holding a rock or leaf or whatever I thought she had said. I almost forgot how much fun that was."

"I loved it too! Auntie used to play this one game with me and Bo. She called it opposites. She would say 'Bo you're Big' and Bo would have to say it in Mohawk, and then I would have to say the opposite."

"*I'ih-se ko'wa-ne?*"

"Yeah!" She playfully gave the old reply for, I am small. "*I'ih-se niwa'a.*"

"Good game," he said, keeping his eyes on the operation of the airplane.

"Albert. I need you to do something for me. Once you're safe, I need you to contact Tori. I think I may need you to teach her that game."

A long silence followed the request. The lack of reply might have troubled other people, but Cleo knew it was simply Albert's way. He needed a moment to think, and badgering him wouldn't help in the least. Ironically, Cleo often did the same thing, taking the time to think through a request before committing. Some people had confused her slow reply for a lack of comprehension. Maybe the aboriginal mind just worked differently than most others. A silent reply from someone like Cleo or Albert simply meant they were already analyzing the request, its permutations, and repercussions. It was also a sign of deep respect.

"Okay," Albert said simply, before carefully asking, "Cyril's dad said you're a member of his society. That you know the medicine in a way even he can't match. Is that where you're going with this?"

She looked back over to the left side of the small cockpit, carefully studying Albert's face to make sure she understood what he was hinting at. Chief Johnson, Cyril's dad, was a member of the same medicine society as Cleo, but for whatever reason, they had never met until Onondaga. Within the small society, most of the Faith Keepers and medicine practitioners were far more experienced than her. Her one claim to fame was that she had traveled to "spirit world" and she had done it more than once. The first time had been by accident, literally. After school, a young Bo and Cleo would rush out to Riverdale Park to go tobogganing.

Back in the day, the City of Toronto had just finished building the Don Valley Parkway to connect the Trans-Canada Highway to the downtown core. City planners had fast-tracked the project by sidestepping developed areas and running the new freeway right down the length of a natural greenbelt. The resulting wide rape of the Don River valley, bisected Riverdale Park right down the center from north to south.

Families living west of the highway were now cut off from the hockey rink on the east side and without a drive from their parents, after school skating was out of the question. The Commanda girls were still allowed to frequent the west side of the park, where the best toboggan hill in the city could be found. If there was snow, you could count on finding Cleo and Bo there every day, at least until the streetlights came on. That's when most of the kids had to head home for supper. It was also the time for a last chance run. Neither Bo nor Cleo owned a toboggan. Mostly they would find pieces of cardboard to ride the snow and sometimes they could use a toboggan belonging to a kid who was too tired or too cold to continue. The year both girls turned eight, a new item made its appearance in the park. It was nothing more than a rolled up sheet of plastic. But unrolled, it was the fastest thing on the hill, and Cleo wanted one. It took weeks before she could convince someone to let her try it. By then, she and Bo had a reputation at Riverdale West as the fastest girls on the hill, and one ride on a Crazy Carpet proved three things: You could go downhill much faster, you could maintain your velocity long after reaching the bottom of the hill, and, there was no possible way to control the plastic sheet once you pushed off.

Cleo's ride must have been a sight to frighten any parent. Not ten feet from the crest of the hill, her downhill progress turned into a wild spinning ride. Worse was the amount of speed she was gaining. She and Bo had watched bigger kids spin their carpets, but they usually fell off long before they reached the bottom of the hill. Cleo would never admit whether it was her never-quit attitude, or her pride, that kept her firmly seated on the plastic sheet. Her reluctance to let go and the increased speed achieved with her smaller size only added to the situation. When the Riverdale Zoo had closed the year before, they had completely cleared the base area. The city's Recreation Department had plans to add three baseball diamonds. Parks and Rec had been so excited about the new acquisition, they had

218

already installed the stadium-style lighting. Of the three huge steel poles that had been erected, one was positioned so that Cleo, closing in at top speed, had no trouble finding it. She had seen the post, but no amount of maneuvering would change what was about to happen. When she woke, she was wrapped in a blanket and stretched out on the living room sofa. Her dad was sitting at her side, nudging gently. He spent the next twenty-four hours watching over her, waking her up every hour, asking questions and giving her the pills the hospital had prescribed.

Knocked out for less than thirty minutes, she had emerged from her unconscious state with memories of family members she had never met, and ceremonies she had yet to be taught. Cleopatra had made her first trip to Spirit World and had returned to talk about it. The situation today was quite different, but the need to hide in Spirit World was a real possibility. Asking Albert to teach Tori a word game played by Mohawk children wasn't about getting Cleo into Spirit World; it was the key for getting her out. And it was one key she didn't want to share with just anyone.

As if he was thinking the same thing, Albert touched her shoulder and pointed to his headset. Cleo nodded, pulling her headset off, and unplugging the cord as she did. Albert unplugged the cord for his headset too, then pushed the right ear cup back. "Maybe you should teach her something she already knows. Maybe something only the two of you know."

Cleo nodded her head and thought about his idea. "Why don't you go ahead and teach her the game anyway. That can be the first level. If I need something deeper, tell her to remember the First Rule of Flying."

"Fly the plane?" Albert quoted with surprise.

"That's not exactly the rule I'm referring to. What I've been teaching you and Bo is the first rule of piloting: 'Fly the plane.' It's one of those snappy things we get student pilots to memorize. Like, 'Operate, Investigate, Navigate, and Communicate.' You probably remember that from ground school?"

Albert was smiling. "Never heard that one, but I now understand that you're talking about two very different rules. One day I'd like to hear about the other one." With that said he plugged his headset back into the communications system and pulled the right cup back over his ear.

Cleo followed suit, and was about to ask something, when the voice of the area Air Traffic Controller called their tail number. While Albert responded to the radio, she pulled out a pencil, preparing to write down any instructions they received. What came next was not surprising. They were being diverted, to someplace called Megiddo.

They had been expecting something but were caught off guard when Cleo couldn't find the airport on her chart. The civil aeronautical charts she had for Israel were provided by the Americans and showed the airport names in Hebrew and English. Even so, Megiddo was nowhere to be found. Finally, Cleo gave ATC the issue number for the chart she was using, refusing to be "vectored" to an unmapped facility. What she had imagined would slow ATC had only worked to rile them up. "You are ordered to divert to Megiddo immediately," ATC responded. "The airport designation on your chart is Shachar 7."

The burning taste of bile surged to the back of her mouth. Realizing where they were heading, she located Shachar 7 by memory. With a deep calming breath, she turned to Albert and nodded her head. He made the corrections to the new heading and changed the transponder code. They were heading for the Jezreel Valley, to an airport marked on the chart as "official use only."

"This is not the plan," Albert commented.

Cleo looked up from the calculations she was making, "No my friend, it most certainly is not. I put our ETA at sixteen minutes."

"Should I start our descent?"

They were flying at seventy-five hundred feet. At a comfortable five-hundred-feet-per-minute descent, they needed thirteen minutes to reach pattern altitude. An efficient pilot would start the descent portion of the flight early enough to ensure they entered the approach at the proscribed airport altitude. At the moment, Cleo had no interest in efficiency. "No. Let's make them step us down. I need some time to figure out what to do."

"What to do? I thought you were committed to this?" Even over the intercom, there was no mistaking the slight twinge of panic in his voice.

"Oh, I'm committed all right. It's just that I've been kidding myself, thinking I might have a say in how this would go down."

"Yeah," Albert nodded, then covered the mic in his fist. "We need a plan."

She nodded, pulling the headset off again. She reached up and hung it up in its standard storage place, on the fresh air gasper, then flipped the cabin speaker switch on, but left the headset audio on for Albert. She wanted to hear ATC and talk "off comms" if need be. For now, Albert could keep his headset on. Instead of unplugging, he pulled the right ear cup back and kept the mic covered with his hand.

"This is not what I was expecting," he said, his voice now competing with the cabin noise. "I'm not sure what our options are. Why don't we refuse to divert, like we did in Iran?"

"We had surprise on our side in Iran. Not to mention time, and some very threatening friends. It's not so simple this time. If we refuse, there's every chance we'll find a Surface-to-Air-Missile up our six!"

"Ouch!" Albert mouthed.

"Okay," Cleo said, planning out loud. "Any strategy we come up with has to provide for your guaranteed departure. Probably the best way to get you off the ground is to keep you off the ground."

"That means a fast turnaround?"

"Actually, I think it means no turnaround at all. We need to do this fast. Almost like a LAPES run. Almost," she said. "I would really appreciate you actually slowing down enough for me to get out in one piece."

Albert's tone was doubtful. "Are you asking me for a touch and go, where you somehow plan to get out of the plane somewhere in-between the touchdown and before the go part?"

"Yes," she confirmed with a smile, "but like I said, it would be nice if you slowed down somewhere in the middle."

"Slowed down," he shook his head, "but you don't want me to stop?"

"Definitely don't stop. Every second you're on the ground increases the chance that you will be prevented from taking off." Cleo climbed out of the co-pilot's chair. "I'm leaving everything on the plane except for one of the Winchesters. If need be, I'll use it to buy you time. So," she said, with a plan now firm in her mind, "while they vector you for the approach, I'll take up position at the cargo door. Once we're on the ground, pull the power back until the tail comes down. That'll be my signal to jump."

"And that's when I take off. I get it, but where do I go now?"

"I don't think ATC will give you much choice. Continue to push for Haifa. That's your approved destination. All I can say is, play it cool. I'm hoping that if I cause plenty of trouble on the ground here, everyone involved will be distracted enough to forget you, temporarily at least. Once you make Haifa, I know you can count on MI6 and probably even the CIA for help. My best advice is to just keep going. Once you make Haifa, head for open water, and don't look back. And Albert," Cleo added, "If the price of your safety is one medicine bundle, then pay the tab and take a dip. I'll understand. Believe me. I will completely understand."

With that said, and only a few minutes to Shachar 7, Cleo moved through the cabin, organizing herself. She pulled her two passports from her flight case, then put the Canadian passport away. If she was going to do this, it would be as a Mohawk, and nothing else. She also passed over everything in her personal kit with the exception of her toothbrush. The more she took, she reasoned, the more they could take away. *So, I will try for the toothbrush and see how that goes.* Once she had her carbine loaded, she pulled on the spare headset hanging by the cargo door. "Report!"

"They just ordered me down, They're vectoring me for the approach."

"Good. I'm going to open both rear doors now. I don't know which I'll use. Just remember, I need the tail down before I can jump. And don't worry when it comes down. You're going to lose all forward visibility. Just keep your eyes on the edge of the runway, count to five . . . slowly—one Mississauga—two Mississaugas—three Mississaugas—four Mississaugas—five. Then push the throttle to the wall and get the hell out of dodge."

"No problem, Colonel," Albert answered respectfully. "Once we touch-down, I'll retard the throttle until I know for sure you're safely out the door. Then it's full power and I'm gone!"

"That's all I can ask. Thank you Warrant Officer Candidate Mackenzie," Cleo said sincerely, addressing him in the rank that would come with his promised acceptance to the US Army's Basic Flight Training program. Once successfully completed, and she had no doubt that Albert would make an exceptional pilot, he would become a full-fledged Warrant Officer. "It has been an honor serving with you, and if you're ever in the Jezreel Valley . . ."

Albert craned his neck around trying to see Cleo's face. "You Okay, Colonel? I can make a run for it?"

If only it were that simple. "Thanks Albert, but no, I think the only way through this is to actually go through with it."

Chapter Seventeen

Shachar 7
near Afula, Israel

Day 1, Zero Hour, 10:20 UTC (approximate time)

Suddenly aware of a severe stabbing pain in the back of her neck, Cleo tried to reach for her head, only to realize she was handcuffed. The pain, radiating along her shoulder and neck, was further exacerbated by the state of the dirt road they were on. Cleo's head bobbed up and down with every pothole the open jeep hit. The guard, sitting beside her in the rear of the old UN pattern CJ5, noticed she was awake, and said something to the uniformed men up front. The forward passenger turned to look at Cleo with curiosity, before giving the guard an order in Hebrew. Sitting next to her on the rear bench seat, the guard, in a surprisingly quick move, stabbed her neck with a syringe. Just before passing out again, She was able to make out the inscription on the cornerstone of the gatehouse: 1931. *Oh frack* . . .

The next time Cleo felt aware again, she was coming to in what looked like an old-fashioned infirmary. She could make out two figures with their backs to her. One was wearing scrubs and a white lab coat. The other looked military, but his uniform was unmarked and devoid of the accoutrements of the any service or rank. The two appeared to be in some sort of heated discussion. *Perfect*, she thought to herself, actually believing she could somehow jump up from the gurney and escape. If the sound of Cleo trying to get up didn't alert the two arguing, then her low, partially stifled groan did.

The woman in the scrubs and lab coat, walked over to the side of the gurney, and in a familiar accent, said, "Welcome back, Colonel Deseronto."

Cleo tried to lift her head again, but the woman stopped her. She hadn't realized she was still in cuffs until that moment. Only now the handcuff shackled her left wrist to the bedrail. She had no idea if her right wrist was cuffed, and before she could move her head to look, wave after wave of nausea hit.

"I gave you a shot of Demerol for the pain, but it appears you are allergic," the woman said, looking over the hives now covering Cleo's arms. "I did not want to risk further complication by giving you morphine until you were conscious. Will you tolerate morphine or should we try something else?"

"Montreal?"

"Morphine," The woman repeated, as if Cleo had misunderstood what she was saying.

"No, you . . . Montreal?"

The woman in the white lab coat studied Cleo's face for a long moment. "Originally," she answered after consideration. "I'm Dr. Bergeson. You have a concussion and a laceration on the back of your head. I have cleaned and stitched the wound. Now, we need to care for the pain."

"What part?" Cleo asked. In a situation like this, information was everything. "What part of Montreal?"

Dr. Bergeson ignored the question, keeping her attention on the task at hand. "We need to address your pain management."

"Why?" She was fighting back the rolling waves of nausea, and had switched her focus to the person who had been arguing with the doctor. As if on cue, the building queasiness forced Cleo to roll on to her side. She threw-up over the edge of the gurney, then lowered her aching head again. One of the many odd things about Cleo Deseronto was her pain tolerance. While most women could tolerate more pain than men, Cleo could tolerate more pain than even the hardiest of women. The only complication was the weird fact that she metabolized pain as nausea. Nausea, like seasickness, is exaggerated every time you move your head, accentuating the sensation of a heaving stomach. Cleo had long ago learned to mask any sign of pain, but knew that once she started barfing there was nothing to do but ride the vomit-comet.

Dr. Bergeson signaled to someone yet unseen. Seconds later, a nurse was cleaning up the mess Cleo had just made. Once the heaving subsided, the nurse cleaned her face and set a kidney bowl on the gurney. "Let me give you something for the pain, now," Bergeson said. The "now" part of her offer hinted that she may not have the opportunity later.

"Ondansetron," Cleo said, watching to see if the request for the cancer medication was unexpected. The prescription had turned out to be the only pill that could control Cleo's nausea, and by effect, manage her pain. Any doctor with access to her medical records would know that. When Bergeson produced a loaded syringe, she knew without a doubt, they were prepared for her and had been for some time, considering how long it would have taken to obtain her medical file and arrange to have the expensive cancer medicine on hand.

SOE Operation Centre (The Tank)
Security and Intelligence Service
Vauxhall Cross
London, United Kingdom

Day 1, 12:30 UTC, Internment Time: 2 Hour, 10 Minutes

It was exactly half past the hour when Sir Richard walked into the Tank. He had just gotten off the phone with Genevieve Schilling, the Israeli Ambassador. She wanted to assure him that Albert and the aircraft would be cleared to leave Haifa for Cyprus without delay. She also informed him that she had suggested to the IDF, that Albert's safe arrival in Cyprus was of national importance. Any relief C felt from the news that SSG Mackenzie would not meet the same fate as Lt.Col. Deseronto quickly dissolved after hearing the Ambassador's update.

"Forgive me *Richard*," Genevieve said over the secure line. "You should know they have taken her to Shachar 7."

"Sha—har . . ." Sir Richard started to ask, before realizing with alarm, what she was referring to. "You mean 1931?" he asked, using the original British designation.

Now facing Tori and her team in the Tank, Sir Richard couldn't bring himself to describe the situation. Instead he asked Rod Nelligan to report. It was not the way the team usually did things, but he wanted Tori and her people to hear something hopeful, before they launched wholeheartedly into Deseronto's situation.

"He just took off," Rod said, referring to Major Butterworth. The Marine had been rushed off and kitted-out in British flight gear, plunked into a two-seat Harrier training jet, and pointed in the direction of the Mediterranean. Butterworth's "wings of gold" attested to his skill as an aviator, while his personnel file clearly recorded his proficiency in the Harrier jump jet. The American version of the fighter trainer was identical to the Royal Navy training Harrier. The two-seater he was flying was a throwback to his fighter school days. It hadn't been difficult for Command Chief Nelligan to twist a few arms to get the jet laid on for an extended-range training cycle. It had taken an altogether different strategy to get the Commodore commanding the Training Wing, to hand over the jet, without a pilot.

"How did you get Commodore what's-his-name to release the Harrier?" Sir Richard asked.

"I threatened the prat! Simple enough."

C shook his head at the salty old mariner. Nothing would surprise him today. "Lady Dufferin," he said to his daughter, with great formality. The Dufferin part referred to the hereditary title she had inherited from her maternal grandfather, the Earl Dufferin, on his death two years earlier. "I must apprise your team of a development. Lieutenant Colonel Deseronto's aircraft has been diverted enroute to Shachar 7. You may know this facility by its original British designation of 1931." Sir Richard pushed ahead before anyone could comment on that news. "As for the Staff Sergeant, he has been allowed to continue the planned flight, which I have been guaranteed, will proceed without risk of harassment. Now, as the chief has just reported, Major Butterworth has departed for Cyprus, where he will collect Staff Sergeant Mackenzie and return him to us. If all goes well, we will have them both back in London sometime this evening."

"Before anyone asks about Cleo's wee plane," the chief interjected, "I've made arrangements with an old colleague in Turkey. He's going to send a few of his SAR boys to collect the Otter and fly her to London."

"How much will that cost us?" C muttered quietly. Sir Richard was visibly depressed with the quick succession of frustrations and betrayals, and let it show.

The chief smiled kindly, "That's the best part. The Turks are havin' a hard time getting AVGAS for those wee birds. When we were planning the details of the operation, Major Butterworth had the same concern, and laid on an Air Tanker in case the team had problems." Chief Nelligan's smile couldn't be brighter. "Major Butterworth, with Langley's blessing, ordered the tanker into the air just before he took off. The Turks will have their petrol within the hour."

Tori thanked him for that one small victory, before turning her attention to the head of the agency. "As you may well guess, we haven't made much progress."

Now re-establishing SOE protocol, Tori ordered Allan to begin. "We," nodding towards Tori, "we have gone through everything the Canadians and the Israelis have given us, which is extensive, and there is nothing in these files to indicate concern, much less a reason to question her." Allan was ready for questions, but the truth was he had no answers, and the pain of knowing it was written on his face. This was more than an exercise for the team. Like everyone else, Allan was emotionally invested. Cleo had worked closely with each of them, during the initial planning marathon, and the weeks of hard work that followed. Nici and Guy were next. They didn't have much but what they did have was a revelation.

"We found some achieved files that were recently scanned and uploaded to the IDF mainframe," Guy reported.

"It looks like the work was done by an outside contractor," Nici said, adding, "they did a sloppy job of blacking out things like names and places on the original English-language documents."

"We found bits and pieces of reports shared between the Mossad and something called the Behavior Analysis Unit," Guy added.

"Gentlemen," Tori said to her father and the chief. "Hank Darien's name is on everything and there are several references to a study conducted on a subject identified only as 'Wahoo.' We thought it a codename, but when I ran it by Agent Commanda, she explained that it was a derogatory term for a person of North American aboriginal ancestry."

"No!" the chief said in disbelief.

Sir Richard shook his head. "What I can't believe is Darien's arrogance, or is it ordinary ignorance?" He speculated, not actually expecting an answer. "What was the task of this Behavior Analysis Unit, and what exactly was Darien doing?"

It was Darcy Gerrard's turn to weigh in. "It looks like the unit was a CIA project, researching the psychological stamina of soldiers of differing races. Noteworthy, is the fact that all of the subjects were appropriated from one UN command or another. None were Americans with the exception of Colonel Deseronto. Judging by his actions to date, I believe Mr. Darien would have considered the Colonel fair game for having chosen to serve with the Canadians and not the US Armed Forces. The man believes he's a true American patriot and would have looked at Deseronto's actions as ungrateful, perhaps even treasonous."

"Bleedin' hell," the chief growled under his breath.

"How many?" Sir Richard asked. "How many foreign peacekeepers did they grab?"

"Twelve," Darcy answered. "That of course does not include our girl."

"Lucky thirteen," C noted absently.

"Judging by the size of the briefing pack he gave the Ambassador," Rod Nelligan speculated, "it looks like Darien's been keeping tabs on our wee Cleopatra ever since. What about the others?"

Tori shook her head, "Not that we can find much, but it doesn't look like it. The real question is why Cleo and why now?"

"I concur," Sir Richard said. "Dr. Gerrard, I believe it's time for you to make a house call. Chief," he ordered, turning to Rod, "get Mackenzie in here the minute they land, and there's something else. Ask Étienne if he can pull a copy of her undergraduate thesis. I seem to recall her querying me on several facilities we built in Palestine between the wars. If I'm right, I think she already knows where she is."

"Really?" Tori asked. "Wait, I do remember reading something about adapting military facilities, but 1931?"

"How does that help our girl?" Rod interrupted. "It's not as if she can escape from that place. It's smack in the middle of Armageddon!"

"Look who's a skeptic now," C raised a brow at the big Scotsman.

"It's not about escaping, Chief," Darcy explained. "It's about information. And in her situation, information is power. The drill in the prisoner scenario is to disorient the subject. They have already failed a very crucial step of her conditioning. They can still exhaust her, or starve her, but they can't intimidate her with her surroundings."

"I don't need you Darcy, or any of your Doctor Who gobbley-gook, to tell me what the prisoner scenario is," Rod barked, letting his frustration escape.

Tori took Rod's arm, effectively halting his outburst, before turning to Guy and Nici, "We need that paper."

Nici shook her head. "We tried, but the RMC electronic archive only goes back to 1998."

"If they have that paper on file," Guy added, "it's only on paper."

Sir Richard, checking his watch, turned to his oldest friend in the world, "Chief," he said kindly. "Get back on the phone to your favorite Frenchman. Ask him to call Saint-Jean and get the school Commandant out of bed."

"Wait! Where's Siobhan?" The chief asked.

"I've got her combing the archives," Nici said. "Why?"

"I've got it, Lass. I've got a copy of all her papers from Uni."

"You kept Cleo's undergraduate essays?" Tori asked, with a skeptical look.

"Aye, My Lady. I kept yours too!"

Now everyone on the team looked surprised, not the least of which was Tori, "Why?"

"How'd you expect me to keep up with all you two were learning?" Rod asked honestly. "It's embarrassing to admit, but I've been so proud of you both. I spent many a night in the kitchen of the Archer, with Nigel and Will, trying to understand all you two were learning about."

At that precise moment, Siobhan burst into the Tank with a look of triumph plastered across her face. "I found something," she announced, dumping a stack of folders on the central workstation, before handing the top file to Tori.

The top page in the folder was an index which Tori quickly scanned before flipping to a specific page. "After-Action reports from the investigation into Cleo's disappearance from the UN compound. This is interesting; this is the Flight Surgeon's report from Germany."

Sir Richard moved closer to read the report alongside his daughter, while the rest of the team dug into the other files Siobhan had delivered. What was even more interesting to learn was that Siobhan, in an effort to keep the chief organized, had scanned in all of his personal files. It only took a second for her to retrieve Cleo's University thesis. The entire team was scrambling to put together the missing pieces when C caught something in the Surgeon's report. "There, a caveat on her injuries." He looked to his daughter, who was reading the same thing.

"It seems the doctor attributed Cleo's stamina to a peculiar fault of her physiology." Tori pointed to a particular section, "he calls it 'Contrary Physiological Responsiveness.' What on earth . . ." she turned to Darcy for input, before her father interrupted.

"I believe we have our 'why.' What we need to know now is why this is so important to Hank Darien, and if the Behavior Analysis Unit is back in action?"

Haifa, Israel

Day 1, 14:20 UTC, Interment Time: 4 Hours

"Charlie-Golf-Foxtrot-Alpha-Bravo," the tower announced the Otter's call sign over the departure frequency.

Albert replied, waiting nervously for his clearance.

"You are cleared for departure. I have been informed by the area controller that an Atalef helicopter from the Sea Corps will join you on takeoff and escort you safely to Cypriot airspace."

Albert groaned, but seeing no other choice, accepted the escort. If Cleo had taught him anything, it was when to fight and when to run. She had ordered him to Cyprus, and it looked like the Israelis were backing that plan. He made note of his departure instructions, switched to the ground frequency, and began to cautiously taxi the Otter. The Colonel had made it look easy, even a little silly, with all that back and forth snaking along the taxiways and ramp. Cleo had been right about that too. It was always the tough stuff that looked simple. In the air, the DeHavilland Otter was as easy to handle as the Cessna 172 he had flown for his private pilot training. On the ground though, the little tail-dragger behaved like a bull in a china shop. Now he understood why Bo had always begged Cleo to take control the minute they touched down.

At the threshold of the runway, Albert stopped the Otter, pushing hard on the toe brakes, to keep her from rolling forward. To his surprise, the tower was on the radio the moment he switched frequencies.

"Golf-Foxtrot-Alpha-Bravo, Haifa tower. You are cleared for takeoff. On takeoff maintain heading three-three-zero. Good day."

Albert repeated the instructions, and thanked the controller, while setting the heading indicator. Gingerly pushing the throttle control to full power, he eased off the brakes and let the Otter roll. For one moment he had a perfect view of the runway before hitting the right rudder pedal to swing the old girl straight down the runway. From the viewpoint of the tower or the escort helicopter, the takeoff roll must have looked wild. Albert had over corrected as he pulled onto the runway. The essentially blind and powerful tail-dragger was now zigzagging from one edge of the paved surface to the other. Just when it looked like the Otter was completely out of control, the tail popped up and all forward visibility was restored. Albert sucked in a deep breath and wrestled with the little cargo plane until she calmly jumped into the air. Instantly back in control, he pulled the nose up to the horizon and let the docile Otter climb out from Israeli airspace. Albert laughed, letting the pent up anxiety drain away. *Bo was right. This just flying around shit, is a lot more exciting than I imagined!*

Holding Level
Security and Intelligence Service
Vauxhall Cross, London

Day 1, 15:30 UTC, Interment Time: 5 Hours, 10 Minutes

By the time Dr. Gerrard entered the observation corridor, Bo Commanda had been hustled from the slumber of her bunk by two uniformed guards and wordlessly man-handled into the adjoining interview room. Judging by her body language, it looked very much like Bo was still hoping this was some sort of joke. Darcy watched her restless movements carefully. His favored modality was to wait until the subject was on the verge of losing their temper, and then enter with a stack of records, usually meaningless papers randomly ordered into official-looking folders. When the electronic door finally whizzed open, Bo launched into the tirade she had obviously rehearsed, stopping only when she heard Darcy's conciliatory apology.

"Captain, I'm so sorry it's taken me so long to cobble everything together. You don't mind. Do you?" he asked, knowing the positive suggestion and the surprise apology had interrupted her behavior, providing a key to gaging the amount of interrogation training she had received. The quick change in Bo's demeanor told Darcy all he needed to know. She had never been on the suspect-side of the interrogation table, and probable hadn't spent many hours on the investigator's side either. Notwithstanding her recent promotion to Special Agent, Bo really was just a very junior G-man.

"Hey Doc, sorry about the hissy fit. I was just pissed at how those guards acted. After everything I've done for you guys, it felt a little fucked-up!"

"You certainly don't share your cousin's aversion to the vernacular, do you?"

"Aversion?" Bo Commanda started to ask, then stopped short, as if some strange reality had just kicked in. "What the fuck's going on here?" Bo shot to her feet, backhanding the tall stack of files Darcy had placed on the corner of the table. The swing sent the folders to the floor, with bogus papers swirling in every direction. When Darcy didn't react to the outbreak, Bo let loose with a second round of obscenities. Pushing the remaining files to the ground, "You son-of-a-bitch! Wait until my government realizes you bastards have me! We know how to reward a hero. What you're doing is bullshit. You should be kissing my ass for all I've done!"

"What about Colonel Deseronto?" Darcy asked, his expression stone cold. "Shouldn't she receive some of the credit?"

"Oh, for fuck sakes," Bo said, steaming with indignation. "You don't see her red ass in here, do you?"

"Would it interest you to know that Miss Deseronto is indeed in holding and most likely being interrogated at this very moment?"

That information interrupted Bo's protest. "You're interrogating her too? Why the fuck?"

"Miss Boudicca, if you persist with your aggressive behavior, and your distasteful gobshyte, I will have you returned to your cell."

Bo, still standing, kept her arms crossed but didn't say a word. Darcy watched her body language move from defiance to bare acquiescence, in seconds. He signaled the resigned Boudicca to return to the seat across from him and watched as she slid back down into her chair. He was sure Bo had plenty of fight left in her, but Darcy knew the pattern for their discussion was set. Bo, like many people, couldn't stomach long periods of isolation. He was now sure she would rather talk than tolerate being sent off alone. The next tool in his arsenal was simple; say nothing and let Bo direct the conversation. This would tell him what mattered most to her, and by contrast, betray her motivations and desire. It only took a minute before a sullen Bo broke the silence. "If you're questioning Cleo, why do you need me? She was in command, not me. If anything went wrong then it's her fault, not mine."

"Have I said anything went wrong?" Darcy asked, still not providing any information she could draw from. He was watching her rapidly changing expression with interest. Clearly Bo Commanda was just as much of a wild card, as he had envisaged at the onset of the operation. As predicted, Bo was letting her perceived childhood injustices rule her actions, and with no mind for the consequences Cleo might face in return. If the two had been arrested as the other parties had planned, who knows how many other facts Bo's indignation would have allowed to slip. He couldn't help but wince at the rebuff the chief had given him over the Prisoner Scenario. Chief Nelligan might be well versed in the psychology of interrogation but Bo Commanda clearly was not. While Darcy maintained his professional silence, he couldn't help be relieved that his interrogation was focused on helping Lt. Col. Deseronto and not the alternative. He repeated an axiom that Cleo had often used. "Thank the Gods." *Thank the Gods indeed!*

Shachar 7
near Afula, Israel

Day 1, 15:40 UTC, Internment Time: 5 Hours, 20 Minutes

Cleo woke to find herself in a holding cell. Opening her eyes slowly, she moved her head with more caution this time. The effort didn't help. The pain shot down her neck and across her shoulders, forcing her to sit up. Resting her back against the cement wall of the tiny space, she took her head in her hands and rested it gently, pulling her knees up for support. With one hand, she reached for the wound on the back of her neck, and was surprised to find a long row of stitches running from her hairline vertically for two to three inches. Her fingers gently traced their way along the slightly curved incision and felt the cleanly shaven edges. The stitches felt good, if you could describe it that way. With no way to see what the back of her head actually looked like, she would have to trust her fingers to paint a picture. The edges of the wound seemed uniform or at least un-raggedy. There was swelling on both sides of the sutures, which was to be expected, along with a good-sized goose egg on the back of her head.

Cleo closed her eyes to thank the Creator. She guessed she had a minor concussion and a well-sutured wound. Her knees and elbows were scraped raw from her unorthodox exit from the airplane, but all in all, she was in one piece. The other thing she thought interesting was her attire. She was still in her flight suit, albeit stripped of the few extra things she had carried off the plane, and ripped at the elbows and knees. Her Winchester had long disappeared, and so were the extra cartridges she had stuffed into her pocket. Her boots and socks were gone, as was her passport and pilot's license. Cleo almost laughed when she realized her toothbrush was gone too. She didn't mind so much. It was the flight suit that confused her. Normally, a prisoner is stripped of all personal belongings, including their uniform. The objective is to remove all external references to a person's identity. Knowing this, she had expected to wake up in a pair of prison pajamas, or worse yet, a dehumanizing hospital gown.

It was time for a SitRep, except there is no one to report her situation to. She looked around the cell cautiously. So this was 1931. The place had been purposely build by the British in 1931, as a means of housing the ever-growing number of Palestinians caught preparing to defend their position when the colonial mandate expired. As a military cadet studying engineering, Cleo had used the British-designated 1931 as an example of well-engineered facilities, that could withstand major structural changes, in an effort to create lasting venues. In her paper, Cleo had proposed that 1931 would provide a suitable foundational structure for a large gallery space, museum, or even a multiplex movie house, which was a relatively new idea at the time.

Looking around the small cell, it was hard to believe she had once championed the place. *Concrete,* she thought. The place was just one concrete pour on top of the next. Even the "cot" she was sitting on was nothing more than an 18-inch-thick pad of cement. The ceiling, floors, walls, everything except the doors and windows were poured concrete. Frank Lloyd Wright and Buckminster Fuller had championed concrete as a miracle materiel, that could be used to inexpensively build long-lasting homes for the working classes. *Boxes made of concrete.* Cleo truly believed that the box mentality of Western society was fast destroying families and communities. Families now lived in separate boxes, with people traveling to work in boxes. Then, stopping on the way home at one box or another for food, gas, etc, etc . . . the boxes were endless. During the bleakest days of the Six Nations, the people banded together to care and protect one another. Today, everyone wanted their own box to live in too. Cleo didn't like the feeling she got whenever she thought about the way her people were changing. There was something in her gut that just wouldn't stop twisting.

She would try and explain her misgivings by asking if anyone thought Handsome Lake would have survived his four years of fever and sickness today? With no children of his own, the great prophet had been nursed day and night by his nieces, and other women from his clan. Today he would have been carted off to a hospital, pumped full of drugs as a means of care, and transferred to the first available long-term-care facility. While she didn't agree with the Code of Handsome Lake as it applied to women, she understood how he had been influenced by the times and circumstances in which he lived. *You've got to believe in something,* she reminded herself, preparing psychologically for her next encounter with the guards. Taking a deep breath, she closed her eyes and began silently, *Grandfather, Grandmother, Thank you for this day . . .* Before she could finish the first line of her prayer, she had moved herself into a deep state of hypnosis. Cleo had practiced this very scenario before, easily transforming herself from battered and worn, to resourceful and ready.

She had only managed to visualize her response to a few scenarios when the steel door was pulled aside to reveal two guards standing behind the still closed and locked inner iron-bar door. Cleo stood and gaped openly at the guards, as they hurled orders at her. One of the guards opened the remaining door, threw in a black hood that reminded her of the cotton gift bags, she used at home. Picking up the bag, she looked inside, as if expecting a gift. Once she discovered the bag was empty, she threw it back at the guard, along with a scathing insult in Mohawk. The first guard shouted instructions at her, while the second began a pantomime to demonstrate the proper use of the hood. Standing on the bed platform, Cleo turned her back to the guards and began a morning chant, secretly counting the seconds before the guards came storming in. When they didn't immediately charge the cell—she smiled inwardly and continued her song, while listening to the bar door being closed behind her, followed by the telltale dragging sound of the outer steel door. *So whoever's running this show isn't ready to rough me up yet,* adding that information to her ever-growing list of observations.

Observation Room, Holding Level
Security and Intelligence Service
Vauxhall Cross, London

Day 1, 20:10 UTC, Interment Time: 9 Hours, 50 Minutes

"No way!" Mike Perkins said emphatically, even as the revolting taste of bile began to build in the back of his mouth. Biting back the sudden desire to vomit was easy, compared to the feeling of being twelve hours behind the ball, and not having a clue who to trust.

"Easy lad," the chief said. "Our resident nutcracker says the same. We just planned to keep her here until she simmered down, but once she kicked off, we realized we could learn a thing or two about how our other girl may be sorting herself."

Mike shook his head, as he watched Bo Commanda go from temper tantrum to Indian Dancer and a whole lot of angry-looking poses in-between. "Learned enough?" There was no point in harassing the chief or his boss, Tori Braithwaite, about nabbing Bo Commanda, and keeping her locked up. He was more concerned with Bo Commanda's behavior. Checking his watch, he groaned inwardly at the time. If Special Agent Commanda was this out of shape after only ten hours in a modern holding cell, how the hell was Deseronto going to survive some CIA shit hole?

"All right," Mike said flatly. "Enough is enough. Let her out."

The chief nodded his head to a uniformed guard sitting nearby. As the guard punched a key on the keyboard, the sound of the electronic lock released, followed by the automatic door opener sliding the steel and glass panel into its pocket. Inside, Bo stopped her tirade and turned to the door just in time to see the chief. She immediately charged, her mouth racing her fists, which were poised for action, only to be stopped dead when Mike Perkins stepped in first.

"Knock it off, Captain!" he ordered, with as much authority as the Marine Corps Commandant. "This exercise is over! Get your head on straight, and get your uniform together, and the rest of this crap squared away. You have an after-action briefing to give."

Bo, caught off guard by Mike's presence, seemed frozen in place until he barked out her new orders. Without a word she began collecting all of the items she had thrown around the room. Her uniform was among the two things she hadn't abused. The other was the buckskin jacket she had received from home. This she was wearing, along with the civvies she had worn on the flight from Dubai.

Chief Nelligan looked Bo over carefully, then pulled his mobile from his jacket and speed dialed a number. "Yeah Vonnie, its Rod. Can you meet Captain Commanda down in the Ladies loo?" still listening to Siobhan, he nodded his head to the guard to escort Bo. "Whatever she needs love. Yeah, take your time. Let her have a shower and get her uniform Bristol, then meet us in the Tank." Nelligan flipped the phone closed and turned to Mike. "Good enough?"

"It's a start," Mike said, "but if you ever pull a stunt like this again . . ." His voice trailed off. What was the point in making threats he couldn't act on. "Chief, this was not kosher, not by a long shot."

Rod let out a heavy sigh. "You're right. Of course . . . we did learn a lot. Care to have a wee listen to our resident head doctor?"

Mike shook his head in dismay. You just couldn't stay pissed at a guy like Nelligan for long. "This better be good," he warned, but couldn't stifle his curiosity.

Royal Navy Harrier Training Jet T32
Enroute from Gibraltar to HMRNAS Yeovilton

Day 1, 23:20 UTC, Internment Time: 13 Hours

"You want to take her again?" Butterworth asked casually. During the hop from Cyprus to Gibraltar, he had given Albert his first chance to pilot a high-performance aircraft. He surprised himself when he made the offer, but what the hell; the aircraft was a training jet and set up for dual pilot operation. Besides, Mike Perkins had let it drop that Albert's next post would be Fort Rucker, and the Warrant Officer Flight Training program. Who knows, a year from now, with all things being equal, Albert would probably be flying a Black Hawk Helicopter in combat.

Once Albert had positive control of the Harrier, Butterworth turned his attention to the approach charts for London. The flight clearance they received in Gibraltar allowed them to proceed to a reporting point at the Eastern inlet of the Thames River. "Watch your altitude," Butterworth ordered. Albert had let the jet sneak up a few hundred feet. "Your stick control is good, but you need to soften up on the power."

"Yes Sir, Colonel Deseronto noticed the same thing. She was always saying small adjustments or big ones, no swishing back and forth in the middle."

"Every situation is different. The important thing is to match the style with the flight situation. I bet the Colonel wasn't shy about pushing that big radial engine to the yellow line when need be."

"She's a Mohawk woman, they're fearless. Hell," he said, "when we were running hard, she had Bo push it into the red, and just kept pushing it. She said she'd blow the engine before she'd let us be forced down. Man, it was close!"

"Sounds harsh. You guys really cut it thin. I can't wait for the full debrief," he commented, while keeping his attention on the aircraft instruments. "When you're trying to make small adjustment with the power, try to walk the power lever forward instead of pushing it too far and having to pull back. Remember those old Yellow Book commercials? You know, where you let your fingers do the walking. Try moving the lever like that, a little twist left then right. Give it a try."

Slowly, Albert gave the power lever a small twist back and forth and found it easier to make small adjustments. "Nice, thanks sir."

"You call me Ken," Butterworth said. "You and Colonel Deseronto really like to stick to military etiquette. What's that about?"

Albert was still fussing with the power and had just realized he was slightly off course. He made his heading correction before replying, "I guess it's easier to create rapport with white people that way. No disrespect, sir. It's just easier when you know the rules."

Butterworth made an odd sound. "In case you hadn't noticed, I'm not white."

"Yes sir, I mean no sir," Albert stopped talking and focused on flying. How could he explain that black and white were the same thing for aboriginal people? "I guess it's different for Americans. When you're in the States, so many issues are labeled Black and White. When you're in Canada, the issues are usually labeled Red and White or French and English. I guess that might be a little like the North and South thing for you guys."

"I think I understand," Butterworth commented, without judgment. "I'm assuming that the *Red* population in Canada is a lot larger than it is in the States. I'm also thinking that the original slave population must have been much smaller up there?"

"Actually, Canada never allowed slavery. After the Conquest of New France, a few English Lords tried to bring slaves north. The parliaments of Upper and Lower Canada couldn't actually outlaw slavery, until the British did, but they put so many bylaws in place, the slave owners gave-up."

"Bylaws?" Butterworth asked. "They thwarted slave ownership with bylaws?"

"Yes Sir! They ruled that any slave imported, had to be given a full education, couldn't be put to work until he was sixteen or eighteen, I can't remember which, and had to be freed on his twenty-fifth birthday. English law already protected families, by making all newborns, black or white, British subjects. That pretty much put an end to any plans to bring that shame north. I'm sure you know this," Albert continued, after making another small adjustment to the power setting. "My home Reserve was a stop on the Underground Railroad. There is great pride amongst the Six Nations to know our ancestors accepted and protected the Stolen People."

"Stolen People . . ." Before he could say more, London Control interrupted their conversation. "Tango three-two, London Centre. Prepare to copy."

"London Centre, Tango Three-two. Ready to Copy," Butterworth responded.

"Tango Three-two, London Centre. Set transponder to one-niner-zero-one and squawk. Descend and maintain two thousand feet. Expect Visual Approach to Landing Zone. Report the Thames Barrier."

"London Centre, Tango Three-two. Roger. Leaving sixteen-thousand for two-thousand. Squawking one-niner-zero-one for the Visual to Yeovilton."

"Negative! You are cleared for off-airport landing. Switch frequency to London approach. Good evening Sir."

Ken Butterworth knew exactly what a Visual to an LZ meant, but where exactly that landing zone was located was a mystery to him. He changed the radio frequency and reported his position. "London Approach, Tango Three-two."

"Tango Three-two, this is London. Stand By."

"I take it we are not flying this girl home?" Albert asked.

"Your guess is as good as mine." Ken folded up his charts and squared away the cockpit in preparation for landing. An unfamiliar approach to land, and an unfamiliar landing, always got his full attention. An off-airport landing could mean anything from landing on a ship, to a rooftop, and all offered different challenges. The fact that it was almost midnight in London would only complicate any landing, especially one in an urban area. "Let's hope they want us to put down on one of those big cricket fields."

"I think it's called a *pitch*, or is that what they call a soccer field?"

"No idea, I'm a baseball sort of guy. You're doing very well Albert. Just keep the VSI pined at five hundred feet per minute, and let's see if you can hit that two-thousand-foot mark."

It was easy to hear Albert suck in a deep breath over the intercom. Yes sir," Albert answered, "Kenny, I mean Ken. Sorry sir."

"Hey, Kenny's okay," Butterworth said. "My brothers still call me that. I'm the baby of the family. Five brothers, all Marines, 'cept one, how about you?"

"Just sisters, three of them, but all older too. Growing up with five brothers must have been cool!"

"Sometimes," Ken admitted, "but they really pushed me hard. My brothers are all NCOs. If they hadn't kept on top of me with school, and keeping my nose clean, I couldn't have made it to Annapolis, much less flight school." Butterworth halted the conversation with Albert when ATC requested a position report. It was just a formality. They were definitely in the London positive radar area. "London Approach, Tango Three-two, Leaving six thousand-five hundred for two-thousand feet."

"Tango Three-two, London Approach here, welcome home. Turn left heading two-seven-zero for a visual to Battersea. Report the Thames River barrier. Extinguish your tail illumination and turn on your landing lights. Please reduce your Airspeed to one hundred and sixty knots."

"London this is Tango Three-two. We are unfamiliar with the area. Request vectors for Battersea Airport."

A short silence followed Butterworth's request. The pause was just long enough for Albert to ask, "Doesn't the controller sound like Bo Commanda?"

Before he could respond to Albert, or ATC, Ken spotted the barrier and ordered Albert to make a standard two-minute turn. Technically, they were cleared to the airport but since he didn't have a clue where that was, it was safer to hold and wait for directions. Noticing Albert was having some difficulty handling the jet in the fifteen-degree bank, Butterworth took control of the aircraft and asked him to pull out the local VFR chart. "Have a look for anything called Battersea. Start looking along the river, then spread out from there."

"Helicopter Tango Three-two, London. You are cleared to follow the Thames River to Battersea Heliport."

"London Approach, Tango Three-two is not a heli . . ."

"Tango Three-two—this is London! You are cleared for the CRUCIBLE! Understand Helicopter Three-two! Crucible clearance!"

Butterworth, caught off guard, asked Albert, "Is that Captain Commanda on the radio?"

"It sounds like her, but I don't understand what she's telling us."

"I think I do," Butterworth told Albert. "Check that chart—follow the river and look for a Heliport marker." He flipped the mic switch from intercom to transmit and announced, "Helicopter Three-two, inbound for the Crucible."

"Very good Three-two. Maintain two thousand feet until clear of London Bridge. Remain on this frequency, report Battersea in sight."

"I've got it," Albert announced, once Ken had repeated the clearance. "It looks like it's right on the river. Once we clear London Bridge, there are two mandatory reporting points: Vauxhall Bridge and Chelsea Bridge." Albert folder the chart for easy reference and focused his map light on the area they were about to fly into. "I get the feeling that we're sneaking in under the radar?"

"There's London Tower," Ken said. "We'll know soon enough." Pressing the transit button, he announced, "Helicopter Three-two, London Bridge, two thousand feet and one-sixty knots."

"Three-two, reduce speed for landing, Altitude is pilot's discretion once clear of Chelsea Bridge. Note that there is a fifteen-degree offset for the approach. Stay over the center of the river until you begin your approach. Remain on this frequency. You are cleared to land."

"Roger London. Three-two inbound, full stop."

"Put it down on the pad and wait for visual signals from Battersea ground."

"Roger, Three-two," Ken acknowledged, again. Once they passed the remaining bridge, ATC reminded them that noise abatement procedures were in effect. It wasn't necessary. Whatever ATC, MI6, or Bo Commanda, USMC, was up to, he didn't have to be told to behave. Obviously, helicopters don't come with after burners, and if they were pretending to be a chopper, it was most probably because they couldn't get clearance for a foreign national to fly a fighter jet through central London. Even if that foreign national was "on the team" and flying an unarmed training bird. With all the fuselage lights turned off and the landing light on, they could look like a helicopter from a distance, but once they were on short final, that would change. To reduce the risks of being detected by everyone within ten miles of Battersea Park, Butterworth knew he had to keep his six pointed down river.

"I see it, sir. It looks like it's built out over the river?"

"I see it too. With this tail wind, I'm going to swing around, just to be safe. Keep your eyes peeled for overhead wired or obstacles." Butterworth piloted the Harrier past the heliport, making an on-point turn over the center of the river. With only five hundred feet separating the Harrier from the landing pad, he pulled the nose up sharply to drop their forward momentum, leveling off while pulling the trust diverter to full Vertical. A moment later the Harrier descended quickly towards the pad, seeming to float above it for a second, before settling in to land.

Finally back on terra firma, he retarded the throttle, pulling the thrust diverter lever back to full Horizontal position. Before he could decide what to do next, several Royal Navy ground handlers appeared on both sides of the aircraft. One, outfitted with lighted wands, signaled for Butterworth to hold the brakes while the mains were chalked. Now it was just a matter of following normal procedures.

The moment he raised the canopy, the ground handlers had their ladders up and were pulling Butterworth and Mackenzie from the cockpit. Before either of them had time to pull their flight helmets off, a new flight crew climbed aboard, and began preparing for takeoff. One of the ground handlers signaled to Butterworth and Mackenzie to follow him, and lead them towards a waiting van.

They didn't have far to go. The very small heliport could only accommodate three helicopters on the apron, leaving the landing pad open, but with no room to park. The Harrier was on the pad with its tail pointing down river. A USAF Black Hawk and a British registered Eurocopter, in an unmarked black livery, crowded the small apron. Several vehicles and personnel of the Royal Navy, and one unmarked Chevy Suburban with diplomatic plates, were jammed into every remaining inch. Their escort walked them directly to the waiting Suburban, and saluted sharply before leaving them with the driver. As they climbed into the SUV, the Harrier lifted off from the pad, turning east to follow the Thames back out to the Channel.

Mike Perkins, who had been waiting in the SUV, signaled for them to keep quiet while he continued a heated cell phone call. Judging by all the "Yes sirs" and "No sirs" flying about, it was easy to guess that Mike was arguing with someone much higher up the food chain.

While Mackenzie, being junior, climbed into the third row seat, Butterworth planted himself in the second row beside Mike and closed the side door of the Suburban. The driver maneuvered the big black SUV around the Eurocopter, and out the airside access gate. Within minutes of landing, they disappeared into the late evening A-Road traffic. Ending his call, Mike turned to Albert, "Your uniforms are hanging beside you. Get changed," he unceremoniously ordered both men before starting another call.

Chapter Eighteen

Situation Briefing, Tutor Room
Security and Intelligence Service
Vauxhall Cross
London, United Kingdom

Day 2, 00:30 UTC, Internment Time: 14 Hours, 10 Minutes

Albert and Ken found themselves alone in the Tutor Room, waiting for the rest of the team. Siobhan had set up her tea trolley at the back, but instead of containing the obligatory pot of tea she had packed it with hot coffee, fresh cream, bottles of cold soda pops, and an assortment of protein bars and fresh baked goods. For all intent and purpose, it looked like Vonnie was determined to keep their high-octane fuel somewhat healthy.

Neither Ken nor Albert had eaten since breakfast and both appreciated the boost, munching away silently while an indiscernible argument raged outside the meeting room door.

"How was she?" Ken asked quietly. "When you dropped her off, I mean?"

"Nervous, I guess. Determined, mostly. Whatever this is about, she meant to finish it once and for all."

Butterworth nodded, he liked this Army NCO, even if he didn't know much about Marines. "The Crucible!" Ken said, "that's how I knew it was Captain Commanda on the radio. It's the final test at the Recruit Training Center at Paris Island. You're not a Marine until you've passed the Crucible."

"Smart," was all Albert said before taking both his and Butterworth's coffee mugs back to the trolley for a refill. "This cream couldn't be fresher if they brought in the cow."

"I know," Ken said, joining Albert. "Even these big biscuits are fresh. They must bake them in house."

"Scones. My Granny would have called them scones."

"Scones," Ken repeated, as if trying out the word for the first time. "Good to know," he added, as he buttered the big biscuit. They had both just finished loading their plates when the electronic lock made its whizzing sound and the door opened. Both men instinctively placed their plates back on the trolley and stood to attention. Mike and the chief were the first through the door, and Mike signaled for them to grab their coffee cups, and take their seats. They were in the process of doing just that when two more officers walked in, prompting them both to pop to attention again.

Bo Commanda walked in first. She was in uniform, and as usual, oblivious to the decorum being displayed. "Hey guys," she said, "bout time you got back."

While polite with Bo, the guys weren't surprised to see her in uniform, but Tori. "Colonel!" Mike Perkins acknowledged with respect.

"Captain," Tori corrected him gently. "Navy tradition and all that." With Tori in battledress, and absent her beret, it was easy to mix up the branch of service.

Mike smiled, "You and the Canucks! Keeping me on my toes, Captain?"

"The uniform was for the benefit of the Air Ministry. Although, I must say, they were more impressed with Captain Commanda's American Marine uniform." She turned her attention from Mike, to Butterworth and Mackenzie, and offered her hand to the senior in rank first. "Major Butterworth, excellent work getting our Staff Sergeant home and navigating the Thames at night." Next offering her hand to Albert, she said, "I'm very glad to have you home, Staff Sergeant." Turning her attention to the room, she explained. "Now that the Gents are back, it's time for a situation briefing. Before we begin, I need to know who's in for the duration and who, if anyone, needs to distance them-selves now?" She signaled for everyone to hold before committing. Cautioning the room, "before anyone, especially you Mike, makes any commitment to this endeavor, I must disclose an important fact. You need to know that Lieutenant Colonel Deseronto and I are involved."

"Involved in what?" Mike started to ask when Bo chimed in.

"They're snogging, or boffing, or whatever they call it here!"

Only Mike was caught by the announcement. "Now I understand! I've been trying to figure out why someone's still shopping Deseronto's file around Langley."

"Shopping?" The chief asked, "I don't understand."

Mike sat down next to Nelligan, "Someone still thinks the Colonel is a security risk, and has presented Deseronto to the Director as a threat based on her sexual orientation. You know, we still discriminate when it comes to this sort of thing, but the angle they have been working is the risk of Deseronto's unknown love interest. Now that we know who it is, well . . ."

"Excuse me, sir," Major Butterworth interjected. "We've had full disclosure since this morning's meeting. Actually, it was yesterday morning now, that's when Darien presented his findings to the Israeli Ambassador."

Mike was still struggling with all the pieces of the puzzle. "Hank Darien has been working this thing for so long now even the Director's suggesting we let things run the course."

"Run the course?" the chief asked. "Bloody hell lad! You've a rogue officer running an operation that's been off the books for, what, twenty years? Are you telling us your hands are tied? Next you'll be telling us they've shipped her off to Guantanamo Bay for her own bloody good!"

Before Mike could respond to Chief Nelligan's challenge, Tori interjected. "Chief, we are all feeling a wee bit let down, but neither Mike nor his team, had any idea this would happen, at least not this way."

Nelligan groaned his understanding, folding his arms, visibly deflated. "I gave her my word. We just can't leave her."

238

"I don't plan to Uncle Rod," Tori said gently before turning to Siobhan. "Please hand out Lieutenant Colonel Deseronto's undergraduate thesis and the attached charts. "First though, do we have a willing team?" she asked, clearly checking that everyone in the room was committed.

"You can count on us." Mike Perkins answered for the Americans in the room. "What about the Canadians? Where the hell are they on this?"

"Étienne is working his side," the chief explained, "but officially, the PMO will only consider a diplomatic solution, which the Israelis say is out of their hands since that cowboy of yours is running his circus off the books and in a place that doesn't exist."

Bo Commanda, who had been uncharacteristically quiet until this point, corrected the chief. "I think you mean rodeo not a circus. If it was a circus he would be a clown, wouldn't he?"

The chief began to bristle at the useless comment, until Tori held up a hand to halt the discussion. "The only thing that matters now is finding a way to help our officer. We are a small team with limited support from our various agencies and governments. Having said that, you must know that I will do whatever it takes to bring Cleopatra home. So, if you are completely committed, and a wee bit bonkers," she warned, "I invite you to stay for a planning session. Anyone with even the slightest misgiving, including any member of the SOE, may leave now without fear of recourse or censure."

When no one moved, Siobhan began handing out the briefing packages, including Cleo's college paper on Shachar 7. "When the Colonel was planning this operation," Tori began, "She managed to create three exceptionally mad and doable plans in under seventy-two hours. In contrast, all we need do is create one plan that will succeed. Shall we begin?"

Shachar 7
near Afula, Israel

Day 2, 14:30 UTC, Internment Time: 28 Hours, 10 Minutes

A program of "softening" a prisoner was almost always the first step in preparing the detainee for interrogation. The process was designed to keep the prisoner in a heightened state of worry, confusion, and exhaustion. Step one: disorientation and sleep deprivation. Cleo was marched back and forth from her cell, to an interrogation room, and to her cell again and again. Whenever it looked like she might be restful or sleeping they would enter her cell, pull a black hood over her head, and drag her around the facility. Once done, they would either take her back to the original cell or they would leave her in an interrogation room for hours on end, before moving her again. No one seemed to be aware that Cleo was familiar with the facility. Even the black hood they kept pulling over her head didn't make much of an impression.

Cleo's lack of fear was quickly becoming a bone of contention among the guards, who she had pegged as IDF. It was hard to tell if the plain blue uniforms meant they were soldiers who had removed all military paraphernalia or civilians with none to display. It was a shame that any military would need to employ jail keepers, although they all pretty much did. And whether civilian or military, all jailers appeared to be woven from the same cloth. These IDF guards were no different than any of the corrections workers she had met over the years. Often, a certain unsavory type of person was attracted to the work. Cleo thought of them as the lowest common denominator amongst the worst of soldiers. These men were no different, except they expected more resistance from their captives than civilian jailers. What they didn't expect was Cleo's complete lack of comprehension. These men were used to softening prisoners who didn't speak the same language. Physical threats and hand signals had always worked to further the prisoner's isolation. Cleo had challenged them at every turn, going out of her way to misunderstand their directions. Worse, she seemed to be enjoying the process, taunting them at every turn. When she wasn't fighting, she chanted eerie tribal songs, and concentrating on a ghost dance that distressed the guards the most. Now they were fast refusing to "work" with her, while arguing vehemently with one another over her behavior. The fact that she couldn't be forced to stand to attention with the hood over her head was bad enough, but the constant chanting and taunting had them spooked.

Cleo had been using the guards' rotation to track time in the windowless block. It was a mistake to get caught-up in keeping track, but the guards were so obvious with their shift changes, that she couldn't help but notice. She even realized that two of the guards were sloppy eaters. Their uniforms progressively becoming noticeably more and more, soiled and sweaty, during their shift. Telling the time by the condition of their uniforms was almost too easy. Everything was a clue you could chase to distraction. Her strategy was to notice everything, then set it aside to evaluate later. Churning through every happening now was just a waste of time. She figured she would need at least two weeks to make any meaningful evaluation of the guards, their procedures, and schedules. All she could really say for now was that she had been here maybe twenty-four hours.

That guestimate was based more on the condition of her wound, or more accurately, the pain in her head. If a doctor were to ask her to rate her pain on a scale from zero to ten, her answer would be seven. Seven was an exceedingly high admission from Cleo, and would be a debilitating level for many other people. Truthfully, Cleo didn't have a ten on her pain scale. She figured ten would mean that things were so bad you were dead. Nine was unconscious and eight required not only unbearable pain but vomiting too, and Cleo had long lost the undigested remnants of yesterday's breakfast. Depriving her of food had only served to help her keep her pain concealed.

On the concrete platform that served as a bed, she sat up straight, crossed her legs and let out a long slow breath. With her eyes closed, she began a low chanting song. The truth was Cleo wasn't singing at all but practicing self-hypnosis. She had used it for years, to eliminate pain, and keep her emotions in check. It hadn't been taught to her. As a matter of fact, she had only recently learned that the method was considered self-hypnosis. Before then, she had simply referred to the practice as "giving thanks." She had practiced her gratitude chant for so long now that she could reach a state where she had reasonable control of her body temperature and blood pressure, which had left more than one Flight Surgeon in dismay.

It didn't take long for Cleo to reach that place where she could block the pain. Timing was important. She knew the second she looked like she was comfortable, the guards would come calling, and it didn't take long. The heavy steel door scrapped open to reveal two guards, both looking irritated. Cleo's eyes opened slowly, smiling as she looked them over. She stood straight up from her legs crossed position so that she was standing on the sleep platform. She said something in a language they had never heard, before charging with the force of a professional linebacker. While one managed to step aside just in time, Cleo hit the second guard full force and together they landed flat out on the deck. The two were wrestling for control when Cleo felt the initial telltale sting of a Taser.

When she woke, she was back where she had started, in the infirmary. Once again the doctor from Montreal and someone in unmarked greens were talking just out of her hearing. The two guards were there too. The one she had knocked down was sitting in a chair with his partner holding him steady. Cleo realized, with some satisfaction, that the one she knocked down must have been shocked by the Taser too. She had to think for a minute to decide if that was possible. *Of Course it was,* she told herself. She remembered having a good hold on his sweaty neck and watching him rub it now only confirmed that the first guard had gotten both of them. It wasn't her idea to hurt anyone but this Taser mishap would force the guards to rethink their tactics yet again. Listening passively to the little powwow, something suddenly got Cleo's attention. The IDF guards were speaking Hebrew with the doctor, who seemed to be translating everything to the soldier in green. Translating into French not English. He wasn't wearing anything that identified him as a soldier of any particular army. Of course, he didn't have to. Everything about this guy said military, from the BDU pants, the crew neck undershirt, pressed khaki shirt, and combat boots, were all a dead giveaway. Long used to the fact that her eye sight was far superior to her hearing, she automatically focused her attention on what she could see. That's when she noticed another disturbing fact. The unadorned soldier was indeed wearing combat boots. Canadian issue boots, but not the standard black leather high-tops, but special issue paratrooper boots. The type of boot only ever issued to the now disgraced Airborne Regiment. *Oh shit! And now the game begins.*

Rooftop Terrace
Canada House
Trafalgar Square, London

Day 3, 05:00 UTC, Internment Time: 42 Hours, 40 Minutes

General Robilard stood at the ornate stone railing of the rooftop terrace at Canada House and gazed over London's early morning bustle. Robilard sucked in long deep gulps of the clear morning air. He had missed spending time on the terrace. Once his office had been moved to Mayfair House, he didn't have the same opportunity to skip out for a breather. Robilard sighed, taking in the view. Standing in the morning sunrise he admitted that he had lost the pulse of the city he so admired. Truth be told, he had lost touch with much, much more. The debate raging in his head amounted to nothing more than his own shame.

Major General Robilard, High Commissioner for Canada, stepped back from the railing and took a seat at the small bistro table that had long been stuffed into the corner. Removing a thick manila envelope from his suit jacket, he laid it down flat and rubbed his hand across the attached label, as if checking to make sure it was secure. The large crested mailing label was clearly addressed to Étienne St. Herbert, and in the general's own handwriting. From another pocket he removed his mounted ribbons with medals. The four rows of "fruit salad" as the yanks would call them, were extensive for a Canadian, even a General, and attested to his long years of service both in and out of uniform. He placed the ribbon bar squarely on top of the envelope and centered it neatly, before adding his Gold Paratrooper Wings, just above his metals. Back on his feet, Robilard brought himself sharply to attention, and with a Browning 9mm Service Pistol in hand, raised his arm as if saluting the crisp morning sunrise, and shot himself in the head.

The Loyal Archer
Vauxhall Cross, London

Day 3, 05:40 UTC, Interment Time: 43 Hours, 20 Minutes

Tori Braithwaite sipped silently at the hot cup of tea Will Green had just poured for her. They were sitting quietly enjoying her favorite breakfast of toast and tea. Will had set a half a dozen small jars of jams and preserves on the table, along with fresh milk and his old big brown betty tea pot. He'd always say you can't make a decent cup of tea in one of those little restaurant pots. No, for his goddaughter and her shattered mood, his brown betty and a good ear was what she needed most. Tori's Uncle Will would never ask what the problem was. He knew exactly what her job entailed and no matter how close he was with the Security Services inner circle, his military training and experience always overrode his curiosity. If Tori needed to talk and could, she would, and if she couldn't, they would discuss the emotional aspect of her worries and skip the details. Sometimes she just needed to spend a little time away from her office and the strain of life and death decisions. William knew she loved her job, and according to Rodney, she was bloody good at it. He had heard the compliment many times, but coming from one of his fellow Chief Petty Officers, made it a fact for the old sailor. "Yer Uncle Nigel stopped by yesterday. He's back from Majorca and brought the marmalade for you." Nigel was another of her nurse maids and an investor in the club.

"Is he still jetting about for British Airways?" Tori asked, with some interest. "He is."

Tori grumbled slightly. "Most men would have tired of the travel by now."

"Aye," Will nodded his head in agreement. "But we're talking about Nigel. You know he can't sit still, always got to be doing something, besides, that Inspector job was the best thing to happen to him. When a man is as tormented by ghosts of the past as our Nigel, then you know he needs to keep moving."

"I wish he'd forgive himself," Tori offered, her voice emotionless, as she pushed a spoon around her cup.

"Aye lass," Will said in agreement, "but that's a conversation for another day. How about you tell me what's got you so shattered?"

Tori's elbow was resting on the table, with her hand propping her head up. The look was reminiscent of the attitude a young Tori Braithwaite used to display at a serving of Brussels sprouts. Before Will could say more, Rod Nelligan, using his own key, let himself in the front door of The Archer.

Calling out to his old sea mate at the back table, Rod asked, "Kettle still hot?"

"Just made a pot Roddy. I'll fetch you a cup, if you can get our girl here to eat."

"Keep yer seat, I'll grab one from the tray," Rod said, ducking behind the bar. Grabbing a cup from the stack of clean glassware, the chief ran water from the bar sink and filled it. "Where do you keep the Ibuprofen these days?"

Will looked up to see where the chief was standing, "Yer close Roddy. It should be just behind the sink."

"I see it," he said, grabbing the bottle. With some awkwardness, he snapped the plastic top open. Taking two tablets from the bottle, he swallowed them with the water chaser, then grabbed two more. "I'll take two for our girl here," he explained, carrying his cup and the pain relievers to the table. Sitting down beside his old chum, Rod handed the Ibuprofen to Tori. "You may need that," was all he said.

"Uncle Rod?" she asked, in a deeply troubled tone. "It's not even seven a.m., what else has gone wrong?"

Rod Nelligan sighed hard, "General Robilard is dead." There was no point trying to spin it for her. She knew just as well as anyone what the implications were.

Tori, who had been in the act of spreading the special delivery marmalade, laid the knife on the edge of her plate and sat quietly for a moment. Finally, Tori Braithwaite, SOE Section Chief, sat up a little straighter and ordered Rod Nelligan to report.

"The RCMP won't give their press brief until the Canadian Prime Minister's Office opens in Ottawa. That's not until eight a.m. Eastern Standard Time."

"Bleeding hell! That gives them five hours to decide how to spin this to their advantage. Do we know what happened?"

"Aye," Rod said nodding. "Étienne said he shot himself on the roof of Canada House."

"Sounds a wee bit like the Suez Canal all over?" Will said, remarking on the similarity to a previous suicide of a Canadian Diplomat. "Another naïve Canadian caught on the wrong side of a dangerous game?"

Ignoring the question, Rod added, "Étienne also said he left a detailed letter explaining his involvement with the CIA. He confessed to planting documents and reports provided by Hank Darien in our Cleo's security file and perhaps stalling her career." Rod stopped to gulp down some of his tea before continuing soberly. "He also made a point of listing every detail of Section 28s operation, which he provided to Darien. That bastard had every scrap of Operation Polar Bear before the team kicked off, and not just the surveillance Darien ordered in

Arizona and Moscow." Rod sighed as he looked his goddaughter over carefully, adding, "Evidently Cleo had fallen off Darien's radar until Robilard let him know we were heading abroad to pick up that wee plane."

Sitting in the very back table of the closed pub, they were cloistered from London's early morning bustle. "Send me in lass," William said. "I can stroll about and maybe undertake a quiet reconnoiter of the area. Perhaps Nigel could join me. That way, if we spot an opportunity, we could exploit it. What'd you say?" he pleaded.

"Thank you Uncle Will," Tori said, smiling at his sincerity, "but I already have a reconnaissance team enroute. They should be in place by the time the Canadians announce Robilard's death. Besides, we can't have you and Uncle Nigel blowing things up in a foreign land, especially this one. The Israeli people," she added honestly, "get very upset about such things. As a matter of fact, I just finished explaining that very same point to our resident SAS Commander. He too, imagined a frontal assault more appropriate than all this diplomacy."

"Speaking of diplomacy," Rod said. "Have you any idea how to manage the Canadian issue?"

"Well, we know the Americans are out except . . ." Tori stopped talking and looked around abruptly. "Uncle Will, when was your last sweep?"

"No worries, Victoria. The counter-surveillance boys swept the place this morning."

"Thank you Uncle Will," Tori sighed with relief, then turned back to Rod. "Again, we know the Americans are out, except for Mike's team. As for the Canadians, I think they will follow the Americans in this. We won't know for sure until the press meet."

"You know," Rod said. "Their PM's sitting on a minority government. He doesn't take risks. That one waits until issues hit the press then he follows public opinion."

"I was expecting that, but my concern surrounds the time it will take before someone leaks this to the press, and how much more damage they can do to Cleo's security clearance. I am not prepared to see her second chance at a career stolen by the same lies that impaired her first go round. There must be more than one version of her security file floating about?"

"Aye," Rod said with another heavy sigh. "Our Frenchman says he can't get his hands on it, but he's sure it exists. If that security file, and not the real one, is presented to the PMO this morning, we can expect some resistance from the Canadians."

"Some resistance?" Will said. "Roddy, it's been a long time since you referred to a stone wall as some resistance. Good to see you up to yer old form!"

Braithwaite Residence
West London

Day 3, 19:40 UTC, Internment Time: 57 Hours, 20 Minutes

Nigel was standing in the garden finishing a cigarette when Ari Ben David, Head of Security for the Embassy of Israel and the Mossad Station Chief, entered the small yard through the rear alley gate. "Up to snuff, mate?"

"Yes," Ari replied. He had just made a personal reconnoiter of the area around the Braithwaite residence, and the covert security curtain that had been raised along a two-block radius. "The sniper on the South-West corner is exposed," he noted professionally.

"Aye," Nigel agreed. "That's CO19's boy. "They tell me it was the only perch he could find. At least the locals won't notice him up there, that's if you can live with it?"

In answer to Nigel's question, Ari flipped open a secure mobile phone and speed dialed a number, said a few words in Hebrew, then snapped the phone closed. "Two minutes!"

With that information, Nigel ducked into the house and immerged a moment later with Sir Richard, Tori, and Chief Nelligan in tow. While Ari took his place at the gate, Nigel, forever the stickler for protocol, shepherded them each into a reception line.

"RSM Wren?" Sir Richard asked of his old shipmate. "Is this truly necessary? This isn't Mademoiselle Schilling's first visit!"

"Sir Richard," the retired Royal Marine answered formally. "This is the Ambassador's first visit since accepting her new office. It's only proper that we demonstrate our respect for her post."

Tori, in a pensive mood had been quiet all day, letting her Uncle Nigel supervise the security detail and pester her father over protocol. "Uncle Nigel's right," she interrupted. "As a matter of fact, where is Uncle Will or Mike Perkins for that matter?"

As if on cue, Will Green bustled out of the house still folding away his chef's apron. "Sorry my girl, I just needed to finish my basting. We can't have the hens drying out, can we?"

Tori gave him a little hug of appreciation for his efforts. The chiefs were doing what they did best, making sure all the incidentals were taken care of, so that Tori and her father could concentrate on the job at hand. Back in the day, it had been their self-imposed mode of operation as Sir Richard's men, and they had kept at it even in their military retirement. The truth was, for old guys they were still a top-notch team.

Rod reassured his god daughter, "Mike should be here within the hour. He asked that we eat without him, but promised to make the meeting."

"How very American," Tori remarked without enthusiasm. "I wonder if those people ever take time to eat a proper meal?"

Ari signaled to the group as he opened the garden gate. Nigel was the first to greet the Ambassador as she passed into the small flower garden. As Sir Richard had said, Genevieve Schilling wasn't a newcomer to this house. As a matter of fact, twenty-five years earlier, she and a young Tori had begun the garden project together. She had spent that spring teaching Tori everything she knew about growing flowers. Although her practical knowledge, which was extensive, came from caring for her family's 4,000 acres of vineyards in southern France, it was easily applied to creating an authentic English Cottage garden.

Genevieve Schilling thanked Ari, and then offered her hand to the first chief in the reception line.

"Regimental Sergeant Major Nigel Wren," he said. "At your service, your Excellency."

"Nigel Wren," Genevieve said with a disarming smile, "How nice to meet you again after so many years. Roddy tells me you now work to keep our skies safe?"

"Yes mum," Nigel answered, offering, "British Airways Operations."

Genevieve nodded with a warm smile, and let go of Nigel's hand, moving onto the next person in line. "Chief Petty Officer Green! *William*, is it not?"

"Yes mum," Will said, proudly shaking the Ambassador's hand vigorously.

"*William*," she pronounced it Will-um, "Are you still keeping our Victoria fed and clothed?"

Will smiled to hear her remember his old job. "She's a big girl now, mum. She hasn't needed her old nurse chief for some time, but I do see to her breakfast. It's the highlight of my day."

"As it would be for me, if I were so lucky as you, to have our Victoria to cook for again." Genevieve smiled at the old chief and moved on to Rod Nelligan, once again offering her hand.

"My Roddy, how nice to see you," she said, before moving into Tori's open arms.

"My Victoria," The Ambassador made no effort to hide the emotions the reunion raised. "How I have missed you little bird, and how beautiful you have grown to be."

Before she could brush away the tears that escaped, Richard Braithwaite reached over and touched her face gently, "Genevieve. Welcome home."

With the formalities over, Will returned to his kitchen, while Nigel took up a perimeter watch alongside Ari. Tori took the opportunity to restore the emotional equilibrium by giving Genny a tour of the small garden. "We've a few minutes before supper," she said to her one-time stepmom. "Would you like to see how our garden has matured?"

"*Mon Cher!* You have made it most beautiful." Taking a seat on the English bench that had long ago been woven into the tapestry of the garden vines, she signaled for Tori to join her. "May we talk about your Colonel, my Victoria?"

Tori nodded, taking the seat offered. "Please tell me you're not shocked or offended?"

"My only offence is my country's participation in this ugliness." Genny said, taking Tori's hand in hers as she had done on so many occasions. "You must know that the Israeli government would not have entertained this, this project, if they had known what and who would be involved. You must understand that Darien has been a good friend to Israel for many years. It has earned him a wide dock."

"Berth, you mean," Tori corrected her English, as she had done so many times as a teen. "I think you mean it has earned him a wide berth."

"*Oui*," she laughed at their old joke, before turning to the present situation. "Now, tell me about this Cleopatra! Your papa says she is a strategist?"

"She is, Genny. Oh, this whole situation is unbearable! Is there nothing you can do?"

"*Ma Cherie*," Genny said, with deep affection, while giving both of Tori's hands a strong squeeze. "I have exhausted all of my diplomatic channels, and many others. I have some intelligence that I will add to yours, and many caveats. Perhaps we will have enough pieces to make a good patchwork."

"If Cleo were here, she'd have come up with several, each more outlandish than the last. She doesn't think like you and me. I think it's why Darien wanted her back, but after so many years . . ." Tori trailed off, her emotions uncharacteristically written on her face.

Genny knew Tori had the fortitude to handle any situation and keep her emotions well under wraps. The fact that her one-time stepdaughter looked so distraught, told her the relationship was serious. "You love this one, *non?*"

"I can't explain it. She's shy, loyal, strong, and vulnerable in a way I can't put in plain words."

"Dutiful and Brave, I think your papa said."

Tori nodded. "That too, but not quite as we understand it. For her people, there is no such thing as cowardice. One is simply brave in their own way."

Before they could continue, Nigel interrupted politely, "Supper's served, Your Excellency."

Genny smiled at the old chief, "Nigel Wren. Will you let us set aside our heads for this evening?"

Nigel was like a deer caught in the headlights, completely lost to understand what she was saying, until Tori corrected her. "Set our hats aside, oh Genny, how I missed you," she said, placing an affectionate kiss on her cheek. With that done, Tori escorted her guest to the same dining room where they had shared many a meal long ago. How that seemed like another lifetime, now. Like old times, Genny sat at one end of the table with Sir Richard at the other. The chiefs, Nigel, and Ari, filled in the other chairs, with Tori next to Genny. Etiquette would normally put Tori at one end of the table, and her guest at the other. No one forgot that socially, Tori actually outranked her father. Of course, she wouldn't have any of it. As far as Tori was concerned, this was her father's house, and would always be so.

Once everyone was seated, plate after plate was carried in from the kitchen. The dinner of Cornish Hens and sautéed fiddleheads met with compliments from everyone. Even the gruff Ari Ben David, was taken aback by the tight group's hospitality. For the chiefs, Ben David was just one more professional in the service of those who do. By the time Mike Perkins arrived, the group had finished dinner and dessert, and were working on a well-chilled bottle of Sabra Chocolate Orange liqueur that Rod Nelligan had bought especially to please the Ambassador, and because he secretly loved the stuff. He offered Mike the Sabra then thought better of it. "I've a twenty-year-old single malt. Would you prefer that with your coffee?"

"Coffee too?" Mike said, taking a seat at the cleared table. "Looks like I missed a hell of a dinner."

"One of *William's* best," The Ambassador said, adding her compliment to the others.

Will, of course, had a plate warming for Mike, just in case he hadn't eaten yet. He was about to pass on the offer when Genny insisted he eat while they talked. Mike looked like he was going to turn down the second offer, but everything smelled so great. "Okay, Chief," he said to Will. "Since the Ambassador's insisting . . ." He shrugged, accepting the plate along with the glass of scotch. Once he was settled in, Will and Nigel retired to the kitchen, giving the others the freedom to speak openly. It really wasn't necessary. The two old NCOs knew what the situation was, and had both offered to go "operational" for Tori.

"Shall we begin in earnest?" Ambassador Schilling asked the small group.

"Before we lay our cards on the table," Sir Richard began. "I want each of you to know that I will provide complete support to my daughter and her team, not because of her burgeoning relationship, but simply because Lieutenant Colonel Deseronto has done all of our countries a great service."

"Do-no forget that we gave that lass our word of honor," Chief Nelligan said, not needing to remind the group again.

"Rod," Mike said, "you know I feel as bad about this as you do, but what if Darien is on to something? What if whatever it is they're learning from Deseronto could be adapted to teach our soldiers?" He held up his hand when he saw the chief's face. "Look, I'm just repeating what I've been hearing all day."

Tori reached across the table, covering Rod's hand with her own. "Let me," she said with a kind smile. "Mike, you've had more than two months to become acquainted with Colonel Deseronto. If what Darien is trying to achieve, or at least learn is that important, do you not think she would have volunteered to help? I know she would have, and while I can't speak for everyone at this table, I would not be surprised to learn that most, perhaps all, feel the same way."

Mike was caught with a forkful halfway to his mouth. Dropping the loaded utensil on the barely touched plate, he snapped, "Jesus H Christ, Tori! Don't you think I've been saying the same thing all day?" Mike stood, moving to the sideboard, before pouring himself a coffee. Taking his time adding cream and sugar, he seemed reticent to continue. "Actually, I've been dreading coming here all day," he said, finally turning back to the table and resuming his chair. "The truth is, they had no right to grab her the way they did, or to hold her at Shachar 7, but what they're learning is invaluable. Frankly, I'm not sure they would have gotten the same results if she'd volunteered."

Everyone sitting around the table was silent for the longest time. Finally Ari broke the building tension, asking, "How is IDF detachment taking orders from CIA?"

"The area commander and Darien go way back, all the way back to the Six-Day War. Hank was leading a squad of rangers on an observation recon when they found a burnt-up tank squadron. The story is, Darien picked the guy out of a pile of dead bodies, and got him help."

The explanation went without comment.

Sir Richard, still ruminating over Mike's previous comment, broke the reverie, "What are they learning?"

"Don't tell me you're subscribing to this nonsense," Chief Nelligan spat with disgust.

"Unfortunately Chief," Tori injected, "it has everything to do with why we're here and knowing may serve us."

Mike opened the small attaché case he had carried into the house and pulled several folders out. The covers of each had innocuous titles like Budget Updates and Expenses. From a folder labeled Staffing he removed a stack of reports with the same title page and handed a copy to each person. "Please discard the top cover. Beginning on page two is the current transcript and report from Darien's team."

"Where does the interrogation transcript begin," Ari asked, as he flipped through a copy.

"There isn't one," Mike admitted. "They haven't gotten that far yet. As I understand it, she has resisted all efforts at softening. Frankly, her success has been serving to validate Darien's argument to continue the project. Another thing you need to know is that they have someone translating her Mohawk, which is all she's speaking right now. And before you ask, it's not Captain Commanda. I've got her on ice. As far as Langley is concerned, Commanda is on leave pending her return to the FBI."

"Any idea who is translating for them?" Sir Richard asked

"Not yet, but he or she is not in house, judging by the four-hour turn-around needed for results. You should also know that Bo Commanda has read through the transcript and tells me it's accurate but devoid of localisms. Whoever they have translating isn't from their home reservation and isn't aware of many of the nuances she uses. And there's one more thing, Bo says she and Deseronto used to play several word games as kids, you know, to help learn the language. Well, some of those phrases show up here. Those phases are translated here, but again, without any mention of a secondary meaning."

"Secondary meaning?" Tori asked.

"Okay," Mike flipped through his notes. "Here! Page thirty-one. The observer's notes are listed next to each time code. If you start where she starts yelling, *il*-something or other, in Mohawk which translates to: *I am small*. Once said, she followed with an immediate attack of two IDF guards. Bo says the phrases are part of a game they called opposites."

"She incapacitated an IDF guard!" Ari commented on the accomplishment.

"I don't understand?" The Ambassador admitted honestly, her attention on Mike.

"Evidently these two, Deseronto and Commanda, were a pretty tough pair back in the day. *I am small* was a kind of war cry they used to help imagine themselves big enough to take on whoever was harassing them, and according to my research, they took on all comers. I guess inner-city kids face the same battles no matter which inner-city it is. Of course, you already know about the Manslaughter charge against Deseronto?"

"What charge?" the chief challenged. "You must be reading that phony-baloney security file Darien and Robilard cooked up. We've known that girl since she was nineteen. Do-no be telling us these lies now!"

Tori, sighed quietly, "It's true Uncle Rod, but she was nine years old when it happened, and clearly just a child protecting herself from a predator."

"Just a child?" Mike questioned her description of Cleo, "Just a child, who could load and handle a twelve gauge shotgun, and take down a two-hundred-pound bull of a man."

Tori was clearly losing her patience, "Mike really? She was a nine-year-old child, at home from school sick, and being sat by her youngest uncle, a boy of only twelve. As I understand the story, Cleo's eldest uncle arrived and began to sexually assault the young babysitter. Believing she was next, and that the uncle would kill them both, she loaded her grandfather's shotgun and threatened the nonce, which only resulted in the man turning his full attention on Cleo. She was forced to shoot, then reload on the move and take another shot to stop Gilbert Commanda." Tori, angered by the examination of Cleo's troubled childhood, followed the same exercise Mike had just gone through, and got up from the table and poured herself a coffee. Before sitting back down, she poured one for the Ambassador and Ari, and moved the cream and sugar set to the table. "Perhaps we should light the smoking lamp?"

There were grumbles around the table until Ari admitted he could use a smoke. That's when Chief Nelligan suggested he and Ari join the NCOs in the kitchen, so as to not bother the non-smokers.

Tori approved, watching the two depart before turning her attention back to Mike. "Why now, Mike? We know she has the survival instinct of a Grizzly. Surely bringing this up now can't help?"

Mike, embarrassed for having said anything, asked quietly, "She told you?"

Tori nodded, explaining. "She wanted full disclosure. I didn't have to ask. Not that I would have known to ask. Such delicate information from an officer's childhood is only, if ever, kept in her psychiatric profile."

"Look, I think I got off on the wrong foot, it's just that I've been getting a lot of static over this. I've had a hell of a day fending off the company line and trying to keep Captain Commanda under wraps. I almost wish I had left her locked up with you. The higher ups are still churning over whether she should be sent in for testing too."

"Testing?" Genny said. "The semantics are interesting?"

"I agree." Tori said. "Well, we now know we have a four-hour window before they have a translation, and that they may not understand what she's actually saying." She took a second to pour a shot of the Sabra in her coffee, before adding, "Mike, we need to see those transcripts before they are sent off to who knows where. And, I hate to say this, but we need Commanda in on this, and I need her at Vauxhall. We can't take a chance that another of our Mohawk assets falls prey to this madness."

"She's pissed," he warned, shaking his head. "I don't know if I can get her in the building."

"Does she know that Langley was considering putting her through the same mill as her cousin?" Sir Richard asked.

Mike's silence was all the confession they needed.

"Bleeding hell, Mike!" Tori was unable to quell her frustration. "She needs to hear the truth, and we need her regardless of whether she likes what's happened or not."

Sir Richard, turning to Mike suggested, "If you need to distance yourself from this, now is the time to do so, but know I will do whatever it takes to put an end to this, even if I have to address the press myself."

"Jesus, Richard! It would ruin your career."

"Perhaps," C said, having obviously considered the ramifications. "I am betting the public, and the higher ups, will see what we have all known from the beginning. This is wrong, whether it is the kidnap and torture of a United Nations trooper, or a courageous NATO Officer. Regardless of the benefits to any and all, our nations have conspired together and must answer for this crime."

Before Mike could weigh in, the smokers returned from the kitchen. Ari, who had been reading the CIA report, interrupted the debate, "She is injured!"

"What?" Tori interjected, sitting up straight. "Where does it way that?"

"Page sixty-one, Medical Officer Report."

"I was going to cover that next," Mike said apologetically. "The IDF doctor at the camp reported a minor concussion, with one large laceration on the back of the head, lacerations and friction burns on her knees and forearms, and several allergic reactions while trying to attend to her pain needs. He attributes the injuries to Deseronto's jump from the aircraft. That is, all except the head injury, which there is no explanation for."

"She," Ari said, correcting Mike. "The doctor is a she. Doctor Hanna Bergeson." When the Ambassador tipped her head in some secret display, Ari continued with the background information. "Dr. Bergeson immigrated to Israel, and volunteered for the IDF, immediately after her graduation from the Sorbonne. She is not a French national. She was born in Canada and grew up on the family farm near . . . Châteauguay, Quebec."

"Châteauguay?" Genny Schilling asked. "Is this not a region of vintners? Perhaps her family has a vineyard?" she asked, having some familiarity with Canadian wine regions.

"Cheese and milk," Ari read from the overview page on Dr. Bergeson.

"You're familiar with the area?" C asked.

"I toured many of the vineyards in the region before I began organizing vineries in the Golan Heights."

Chief Nelligan shook his head with the irony of the entire affair. "How is it, we keep ending up in the same place? Tell us Genny, 'ave you some idea how far this farm is from our girls' home town? Could they have known one another?"

"No my Roddy," she said, explaining, "Toronto is many hundreds of kilometers from Montreal."

While Genny and Rod compared the wine regions of Quebec and Israel, Tori with Mike at her side, opened her laptop and called up a satellite map of the region. "There may be some unknown association," she said, "but we're just pulling at wool, without more insight. I'm afraid that anything we find is pure conjecture until we can add local substance to the equation, and for that we need Commanda."

Mike stood, excusing himself from the table, and hitting speed dial on his cell, walked away.

"Ari, what else can you tell us," C asked the Mossad Chief directly.

"She has been given no medication for pain, and has not been fed since arriving. They are allowing her minimum water only. This does not appear to be of any consequence to Colonel Deseronto. She has not asked for anything or responded to any orders." He flipped to a page with a folded corner and read from his notes. "There is a second incident of unconsciousness. The doctor has not yet reported, but the IDF guards now refuse to attend to her after, what is translated as, an unprovoked attack. I do not have the original report only this English translation."

"I think we should ask our American friend for the original report?" Genny said. "Perhaps we may find subtleties lost to the translator as well."

"It's a good idea," C agreed.

Mike, still on the phone, wandered back to the table. Touching Tori's shoulder to get her attention, "Where do you want her?"

"Will she come here?"

"She'll go where I send her," Mike's response gruff was. Moving the cell phone back to his ear, he ordered, "tell your driver to bring you to the Crow's nest," he said, then flipped the phone closed. "Done." Sitting back down beside Tori, he pulled the laptop closer, typing in two locations on Google Earth. "Ari? Do you know what Bergeson was doing before the University of Paris?"

The Mossad Chief flipped through his notes. "She attended the Concordia University in Montreal. She did not return after her second year, and did not attend the Sorbonne until the following year, in September, 1991. She completed undergraduate studies in . . ."

"Wait," he ordered, "what year did she attend Concordia?"

Not used to being interrupted, Ari was a little impatient with Mike, as he flipped back through his notes, "1988 until the spring of 1990. She spent each summer working on the family farm."

"Jesus H . . . Bo thinks we should consider the Oka Crisis. I thought she was just doing the over-sensitive Indian thing, but there does seem to be a connection, at least time wise."

Chief Nelligan, aware that Bo wasn't cleared to enter the perimeter, left the room a second time to attend to the details. For Nelligan, it was as simple as joining the other NCOs, and the CO19 Commander, who were standing around the kitchen. Once the appropriate orders were doled out, Nigel and Rod organized fresh coffee for the others and carried everything into the dining room, while Will cleared the table a second time, collecting dirty cups and empty wine glasses. "Anyone for spirits then?"

"Perhaps just the Sabra and the Scotch, Chief, "Sir Richard said quietly, as the old steward laid out fresh cups and saucers, then returned to the kitchen to top up an ice bucket for the Sabra, and bring in a second ice bucket for the Scotch drinkers. Once he had the room up to snuff, he hustled Nigel back to the obscurity of kitchen.

During the interlude, Tori had brought up the MI6 overview of the Oka crisis. "Did Bo mention the blockade?" she asked Mike. "Evidently the Mohawks closed the highway to Montreal."

"Ma Cherie," Genny asked. "May I see your map of this region?"

Embarrassed that she hadn't thought to show the Ambassador what she and Mike had been looking at, Tori flipped the laptop around for her, "This is Châteauguay, and this must be the road to Montreal heading north."

"As I remember," Genny said. "This highway leads to Montreal but via a bridge. The community would have been cut off from the island of Montreal if the Red Indians were to blockade here," she said, pointing to the Mercier Bridge.

Turning the computer around, Tori read from an MI6 briefing page. "There were actually two separate roadblocks staged by residents of two Native communities. One here," she said pointing to the village of Oka, 70 kilometers west of the Mercier Bridge, "on a dirt road that led to the town's golf course? It was staged by residents of Kanesatake. The second roadblock was staged in protest of a botched police action against the first group. This roadblock was placed on the Mercier Bridge and was staged by warriors from Kahnawake. So, Kanesatake and Kahnawake are two different places? I had no idea."

"And that's exactly where I am," Mike said, "So Kanesatake is next to Oka and Kahnawake must be around Châteauguay. Bo tells me the whole region used to be Iroquois until the French and the Catholic Church divided the land between themselves. Christ," he said, letting his frustration slip. "This is why I hate dealing with the Canadians. They just create one quagmire after another."

"Well regardless of who created this mess," Tori said, "we still don't know enough about the situation to understand how or if it has any bearing on Dr. Bergeson and her loyalties."

* * *

"This is fucking bullshit!" Bo Commanda burst out in frustration. "Sorry your Ladyship," she said, cooling her frustration.

Tori knew the apology was meant as a jab and took no notice. She was just as frustrated and had said as much.

"Why can't I go in?"

"As I have already explained, you are an asset here, and a liability over there. Can you not imagine what would happen if Darien got his hands on you too?"

"I can handle myself," Bo said, with belligerence. Backing down was difficult but she was aware that some, if not all of the people in the house, knew of her behavior at Vauxhall. Maybe Bo Commanda could handle herself on the streets but not confined to a cell.

Tori couldn't help but wonder if Bo, like Cleo, suffered from claustrophobia. She hadn't thought of it before, and remembering how well Cleo disguised it, it was no wonder she hadn't noticed the same thing with Bo. "How do you manage it Bo?" Tori asked gently, "Your claustrophobia?"

Bo Commanda sat in silence as if trying to decide if she wanted to play or go home. Things had just gotten personal again, and much more painful. If she wanted to play, it would be by the rules Cleo had established when they were young, and admitting that was tantamount to admitting to having her own personal demons. Finally, with no real option, she gave in, "If we were in a bad place, she would make me play opposites, or move the walls."

"We've learned about your childhood game, but I don't understand what moving walls is about?"

"We would close our eyes, and Cleo would make herself small, so the room would seem bigger, and I would become the big one, so I could push the walls out or break them down. Then we would pretend to be in a forest. We could even make the trees grow and see the sun shine through the pine boughs."

The revelation shook Tori. "Clearly Cleo knew how to hypnotize you and herself!"

"Like hell! Yah think I'm some sort of simpleton?"

Tori ignored the comment, having no patience for Bo's ignorance. "Were you always the *big* one, and she always *small*?"

"Of course!"

"That would make Cleo the leader, and you what, the team striker?"

"Are you calling me a hockey goon?" Bo challenged, before smirking. "That's way cooler than a footballer, any day."

Bo's joke struck a little too close to Cleo's own humor, and rattled Tori. She was unable to curb the sharp edge of her tone. "Where were you when Cleopatra shot your uncle?"

"Killed him you mean," Bo said, her attitude masking any discomfort on the subject.

"Are you playing word games with me, or are your semantics indicative of something more personal?"

It was not the first time, in the long evening, that Bo found herself with her head down and spirits squashed. "I should have been there. I was home from school too, but I insisted on going grocery shopping with our moms. Uncle Huey was home too, so they gave in, and took me along." Bo explained in a ragged tone. "It was my job to keep Cleo out of trouble. Uncle George made me promise, but it wasn't Cleo who started things. It was always her little sister. She started fights with everybody, always expecting us to fix it."

"And somehow you believe Elizabeth was responsible for the attack?" Tori asked skeptically.

"Liza," Bo corrected her, "are you kidding? This must be the one time that little bitch didn't get us into trouble. No one even knew Uncle Gilbert was in town. I should have been the one to kill the bastard, not her."

"Why Bo?" Tori asked gently. It was just the two of them at the ornate table. Genny and the men had drifted off to the media room to review the A/V files. In the background, they could hear the Ambassador explaining the changes and growth that had taken place, over the last twenty years, in the northern region of her country.

"Killing Gilbert made her a warrior in the eyes of our grandfather!"

"He wasn't distraught over the death of his eldest son, or the attempted assault on his youngest?"

"He never talked about it," Bo said, shrugging. "My grandmother used to say they took her little boy away to Residential School, and fourteen years later, returned an angry white man in his place. Gilbert was the last in our family to be sent away to the Mohawk school."

"Why did Cleo's father ask you to take care of her?" Tori asked, sidestepping the issue. "More trouble from Liza?"

"Sort of," Bo admitted, the difficult memories were clearly weighing on her. "You know what Cleo's like. She thinks an order is an order. If you tell her to do something, she just does, and without a second thought. This one time we were having dinner at Uncle George's house and the French guy comes to the door kickin' up a storm about George's kid having attacked his kid, this little bastard named Pierre LeRoux. By the way, we were only four years old at the time. Anyway, Mr. LeRoux shows up at the door with Pierre, and Pierre's head is shaved and he's got thirty-five stitches and a major shiner. Turns out that Uncle George told Cleo it was her job to protect Liza whenever Pierre started dragging her around the playground caveman style."

"I see where this is going," Tori said. "Why did she do it, and where were you?"

"I had to go for a bath before we went to Uncle George and Auntie's for dinner. Cleo's frog mother always insisted us girls wear dresses at dinner. So off I go to get cleaned up, and Pierre takes the opportunity to kick off. Uncle George had told Cleo that the next time Pierre went after Liza, to find a big stick, and give him a good beating. So she did." Bo couldn't hold back the grin. "The best part was when Cleo's mom insisted she go apologize to Pierre and his father. You should have seen Mr. LeRoux's face! He took one look at little Cleo in her stupid dress, grabbed Pierre, and stormed off. The bastard never said a word again. It was so cool."

"Cool?" Tori probed, questioning Bo's enthusiasm. "You are speaking of the beating of a small boy."

"It wasn't that bad. She only hit him once, then did what she always does, and started negotiating with the little prick. She only gave him the shiner, when he wouldn't stay down, and besides, Pierre was twice our size."

"I see," Tori was starting to comprehend the nature of the symbioses between the cousins. "So you became the fighter and she the negotiator. No wonder you were disappointed when she did not join the American Marines."

"I didn't know about any of this shit she was up to in the militia. She never said anything and I never asked," she admitted painfully. "I just thought she had gone soft. I feel like a real asshole now."

Tori was caught off guard by Bo's sincerity. "If it helps, she wanted to join you."

Sounding very much like Cleo, Bo smiled, "Well that's something, isn't it?"

Chapter Nineteen

Route 65/HaBanim Junction
Southwest of Afula, Israel

Day 4, 16:40 UTC, Internment Time: 78 Hours, 20 Minutes

Major Kenneth Butterworth, USMC, dressed in khaki pants and a sweat-stained shirt, was fussing under the hood of the twenty-year-old Land Rover. The old series 90 Defender was in tip-top shape, needing none of the attention he had been giving it for the last hour. Everything from the spark plugs to the air filter looked brand new, including the vinyl placard on each side of the truck that read American Wildlife Trust.

Albert, who had spent the time moving things to and from the rooftop luggage rack, had given himself the job of sorting their photo gear and cleaning and checking the camera lenses. At the moment, he was focusing a telephoto lens and panning across the orchards west of them. They were stopped at gas station just off the HaBanim junction of Route 65. They were literally across the highway from Shachar 7. Anyone leaving the facility and heading to Afula would have to pass them on either the 65 or HaBanim road. Albert lowered the camera, reached for the side rail of the rooftop luggage carrier, and catapulted himself off with the ease of a well-built predator. "She just turned onto HaBanim."

Ken closed the engine hood and headed for the driver's door. "She must be heading into town. This might work to our advantage." Behind the wheel, he spun the Land Rover around from where they were parked, and headed to the HaBanim exit. A moment later they were heading into Afula following the Lady Doctor from the IDF.

They had flown to Tel Aviv only twenty-four hours after the initial early morning planning session. Mike Perkins had taken them out to RAF Nort-holt and put them on a USAF executive jet, coincidentally, the same jet that Hank Darien had used to get to Israel. Mike Perkins knew he didn't have the company behind him but he did have friends, many of whom owed him, and didn't hesitate to pull strings here and there. Darien might have the ear of the top brass, but he couldn't reach the mid-level bureaucrats who pushed the papers to make things work. Darien's "go order" would no longer get him any logistical support. Deseronto, and the secret facility might be under Darien's thumb, but he wasn't going anywhere fast. If the Israelis decided to pull Deseronto from the facility, Darien and his team would be unable to bug out. Hank Darien was probably unaware of the noose tightening around him, but Shachar 7 was fast becoming his permanent home.

Out on the streets, the Afula traffic seemed heavy for the size of town, but the narrow roads and the parallel parking were the real culprit. Butterworth had no problem keeping the little Renault in sight from the higher purview of the Rover. They followed the doctor in silence through the small streets until she parked her car and entered a small shop. Of the several signs and posters in the store window, a bright neon envelope identified the place as a postal outlet. Albert was going to exit the Rover and follow on foot, when Ken stopped him. A parking spot had just opened up on the opposite side of the street. Ken spun the nimble 4x4 around and drove straight-in, without bothering with the standard parallel parking maneuver. "Sit tight buddy. Let's wait till she comes out. If she gets back in the car, she's probably heading home. If not, we can both jump out and follow her. You take this side of the street, and I'll hang back on the other, okay?"

Albert nodded, handing Ken one of the earpieces from the CIA communications set they had been issued. "Try this one, Major big ears!"

"Hey! I don't have big ears! My Momma didn't raise no big-eared aviator!" Butterworth smiled, in mock indignation. "Although, my brothers did drag me around by my ears on more than one occasion."

"I'll bet; my Granny could get me to stand six inches taller with just one tug on my ear! She sure didn't have to do that too many times, before I learned."

"Funny how much we learn from women. There she is—looks like she's heading for that café." Both men sat quietly watching the doctor make her way past the outdoor displays of fruits and dry goods stacked in front of each shop. "Move out," Ken ordered. As planned, Albert kept to the same side of the street, taking his time to stop at each shop, looking over the goods for sale.

Ken made his way across the street, quickly moving to the only place where he thought he could get a good view of the café's interior. The café's wide-open windows, and the sun at his back, were all working to his advantage. He stopped in the shade of a shop entrance, and trying to look inconspicuous, played with the settings on the camera Albert had handed him in the vehicle.

Across the street, Albert had made it to the last shop before the café. He was bagging what looked like tangerines when the lady shopkeeper came storming out. She started hitting Albert with a broom and yelling at the top of her lungs. Albert, caught completely unprepared, did the stoic thing and stood to attention, taking the woman's blows and obscenities without resistance. Whatever he was being accused of, the woman and her shouts were beginning to gather onlookers, and it wasn't long until a waiter from the café joined the group. This was too much, Butterworth knew instinctively that Albert wouldn't stand up to this woman, and waiting for the Police to intervene was not a good idea. Ken crossed the street at double time, calling to the shopkeeper and the others in English, "Hey guys, what's the problem?"

The shopkeeper halted her tirade, but kept her broom up, as if Albert might still charge at her. The others, who had crowded around, made room for Ken to pass. The whispers of "American" sailed from one witness to the next, until the waiter asked Ken directly, "American?"

"Yeah, we're Americans," he said, giving a hand signal, indicating he and Albert, to the waiter and then to the crowd. "We're Americans. What happened?" With a smile, he jokingly asked the shopkeeper, "Did my friend pay the wrong amount? Excuse him; he never learned to count properly."

The shopkeeper, for her part, barely took her eyes off Albert, and only to give Ken a short suspicious look. When someone in the crowd began translating for the shopkeeper, Ken was instantly relieved, until he saw the look on Albert's face. He cursed inside while plastering on his best poker face. Turning to face the Good Samaritan, he smiled and offered his hand to the IDF Doctor, "Hey, thanks for translating for us. I'm not sure what we did to upset the lady so much?"

"She thinks your friend is a Palestinian. Her son was killed by a Palestinian last year. She has refused to serve any Arabs since. I'm afraid your friend did not see the sign. It's very clear, is it not?" The French influence of her upbringing was more than evident in her tone."

"Montreal?" Albert asked without thinking.

The doctor didn't answer but turned to the Shopkeeper, and the crowd, announcing, "These men are Americans, both of these men!" With that said, the shopkeeper retreated and the crowd began to disperse. A few stragglers stopped to shake hands with the American visitors, or to wish them well, before returning to their earlier distractions. Ken and Albert now found themselves facing the IDF Doctor alone.

"Thanks for stepping in," Ken said again, adding, "Listen; we were just going to grab a bite to eat. Why don't you join us?" Butterworth was sure he had just overplayed his hand, before he realized something was brewing between the doctor and Albert. In an effort to break up the sparring match, Ken stepped between them, asking, "You'll join us for something to eat? This café looks good, if it's okay with you?"

"I have a feeling I should accept," she replied without joy. "I have a table already, join me."

"All right then," Butterworth said, offering his most charming smile. "C'mon buddy, we're buying the lady dinner."

Shachar 7
Afula, Israel

Day 6, 04:20 UTC, Internment Time: 114 Hours

Cleo hadn't uttered a word in any language but Mohawk since arriving, but that hadn't stopped the interrogations once they began. What Darien's team hadn't realized is that their standard softening technique had only worked to force Cleo deeper into her own mind. They had made other mistakes, like trying to tempt her with food. The interrogator had set a plate with a chicken sandwich, several pieces of fresh fruit, and a hot coffee, on the interrogation room table. When the guards brought Cleo in she didn't sit quietly and wait to be invited to eat the food. The exercise usually required the prisoner to offer up information in exchange for each item. Much to the guard's disgust, Cleo, seeing the food plate, broke free and grabbed everything she could. In her attempt to conceal her finds and confusing the guards, she shoved things in several different pockets of her dirty flight suit, while trying, at the same time, to peel and eat a banana.

Once they wrestled her to the ground, and retrieved everything she had stolen, they took her back to her cell with threats and indignation. As far as prisoners go, this one seemed to be breaking all the rules. It wasn't just frustrating; it simply didn't appear to make sense to any of the cadre. Nothing she did made sense to them.

Back in her cell, she sat quietly for several minutes before slowly removing the chicken slices she had managed to conceal during the struggle. While she was under constant surveillance, she had realized that the IDF guards were no longer willing to enter the cell of the "savage." The unplanned meal would help to ward off the hallucinations that come from going without food and sleep for so many days. Cleo laughed inside at her condition. In some deep recess of her exhausted mind, she recognized this was fast becoming a Vision Quest. Which would be the greater challenge? Cleo wouldn't succumb to her exhaustion and sleep. Instead, she sat, as she had done for so many long hours, cross-legged on the raised concrete bed. She had been using her old practice of giving thanks, to block the pain and hunger, but she had also been using the practice to control her ability to communicate. She knew instinctively, that you can't pretend to be ignorant of a language for any length of time without being tripped up. A comment, a name, or any kind of anchor, spoken at the right time, could break the faker's concentration and destroy their defense.

Cleo hadn't been pretending to only speak Mohawk; she had blocked all of her language skills except the language of her grandparents. Even doing this had a limit, not that she couldn't keep it up. She had long reached an expert level. Her concern stemmed from the knowledge that eventually they would identify the language, or probably already had. Once done, it wouldn't be long before the CIA had a translator working for the interrogators.

That was another interesting point. A prisoner ready for interrogation would usually face one interrogator. If that person was unable to make any gains, a more senior soldier, usually the next man up the food chain, would take over. At some point in the succession of interrogators, the person who was able to demonstrate the best rapport with the prisoner would become the primary, regardless of their rank. Rank was hard to tell here, what with no names or ranks badges on any of the green or blue uniforms. She was well aware that the "guys" interrogating her were not IDF. The truth was, the IDF guards hadn't come near her for several days. That hadn't stopped her from causing trouble for the North American interrogators, but it hadn't been as much fun. Whenever it was time to transfer her to the interrogation room, they, the non-IDF guards, would show up in force. She'd hear the cell door scrape open to reveal three guys in green, and all with Tasers drawn. And, they would bring backup too. The guys in green certainly didn't have any of the fears about the "savage" that the IDF guards had developed. Even so, they would still have the IDF guards on hand each time they moved her. She would hear them swell into the corridor and wondered if they actually intended to backup the North Americans, or just came to watch.

Thankful for the short rest, Cleo used the pain to stay alert and keep her eyes open. The constant physical and mental jousting had exhausted her more than a few chicken slices could remedy. Finally closing her eyes, she began where she always did, "Grandmother, Grandfather, thank you for this day . . ." Within seconds she entered her mental sanctuary, moving to a deeper level than she had ever achieved before. She was startled when she felt something nuzzling her neck. The thought that some guard would lick her face almost broke her concentration, until she realized the offender was not an outsider, but a bear. One who seemed to be sharing the same waking dream. Laughing at her own confusion, Cleo joked and tussled about with the young polar bear. She knew this one, they were old friends. Together they sat eating a feast of Salmon and gooseberries.

Topsy, the bear she had befriended as a small child at Riverdale Zoo, loved to eat the fish heads, flesh, and innards. She would always leave the meat, which was the least desirable portion of a fish, from a bear's perspective. This became Cleo's meal. One she would always enjoy. Once all the fish and berries were gone, they cuddled up for a long languid sleep, warm, full, and comfy. Cleo woke hours later to find she was in an empty dark room, built suspiciously out of cinder blocks, and not the poured concrete of the British-built facility. The room was freezing. A plastic wall thermometer conspicuously verified that fact. There were no doors to the room, just a metal ladder on one wall that led to a trap door in the ceiling. She stepped up a few rungs on the ladder and pushed the hatch open. Her bare hands and feet were numb from the frozen rungs, and her eyes watered from the fierce wind. Looking out over the land, she could clearly see the frozen tundra, even with the flying snow. *We're not in Kansas anymore*, she noted, not quite understanding.

Pulling the trapdoor shut, she made her way back down the ladder. To her astonishment Joe Commanda was waiting inside. "Sit down child," he ordered, before wrapping a four-point blanket around her shoulders, and handing her a cup of tea. Like his granddaughter, Joe had a blanket around his shoulders and was sitting cross-legged on the floor. "Clear the questions from your mind," he said. "They won't serve you here."

"I'm so cold, papa. Where are we?"

He ignored her question by simply not hearing her words. "I have a question for you, child. What's more important, tradition or change?"

Cleo was quiet for the longest time, cradling her hot tea cup protectively. She knew her grandfather preferred she think things through instead of just tossing ideas out. "Tradition and Change are equally important," she finally answered. When he encouraged her to continue, she added, "They are a part of one another, like opposite sides of the same coin."

He smiled at his oldest grandchild. "The people have been changing for years." He drew a circle around change, then love, tradition, and fear, on the frost covered floor, before launching into several hours of instruction on the people and their changing needs. "We can no longer sit on the disappearing lands the white man allows us to use, until he finds something more profitable for it. Our Nation is shrinking, our land is shrinking, and our knowledge is shrinking. I once told you that the white man's words should not be used to disseminate the teachings to the people. I was wrong. The white man's talk is strong, not strong like ours, but it has become the way of this world. Now, I ask you to use their words to teach our ways. No longer can we wait for the young people to come to us to learn. We must go to them, and many others who pray every day for what we once knew. Use the white man's talk. Use his paper and words, and share all that I have taught you, all except the Bear Medicine," warning, "that must always remain your gift."

"May I teach it to Boudicca?"

Joe shook his dark, deeply lined face slowly. "The gift is yours alone. I would give her any gift, but she does not understand that such a gift is also a curse. Boudicca carries many gifts herself, each with their own frontiers. She has her own path to follow and you have put her back on that path. For that, take solace in your relationship. You are clan sisters and warrior women, in a time when so few hear the call to stand. Neither of you will ever know the heartache or joy of motherhood. You will not hold the people's land, or fill your harvest baskets with the three sisters. But you will know love and honor, as will Boudicca." He moved closer, reaching out, squeezing her hand, he then handed her a brand-new pair of mukluks and mitts. "Go my child. She is waiting."

Sorry to leave the relative protection of the cinderblock room, Cleo reluctantly pulled on the hide boots and returned to the pipe later. Outside, the snowstorm had subsided, revealing more of her surroundings. The sky was totally obscured, making it impossible to judge the time of day. In front of her lay open tundra and blowing snow, behind her, the tree line was barely visible but visible none the less. Cleo turned in that direction, creating an unseen track line in her mind's eye. She wrapping the Hudson Bay blanket tightly around her shoulders and started out for the trees. Her plan was to reach the pines, then find a safe place to build a campfire.

The march to the trees turned out to be much shorter than she thought it would be. Once she reached a suitable spot, she started hunting for firewood and kindling. That's when she noticed a wolf not far off, a wolf who appeared to be watching her intently. Unarmed and without a fire, keeping a wolf at bay was a challenging prospect. Cleo looked around to see if she could spot the rest of the pack, but had to consider that this wolf was alone. A lone White Wolf, she noted to herself, wondering why the wolf had taken an interest in her. Choosing a stick from the bundle she had been collecting for firewood, she checked it to make sure it was sound, then returned to the open tundra and started walking. She planned to keep moving hoping the wolf would lose interest and return to her pack. The fact that the wolf was all white, a symbol of an animal guide, confused her.

As she started in one direction, the wolf ran ahead and cut her off but didn't growl. Cleo retreated quietly, before turning in another direction. To her relief, the wolf kept pace with her but didn't try to stop her again. After several hours of trudging through the snow, she spotted smoke. With the wolf still in tow, Cleo headed for the smoke and hopefully the campfire and the campers who built it. It didn't take long to make her way through the pines to an opening in the woods. Stepping into the clearing, Cleo felt a lot like an interloper at a private function, worse yet, was the fact that the wolf had followed her to the edge of the clearing. An old woman, tending the cooking fire, signaled for her to take a seat at a nearby picnic table. As she did, the woman set a paper plate with corn, fish, and fry bread on the table in front of her, before taking a plate of scraps to the Wolf.

"She followed me here!"

"You followed her here," the old woman corrected. "I'll make an offering for you."

Cleo, tired and hungry, concentrated on chewing quietly until done. When she finished eating, she wanted to thank the old woman, but when she turned back to the fire, the old woman was gone and so was the wolf. She tossed her chewed corn cob into the woods then dumped the paper plate into the fire. Turning to sit back down, she found Samantha sitting on the bench. "You're here?" She hadn't meant to state the obvious, but in her confusion had to ask, "Am I dead?"

Samantha Stewart gave her the same smile that had melted Cleo's heart sixteen years earlier. "You're not dead, just somewhere else, lover."

"Am I still your lover?" Cleo asked, still overwhelmed by the pain of her loss.

"I hope you will always remember that I was your first great love," she said cryptically. "More importantly, I want you to remember our love. It will always be part of your past, but you have reached a junction. This is a time of transformation, where you must choose between the future and the past. You have completed many challenges with grace, but the time has come to defeat what you carry inside. You must face your fear of healing, letting go and moving on, if you wish to be reborn into your new role and responsibilities."

"What if I don't want to lose the past?"

Sam smiled in that gentle and kind way that had always helped Cleo through the hard choices. "Oh honey, you have reached a place in-between this life and the next. Only you can choose to go forward or retreat. I need you to know, the past is as illusory as the future. The truth of your place lies in the present, in this moment of your life, and in the love you have found in this moment."

"Oh Sam! Please forgive me."

"Oh, honey," Sam wrapped an arm around her shoulder, explaining, "Love knows no limits—you know no limits. Cleo, I've have always wanted you to love again. Never stop on my account. It would break my heart to see you alone when I know just how much you have to give."

Cleo was quiet and pensive. "What if it doesn't work out? I'm not sure I can endure that kind of heartbreak again."

"You can, my beautiful warrior, but you won't need to. Just remember that real love begins with trust. Trust her; she's fighting for you, even as we speak."

"I want to stay with you," she admitted selfishly, almost under her breath.

"Cleopatra Isabella!" Samantha snapped, but her eyes were gentle. "You and I have already had our moment, and it was a beautiful moment. Now our paths have moved in different directions. I too have a calling, as you know. Oh my love, I wish I could show you everything that you will learn along your journey. Just know that it may be challenging at times, but what you gain, what you achieve, and the gifts you bring to the people, cannot happen without you." Sam moved closer, wrapping the blanket tightly around Cleo, holding her close. "I will always love you, and no matter who else you learn to love, I know that you loved me too." Still holding her protectively, Sam kissed her temple, then began rubbing gentle circles on her back. "As for Victoria Caroline, she is a good soul on a difficult path. I know how frightening it is for you to open your heart, honey, but it's truly time for a leap of faith."

Embassy of Israel
London, United, Kingdom

Day 6, 08:30 UTC, Internment Time: 118 Hours, 10 Minutes

Ambassador Schilling was on her feet to greet Sir Richard. Behind her were two IDF Officers, who both jumped to their feet the moment the Ambassador stood.

"Sir *Richard*," Genevieve Schilling said formally to the Head of the British Security Services. "May I present Major Jacob Huffman and Captain Aryeh Perec? Captain Perec is in Command of the Shachar 7 demolition project. I thought perhaps we should ask him for a situation report, first."

Perec remained standing while Ambassador Schilling signaled for Sir Richard to sit with her on the spacious leather chesterfield. Perec, took up a spot exactly three paces in front of the pair, while Huffman took a seat nearby. "Your Excellency, Sir Richard," The very young IDF captain began nervously. "As Madam Ambassador says, I was, I am, CO of Construction/Demolition Company. Several weeks ago I began to plan the demolition of Shachar 7. Such a plan is very detailed," he added apologetically, "especially with such heavy construction. The British engineers built your 1931 to last, with two-meter-thick concrete and hardened rebar."

"I understand the challenges," Sir Richard said, wanting to reassure the young engineer. "What's happened, son?"

Just to be sure, Captain Perec looked to Her Excellency before continuing, "I scheduled my company into the field with plans for thirty days to drill and set charges before destruction. On arrival, Mossad ordered us into the field for combat training for two weeks. I postponed my schedule and reported to my command. Then they sent my company for six weeks armorer's school while I was sent on leave. It is June now, and I do not know when I will resume my command, where my company is, or my orders. I am the soldier who has become an orphan."

"Orphan? Oh, I think I understand your metaphor."

Perec nodded his head with the shame of a professional soldier who just found himself on the outside of his own command.

Sir Richard nodded his appreciation to the young man. He had several questions but wanted to learn who the other officer was first. "Thank you Captain. I have many questions for you, but perhaps we should hear what Major Huffman has to report first?"

Huffman stood, taking the floor from Perec, who seemed reluctant to sit until ordered to do so.

"Madam Ambassador, Sir Richard," he began formally, revealing his American accented and exceptionally good English. "My name is Jacob Huffman; I am an IDF cryptographer, currently serving with the Mossad. And, until nine days ago, I was working undercover as an Iraqi expatriate interpreter for the Iranian Security Service."

Groaning inwardly, Sir Richard had a terrible feeling he knew where this was going. "You're him?" At the affirmative, he apologised, "We had no way of knowing who you were. I can't tell you how sorry I am for blowing your cover. I am however, relieved to see you made it out successfully."

Huffman smiled the smile of a sly fox, "Sir Richard, you don't understand. The entire incident had the exact opposite effect! The Iranians now think I'm some sort of hero for surviving. They have no idea that you have Major Suyfias. They think your Native Americans killed him and dumped his body during the confrontation between the two Air Force squadrons. They know nothing of the operation your Native Americans completed. It's their solemn belief that having a woman in command, sent the savages into turmoil, eventually resulting in the murder of their Intelligence Officer."

Sir Richard stood, taking the two steps necessary to reach the Mossad officer. Extending his hand, he said, "Major Huffman. It is pleasure to meet you."

"And you, sir," Huffman said, shaking the outstretched hand with pride. "Now, I must insist on helping your team. I can arrange to be posted to Shachar 7 as an Interrogator. I made it known, within my command, that I deserved the right to face the woman who undertook to send me to my death."

The comment halted Sir Richard's return to his seat. He turned back to the major and said carefully, "Some might think you bear ill will to the officer in question?"

"As I hope, sir!"

"Forgive me Major, but I'm wondering if you're actually interested in helping Lieutenant Colonel Deseronto, or perhaps you feel the need for retribution?"

"Sir Richard! I meant no disrespect. Ari Ben David and I are old school chums. It was he, who approached me with the tale of your special team!" He shook his head, looking very much like a man desperate to find the right words. "I have great respect for these Native Americans. Not just for their service, but their conduct. They were professional at all times. They even returned my belongings and money after searching me and Suyfias."

Sir Richard sat back down beside the Ambassador. "Tell me Major, are you not angry at the Colonel for having ordered you thrown from her aircraft?"

Before Huffman could answer, someone knocked and then opened the office door. Ari Ben David entered first, holding the door for the Acting High Commissioner to Canada, and his Intelligence Chief, Étienne Ste. Hubert. While everyone stood for the new arrivals, Genevieve Schilling crossed the room with her elegant long strides, and offered her hand while Étienne made the introductions. "Madam Ambassador, may I present Acting High Commissioner Semple." The modest introduction was appreciated by everybody but meant much more. Sir Richard and the Ambassador immediately knew that Étienne was signaling something important.

"Your Excellency," Semple said, accepting Genevieve Schilling's outstretched hand before briskly questioning Sir Richard, "And you are?" he asked, unceremoniously, and with unbridled arrogance.

Genevieve Schilling, more than acquainted with brash bureaucrats made the introduction. "This," she said in a tone both soothing and authoritarian, "is Sir Richard Braithwaite, Head of the United Kingdom's Security and Intelligence Service."

That information slowed Semple, but didn't curb his haughtiness. "Are these officers security and intelligence as well?" he asked, pointing to the two IDF officers.

"Major Huffman is indeed Mossad, and Captain Perec is a specialist on my staff." As Ambassador, she believed it her prerogative to economize with the truth whenever it suited her country. Calling his arrogant little bluff, she asked, "do you prefer to be addressed as Acting High Commissioner or Captain? I understand you have been holding the Communications post at Canada House? How this tragedy must weigh on you terribly." Her point was to remind him that while temporarily promoted, she and by extension Sir Richard, knew he was nothing more than a raised up bureaucrat, and not the next High Commissioner or even deputy.

Semple's expression said everything. "I don't know who you people think you are, but I'm here to tell you to stay out of Canadian business. I hereby order you to stop any action you may be considering. The Prime Minister's Office has given me clear instruction. We will not, under any circumstance, participate in some hair-brained scheme. It's not going to happen," he added defiantly.

Ambassador Schilling took her place behind her desk, directing Sir Richard, and Captain Semple, to the visitor's chairs. The other men, from experience, knew to move to the sitting area and wait to be invited to participate. "Captain Semple," Ambassador Schilling asked formally, "May we discuss the current situation in which our three nations are involved?"

"Involved?" Semple exploded. "Let me tell you something, lady. I know this officer. I met her years ago, and I know all about her career, and her treasonous activities. There is nothing that you could tell me about *Trooper* Deseronto that I don't already know." Everyone could see that Semple was fighting to control his anger, or perhaps his contempt. Every word from his mouth was backed by spit and hate.

Sitting quietly in an identical leather block chair, Sir Richard leaned back comfortably, asking, "Captain, is there any doubt in your mind, or should we dispense with the facts altogether?"

"How dare you, *Commander* Braithwaite," Semple said with contempt, using Sir Richard's rank from the period when he first met Cleo. "Yes, I know who you are," he hissed, "and I know you covered for her in Germany. As far as I'm concern, and the PMO, you and the Israelis can keep her treasonous ass for as long as you like, but be warned. If and when she comes home, we plan to prosecute her under the National Secrets Act."

Before Sir Richard could comment, the Ambassador gave him a silent signal to wait. "I understand you and Colonel Deseronto met when she was released by the Mossad after undergoing six weeks of questioning by the American Central Intelligence Agency."

Showing the first tiny crack in his armor, Semple challenged her. "*Trooper* Deseronto was never incarcerated. She made up the entire story to cover for deserting, and running off to be with . . . with him," he added, with disgust while tipping his head towards Sir Richard.

"Captain Semple!" The authority in Ambassador Schilling voice was unmistakable. "Do you wish to learn what actual happening from me or Admiral Sir *Richard?*"

Semple sat frozen. Suddenly unsure. "I am quite sure of my facts, Madam. Are you?" he blustered, determined to hold his own with these higher ups.

Étienne Ste. Hubert, who had been sitting quietly until that point, got his feet and took up a position at the side of the Ambassador's desk, while Ari joined him, handing over the Mossad's complete dossier on one Cleopatra Isabella Deseronto. Once Genevieve nodded her permission, Ari and Étienne presented the dossier in detail, covering both Cleo's career from her time with the United Nations, up to and including, her command of Section 28T and Operation Polar Bear.

Semple sat passively, unwilling to actually accept anything presented. Even if the length of the presentation, and the detailed evidence, were hard to ignore. Once they had finished, the two Security Chiefs sat back down, leaving the arm-twisting to the brass. Not willing to completely abandon his position, Semple said plainly, "The Prime Minister wants to give General Robilard a State Funeral."

"A State Funeral for a High Commissioner?" Sir Richard asked. "It's an unheard of show of respect for a diplomat, especially one who committed suicide!"

That took Semple by surprise, and made him angry again, "Do you people never stop with your lies? General Robilard was a patriot! How dare you!"

"Patriot?" Genevieve Schilling asked. "Is that not an unusual thing to call a Canadian Diplomat? If I recall, patriot is a title Americans use to distinguish their heroes."

"General Robilard was a hero! Why are you people so determined to ruin his reputation, and why protect *her?*"

Genevieve Schilling opened another dossier on her desk, and handed a single photocopied page to Semple, giving him time to read it without interruption.

He read the page once, turned to Genny suspiciously, but chose to read it a second time before commenting. "This could be a fake," he said, with waning conviction.

"I assure you, it is a genuine copy of the suicide note. Perhaps you recognize the writing? As Communications Officer, I imagine you have seen the High Commissioner's hand many times," Ambassador Schilling stood to deliver her ultimatum. "Captain Semple, as acting High Commissioner to Canada, Israel wishes you to know that we will not abide by the kidnapping and torture of any persons within our borders. Canada has proven to be a good friend to Israel, but be warned, you will not silence us on this abuse of our friendship. General Robilard was a good man who made the mistake of listening to his prejudices. If your Prime Minister moves ahead with this charade and announces a State Funeral, Israel will be forced to reveal the details of Robilard's death, the success of the Red Indians, and the illegal incarceration of their commander."

Semple, unfamiliar with diplomacy of any kind, had been prepared to play hardball, but had entered the Embassy blind to the facts of the entire situation. He did know Cleo Deseronto, and had publicly blamed her for stalling his career. Semple's face and body language showed everything. He would acquiesce, but did he have the chutzpa to fight the PMO?

As if understanding the unnamed concern, Étienne resumed his place beside the Ambassador's desk, telling Semple as plainly as he could, "We 'ave all been misled, but the time has come to undo what has been done. Acting High Commissioner Semple, this is a good officer. She lied to you in Copenhagen and abused your inexperience. I understand this has been a sore point for you, and I understand that you may not be willing to help, but the truth will come out. You may have blamed her for many things, but your security and personal files are free of any concerns regarding Copenhagen. If you still blame her, then know you have been lied to by Robilard, and those involved in this . . ."

"You must see what's happening, son?" Sir Richard cut in, reasonably. "This isn't your great opportunity to get your career back on track. They chose you because of your loyalty to General Robilard and your past connection to Deseronto. Regardless of what you have been promised, they will not fast-track you for keeping their dirty linen. If things continue on this course, this situation will blow up magnificently, and you sir, will be expected to fall on your sword."

Semple looked too deflated to argue, "I'll deliver your concerns to the Prime Minister's Office," he said, then stood to leave, but not actually sure of the protocol, he waited like a school boy, while Étienne paid his respects, before leading his charge out the door.

Once they were gone, the Ambassador turned to Sir Richard. "I think it best that we move forward immediately. I do not trust that the Canadians will act correctly." She was clearly disappointment with the parley. Sir Richard too, had had just about enough.

Shachar 7
near Afula, Israel

Day 7, 03:30 UTC, Internment Time: 162 Hours, 50 Minutes

When Cleo opened her eyes, she was surprised to see she was back in the infirmary. At first she thought it was just another scene from her vision quest, until a nurse started jabbing her hand with an intravenous catheter. Once the nurse was satisfied with all her poking and prodding, she taped the IV in place, and hung two clear bags. Cleo assumed one was standard IV fluids, while the other bag was marked in Hebrew and English. The English read Potassium in large san serif capitols. Reminding herself that understanding English, in any form, could weaken her resolve, she was about to hypnotize herself again when the doctor from Montreal touched her arm. "Your electrolytes are dangerously low. I need to rehydrate you before anything else."

Before anything else, Cleo groaned inwardly. What else could they throw at her? She closed her eyes and began giving thanks. She had almost reached a state where English would be completely gone, when the doctor whisper, "Don't worry. We have a plan to get you out!"

The words rattled around her mind. Not willing to let her guard down, Cleo quickly moved into a state where she blocked all English from her consciousness. Whatever the doctor had said was now gone, yet something beyond words, beyond language, kept telling her to trust this woman, this doctor from Montréal. To stay focused, Cleo concentrated on pinning the doctor's accent down. For all the limits of her hearing, she did have a natural talent when it came to inflection. Countries were easy for her to distinguish, whether or not the speaker revealed their accent while speaking French or English. For countries she had little or no familiarity with, the best she could do was maybe narrow down their origin to a large region, but when it came to North America and parts of Europe and the Middle East, Cleo could pretty much identify a speaker's city of origin, and sometimes even their neighborhood, after just a few sentences.

The doctor, she knew, was from somewhere near Montréal, but not the island itself. She churned through a mental list of boroughs in and around Montréal, with no match. For the first time in her life she regretted not having spent more time there. The annual trips her family made to visit her maternal grandmother were her only insight in to the cosmopolitan city. Her Labor Day Weekend memories did give her some insight into her Grandmother's Outremont neighborhood, but it wasn't until she considered that the doctor's path, may not have been direct, that she started to make progress. She was starting to hone in. Recalling the sounds of Verdun and La Salle, she eliminated them quickly. Then she remembered it suddenly, and with startling clarity. The memory was from the news coverage she had seen over and over again, and the realization made her stomach turn. All she could picture was the news footage of Mohawk Elders and children, being driven off the reserve during the Oka Crisis. The motorcade was making its way out of Kanesatake, through an obstacle course of roadblocks, and cement pylons. Both sides of the rural road had been lined with onlookers, most of whom were young people from the neighboring communities. Some had driven over from Châteauguay.

Like most tragic events, it began innocently, with a handful of boys pushing each other around and yelling insults at the line of slow moving vehicles passing off the Reserve. Soon, the insults escalated until everyone seemed to have some complaint they needed to share. From the beginning of the crisis, the Mohawk protestors faced one set of belligerent bystanders after another. The one thing the bystanders and police shared was their fear of their aboriginal neighbors. The mystique of the Mohawk Warrior so frightened the local police, that they refused to investigate the roadblock, forcing the mayor of Oka to call in the Provincial Police. The Quebec Provincial Police, or *Sûreté du Québec*, made a tactical assault on the dirt road protesters. During the fifteen-minute firefight, the *Sûreté* emptied their entire arsenal of tear gas which blew back on them, forcing them to fall back, abandoning their vehicles and a frontend loader to the Mohawks.

In their haste to withdraw, several of the officers clad in riot gear and gas masks, lost their footing in the woodland underbrush. The constant tumbles and the noise of their own shouts spooked the retreating Sûreté even more. It was only natural that the crack of a pine bough would sound suspicious to the panicked men. When the jammed police radio cracked with warnings of an "Indian" attack, the entire force opened fire. When the smoke cleared, the Sûreté had shot up six cars, all their own, and their abandoned frontend loader was being used by the warriors to move the shot-up cars and trucks out onto the highway. The Sûreté had forced the Mohawks to abandon the harmless roadblock of the golf club, for the local highway, that passed through their land.

More embarrassing was the television footage of the attack, clearly showing unarmed Mohawk women forming a line in front of the blockade. As holders of the land, the responsibility fell to them, first. Even worse was the death of a *Sûreté* Corporal who had been shot in the back by a fellow officer. The RCMP inspectors later sent to investigate the shooting were unable to identify a single round of ammunition that could have been fired from the warriors. The investigators were forced to admit that the Mohawks had held their position without firing a single shot. That wasn't how the *Sûreté* saw the firefight, regardless of the evidence, and made sure the local community saw it their way too.

With difficulties between the local communities escalating, the Clan Matrons were forced to order the Warriors to defend the people. Their order made it clear they would only tolerate violence as a last straw. Fire only if fired upon. They also wanted all elders, small children, and the sick, taken to families and friends outside the community. Now in charge, the RCMP agreed to let the motorcade pass, but failed to provide protection for those leaving. Worse yet, the *Sûreté* were still in the loop. While they had lost jurisdiction and face, they made sure every non-native living south of the Mercier Bridge knew the Indians were coming out. No one in the departing vehicles were surprised by the behavior of the teens hurling insults, but when the rocks started flying everyone seemed shocked. So much so that the motorcade didn't increase its speed until the drivers realized cars windows were breaking. That's when everything changed. As the crowd roared at its supposed success, other young people, and even those who should have known better, were pulled into the excitement. Suddenly, everyone was throwing rocks at each car that passed. The women who had volunteered to drive the motorcade were now speeding through the barely passable road, while the onlookers threw rocks and cheered at their success. By the time the small motorcade reached a safe distance, several of the drivers and children were seriously injured, and one Elder was dead, from the blow of a football-sized rock that had speared a window, and struck the back of his skull.

After the tragedy, Cleo thought saner heads would prevail, but the perceived success of the anti-native groups only fueled further failures of democracy, diplomacy, and downright decency. It wasn't until this exact moment that Cleo realized what the doctor had said, *We have a plan to get you out. Gosa! So Mademoiselle Châteauguay wants to help me. I wonder if she brought a rock from home?*

**Overhead Highway 66,
near Salem, Israel**

Day 9, 04:30 UTC, Internment Time: 209 Hours, 10 Minutes

"There they are," Butterworth said. He was sitting in the co-pilot's seat of an Israeli Air Force trainer. The Beechcraft King Air was older than both its pilots, but that didn't matter to either one. The King Air, no matter how old, was still a sweet ride for a light twin engine airplane.

"I can see the airport," Albert said, while concentrating on piloting the aircraft.

"Stay over the road until we hit highway 65, then turn directly for the field," Ken ordered. Lifting his binoculars, he spotted a convoy of military vehicles. The Company of Engineers and their heavy equipment poured out onto Route 65, heading east for Shachar 7, now only five kilometers away. "I don't want to fly over the camp until just minutes before the engineers pull in."

Albert, like Ken, was wearing a new, straight from the package, US military issue, sage green flight suit. The starchy unwashed Nomex was irritating Albert's skin and agitating his mood.

Watching Albert fly the aircraft and scratch at his sleeves and calves was irritating Butterworth too. "Suck it up, Buttercup!"

"Hey, I would have thought Buttercup was your call sign?"

"Nice try, but my fellow aviators found Vader a more suitable handle for the Prince of Darkness."

"Vader, wow! Now that's a lot better than Buttercup."

"Yes it is," Ken agreed. "Start your turn and head straight for the camp. I want you to fly right over the big H Block. Go ahead and take her down to 500 AGL." He watched Albert roll the King Air onto the new heading and start his descent. "Actually, I had a different call sign my first year at Annapolis. How would you like to be saddled with Butterball?"

"Oh, no thank you, sir!" Albert considered his options, "I would want something like Silverheels. That was the name of the actor who played Tonto on the Lone Ranger. He was a star Lacrosse player from my home Reserve."

"Silverheels! I like that." While Albert was concentrating on getting down to the proscribed altitude, Ken knew from experience, he would fall short and took control of the aircraft. "I've got it Silverheels," he said, before retarding the throttles and pushing the nose down sharply. A moment later they were skimming over Shachar 7 at less than one hundred feet above the ground. The idea was to get the attention of the guards, and judging by the movement on the ground, they had succeeded. Butterworth pushed the throttles forward again, giving the Pratt & Whitney engines a second to catch up, before pulling the nose up into a climb and turning back towards the empty airfield. "Albert, you ready to land her?" Ken asked, his student pilot and partner in crime.

With his hands back on the controls, Albert made a heading adjustment and steered the King Air into a standard circuit of the single runway airport. He flew the pattern by the book, completing the checklists and calling out all his changes. When we made his final turn for the runway, he lowered the gear, waited for three green indicator lights, and called the gear locked, before cranking in two complete turns on the trim wheel.

"A little light on the nose, don't you think?"

"It's a trick the Colonel always uses. The idea was to keep the plane trimmed for the go-around and not the landing."

It was a technique Naval aviators knew well, but he had only used it when landing on an aircraft carrier. Albert, displaying his burgeoning skills, greased the landing at Megiddo Airfield. Back on terra firma, he eased on the brakes, slowing the aircraft to taxi speed.

"You know, every landing I make in the AV8 has to include a go-around plan. I had completely forgotten how much harder that would be in a vertically challenged bird."

"Are you calling me a fixed wing weenie?" Albert joked, taxiing to Pad 2 of the Airfields ramp. Turning the nose of the aircraft to face the runway, he shut down the Beechcraft's twin PT6 engines and sat listening to the old transport trainer cool. "I like this plane."

"Well Mr. WOC, if you ever get tired of flying those Army whirlybirds, I'm sure the Marines could find room for you."

"Yeah," Albert said, "Room to fix them, not fly 'em. Remember, I ain't got no edumacation!"

"Don't let that hold you back, buddy. You're a smart man, and a hell of a pilot. Actually, with all your experience, I bet you could put a degree behind you in no time and I know the service would pay for it."

"The Colonel said the same thing. She suggested I apply to West Point or RMC instead of a civilian college. Does Annapolis have a program for retreads like me?"

"Here comes a Jeep." Ken pointed in the direction of an old CJ5, speeding towards them. "Show time," he said, releasing his seatbelt and heading down the small aisle to open the rear passenger door. Ken Butterworth and Albert Mackenzie stood side by side at the foot of the cabin stairs and waited for the Jeep to come to a halt. The driver and guard, in blue uniforms, were clearly IDF but the passenger, the guy getting out, was wearing unmarked green BDUs. This was exactly what they had been hoping for. As the unnamed soldier stepped up to the two pilots, Ken offered his hand, introducing himself. "The name's Jackson. We're here to pull you out." As he said it, a convoy of military trucks, belonging to the engineers, rolled by on the 65, heading for the camps main entrance.

"What the hell's going on?" the other guy asked him.

"Fucked if I know," Ken said. "I just fly the fucking plane."

"Wait here," the other soldier said, climbing back into the front of the Jeep. They started to race away, when the Jeep suddenly screeched to a halt. The IDF guard, who had remained in the back seat, climbed out and walked back to where the airplane was parked. He took up a position near the nosecone, facing the now empty highway, rifle at the ready.

Albert looked to Ken, with just the slightest hint of panic in his eyes.

"Easy Slick, he's just protecting their escape route. The important thing is seeing if Darien takes the bait, and if the engineers can look like real soldiers who mean business."

"I don't like the idea of taking Darien out of harm's way and leaving the Colonel behind," Albert muttered for the umpteenth time.

Before Ken could respond, a loud boom was heard from the camp. "That's it. They blew the gate. It's just a matter of minutes now. If Darien is smart, he and his team will be here soon. Then it's up to the doctor and Ari's team. Trust them, Buttercup. They're the best we have."

Albert nodded, but called on his native prerogative to remain stoic, waiting for the chance to fight or fly. Moments later the decision was made for him, when two Jeeps sped out of the camp, storming along the dirt road to the airfield.

Ken lifted the binoculars he had been holding. "I've count three, no four guys in green and a . . . God-dammed cowboy? No shit! The dude's wearing a Stetson. Yeah . . . yeah, it's him, it's Darien. Get in the plane and start up the number two engine. And Silverheels! Make the call."

Back on board the King Air, Albert flipped on the Batteries, Magnetos, and the Avionics Master, before transmitting. "Yea, though I walk through the valley of the shadow of death, I will fear no evil; for I am the biggest bad ass this valley has ever seen!" There was no reply to the cryptic radio call. There wouldn't be. Following orders, Albert started up the right engine. He was about to make the call again, when an AStar Eurocopter ripped overhead, circling the camp, before setting down just out of sight.

Turning his attention back to the King Air, Albert was just about to check the Mags when he heard sounds in the cabin. Turning to look, he watched Darien and four soldiers board the aircraft. That's when he recognized the last of the four soldiers. He turned forward quickly, hoping to block the passenger from seeing his face, and continued with the Start-up Checklist.

Albert was still sitting rigidly with his back to the cabin when Butterworth climbed into the seat beside him. "What's with you buddy?" Ken asked, over the pilot's intercom. "You look like you've seen a ghost?"

Handing over the checklist, Albert asked quietly, "is the intercom secure?"

They could hear explosions coming from the camp, and immediately turned their attention to getting the aircraft off the ground. While Albert ran through the start-up sequence for engine one, Ken, spotting several vehicles moving in their direction, ordered, "Skip the run up checklist and taxi to the intersection. Looks like it's time to bug out."

Albert had just reached the runway intersection and was about to backtrack to the threshold when he realized that whoever was pursuing them would get their first. Changing his mind, he swung the King Air down runway two-seven and pushed the power levers to the wall. "I'm expediting," Albert declared. "Hang on." Moments later they were airborne. It had taken a lot more runway with the added load than he had expected, but at 7,000 feet, they had the room to run long. "Ken, we have a problem. One of our passengers is a spy."

"Relax Buttercup," Ken said, counseling his charge. "They're all spies. That's what these guys do."

"No! I mean yes! One of their guys in a spy, but not one of ours. Believe me," Albert wanted desperately to explain. "It's the same guy we threw out of the Otter ten days ago. He was the translator. What do we do now?"

Ken watched Albert silently, trying to decide if he was serious. "You're sure it's him?"

"Well, if I compare him to all the other translators I've thrown out of perfectly good airplanes . . . hmm!" he said, sarcastically. "Yes it's him!"

"Woe boy! Pull your horns in. We're supposed to be the emergency transport for Darien and his team. If that team just happens to include your guy, so be it. We will report that fact to 'our' command the moment we get a chance. In the meantime, stay out of his face," Ken warned. "If we have a spy, we can reel him in later, and much to the continuing disgrace of our favorite cowboy."

Chapter Twenty

Heathrow International Airport
London, United Kingdom

Day 9, 22:30 UTC, Internment Time: 228 Hours, 10 Minutes

Like every major airport the world over, the flow of arriving passengers usually log jams in the Customs Hall. Cleo, confused and in pain, followed the first-class passengers to a line and waited without comment. She was dressed in a brand-new flight suit and had fresh bandages over her wounds. Without remembering how, the doctor from Châteauguay had gotten her from the infirmary, and into the helicopter without much fuss. The only person to challenge them was a single IDF guard, who backed away, when one of the "green guys" ordered him to clear out. Without further opposition, the doctor got Cleo and dragged her from the building, to an open courtyard. Seconds later a helicopter set down and both women boarded quickly.

As the helicopter began a vertical assent out of the camp, Cleo thought about her latest interrogator. She had been suspicious of the new guy, but trying to figure it out was hurting her ability to block out the pain. The problem was, there really wasn't much pain, or not like it should have been. Just hours earlier, she had been dragged from her cell and tossed into an interrogation room. She had almost completely retreated into her deep trance when the new Interrogator walked in. Normally this wouldn't matter, except for one little problem. The man standing in front of her was not CIA, not CSIS, and not even Mossad. Hasid, the translator from Iran, the guy she had ordered shoved out of her aircraft, was standing in front of her.

"Remember me?" he asked in perfect English.

Cleo's first instinct was to act. For someone who hadn't slept or eaten for seven or eight days, she was still quick on her feet. Sweeping around the table, she heaved the chair in his direction and made for the door. It, of course, was locked from the outside and she chided herself for not remembering that detail.

Hasid grabbed her by the back of her filthy flight suit and hurled her towards the table.

Hitting it square across the ribs, Cleo collapsed, bringing the table down with her.

Kicking the interview table clear, Hasid ordered her to her feet, "We have a lot to discuss, you and I."

"Me and you," Cleo corrected the bastard, while she pulled herself to her feet.

"It speaks!" Hasid said with pride. "Now, my savage friend, it's time to talk."

Before Hasid was ready, Cleo let out her childhood war cry, "I'ih-se niwa'a" and charged straight at him. Now the two of them were down and the fight was on. While Cleo didn't exactly win, she had held her own for what seemed like hours of weak-ass holds and pathetic hits, until a single punch to the wound on the back of her head knocked her out. The next thing she remembered, was waking up in the infirmary, to the doctor's insistence that she move.

"Come on, Colonel," she urged. "We have to go!" She helped Cleo to her feet, and steadied her, before leading them to the approaching helicopter. The doctor from Châteauguay didn't just get her to the helicopter; she boarded with her. A utility bag had been left on the rear seat of the Eurocopter. The doctor retrieved the bag and immediately began sorting the contents. Her first chore was to strip Cleo of her dirty cloths and get her kitted out in fresh drawers, T-shirt, and a flight suit.

She was aware that the woman seemed to be trying to clean her up and tried not to make the exercise more difficult than it need be. Wanting to dress herself, she picked up the new socks sitting on the seat, and tried to reach for her foot to put one on.

"Let me do that," the doctor said, pulling new boots over the socks and lacing them. "Keep those loose for a few days. Your feet will probably swell a little." With that said, she opened the first aid kit. It wasn't your average camper's outfit. This one contained bandages, a suture kit, a large variety of meds, and two bags of IV fluids. She hung one from the helicopter's headrest before selecting a new sight for the IV catheter. This was a job usually done by skilled nurses and rarely in a moving aircraft. She took her time, not wanting to stick Cleo more than was necessary. It was only a minute before she had the IV squared away and could concentrate on replacing her bandages. Less than twenty minutes into the flight, the doctor had her cleaned up, re-bandaged, and on her way to being rehydrated. She was trying to talk to her about her injuries and the medical attention she would need, but stopped when she realized Cleo had fallen asleep.

When they finally touched down at Ben-Gurion Airport, the unmarked helicopter, in glossy black livery, was directed to hover-taxi directly to the ElAl departure gate. The Boeing 747 was scheduled for a 09:05 departure for London Heathrow and was ready to go. The doctor and two airline agents helped get Cleo up the air stairs and onto the plane. With Cleo clearly out of it, her boarding pass, and a lengthy note from the doctor, were pinned to her flight suit in the same manner used with unaccompanied children. Cleo, only half aware, tried to read the ticket, *J-class; seat K73*. From experience she knew that seat would be on the upper deck and actually laughed to think about the flight attendants trying to get her up the narrow circular staircase. After struggling to get her as far as the main cabin, the purser suggested she be moved to an empty seat in first class. They maneuvered her into seat C4 and buckled her in. Once done, the purser escorted the agents off the plane, thanking them for their help and joking, "These foreign officers, they come over for our training, and end up going home like tired kids."

"At least you won't have to serve that one," the second agents commented. "She looks like she'll sleep for a week." They couldn't have known just how true that was.

Now standing in the Customs Hall, and not at all sure how she got there, Cleo tried to concentrate on the business at hand. She'd worry about the here, later. The truth was she wasn't entirely sure where *here* was? She had heard the purser announce the weather in London and the arrival time, but that didn't mean much. If they were still fracking with her, this could just be part of an elaborate ploy to get her talking. Listening carefully to the passengers around her, she was aware that few were speaking English, but that didn't mean much. Terminal One was an international terminal, and just how many Brits would fly ElAl, she couldn't guess. She pushed the nagging questions out of her mind, desperately trying to focus. Wherever she was, it wasn't home, or Tori would be waiting. She was sure of it.

Pulling herself back into her Mohawk only persona, she followed the line until she was face to face with the Customs Warder. Working hard to block the pain, she watched with interest as the Warder kept repeating something to her. Finally, he pointed to her flight suit. Looking where he was pointing, Cleo remembered the papers pinned to her chest, and handed them over. She was surprised to see her Six Nations passport in the bundle. He examined it carefully before asking her something else and gesturing repeatedly. Still unable to understand what he wanted, she searched her pockets. All were empty except for a new, unopened toothbrush. She held it up for inspection, hoping it answered his question. The look he gave her pretty much said everything she needed to know. Whatever this test was supposed to be about, she had just failed it.

As if proving her point, two guards in blue joined her, each taking an arm. The moment they latched-on, Cleo began to fight. Within seconds, two more warders jumped into the scrum. They dragged her, kicking and fighting, to a secure holding room. Shoving her inside, they locked the door, leaving her alone to contemplate the situation. Once the door closed, she immediately moved around the room checking the door and the two-way glass. It's too much, too small, too wrong, and she didn't care who knew. She started to climb onto the table, with the intention of checking the ceiling panels for an escape route, when she realized she couldn't lift her leg high enough to climb onto the chair, much less the table. Trying to remain calm, she collapsed into a corner, sliding down to sit on the floor. Alone again, and feeling even more trapped, she began to drift back into the safety and relative calmness of spirit world. She was determined to block out anything they might throw at her now. "T'ih-se niwa'a," she repeated quietly, closing herself from the world around her and her own conscience.

When the door finally opened, Cleo Deseronto had worked herself so deep into a trance that she was completely disconnected from her own chanting. Even the sound of angry voices all around her were beyond her perception. Trance like, she sat rocking and singing, allowing the noise and the people to disappear. Cleo had finally achieved a state where no one could reach her, yet something about it, something about the room, the sounds, and even the smells seemed curious somehow. She thought about abandoning per place of complete peace, but the idea of returning to whatever was going on, and whatever they were trying to do, just didn't appeal to her. *Could she really stay here?* she asked herself, only to come face to face with Joe Commanda.

"The time has come granddaughter, open your eyes."

It took a long time to realize someone was talking to her. She knew her grandfather had said something important, but what, she wasn't sure. No amount of coaxing or begging could bring her into the here and now, but she had heard something. *Some things are worth the risk, but what about the key?* Gradually she became aware of someone close, pulling her aching body closer, and wiping tears from her eyes. That was curious too. *Am I crying?* More curious was the fact that she could hear someone clearly and very close by. The words seemed familiar, even important. Cleo resumed her chant until she heard the words again. *That's not supposed to happen!* While she listened, she realized, she understood the words.

"The first rule of flying is love."

At first, she was unmoved. Her physical exhaustion was working to strengthen her emotional barriers, making it much more difficult to bypass the mental blocks she had created.

"Love," Tori said repeatedly, "it's the first rule of flying."

Focusing on the face in front of her, Cleo began to wonder if it could be Tori. She did wonder for the briefest of moment if she was hallucinating again, but she brushed it aside at the sight of Tori crying, and apologizing for who knows what. Still silent but focused, Cleo just stared into the eyes of the woman she knew she wanted to love more than anything.

"We've an ambulance waiting, my love," Tori explained, as the medics rolled a stretcher into the small holding room and began to set up a fresh IV.

Cleo removed her boarding pass and the doctor's note from her pocket, handing them to Tori.

She accepted them without question. Darcy had already spent many hours preparing her to face the aftereffects of Cleo's prolonged period of disassociation.

Wordlessly, Cleo lifted her hand again and brushed Tori's cheek with just the tips of her fingers. For the longest moment, she just stared, not moving, not talking, locked inwardly in time and thought.

"Tori?"

"You're here my love, your home!"

"Tori?" Cleo's dry-raspy voice was warm and calm, and completely incongruent with her physical appearance.

"Yes, my love. It's me. Not quite on the runway, but as close as they would let me."

Cleo smiled, letting Tori hold her hand, while the medics manhandled her into the gurney and out into the corridor. "Stay close?"

"Wild horses, my love," Tori's joy was blatant, "Wild horses."

"Just in case they have some Mustangs," Cleo whispered, "do you think you could tell me that thing again? Just so I know for sure, that I'm not in Spirit World, anymore?"

Tori, still holding her hand, walked steady beside the gurney. "What's the first rule of flying? I understand it now. Love, is not just about flying, it's about what you're flying for."

Bo Commanda, who had been waiting in the corridor, now led the parade of personnel escorting Cleo to the waiting ambulance. In front of the group, and wearing her US Marine Corps uniform, she wasn't shy about her purpose. "Make way for a Mohawk Warrior!"

Some of the older folks in the terminal, seeing Bo's uniform and prompted by her, saluted or clapped as the group went by. Cleo let the last few unbelievable months roll past her like some wild nickelodeon. Only moments ago, she had been contemplating whether she would consider listening to whoever was trying to reach her. Now she was home, albeit in a new home, with a new love and a new life. The reward, it would appear, was well worth the risk. With Tori's hand still firmly in hers, Cleo held it against her face, affirming in a gravely rasp, "I missed you, too."

Quick Reference of Acronyms, Short Forms,
and Localized Slang

309 AMARG	309th Aerospace Maintenance and Regeneration Group
AFB	United States Air Force Base
AGL	Altitude above Ground Level (measured from the ground directly below)
APC	Armored Personnel Carrier
ASL	Altitude above Sea Level (measured from Sea Level)
ATC	Air Traffic Control
AVGAS	Leaded Aviation fuel used by piston airplanes
AWOL	Absent WithOut Leave (archaic term for Unauthorized Absence)
Annapolis	United States Naval Academy
BAe	British Aerospace Aircraft (BAE Sytems)
BBC	British Broadcasting Corporation
BDU	Battle Dress Uniform
BIA	United States Bureau of Indian Affairs
Blueberry	Slang for a UN Peacekeeper (Blue Helmet, Blue Beret . . .)
BOQ	Bachelor Officer's Quarters
CAF	Canadian Armed Forces
CavOK	Ceiling and Visibility unlimited for flying
CBC	Canadian Broadcasting Corporation
CFB	Canadian Forces Base
CFS	Canadian Forces Station
CIA	Central Intelligence Agency of the United States of America
CJ5	Older version of the current Jeep Wrangler
CO	Commanding Officer
Company	Casual reference to the Central Intelligence Agency
CPO1	Chief Petty Officer, 1st Class, casually referred to as Chief
CSIS	Canadian Security and Intelligence Service
ELT	Emergency Locator Transmitter (Aircraft emergency signal)
EVA	Extra-Vehicular Activity (Space Walk)
FAA	Federal Aviation Administration of the United States of America
FBI	Federal Bureau of Investigation of the United States of America
FCO	Foreign and Commonwealth Office of the United Kingdom
GCHQ	Government Communication's Headquarters (UK equivalent of the NSA)
G-Man	Slang for Agent of the Federal Bureau of Investigation
GMT	Greenwich Mean Time
HALO	High Altitude, Low Opening, parachute operation requiring oxygen

HM	Her Majesty, (or Her Majesty's), often appended to military facilities and government operations, in the UK and the Commonwealth
HMMWV	High Mobility Multipurpose Wheeled Vehicle (Military Humvee)
HMNAS	Her Majesty's Naval Air Station
Hoo-ah!	Un-official cheer of the US Army
IAEA	International Atomic Energy Agency
IDF	Israeli Defense Force
Intel	Reference to Intelligence information gathering, not the microchip guys!
JAFO	Just Another Fucking Observer
JIC	Joint Intelligence Committee for the United Kingdom
JPL	Jet Propulsion Labs (NASA)
Langley	Casual reference to the Headquarters of the CIA
LAPES	Low Altitude Parachute Extraction System
LCol	Lieutenant Colonel, USA
Lt. Col.	Lieutenant Colonel, UK and the Commonwealth (Wing Commander in the RAF)
Med Aide	Military Medic or Corpsman
MI5	Security and Intelligence Service, UK, Domestic Intel
MI6	Security and Intelligence Service, UK, Foreign Intel
MOC	Military Occupation Code
Mossad	Israeli Intelligence Service
NASA	National Aeronautics and Space Administration, USA
NATO	North Atlantic Treaty Organization
NCO	Non-Commissioned Officer
NDHQ	Canadian National Defense Headquarters
NYANG	New York Air National Guard
Oo-rah!	Un-official cheer of the USMC
PA	Personal Assistant
Pentagon	Headquarters of the five military branches of the US Armed Forces
PersFile	Military Personnel File
PLB	Personal Locator Beacon
PM	Prime Minister
PMO	Prime Minister's Office
POH	Pilot's Operating Handbook
RCAF	Royal Canadian Air Force
(ret.)	Retired from a military organization
RMCsj	Royal Military College at Saint-Jean-sur-Richelieu
RN	Her Majesty's Royal Navy
ROV	Remote Operated reconnaissance Vehicle
Saint-Jean	Casual reference to the Royal Military College at Saint-Jean-sur-Richelieu
SAR	Search and Rescue, common to all Countries

SAS	Special Air Service (British and Australian Airborne Commando Regiments)
SIS	Security and Intelligence Service of the United Kingdom
SIU	Special Investigations Unit
SOE	Special Operations Executive
SOP	Standard Operating Procedures
SSG	Staff Sergeant (US Army)
StoL	Short Takeoff and Landing, design characteristic designated to certain Aircraft
sUAV	small Unmanned Aeronautical reconnaissance Vehicle
Sub.LT	Royal Navy Sub Lieutenant is equivalent to Lieutenant J.G. in the US Navy
TC	Transport Canada (Canadian equivalent to the Federal Aviation Administration)
Tuque	French Canadian reference to a knitted Watch Cap
UAV	Unmanned Aeronautical reconnaissance Vehicle
UN	United Nations
UNDOF	United Nations Disengagement Observers Force (Golan Heights)
USA	United States Army
USAF	United States Air Force
USMC	United States Marine Corps
UTC	Coordinated Universal Time, replaces GMT as the World Time Standard
Vauxhall Cross	Casual reference to MI6
VSI	Vertical Speed Indicator
WAC	World Aeronautics navigational Chart
WestPoint	Casual reference to the United States Military Academy at WestPoint, NY
WOC	Warrant Officer Candidate (US Army)
ZULU	Military and popular slang for UTC

CPSIA information can be obtained at www.ICGtesting.com
Printed in the USA
LVOW07s0500190116

471180LV00001B/184/P